HER
LAST
BREATH

Alison Belsham initially started writing with the ambition of becoming a screenwriter and in 2000 was commended for her visual storytelling in the Orange Prize for Screenwriting. In 2001 she was shortlisted in a BBC Drama Writer competition. Life and children intervened but, switching to fiction, in 2009 her novel *Domino* was selected for the prestigious Adventures in Fiction mentoring scheme. In 2016 she pitched her first crime novel, *The Tattoo Thief*, at the Pitch Perfect event at the Bloody Scotland Crime Writing Festival and was judged the winner. The novel became an international bestseller upon publication, and has now been translated into eleven languages. *Her Last Breath* is her second book.

Also by Alison Belsham

The Tattoo Thief

HER
LAST
BREATH

ALISON BELSHAM

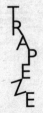

First published in Great Britain in 2019 by Trapeze
an imprint of The Orion Publishing Group Ltd
Carmelite House, 50 Victoria Embankment
London EC4Y 0DZ

An Hachette UK Company

1 3 5 7 9 10 8 6 4 2

A CIP catalogue record for this book is
available from the British Library.

ISBN (Mass Market Paperback) 978 1 4091 8267 2

Typeset by Input Data Services Ltd, Somerset

Printed and bound in Great Britain by Clays Ltd, Elcograf S.p.A

MIX
Paper from
responsible sources
FSC® C104740

www.orionbooks.co.uk

For Mark, Rupert and Tim

Vulnerasti cor meum,
soror mea

*You have wounded my heart,
my sister*

Prologue

Wednesday, 19 July 2017

A dragonfly dipped low over the prow of the rowing boat, transparent wings shimmering in a shaft of sunlight, its body a sharp blue needle. The man watched it for a moment, before turning his attention back to navigating the narrow channel the river had become. Seven long, hot weeks without rain had exposed flat expanses of riverbed that were usually covered with water. The vegetation on the banks was brown, leaves curled like old parchment. The mud stank in the unending heat, flies buzzing and jostling above it.

The man wondered if he'd reach his destination before the water became too shallow for him to keep rowing.

His eye snagged on something protruding from the quagmire up ahead. A dried stick bleached white by the sun, revealed in the cracked, dried mud as the water receded. The dragonfly swooped, then settled on the tip of it, fanning its wings in the sunlight.

The man tugged harder on the oars, scraping the riverbed and churning up clouds of silt as he slipped through the water. He squinted as he came closer. It wasn't a stick at all.

It was a bone.

And he knew enough about anatomy to recognise it for what it was.

A human thigh bone.

His father's thigh bone.

The man lost his grip on one oar, his palms slick with sweat. It clattered in the rowlock, scaring a brace of pigeons into the air. But there was no one there to see how much his hands were shaking as he clumsily turned the boat around to return the way he had come.

The sun was low in the sky now, its brilliance turning to dull orange, but its heat hadn't dissipated. Its reflection turned the water ahead of him blood red, just as it had been on the day she died.

He read the signs, he interpreted them.

The past wouldn't be silenced. Or forgotten. The man could no longer refuse its call.

I

Saturday, 12 August 2017

Alex

Walking into The Haunt at just after midnight was like walking into a solid wall of sweat. Alex Mullins felt instantly clammy as he pushed his way across the dance floor to the bar. As the tempo of the music ramped up, dripping bodies bumped against him, deflecting him from his course as if he were inside a giant pinball machine. He grinned and looked over his shoulder to check that his girlfriend, Tash, was still with him.

She smiled back, then wrinkled her nose, the combination of cloying perfume and body odour making her grimace. But her hips were already moving to the beat, so Alex abandoned his attempt to get drinks and caught her hand to lead her deeper into the throng. They'd shared a spliff in an alleyway outside the club before coming in, and now Alex let the music seep through his body and take control. Nineties Hip Hop Sweatshop. They certainly got the name right tonight. He danced round Tash, grinding his hips and watching her moves from under heavy eyelids. He couldn't help thinking about how they'd spent the afternoon in his bedroom, exploring each other's bodies until his mother got home from work, at which point they'd headed to the beach and the pub.

God, he needed to get a place of his own.

3

'Looking so hot, babe,' he breathed into her ear as their heads bobbed closer together.

It was no exaggeration. Tash Brady was easily the fittest girl on his course. A heart-shaped face with a wide mouth, long chestnut hair and even longer legs. Great rack. Alex had wanted her the moment he saw her, and his desire for her showed no sign of waning several months on. He'd never dated anyone for this long before.

He watched her dancing. She had great moves, but she kept adjusting her position so she could see herself in the mirror behind the bar. She smoothed down her top, then a moment later fiddled with her hair. Alex moved to block her view of herself and Tash frowned.

'You're beautiful,' he mouthed over the music. She shook her head.

Why was she so insecure? Were all girls like this? Yeah, his mother was a bundle of insecurities, but her relationship with his dad had been a mess for years. But what about Tash? There was no reason for her to constantly doubt herself. He didn't get it, so it pissed him off.

A moment later, she'd danced round him so she could see herself again. This time she pouted, checking her lip gloss, and then stopped dancing. She leaned forward and grasped his arm.

'Just going to the toilet,' she said, her mouth close to his ear, warm breath on his neck.

Alex felt a surge of longing and pressed his hips forward against hers. Tash laughed and pulled away. He watched her go and saw her talking to Sally Ann at the edge of the dance floor. If she was here, perhaps the rest of the crew were too. Tash would be gone for some time, so Alex circled the floor looking for other mates.

He didn't see anyone he knew, so he carried on dancing,

letting the music clear his mind until all he was aware of was the rhythmic pulse of the thudding bass.

Alex felt a tug on one of his dreadlocks and snapped out of his trance.

A skinny blonde girl in tight sequins was gyrating in front of him, reaching up to pull his hair again. He swung his head to one side to avoid her hand. It annoyed him. His dreads weren't public property but it was amazing how many people thought it was okay to touch them. He kept dancing, watching to see what the girl would do next. She was pretty enough, but not his type. Her flinty eyes and pointed nose made her face sharp. She was probably the sort of girl who would actually look better when she wasn't plastered in make-up.

She came closer, smiling and beckoning him in with a hand. She wanted to say something.

He leaned in.

'Is it true about black men's cocks?'

'What?' he mouthed, taking a step back so he could see her face. He'd heard perfectly clearly what she'd said. It was some-thing he'd heard too many times before – from toxic girls just like her and from cocky lads wanting to pick a fight. He tried not to let it bother him. With the blokes, he could handle himself, and as often as not they backed away as soon as he made it clear he'd take them on. But the girls wound him up, giggling behind their hands, whispering to their friends.

'Your cock,' she said. 'Big, is it?'

For fuck's sake.

He forced himself to grin at her, then leaned forward again.

'Why don't you find out for yourself, babe?' At the same time, he grabbed her hand and pressed it to his crotch.

She tried to struggle away as soon as she realised what was happening but Alex tightened his grip. Stupid bitch needed to learn a lesson. It took her a moment to gather herself, then she narrowed her eyes and he felt her grabbing at his privates. He pushed her hand away, making her stumble slightly.

Tash appeared behind the girl's shoulder. 'What the fuck?' she mouthed.

She pushed past the blonde to get at Alex. Her brows were lowered in a scowl. She'd seen what had happened.

As the blonde girl melted back into the crowd of dancers, Tash glared at Alex. 'Jesus, I'm gone for one minute and you let another girl feel you up?'

Alex raised both hands in supplication.

'It wasn't like that.'

The music was too loud for an explanation, and it seemed like Tash wasn't interested in hearing one anyway.

'I saw what you did,' said Tash, her voice raised and harsh. 'Bastard!'

She slapped him hard and fast, and as Alex raised one hand to his cheek in stunned silence, she shoved her way across the dance floor towards the exit.

'Tash?'

She didn't hear him. His cheek stung and he realised that people were staring at him. Sally Ann Granger was coming towards him.

'What's wrong?' she said.

Alex shook his head. 'Nothing. Just a misunderstanding.'

Sally Ann's eyebrows shot up.

He needed to get out of here, so he pushed past her and followed Tash out.

It was gone one in the morning, but the welcome flood of cold air he expected on leaving the club didn't materialise. It was still muggy and he felt clammy inside his clothes. There was no sign of Tash – she hadn't waited for him – so he went around the corner into the alleyway and pulled his gear out of his pocket.

Leaning up against a wall, it took him less than a minute to roll a joint and, after glancing around for cops, he lit it.

He held the smoke in his lungs for as long as he could, and waited to feel his body relax. Leaving the joint hanging from the corner of his mouth, he fanned his T-shirt up and down to get some air onto his sweaty chest. Fuck that stupid blonde girl. He'd finish his smoke, then go and find Tash.

Bloody women. Sometimes he wondered if they were worth the bother.

He inhaled again. It was good stuff, strong. He let go of his T-shirt and leaned back against the wall, closing his eyes. He'd sort Tash out in a moment . . .

2

Tash

Tash Brady took a lungful of sea air to clear away the sweat and fug of the club, then lit a cigarette and inhaled deeply. *Damn Alex Mullins!* She turned her back on The Haunt, wishing she'd never agreed to go there tonight, and headed down Old Steine towards the seafront. Even though it was well past one in the morning, heat still radiated off the stone walls, which was just as well as she didn't have a jacket.

She'd had too much to drink in the pub garden earlier, and the potent mix of lukewarm Prosecco and hot sun had made her head ache. The joint she'd shared with Alex outside The Haunt hadn't helped either. She'd been snappy with Alex in the pub and by the time they'd arrived at the club, at just gone midnight, she wasn't in the best of moods. Half an hour of the thumping bass of the Nineties Hip Hop Sweatshop set had made her head pound. She felt sick and she wanted to go home. She'd retreated to the toilets with Sally Ann, where she sat gossiping from one of the cubicles, door open, while she waited for a couple of Nurofen to kick in. Sally Ann's stories of the hunk she was shagging at work brightened her mood, but by the time she came back to the dance floor, Alex had been cracking on with another girl.

Screw that. They were done as far as she was concerned. Over. Finished.

Her six-inch heels clattered on the pavement, and she could hear the throbbing beat of house music coming from another of their favourite clubs on the corner. A drunken couple emerged, grappling with each other on the pavement, and Tash sniffed self-pityingly as she carried on walking on her own. Friday nights were always busy in the clubs, but once she got down to the front, there was far less action. It was completely different to earlier, when the beach had been jam-packed with bodies – tanned girls in tight bikinis, ripped guys showing off their abs, mums screaming at toddlers, and old guys turned lobster-red because they'd fallen asleep in the sun. The air still carried a whiff of suntan lotion and chips.

She crossed the main road to the promenade without having to stop for traffic. She looked around and listened, hoping to hear Alex's heavier footfall behind her, or to see him coming to get her as if he really cared.

But that was the thing. The bastard didn't.

She couldn't turn back. She couldn't bear the thought of seeing him with that girl, so she marched purposefully along the front in the direction of The Grand Hotel. If he hadn't texted her by the time she got there, she'd get a cab home. His loss. He'd realise that when he woke up in the morning and didn't get her usual 'good morning' text.

The moon was a sharp, silver crescent and her tears blurred the light dappling the surface of the sea. Had she really been that clever to get into a relationship with Alex Mullins? Sure, he was buff, but he was a mare to deal with. Everyone knew he was a player. A fuckboy with double standards – he could chat up other girls in clubs as much as he liked, but if she so much as looked at another guy, he flipped.

But then she thought about the afternoon spent in bed with him, and lit another cigarette. She hadn't been a virgin when she's started seeing Alex but she might as well have been. He'd made her aware of her body in ways she'd never experienced with other boys. Like he really knew what he was doing. . . Because he was a player, right?

She craned her neck over her shoulder, looking back towards the pier. There was still no sign of him, but there were no taxis outside The Grand either, so she carried on walking. Fuck him. She wouldn't go back to him, even if he begged. She deserved someone better.

She took another drag of her cigarette, then dropped it. She didn't want to stink of smoke. She'd be home in fifteen minutes even if she walked the whole way. If her mum was still up, there'd be hell to pay. Smoking. Staying out late. She could never do anything right – her mum treated her like she was still a kid. Then she remembered – her parents were away and she'd be going home to an empty house. She ground out the butt with her foot, then slipped off her heels and picked them up. The pavement was hot under her bare feet, and she had a sudden urge to feel the cooling balm of wet sand between her toes. She headed down a ramp that led from the promenade onto the beach, scurrying across the pebbles, gasping aloud at the sharp stones underfoot, until she reached the soft sand at the water's edge. She looked up at the town, walking back along the beach a little way until she could see the floodlit domes of the Pavilion. Then the bright lights of the pier made her feel even lonelier.

The sand was deserted. Just a broken deckchair and a line of litter at the highwater mark. Tash started to cry again as she turned back to head for home. The noise of the waves raking the gravel drowned out the sound of her sobbing. She didn't want to break up with Alex. They had fun together, they had amazing sex. Having a boyfriend like him made her feel good about herself. And what would happen when she went back to college in September? If they broke up, how would she bear having to see him every day, hanging out with those slags who were always pushing themselves at him?

With a sniff, she wiped her eyes and kept walking. Up on the road, the traffic had all but disappeared and there was no one else out walking at this time of night. That was a good thing, wasn't it? She shivered and started to wish she hadn't been so impulsive. Maybe if she'd acted cool and hadn't shoved the bitch, she'd still be at the club with Alex . . .

A hundred yards ahead, she could see the intricate silhouette of the Victorian bandstand, jutting out above the beach from the promenade. It reminded her of a wedding cake. She'd walked further than she thought, and she was cold now, but she still had quite a way to go. The moon vanished behind a cloud and it seemed instantly darker. She quickened her pace, moving away from the water's edge – her feet were freezing.

She thought she heard something but she couldn't work out what it was over the sound of the waves. A lone gull swooped inquisitively and then flew off with a screech. Tash gasped. It was nothing, but it unnerved her so she walked faster still, thinking of how bright and cosy her bedroom would be in a few minutes. She thought about how Alex would sprawl on her bed when her parents were out and what they got up to, always in a hurry in case her mother came home. God knows what would happen if they were ever caught.

Footsteps crunched on the stones behind her and she whipped round.

Alex?

A figure had materialised further down the beach, making a beeline for the water's edge. He wasn't looking at her, but she felt scared and headed back towards the promenade at the base of the bandstand. There were steps by the bandstand café that led back up to the street. She'd feel safer on the promenade, where the street lights would guide her home. She sat down on the bottom step to put on her shoes, brushing the sand off her feet with frenzied strokes.

A flare of bright, white pain exploded on one side of her head. Her shoes flew out of her hand and she tumbled forward. Her chin hit the paving.

What the hell?

She tasted blood in her mouth.

'Alex?'

Two hands grabbed her by the ankles. She struggled but it was no good. The grasp around her legs tightened. She was being dragged over the rough stone surface. Panic stole her breath and made her dizzy.

She wanted to kick out at her attacker, but her legs and arms wouldn't co-operate. Her head smacked against a low kerbstone. Pain ripped through her skull. She couldn't focus her eyes, and tears were pouring down her cheeks. She screamed, tearing the back of her throat, but there was no one on the beach to hear her.

Who? Why? Half-formed questions bubbled into her brain.

'Please,' she spluttered. 'Let me go.'

Her captor stopped pulling her along and released one of her ankles. She could see the dark silhouette of a man looming over her. Still holding the other ankle, he moved to one side of her. Then he took aim with a booted foot and kicked her in the ribs.

Venomous pain flooded her body and she couldn't breathe.

A dark shadow cloaked her vision and her mind went blank.

i

19 July 1982

Your fifth birthday is a very exciting day, Aimée. Of course it is – all birthdays are. But especially turning five, because this afternoon you're going to have your very own birthday party for the first time. There will be games and presents, and a cake shaped like a giant yellow sunflower. You were allowed to choose five girls from your class at school to invite and you've got a new dress. A red dress with satin bows, and shiny black sandals to wear with it, and Mummy's going to put a red ribbon in your long black hair.

Your guests won't be here for at least an hour, but already you're practically sick with excitement.

Mummy has sent you to your room with a book. She's too busy with party preparations to keep an eye on you. She's quite snappy, so you're glad to be out of her way. You get the feeling that she doesn't really like parties. Not unless they're grown-up parties, when she can have drinkies and do her fake laugh.

You're bored with the book and your brother, Jay, won't play with you. Yours is a girls-only party – no boys allowed. Jay said he doesn't care and wouldn't want to go to the party anyway. He called it a baby girls' party. He has better things to do up in his room. You try to go in but he shoves you out and tells you to go away because he's reading. Just because he's four years older than you, he thinks he's better than you. You know that's not true.

But it means you have no one to play with now. You wish Jay wasn't acting so stupid. You want him here to make you laugh, or even to tease you rotten. You sit on the window seat in your room and stare out of the window, tapping your foot anxiously as you wait for your first guests to arrive. You're sure they're late. You keep asking Daddy, 'Shouldn't they be here by now?' This makes him laugh, which you don't think is very nice of him.

At last, the doorbell rings.

Things don't go well at the party. Isabella has decided she doesn't want to be your friend any more. This might be because you fibbed to her about having a swimming pool in your garden and a pony. Now she just wants to be Bethany's best friend. You're sat next to Bethany to play pass the parcel and she won't pass it to you quickly enough. The music stops and Bethany still has it, when you know it should have been your turn to unwrap the next layer.

'Come on, Bethany,' you say. Mummy glares at you.

Bethany unwraps the parcel as slowly as she can, making a face at you.

'It's not fair,' you say.

'Aimée, don't shout!' says Mummy.

Bethany sniggers loudly.

You pull Bethany's hair. It's not that bad, what you do, but Mummy sees you doing it and then Bethany, seeing that a grown-up's watching, screams like a baby.

'Aimée!'

Goodness, Mummy looks ugly when she's cross. This makes you laugh and you pull Bethany's hair again, just to hear her scream again. You pull harder this time to make her scream for real.

'Valentine, she's had too much sugar and too much excitement. Can you take her up to her room?'

This makes you furious. But worse is to come.

'Bethany,' says Mummy, 'you are the winner of the game. You can unwrap the rest of the layers.'

Daddy picks you up. He knows how cross this will make you. You pummel his arm, then you start to cry. Up in your room, Daddy sits down on the bed, shifting you easily onto his lap.

'Bethany's a nasty girl, isn't she?' he says. 'I saw her holding onto the parcel.'

Daddy always knows how to make you feel better and he practically never gets cross with you. He's not like Mummy or Jay, who never have time for you and always have more exciting things to do. When Daddy's home, he makes time for you. And he stops Mummy from being cross with you all the time. He's your favourite person, always.

He lies down on your bed, even though his feet are too long for it, and gathers you in to a big hug. You begin to feel better.

'Shhhhh, princess, no need to cry.' Daddy smells nice, better than Mummy. 'There, there, princess. No harm done. We'll go back down in a while and then you can say sorry to Bethany for pulling her hair.'

You hate this. You never want to say sorry.

'Let's just stay up here,' you say.

Daddy laughs and holds you tight. So tight you can hardly breathe. He's the best daddy in the world. Everybody says that. He presses you closer to him. It's as if he never, ever wants to let go of you. You feel safe.

Until you hear Mummy's footstep on the stairs.

3

Marni

'For God's sake keep her talking, Alex,' said Marni. 'Tell her we'll be there in a couple of minutes.'

She could hear a keening cry coming through Alex's phone and pushed her foot down harder on the accelerator. It didn't make any difference – she was already driving flat out. Ten minutes earlier, Alex had barged into her bedroom without knocking, dragged her out of bed and pulled her downstairs and out of the door.

'Mum, we've got to help Tash!' he shouted. There was a tremor in his voice and the hand clasping his phone was shaking. 'She's been attacked.'

'How'd you know?' said Marni, still groggy, pulling on a misshapen sweat top over crumpled pyjamas. With no time to check her blood sugar, she grabbed her insulin kit and followed him towards her car.

'She just told me.' Alex put the phone back to his ear. 'We're coming, Tash.'

Thierry, of course, had slept through the whole commotion. Not surprising given the amount of weed he'd smoked the previous evening, not to mention the half-bottle of Cognac he'd drunk.

Marni glanced at the clock on the car's dashboard. It was just

16

after half past six and the dawn light was struggling against a bank of dark clouds rolling in off the sea. Though there was traffic on the streets, it was light enough not to bog them down, and a couple of minutes later, Alex craned his neck out of the car window as the bandstand came into view.

'Tash? Tash, are you there?' Alex's voice went up a pitch. 'Mum, I think she's passed out.' He repeated her name again and again, louder and louder. 'Should I call the cops?'

'Wait till we get there and see what's happened.' Marni's ill-ease about the police made her guts churn. Maybe it would be nothing. Maybe they wouldn't need to call the police. But Tash's piercing shrieks over the phone line hardly signified nothing. Marni gripped the steering wheel with white knuckles as her shoulder and neck muscles tightened.

She momentarily lost focus, then too late realised the van they were speeding up behind had stopped. She slammed on the brakes, and Alex jolted forward against his seatbelt.

'Jesus, Mum!' He closed his eyes and clutched the edge of his seat.

They sat in silence, waiting for the van to move again, but the driver's door opened. It wasn't going anywhere.

'Sorry,' said Marni, taking a deep breath before pulling out to pass the stationary vehicle. 'What about Tash?'

Alex redialled her number. 'Nothing.' He tried again and again.

'She just said she was at the bandstand? Anything else?'

'She was crying – she's hurt. Maybe badly.' His voice cracked and his head dropped forward to his chest. He pressed his thumb and index finger into the corner of his eyes.

'Weren't you out with her last night?'

He looked up, sniffing. 'She went home without me.'

Marni sighed. 'You let her go home on her own? Was it late?'

Alex stared out of the window without speaking. He twisted his phone in his hands, unable to keep still.

'Alex, what time was it?'

'I don't know, Mum. We had a row. We were in The Haunt and she stormed off.'

'Well, you should have gone after her.'

'I was going to . . .' His voice tailed off.

'The bandstand,' said Marni. 'Look.'

'I don't get it,' he said, pointing. 'It's deserted.'

Marni pulled the car up in the first empty parking space, a few yards beyond, and Alex had the car door open before she'd even stopped.

'Maybe she's on the other side. Come on.' He ran ahead.

The bandstand stood several feet higher than the main promenade and could be accessed by a small bridge with wrought iron railings. Steps also ran down from the promenade to the beach level, where underneath the bandstand there was a small tearoom, with a terrace overlooking the sea.

Given that the octagonal floor of the bandstand was empty, Marni and Alex ran straight for the steps down to the beach.

'Tash?' called Alex. 'Are you there?'

There was no answer but as they drew closer to the café, Marni saw blood on the paving. Fear channelled through her body like lightning and her legs seemed suddenly too weak to carry her weight. She put out a hand to the bandstand wall to steady herself.

'Look,' she said.

'Tash!' called Alex again. He ran around the side onto the seafront terrace. 'Oh my God! Mum, she's here.'

As Marni rounded the corner, she saw her son bending over the prone figure of a girl. Blood stained the paving all around her.

'I think she's unconscious,' said Alex. He knelt down and

pulled her head onto his lap. Her long dark hair was matted with blood, her dress stained with it. Her hands, and her arms and legs were covered in it.

Marni looked at the amount of blood on the ground around her, then back at the girl. She must have multiple wounds. Her blood-spattered mobile lay next to her where she'd dropped it. Marni's stomach contracted but she had to take charge.

'Call an ambulance, Alex. I'll find something to stop the bleeding.'

The blood trail came from the other side of the bandstand. It looked like Tash had crawled from that direction before she lost consciousness – trying to get away from her attacker or trying to get help? Marni ran to investigate. The door to the café was ajar and there was a bloody handprint on the doorframe. It looked to Marni as if someone had broken in.

'Oh shit.' Cold fear washed through her. What would she find inside?

Marni knew she shouldn't go in – it was a crime scene. But she couldn't let Tash lie there bleeding out – she'd already lost a lot of blood and the ambulance would take time to arrive. She gingerly pushed the door further open, using her elbow so she didn't leave fingerprints. It was warm inside and the stench of blood hung heavily in the stale air. With daylight still just a smear in the eastern sky, the interior of the café was half dark. But Marni could see enough. Her breath caught in her throat – the place was a bloodbath. A pair of high-heeled sandals lay abandoned in the middle of the floor, one on its side, both stained with blood.

Tiptoeing carefully so she wouldn't tread in any of a dark slick in the centre of the floor, her whole body shaking, Marni went around the back of the café's glass counter. She needed to find something she could use to staunch Tash's wounds. A frantic search of the drawers and cupboards turned up nothing useful, but then she saw a package of kitchen rolls on a shelf under the sink. Fingerprints be damned! She picked a clean knife out of a drawer of cutlery and sliced through the plastic outer wrapping.

'Mum!' called Alex from outside. 'Hurry.' There was desperation in his tone.

Marni came out of the café. She was sweating, suddenly conscious of the smell of her own body. She wanted nothing more than to retreat into a cool shower, to pretend this wasn't happening.

'Did you call the ambulance?'

'It's coming.'

She unrolled several sheets of kitchen towel and knelt down to press them against a wide gash just beneath Tash's ribs. The girl stirred and whimpered as she did it.

'Tash?' said Alex.

Tash's eyes opened and stared at him blankly. Her face was grey, with a shiny coating of sweat.

'Tash?' Alex's voice faltered on his girlfriend's name.

Marni took one of the girl's bloody hands, and with her other hand, stroked Tash's hair back from her forehead.

'Tash,' she said softly, 'can you tell us what happened?'

'I ... a man came at me from behind ...' She could barely manage a whisper. She looked at Alex as she said it, and shrank away from him.

Marni carried on pressing the paper against Tash's side.

'He must have stabbed her,' she whispered to Alex.

God, what had she been through?

It was a serious attack – they needed to call the police. Marni felt light-headed. Could she bring herself to speak to DI Frank Sullivan? His rejection had hurt her, but that had been more than ten months ago and now she was back with Thierry. Maybe she wouldn't have to deal with him. After all, his beat was murder, and as serious as Tash's wounds were, she was very much alive.

'Mum? Mum?'

She glanced back at Alex. 'What?'

'Look!' He was holding Tash's hands, palm up. 'What are these?' In the centre of both of Tash's palms were deep pits that looked to have been gouged out with a blade. Her hands were completely covered with blood as if she was wearing red gloves. 'And her feet . . .'

Marni looked down.

Tash Brady had similar wounds dug into the top of each foot.

Alex's hands were shaking, making Marni look at her own. A dark fear swept through her. Tash's bag had been lying on the floor of the tearoom – it hadn't been taken. This was no ordinary mugging – this attack, these wounds, signified something.

Tash suddenly stiffened and tried to free herself from Alex's supporting arm. She murmured something but an exchange of glances showed that Alex hadn't caught it either.

'Tash?' said Alex.

She spoke again but it was garbled.

Wiping the blood from her hands on the front of her pyjama trousers, Marni dug her phone out of the pocket of her sweat top. She dialled and waited, listening for the sound of the ambulance's siren in the background.

What if he didn't pick up?

But he did.

'Frank, I need you here now!'

4

Saturday, 12 August 2017

Francis

Ten minutes after receiving Marni's call, Detective Inspector Francis Sullivan pulled up behind an ambulance parked by the bandstand. He glanced around and quickly spotted the site of activity, down on the lower level by the café. He was the first policeman on the scene and the paramedics had only just arrived. He put in a quick call to his sergeant, Rory Mackay, to get some SOCOs sent over, and then took a deep breath before getting out of the car. He was going to see Marni Mullins again and he wasn't sure how he felt about it.

Marni Mullins. The tattoo artist had helped him solve the so-called Tattoo Thief murders the previous year. He'd been trying not to think about her. She'd saved his life and for that he owed her something. But he'd been avoiding her. He couldn't handle the feelings that had sprung up between them when their working relationship spilled over into something more personal. Or, to put it more brutally, he couldn't afford the level of drama that most interactions with Marni Mullins involved. She was eight years his senior, had a violent ex-husband and a truckload of baggage that gave her particular cause to hate the police. He hadn't seen or heard from her in months. Until this morning. The half-finished tattoo on his shoulder started to tingle as he remembered the feeling of her needles

22

piercing his skin. His palms were sweating and his heart was pounding.

Get a grip of yourself.

And now here she was, hurrying up to him as he came down the steps from the promenade. He had a split second to take in her tousled hair and bloody clothing before she started to speak.

'Frank, thank God . . .'

'What's going on?' It came out sharper than he'd meant it to.

'Alex's girlfriend has been attacked.'

'When?'

Marni shrugged.

'Did she know them?'

'I don't know. She's not making sense.'

They walked around the bandstand. Francis didn't speak. He pushed his hands into his pockets to prevent Marni noticing that they were shaking. But he probably needn't have bothered – she was more concerned for the girl than about any feelings seeing her might have dredged up in him. She led him to where one of the ambulance men was carefully inserting a cannula into a vein in Tash's arm. She was barely conscious and the paramedic, now attaching a bag of fluid to the tube, looked deeply concerned. There was a boy hovering nearby, glaring at Francis as if he were an uninvited party guest. Alex, Marni's son. He fleetingly wondered how much the kid knew about his and Marni's relationship.

Looking down at the injured girl, he managed to get his mind onto the job. Her face was puffy and bruised on one side, her eyelid swollen shut, dark purple under smudged make-up – she'd taken a beating from someone. He leaned over to watch the second paramedic applying a pressure bandage to an area just underneath Tash's ribcage on the right-hand side.

'Is it serious?' he asked.

The paramedic glanced up and nodded. 'It's deep,' he said.

'We won't know what damage it's done until we get her to the hospital. But she's lost a lot of blood.'

The paramedics had cut part of Tash's dress away and the fabric was drenched with blood, as was her underwear.

Marni came up beside Francis.

'Look at her hands and feet,' she said.

Francis looked. On each hand and foot, he saw a round, bloody wound.

'What are those?' he said.

The medic who'd attached the plasma bag to Tash's arm was now jotting notes on a clipboard.

'No idea,' he said. 'But all four go right through.'

They weren't defensive wounds, and they certainly weren't accidental. Something horrific had happened to the girl and she was lucky to be alive.

'Tash?' said Francis, bending down so he'd be within the girl's range of vision. 'My name's DI Sullivan. How are you feeling?'

She stared up at him with wide and frightened eyes. The paramedics looked on warily and Francis knew his time was limited. They needed to get her to hospital.

'It hurts,' she whispered.

'Do you know who did this to you?'

'Alex?'

For a moment Francis reeled with shock, but when she repeated herself and Alex went to her, he realised she hadn't been answering his question at all.

'Tash,' he said again. 'I need to find out who did this to you. Can you tell me anything about what happened?'

Tash Brady shook her head and started to cry.

The first paramedic stood up and looked at Francis.

'We've got to go, mate. Her blood pressure's dangerously low. I'm sure you'll be able to talk to her later when she's been stabilised.'

24

As the two men gently lifted Tash onto a stretcher trolley, Francis turned his attention to Marni's son. At first glance, Alex appeared the same as Francis remembered him – tall and rangy like his father, and still sporting dreadlocks that reached down past his shoulders. But on closer inspection, he noticed that the boy's features had matured. His cheeks had hollowed and he'd lost some of his fresh-faced charm. Francis couldn't tell if the slight stubble on Alex's chin was by design or simply because he hadn't shaved yet that morning, but it made him look older.

'Tell me what happened, Alex.'

The boy avoided eye contact. 'I don't know what happened – I wasn't with her when she was attacked.' His voice sounded shaky.

'Tash called him at about six a.m.,' said Marni.

'Why him? Why not her parents?'

'She has a difficult relationship with her mother,' said Marni.

Alex scowled at her. 'They're away,' he said. 'In London.'

'How old is she?' said Francis.

'Seventeen.' Which meant calling her parents had to be a priority. He'd get Angie Burton onto that as soon as.

'You're going out with her, Alex?'

Alex frowned, but nodded.

'Were you with her last night?'

'I told you. Not when it happened.'

'But earlier?'

'Yes.' His voice sounded defiant.

'What time did you last see her?'

'She left The Haunt at about one a.m.'

'On her own? Or with friends?'

'On her own,' said Alex.

Alex shifted his weight from one foot to the other and back again. His fists were clenched in his trouser pockets. Something wasn't right.

'She called you when?'

Alex scowled again. 'About six.'

'And did she tell you what had happened during those five hours?'

'No. She said some stuff that didn't make sense.' His attention was snagged by the departure of the paramedics, pushing the stretcher trolley between them. 'Can I come with you?' he said.

'Sorry,' said the first one. 'We're taking her to the County. You'll be able to see her there.'

'Mum?'

'In a minute. But I need to show Inspector Sullivan where it happened.'

Marni took Francis by the elbow and steered him towards the café. Francis shrugged out of his jacket as they walked – he could already feel the heat of the sun on his back.

'In here,' she said.

Francis stood in the doorway and looked in.

'Jesus wept.' It was all he could do not to look away.

Blood was pooled on the floor and spattered in wide arcs on the surrounding walls. A chair was overturned, and there were handprints and a couple of bare footprints amid smears of blood leading towards the door. He noticed the shoes in the middle of the floor and wondered if they'd come off before or after the attacker had wounded her feet. He looked for signs of a struggle and saw that the glass had been smashed in the door and the lock had obviously been forced.

Someone had broken into the café, brought the girl in here, then had viciously attacked her. A frenzied attack that left her almost dead. Questions surfaced rapidly, all without answers. One person or a gang? What was the motive? Was Tash the specific target for this attack or could it have been anybody? Had she been raped? It didn't appear to be a simple mugging – Tash had still had her phone to call for help.

It wasn't the first gory crime scene Francis had come across, but there was something about this that was particularly sickening. Tash Brady had been literally butchered.

He needed to get out.

'Okay. I'll leave this for the scene-of-crime team.'

'Are you coming to the hospital?'

'No, I'll send DC Burton over – it'll be better for Tash to be questioned by a female officer. She'll also need to take a statement from you and Alex. Any idea who might have done this, Marni?'

He turned to face her. She looked the same, if a little more careworn, hair struggling to escape an untidy plait, and her frown lines just a little more entrenched than they'd been before. He wondered what – or who – was wearing her down.

She shook her head.

'Don't for one minute think that Alex did this,' she said.

The fire in her eyes was all too familiar.

'Why would I?' said Francis. It was an odd thing to say.

'I hope you wouldn't. But isn't that what you're trained to do? Look at the husband/boyfriend/lover first?'

Same old Marni, always with an axe to grind when it came to the police.

'I won't be looking at anyone until I've established the facts of what happened.'

Marni cocked an eyebrow, clearly unconvinced.

They'd never have made a go of it.

He led the way back round to the terrace. The paramedics had gone and Alex Mullins was standing, staring out to sea, squinting towards the sun with one hand shielding his brow.

It was time to get the team down here. Francis took the steps back up to where he'd parked his car without speaking to Marni or the boy again. But he had plenty of questions that needed answers.

And Tash's wounds … He knew what they were. But why would someone see fit to inflict her with a set of stigmata – the same wounds Christ suffered on the cross?

5

Saturday, 12 August 2017

Angie

DC Angie Burton was on a mission. The boss had briefed her over the phone as she'd hurriedly shovelled down a bowl of Weetabix, standing at her kitchen counter. A woman had been attacked and brutally injured. She'd left a nightclub, The Haunt, at approximately one a.m. and had called her boyfriend for help at about six a.m. It was up to Angie to find out from her what happened during those five missing hours – and, more importantly, any indication of who'd done it.

It only took Angie three minutes to locate Natasha Brady in A&E, but she wasn't allowed into the resuscitation cubicle where they'd taken her on admission. The doctors were working on her to stabilise her blood pressure and stop the bleeding from the deep cut in her side. Nurses hurried in and out with calm efficiency, and Angie craned her neck to see inside each time the door opened and closed.

Please don't let her die.

'How is she?'

The nurse who bustled out of the door looked at her disapprovingly.

'You won't be able to talk to her for quite a while.'

'Of course. I absolutely understand that.' Angie was prepared to be as diplomatic as she needed to be. But talking to Tash as soon as possible was critical, while any memories of the attack were still fresh in her mind. 'Who's the doctor in charge of her case?'

'Miss Parry's leading the trauma team.'

'Okay – I'd like to talk to her, if that's possible. Can you arrange that for me?'

The nurse looked distinctly put out. She clearly didn't feel that her job description covered this.

Angie put a hand on the woman's forearm.

'It was a terrible attack, and we need to do all we can to find out who did it.'

The nurse let out a deep sigh. 'I'm sure she'll talk to you when she has a moment, but right now the patient is our number one priority.'

'Of course.' Angie stepped back to move out of her way, then went across to a row of chairs further down the corridor. There was nothing she could do until she'd spoken to Natasha.

First thing on a Saturday morning, A&E was relatively quiet. The sports injuries wouldn't be in until the afternoon, the drunks not until later in the evening. She remembered from previous visits that there was a coffee machine around here somewhere. The coffee it produced was crap, but it still contained caffeine. She headed off in what she thought was the right direction. When she found the machine, the coffee tasted worse than ever, but at least it was hot. When she came back, her seat was taken – and she recognised the woman immediately.

It was Marni Mullins. Angie knew from Francis's call that Mullins's son Alex had been involved – presumably he was the young man, pacing the corridor in front of where his mother sat. Angie knew she'd need to talk to them about what had happened, but hadn't expected to see them here.

'Hello, Marni,' she said. 'I'm Angie Burton. Remember, we met last year.'

Marni's eyes were hostile. 'I remember,' she said.

'You're Alex?' said Angie, turning to the boy. With his long dreadlocks and scruffy clothes, he looked exactly how she would have imagined the son of Marni and Thierry Mullins.

He nodded and glared at her. Sullen teenager – she had his measure.

'I understand from DI Sullivan that you were both at the scene and called the ambulance?'

'That's right,' said Marni.

Angie looked them up and down. Marni seemed to be wearing a pair of pyjamas, with a faded hoody on top. She noticed for the first time that both their clothes were stained with what looked like dried blood. Natasha Brady's blood?

'I'll need to take statements from both of you later on, once I've had a chance to talk to Natasha.'

Marni Mullins looked disappointed. Was she hoping that Francis would be the one to take her statement? Angie knew she'd been helpful in the Tattoo Thief case, but she'd never really warmed to the woman.

'Are you DC Burton?' said a woman's voice behind her.

Angie turned around to see a young woman in scrubs hurrying towards her.

'I am.'

'I'm Tanika Parry. I'm looking after Natasha Brady.'

Out of the corner of her eye, Angie saw Marni Mullins half rising from her chair. Alex came towards them at the same time.

'How is she?' he said.

Tanika Parry ignored both Alex and Marni, fixing a gaze squarely at Angie.

'You can talk to her for a minute. And there's something I think you need to see.'

Angie followed the surgeon down the corridor and into the cubicle where they were treating Natasha Brady. She paused in the doorway. The room was just large enough for a hospital trolley and an array of medical equipment on either side. The girl in the bed looked unnaturally pale, and her face glistened with a bright sheen of sweat. Her hands were on top of the covers, both wrapped in heavy bandages. She had a drip in one arm and was wired up to a cardiac monitor.

Angie sat down on a chair by the side of the trolley.

'Tash?'

The girl opened her eyes slowly, then glanced around the room, slightly panicking.

'It's okay, Tash. You're in the hospital. You're safe.'

On hearing Angie's voice, Tash fixed her gaze on the police-woman's face.

'My name's Angie. I'm a police officer and I need to ask you a few questions about what happened last night.'

A look of pain flitted across Tash's features and she looked down at her hands.

'I . . .' She faltered and her hands clasped at the sheet. Her eyes were wide with fear now.

Angie took one of her hands, careful not to touch the band-aged area.

'It's okay, Tash. Just tell me anything you remember.'

'I was with Alex,' said the girl hesitantly. 'We were on the beach.'

'After you left The Haunt?'

'The Haunt? Were we there? We were on the beach in the afternoon.'

'Okay. I think you were at The Haunt in the evening, but you left alone.' Francis had told her that on the phone.

Tash nodded but it was evident she had no recollection of even being at the club.

'What happened to me?' she said.

'Somebody attacked you, Tash. At the bandstand on the front.'

A flicker of remembrance lit in Tash's eyes. Her hands grasped at the sheet again.

'Do you know who did it?'

She shook her head. 'No . . .'

'Do you remember anything about it?'

Tash closed her eyes.

Angie hated pushing her back into something that must have been utterly horrific.

'A man. I couldn't see him properly.'

'Why couldn't you see him, Tash?'

'There was a light, shining right in my face.' Her eyes darted from side to side in panic. Then she covered them with her hands and started to cry.

'What did he do to me?'

'You're safe now, Tash.'

Angie stood up and turned to Tanika Parry.

'I'll have to come back,' she said quietly, so Tash wouldn't hear. 'She's too distressed for any more. Would it be possible to arrange for a sexual assault examination, as soon as possible?'

'You think she might have been raped?'

Angie shrugged. 'We've got to consider the possibility. I'll also need to take her clothes for forensic examination.' She paused. 'You said there was something I needed to see.'

'Yes.' Tanika Parry came to the side of the bed. 'Is it all right if we have another look at your back, Tash?'

Tash nodded, but her eyes looked vacant and Angie wondered if she'd really taken the question in. Tanika Parry nodded at one of the nurses and together they gently helped Tash to roll over so she was lying on her side. The nurse undid the ties at the back of her hospital gown and pushed it open to expose the girl's back.

'Her wounds aren't life threatening, though they might have been if she hadn't managed to call for help,' said Parry. 'The stab wound under her ribs has caused some damage to her liver, but we managed to stop the bleeding. We cleaned her up, and packed and dressed her hands and feet. On all four extremities, the wounds went right the way through.'

Angie stepped forward, wondering what they wanted her to see. The nurse peeled back a strip of gauze held in place by medical tape. Angie caught her breath sharply as she got a clear view of Tash's back.

Across her shoulder blades were three lines of ornate gothic script – a very fresh and very bloody tattoo. Angie read the words out loud but she didn't have a clue what they meant.

> *Clavos pedum, plagas duras,*
> *et tam graves impressuras*
> *circumplector cum affectu*

'Who did this?' she said.

Tanika Parry carefully replaced the dressing.

'That's your part of the job, isn't it?'

6

Saturday, 12 August 2017

Francis

Francis stared down at the tattoo on Tash Brady's back. Three lines of Latin verse. He didn't know what they meant, but for some reason they seemed familiar.

Tanika Parry glared at him as she held the dressing aside. She hadn't wanted to let him see, but he'd been insistent.

'She's been through enough,' the doctor had said, blocking the doorway to Tash Brady's room. She'd been moved from A&E to a side room on one of the surgical wards.

'We're probably looking at attempted murder,' said Francis through gritted teeth. 'I need to find out who did this. Sooner rather than later.'

The girl had been sedated and was barely conscious as Parry and the nurse had once again gently rolled her over.

Angie, pale and fidgety, stood on the other side of the bed.

'What is it, boss? What does it mean?'

'*Clavos pedum, plagas duras, et tam graves impressuras circumplector cum affectu,*' said Francis. 'It's Latin.'

Harsh words, gouged into a young girl's back. This was no Friday-night mugging.

He nodded at Tanika Parry. He'd seen enough.

Once he and Angie were out in the corridor, he pulled out his phone.

'Rory, I need you here now. And I want you to put Rose Lewis in charge of this morning's crime scene. I don't care that it's Saturday – get the team in. We need CCTV of Tash Brady last night, we need someone down at whatever nightclub she was at, and I want statements from Alex Mullins, Marni Mullins, and anyone who was with her at any point yesterday evening. Fast, Rory – I've got a bad feeling about this one.'

'I'll sort it,' said Rory. 'I'll be with you in fifteen minutes.'

'Angie, where can we get coffee? I need you to tell me everything Tash Brady said to you.'

As Angie headed in the direction of the coffee machine, Francis caught Tanika Parry as she came out of Tash's room.

'You'll need to call me as soon as she's fit to be questioned.'

The doctor frowned.

'Someone tried to kill her. Don't you get it? There's a potential killer out there who might strike again.'

'Of course. We'll let you know.'

As Francis headed after Angie, he called Rory again. 'Get a uniformed officer stationed up here, Rory. We don't know if she's still in danger.'

'Francis!'

He looked up, already recognising the voice.

'Robin? What are you doing here?'

His older sister squinted at him, leaning hard on one of a pair of walking sticks she was holding. 'You got my message, right? That's why you're here, isn't it?'

Francis glanced down at the phone in his hand.

'You didn't?' Robin's tone was sharp. She already knew the answer.

'I'm on a case. A girl's been attacked . . .'

'Mum's here, in the hospital, Fran.'

'Since when?'

'Since yesterday afternoon. You need to check your phone.'

Francis did remember seeing a missed call from his sister the previous evening, but he wasn't going to admit it.

'What happened?' he said. He couldn't look her in the eye.

'She's got a chest infection. It wasn't clearing with antibiotics, so Doctor Chamberlain referred her.'

Doctor Chamberlain was the GP who looked after the residents in his mother's care home. His name was becoming increasingly familiar. The MS that had plagued Lydia Sullivan for more than twenty years seemed to be progressing ever more rapidly, and Francis knew that a chest infection could be dangerous for her.

'Sorry I missed the call. Work . . .'

'She told me she hasn't seen you for over a month, Fran.' Robin shifted position on her sticks. She also suffered with MS, so she found their mother's deterioration especially hard to cope with.

'Okay, what ward is she in? I'll come up as soon as I've finished here.'

'She's on the second floor of the Barry Building, in the respiratory unit. But take your time. Another hour or two won't make any difference.'

'Robin . . .'

'I know. Work comes first. Brighton's very own superhero.' She spoke with venom and turned away from him.

His phone rang and he glanced down to see it was Rory. Robin walked off without another word.

Damn.

He met Rory and Angie in the hospital coffee shop.

'We need to get on top of this as a matter of urgency,' he said, slapping his palm down on the table. 'It's not a robbery, so what's the motive? Was it someone out to get Tash, or was she the unfortunate victim of a random attack?'

'And why those particular wounds?' said Rory.

'Stigmata,' said Francis. 'They exactly replicate Christ's wounds on the cross, and the Latin verse tattooed on her is probably religious too.'

'So we're dealing with a God-botherer?' said Rory.

Francis shrugged. 'It's some kind of message, that's for sure.'

Angie was quiet, still pale, but jotting down the tasks Francis assigned in her notebook.

Half an hour later, having briefed them on what they and the team needed to do, Francis made his way up to the respiratory unit. A nurse pointed him in the direction of his mother's ward.

Lydia Sullivan was lying in the bed furthest from the door, closest to the window. A plastic oxygen mask covered her face, and if it hadn't been for Robin sitting next to the bed, he would have had to look twice to make sure it was her. The curtain between her bed and the next one was pulled across.

When she saw him, she struggled to pull the mask to one side.

'I must be dying for you to show up,' she said and for a split second, Francis saw the ghost of a familiar smile.

He bent to embrace her, noticing as he kissed her cheek how cold her skin was. Every time he saw her, she seemed to have aged, diminished in some way that he could never quite put his finger on. The MS taking its toll. She looked tiny in the hospital bed. She'd always seemed so tall and graceful to him when he was a child, but he could hardly equate the crumpled body in the bed with the woman she once was. Her hair was in need of attention and the hospital gown swamped her.

He held her tightly for a minute, feeling a lump forming in his throat.

'Maman,' he said, reverting back to what he called her as a child. 'When were you brought in here?'

Robin, sitting on a chair between the bed and the window, gave him a withering look without bothering to say hello.

'When . . .?' said Lydia. She looked confused and Robin cut in.

'I told you everything earlier, Fran.' She sounded irritated.

Lydia cleared her throat to speak but was immediately racked by a crushing cough. Her chest rattled and she barely seemed to have the strength to raise a hand to cover her mouth.

'Sorry I didn't come sooner,' said Francis.

Lydia gazed up at him, the mask back over her face. He forced himself to smile at her, though he hated seeing her like this – it was why he visited less and less often. But he hated himself more. He used his work as an excuse and he knew it was a feeble one.

Robin rolled her eyes. Francis could understand her anger. Watching your mother laid waste by a horrible disease was distressing enough, but looking on in the sure and certain knowledge that you were following her down the same path? It was unspeakably cruel.

Francis looked across the bed at her. 'How are you, Robin?'

She shrugged. 'Exhausted. It hasn't been a great week.'

Francis had noticed how she'd laboured with her sticks in the corridor earlier.

His phone rang. It was Rory calling from the police station in John Street.

'Boss, we've got CCTV footage of Tash Brady leaving The Haunt. We're about to spool through it.'

Francis glanced across at his mother. She seemed to be asleep. 'I'll be right with you.'

'Of course you will,' said Robin. 'Of course you bloody will.'

A surge of relief swept through him as he left the ward and the knot of tension in his shoulders loosened. Then, feeling disgusted with himself for it, he turned his attention back to the messages queued up on his phone.

7

Saturday, 12 August 2017

Marni

It was close to eleven, but there was no point in trying to go to bed. Marni knew sleep wouldn't be her ally. Her mind was still plagued with what she'd seen at the bandstand that morning. Tash, as they'd found her, sprawled on the paving behind the bandstand, bleeding and unconscious. And the interior of the café ... the stench of congealing blood still hung in her nostrils. Who the hell could have done such a thing? And why Tash?

It was close and the air seemed heavy. The back garden was dark and quiet, but it didn't bring her any comfort. Neither did a tumbler of red wine. She hadn't eaten all day and that had messed up her insulin schedule. She lit a cigarette – God knows how many she'd smoked since she'd been sitting there – and stared up at the sky, wondering if it would rain. But the only clouds she could see were as wispy as the smoke curling up from the end of her cigarette. She tried closing her eyes. The noise of a car somewhere on the road at the front made her open them and the endless rotation of questions and images started all over again.

Sweat trickled down between her breasts and she pressed the cold glass against one of her cheeks. Pepper, the bulldog, muttered restlessly in a fitful sleep on the lawn.

Why would someone have attacked Tash? Surely she didn't have any enemies?

The front door slammed and she stubbed out her cigarette in a pot of sand next to her chair.

'Alex, is that you?'

'Mum?'

'I'm in the garden.'

She stood up and hugged him as he came out onto the back doorstep.

'Are you okay?' He smelled of stale sweat and he looked wiped out. He'd been at the hospital all day.

'Where's Dad?'

'He's at Charlie's, watching the football. He'll be back soon.'

Alex grunted and went into the kitchen. He returned a moment later with a bottle of beer in one hand.

'How's Tash?'

'Um . . .' He took a swig from the bottle. 'Scared. Confused. Mostly she's been drugged up to the eyeballs, so I haven't really been able to talk to her.'

'Did her parents arrive?'

'They made me leave, Mum.' There was a tremor in his voice that carried Marni back to the days when he'd been a little boy on the verge of tears.

'Who? The doctors?'

'Tash's parents.'

She took a step back from him. He moved past her and dropped into the deckchair she'd just vacated. His shoulders slumped and his head drooped forward. He looked defeated.

'Why did they want you to leave? You're her boyfriend. Don't you get on with them?'

'They don't know who I am,' said Alex. The words tumbled out quickly, awkwardly.

'What? Why don't they know you?'

Alex sighed and stared at his feet. 'Tash wanted to keep it a secret. They wouldn't have approved of her going out with me.'

'Look at me, Alex. Do they think their daughter's too good for you?'

Alex exploded with anger. 'D'you really not get it?'

'No, I don't.'

'Jesus, Mum. Sometimes you forget that I'm black. Other people don't.'

For a few moments Marni was unable to speak. She wanted to throw a brick through a window, but that wouldn't help Alex. She'd fought so many battles for him when he was a kid – against the headmistress who demanded he cut his dreadlocks, against the little shit down the road who would make monkey noises out of the window when he saw Alex walking by. At nineteen, he was old enough to fight his own battles now, didn't want her wading in. But would it never fucking end?

'I'm so sorry, Alex. You should have told me.'

Alex shrugged. 'I have and now you're upset.'

Marni lit another cigarette.

'Bastards,' she said.

'I don't care,' said Alex. 'I didn't want Tash to cop a load of grief.'

'Yeah, but I care.'

Neither of them spoke for a few minutes while Marni smoked.

'Alex, have the police spoken to you yet?'

He shook his head. 'Not apart from DI Sullivan, this morning.'

'What happened last night?'

'What d'you mean?'

'Why did Tash leave the club on her own?'

Alex stared out across the garden. Even in the darkness, Marni could see he was biting his bottom lip.

'Alex?'

'We had a row.'

'About what?'

'She thought I was messing with another girl while she was in the toilet.'

'And were you?'

'No, Mum. But she wouldn't believe me, so she left.'

'What did you do?'

'I went after her.'

Marni waited. The silence lengthened.

'And?'

'And nothing.'

'Alex, you can't just say that to the police. What happened? Didn't you find her?'

'I stopped for a smoke.'

Marni sighed. She knew he meant a joint – Alex didn't smoke cigarettes.

'Then?'

'I wandered about a bit. There was no sign of her, so I came home.'

'At what time?'

'I don't fucking know.' He was getting impatient with her questioning.

'Listen, Alex. The police are going to be all over you like a rash. I suppose people saw you arguing in the club?'

Alex heaved himself out of the deckchair.

'You need to get your story straight.'

'You're being ridiculous, Mum.' He went towards the back door.

'No, Alex, I'm not. It's always the same. The police want to find the quickest and easiest way to close the case.'

'You're paranoid. You've always been weird about the police.'

'With good reason.'

'What are you talking about?'

Marni shook her head. Now wasn't the time to go into the past.

'Don't be a fool, Alex. It'll be the easiest thing in the world for them to arrest you and charge you for this. They won't care if you actually did it or not.'

'Fuck the police,' said Alex, disappearing back into the kitchen.

8

Sunday, 13 August 2017

Alex

Alex couldn't remember the last time he'd been up this early on a Sunday morning, but he needed to see Tash. Getting up wasn't exactly difficult when you couldn't sleep, and despite the mugginess, he practically jogged the five-minute walk to the County Hospital. Stepping through the main doors, he stopped for a moment to catch his breath under the cooling blast of the air-conditioning vent. But only for a moment. Then he raced down the hall to the lift to go up to Tash's ward.

He had hoped that Tash's parents wouldn't be there yet and that he might snatch some time alone with her before they arrived, but it wasn't to be. As soon as he got out of the lift, he saw Kath Brady standing in the corridor outside Tash's room. Thankfully, she had her back to him and her phone glued to her ear. He ducked down a corridor leading in the opposite direction, then cautiously looked around the corner, back towards Tash's room.

What a difference twelve hours had made. When Kath Brady had arrived at the hospital the previous afternoon, she'd been groomed to within an inch of her life, with expensive blonde highlights that matched the colour of her discreet gold jewellery. Now, her hair was dishevelled and her clothes were creased. They must have stayed in the hospital all night.

She finished her call and leaned in at the doorway of her daughter's room.

'Richard?'

Tash's father appeared. He was a tall man, with thinning hair. Yesterday, he'd been wearing an elegant navy suit. Today, it was shirtsleeves and rumpled trousers. Alex couldn't make out their hurried conversation and quickly retreated as they turned to come towards the lift. He slipped into an empty toilet cubicle so they wouldn't see him as they waited for the lift.

Five minutes later, he ventured out again. The corridor by Tash's room was empty – the whole unit seemed quiet. He was hoping the Bradys had gone to get some breakfast, or better yet gone home for a change of clothes. He waylaid one of the nurses who'd seemed friendly the previous day.

'Are her parents with her?' he said in a low voice.

The nurse shook her head. 'I don't think so.'

'What's going on?' he said. 'Is she getting better?'

The nurse looked around, shuffling her feet.

'Don't worry. The doctors are looking after her.' It didn't sound as reassuring to Alex as it was supposed to and he hurried in the direction of Tash's room.

As he reached her door, he felt increasingly nervous. He knew he could only afford to stay for a few minutes, or he would risk being caught by her parents. His stomach lurched. He felt sick, despite the fact he hadn't eaten anything before coming out. With a dry mouth, Alex put his hand on the door handle, wondering what he would find inside. Why wasn't Tash getting better? He hoped she'd be sitting up, smiling and whinging about when she'd be allowed home.

It turned out the nurse had been wrong. They hadn't gone anywhere. Richard Brady emerged from a men's toilet further up the hall and turned towards Tash's room. He stared at Alex. But Alex had had enough. Tash was his girlfriend and he had a right to be with her. He stood his ground, blood rushing in his ears, dreading the thought of how her parents would react when he insisted on seeing her.

Tash needed him, though.

Taking a deep breath, he opened the door and stepped inside, with Richard Brady right behind him.

Kath Brady turned towards him as he came into the room, but Tash didn't even seem to see him. She was lying propped on a heap of pillows, slumped with her head resting on one side. An oxygen tube snaked up into her nostrils and there was a drip taped to her left forearm. Wires led out from the neckline of her hospital gown to a heart monitor, every beat of her heart bumping along its black screen. Seeing her like that reminded Alex of a video he'd seen about lab rats and animal experimentation. She didn't look right and his stomach contracted with a rush of fear. He longed to pull all the equipment off her, but he knew she needed it.

Her eyes were closed and each breath sounded like hard work.

'Oh God, why do you keep turning up?' said Kath Brady, on seeing Alex standing in the doorway. 'Please just leave.'

The make-up under her eyes was smudged and she sounded exhausted. Alex felt sorry for what she was going through, but there was no way he was leaving.

'I've a right to be here,' said Alex. 'I'm her friend.'

Richard Brady stood at the end of the bed.

'Can I have a word?' he said. He made a sideways movement with his head, towards the door. 'Outside.'

'If you want to say something to me, you can say it here.'

'I don't want to disturb Natasha,' said Richard Brady quietly.

'Then don't.' Alex widened his stance and drew himself up to his full height. He knew it was aggressive but he wasn't going to allow himself to be pushed around by a man in a suit and his racist wife.

'Look, Alex,' said Brady, propelling him towards the door with a hand on his shoulder. 'I know you mean well and I know you think you're her friend. But your presence here isn't helping. It's upsetting my wife, and she needs all her resources to care for Tash.'

Alex caught hold of the doorframe and shifted his weight back onto his heels.

'I think my presence is helpful to Tash. What treatment has she had?'

'It's not really any of your business.'

'What's wrong with her? Why isn't she getting better?'

Brady let go of him and went out of the room. Realising it was the only way he'd get any information, Alex followed him.

'The doctor thinks she's got an infection and she's been given an antibiotic to tackle it. They're monitoring her heart – they think the shock of the attack has given her an arrhythmia.'

'What's that?'

'An irregular heartbeat. She's really quite ill, Alex.'

Alex felt the sweat on his body turn cold.

'So, a reassuring friend might bring her some comfort.'

As Richard Brady considered this, the room door opened and Kath Brady appeared. Alex took a breath and waited for the onslaught but it didn't happen. Although the bitch could barely bring herself to look at him when she spoke.

'She's asking for you, Alex. I think she just opened her eyes and saw you as you went out.'

'Good,' said Alex, and without waiting for either of Tash's parents to say anything else, he shoved past them back into the room.

This time Tash looked at him, but if anything, it made Alex feel even worse. Her eyes were barely open, grey pools in a sallow complexion – she looked far more ill than she had done the previous evening.

'Tash!'

'Alex?'

He came closer to the bed and took hold of the hand that didn't have the drip attached. Both hands were swathed in bandages and she winced as he touched her.

'How are you, babe?' He felt a desperate urge to pull her into his arms for a hug, despite all the wires and tubes. He just wanted her to be her usual self – funny and sexy. Seeing this version of her scared him.

She grimaced. Her lips were dry and cracked. 'Awful. My chest's tight, I feel sick. Everything hurts.' The exertion of talking made her breathe more rapidly and the travelling green light on the heart monitor bounced faster and higher for a moment. She was panting.

Alex stroked her forehead. 'You're going to be fine, Tash. You're in the right place.'

'I'm scared,' said Tash.

'Don't be.' He hoped he sounded convincing.

'I'm sorry about what happened in the club,' she said.

'It's all okay.' He paused and watched the monitor, mesmerised. It seemed to be moving more slowly now.

'Love you, Tash.' He'd never said that to a girl before, but it seemed like the right thing to do.

'Kiss me?'

The Bradys were still out in the corridor, so Alex bent carefully over the bed and kissed Tash softly on the mouth. The dry skin of her lips was rough, and her breath was sour. But she clung to him, so he pulled her up against his chest and kissed her properly.

She took her mouth from his. 'Can you feel my heartbeat? It keeps flicking about – it feels weird.' Her voice was barely above a whisper.

Alex slipped a hand inside her hospital gown to feel the left side of her chest. He could feel her heart pounding, but it wasn't quite regular. His own heart rate increased. What was wrong with her?

'Shhhh, you'll be fine.'

She smiled at him and leaned in to kiss him again.

'What the hell are you doing?'

Kath Brady had come in. *Damn!* He snatched his hand out of her gown, then gently lowered Tash back onto the pillows. He turned to face her mother, jaw set defiantly.

Not that Kath Brady wanted to hear any sort of explanation.

'Richard! Richard!'

A nurse came into the room to investigate the commotion.

'Please call the police,' said Kath Brady. 'This man was assaulting my daughter.'

The nurse dithered, confused by the situation.

'No, he wasn't,' said Tash, her voice wispy and reed-thin.

Alex echoed her. 'I wasn't attacking your daughter, Mrs Brady.'

Kath snorted. 'I saw what I saw. You were mauling her. You had a hand inside her gown. You were interfering with her heart monitor.'

With a supreme effort, Tash pulled herself up into a sitting position. She was shaking her head.

'No, Mum, you're wrong. Alex is my boyfriend. I asked him to kiss me.'

Kath Brady's upper lip curled with disgust and Alex could guess what she was thinking. She couldn't bear the idea that her precious daughter might be dating a black man. Might have had sex with a black man. He wanted to shout in her face. God forbid, he wanted to hit her. But for Tash's sake, he had to curb the impulse to walk out of the room. She needed him here now more than ever.

The nurse scurried away, obviously not wanting to be drawn into a family argument.

'How long has this been going on?' said Kath. Her voice was icy, her eyes narrowed.

'What?' Richard Brady appeared in the doorway.

'This,' said Kath, waving an arm at the pair of them. 'She says he's her boyfriend.'

Richard Brady didn't look as shocked as his wife had, but his expression was in no way friendly.

'Six months,' said Tash. She was labouring for breath and the light on the heart monitor moved sluggishly as it traced her heartbeat.

Alex pointed at the screen. 'She needs help. Get the doctor.'

'Get him out of here,' hissed Kath, close to her husband's ear. 'He's making her worse.'

'Shhhhhh,' said Richard Brady.

'Don't shush me,' said Kath, her voice rising from a whisper. 'If she hadn't been seeing him, this probably would never have happened. He must have had something to do with it.'

Alex looked at Tash. She was unconscious. Bile surged up his throat and he fought against rising panic. Tash needed assistance and her parents were too busy fighting to realise it. He ran from the room. There was a nurse heading away from him up the corridor.

'Help. We need a doctor in here. Now!'

The woman hurried into Tash's room, took one look at the monitor and slapped the crash call button by the side of the bed. Outside, Alex heard a claxon sounding, then running feet. Kath Brady gasped loudly. Alex couldn't see any signs that Tash was breathing. Her chest wasn't moving.

'Get out! Get out now!'

A voice hailed from the doorway and another nurse rushed in, followed by three doctors.

'Clear the room! Get out!' shouted the first doctor through the door.

The first nurse put an arm around Kath Brady's shoulders and hustled her out.

'You too,' said the second nurse, addressing Alex.

He slowly backed away from the bed.

'I need to be here for her.'

The doctor who seemed to be in charge pulled Tash's sheet away from her chest and roughly shifted her down the bed so she was lying flat. 'Nurse, get me atropine – she's bradycardic.'

One of the nurses put a mask over Tash's face and began squeezing the bag attached to it. The doctor quickly prepared an injection.

Alex stood paralysed, suddenly aware that the beeping of the monitor had become a single, flat tone.

Without ceremony, the doctor positioned the needle in the centre of Tash's chest and rammed the syringe home. As soon as the needle was out, one of the other doctors leaned over her to administer chest compressions. The nurse carried on squeezing the oxygen bag, watching the monitor. After a moment the bleep started up again, but it was all over the place with no steady rhythm.

'Ventricular fibrillation,' snapped the doctor. 'Defib.'

A nurse attached sticky electrodes to Tash's chest, then attached wires to them. She nodded at the doctor.

'Clear!'

The nurses stood back as the doctor shocked her, and Tash jerked on the bed.

Oh, fuck . . .

Though the doctors and the nurses worked calmly, Alex could see their eyes widen with fear. They shocked her again but it was no good. The bleeps stuttered and then stopped altogether, after which the piercing tone of the monitor went on and on.

It meant only one thing.

Tash was dead.

ii

19 July 1986

It's your ninth birthday, Aimée, but this one wasn't very special at all, was it? There is no party this year because of Mummy's illness. It's not fair. She's got a poisonous lump growing inside her and she needs to go to hospital a lot. You know it's cancer, even though she and Daddy are very careful not to say the word in front of you. You know it's cancer because your friend Carla told you. Then she asked you if Mummy was going to die.

You asked Daddy and he said, 'Of course not.' But these days you can tell when Daddy's lying, can't you?

Would you care if she died? She's never here anyway.

Your summer holidays are going to be dull, dull, dull. No birthday party is just the start of it. No party, no friends round, no noise in the house when Mummy's home and sleeping in her room. Jay, who can't keep quiet for a minute, let alone for a whole day, is grumpy all the time. He goes off to play in the woods on his own. But Daddy won't let you go. He says you need to stay here to help keep Mummy calm. He says she loves to hear you reading out loud. That's not true. She covers her eyes with her hand whenever you read to her. She wishes you would go outside to play. Quietly.

Even on rainy days when Jay can't play outside, he won't spend time with you. He calls your games silly. But he's silly. He stinks of smoke all the time and he thinks he's so grown-up for swearing. Once you caught him drinking from a bottle of Daddy's whisky. He twisted your arm behind your back until you promised not to tell.

Always on your own. Apart from the time you spend with Daddy.

Jay is very jealous of this, so you make sure he knows all about it. But secretly, you'd rather be with Jay. He's tons more fun than Daddy when he's not grumpy – last summer you built tree forts and played football and read comics. He taught you how to swear and how to fight. You're scared of nothing when Jay's around. But this summer he hasn't time for you.

Today's your birthday and nothing's different. Jay's gone off some-where and Mummy is too sick for a special birthday breakfast.

Daddy wondered if you wanted riding lessons for your birthday present, but you didn't. You couldn't think of anything you did want. From him.

He won't let you call him Dad. That's what your friends call their fathers.

You have a temper tantrum and get sent to your room. He says he'll deal with you later.

He watches you sleeping.

You know this, don't you, Aimée, because you're not always sleeping when he comes in.

Quite often you're lying in your bed awake. Then you pretend to be asleep. You can hear when he's coming up the stairs, and when he tiptoes along the hall outside your room. Very, very slowly, he pushes down the door handle. You watch the handle on the inside of the door moving, as if a ghost is trying to open your door. But it's not a ghost. It's Daddy. He turns the handle slowly because he thinks this makes it quieter. He doesn't want to wake you up. But you're already awake. Sometimes, even if you're sleeping, the creak of the door handle wakes you up.

You pretend you're sleeping.

You can hear him breathing as he stands in the doorway. He's

watching to see if you're awake. It's dark and you can smell his co-
logne, and the mothball smell that clings to his suit. His shoes creak
when he walks across the room.

He stands right by your bed and stares at you while you sleep.

He's there for what seems like for ever and you wish he'd go away.
Sometimes you fall asleep while he's there and once, you sneezed. He
snuck back into the dark shadows in the corner of the room.

Tonight, he reaches out a hand and strokes your cheek. He pulls the
covers away a little bit.

You don't know if it's creepy or kind of sweet.

You think maybe it's a little bit creepy?

Oh, Aimeé, it is. More than a little bit.

9

Sunday, 13 August 2017

Francis

Francis called the team together in the incident room at midday.

As he got his papers in order, Rory Mackay arrived panting with the exertion of climbing the stairs to the second floor. He ripped off his jacket and yanked his tie down from his collar. Dark patches of sweat stained his white shirt under the arms and dotted his chest. Francis felt the back of his own shirt sticking to his skin where it had rested against the leather of his car seat.

'Bloody heatwave,' said Rory. 'Roll on September.'

Angie met them at the door of the incident room. Behind her, at his untidy desk, Kyle Hollins pretended to be working, while surreptitiously listening in on the conversation.

'Tash Brady's still in hospital,' Angie said. 'According to Tanika Parry she's not recovering as they would have expected.'

'In what way?' said Francis.

'They think she might have some kind of infection – she's been having dizzy spells and her blood pressure's too low.'

Rory shrugged. 'Not surprising. Don't imagine for a moment the guy sterilised whatever he used to make those wounds.'

'They're worried about sepsis,' said Angie, with a bleak expression.

'Right, progress so far?' said Francis. His expectations were low – until they had more information from Tash Brady, they couldn't know what they were dealing with.

Angie Burton nodded her head. 'Tony and Kyle visited The Haunt nightclub to look at their CCTV footage. Turns out Tash Brady and Alex Mullins had some kind of fight shortly before she left the club. The film shows him talking with another girl. Tash comes over and has a go, slaps him round the face. She storms off and doesn't reappear. That's the reason why she left the club on her own.'

'What about Mullins?' said Rory.

'He follows her out, but then there's a few minutes' gap before we pick him up on CCTV along the front.'

'Right, we need to talk to Alex about that,' said Francis. 'And any other witnesses you can identify who saw what happened? And you'll need to see if you can talk to Tash again, Angie.'

'Kyle and I are going to go to the club tonight with pictures of Tash and Alex,' said Angie. 'We'll see if we can find anyone who was there and knows anything about what happened. And I'll go back to the County now to see Tash.'

'What about Tash, after she left? Got anything there?'

'Tony's checked the promenade CCTV. There was a man walking along the promenade a little time after Tash went along it, but his features aren't clear. Alex went that way too, when he left the club – that's not the right direction for him to be heading home.'

'Did either of them go past the bandstand?' said Rory.

Angie wrinkled her nose. 'No. Both disappear before they get that far along. But there are gaps between the cameras, so we don't know where they went. I've asked Kyle to follow up on it.'

'No weapon of any kind at the bandstand?' said Francis.

'The SOCOs found nothing at the scene,' she said, shaking her head. 'The guy must have taken it away with him.'

'The doctor couldn't say what made those wounds in her hands and feet,' said Rory. 'But whatever it was, you're not gonna leave it lying around, are you?'

Angie pulled a face. 'Sick bastard. What about the cut in her side?'

'Straightforward knife wound, apparently,' said Rory.

'It's not the how we need to worry about,' said Francis. 'It's the why. She wasn't robbed and, according to the rape kit results, she wasn't sexually assaulted. Once we work out the motive, we might know who to look at. Kyle, Google that Latin verse for me.'

'Yes, boss.'

Angie handed him a sheet of paper with the Latin wording of Tash's tattoo written on it. He typed it laboriously into his computer.

'Doesn't make sense . . .' He studied the screen. 'No, wait. My fault – typo.'

'When you're ready,' said Rory impatiently.

'Got it,' said Kyle. '"*Clavos pedum, plagas duras, et tam graves impressuras circumplector cum affectu.*" It apparently means, "The nails in Your feet, the hard blows and grievous marks—"'

'"I embrace with love,"' finished Francis for him.

'You're right,' said Kyle, with raised eyebrows. 'How did you know that?'

'It's from a seventeenth-century choral piece,' said Francis. It had suddenly come to Francis why the words had seemed familiar on first reading – he'd sung it with the church choir.

'Impressive, sir,' said Angie.

Luckily, before Rory could contribute a snarky comment, the phone started ringing in the small cubicle off the incident room that Francis used as his office.

'Get that, would you, Rory?'

Rory grimaced, but headed in the right direction.

Tony Hitchins came in carrying two takeaway coffees, with

two wrapped toasted sandwiches balanced on top of them.

'Here you go, Ange,' he said, extending one of the coffees and sandwiches in her direction.

Rory had confided to him that he thought there was something more than a professional relationship between these two. Now Francis was beginning to wonder.

'That other one for me, Tony?'

'Fuck off, Kyle. I didn't have any breakfast this morning.'

Kyle looked at his watch. 'Careful, mate, you'll start losing that hard-earned gut.'

Hitchins put his lunch down on his desk and dropped into his chair just as Rory reappeared in the doorway of Francis's office. His expression was grim.

Francis nodded at him, feeling suddenly cold despite the heat. 'What?'

'Tash Brady's dead,' said Rory. He took a deep breath and shook his head. 'They can't explain it. She should have been getting better.'

'No!' Angie covered her eyes with one hand and Tony put down his half-eaten sandwich.

A death like this wasn't supposed to affect the team, Francis thought. But they weren't automatons. And they wouldn't be able to do their job half as well if they didn't care about the victims.

Rory came back into the incident room, eyes wide, shocked by the news.

'They couldn't save her. Her heartbeat became wildly irregular. They tried shocking her, but it didn't work.'

There was silence, the team too stunned to speak.

Then Francis cleared his throat.

'That means this is now a murder investigation. Everybody, redouble your efforts. Someone killed Tash Brady and I want them brought in.'

He went into his office. He needed to reassess the situation and set new priorities.

Rory knocked on the door jamb, then invited himself in without waiting for Francis to respond.

'Boss, do you think it could have been Alex Mullins who attacked Tash?'

'It's too early to say, Rory. It's a possibility, but it might just as easily have been a stranger. There was that other man on the CCTV, walking up the promenade behind her.'

'Not that closely behind her.'

'Closer than Alex. And even if Mullins was angry with her, and followed her to have it out, why would he have wounded her in that way?'

'I don't know – but the fact that they had a fight earlier puts him in the picture, doesn't it? And if anyone has access to tattooing kit, it's Alex Mullins.'

Francis didn't reply. He was thinking about how Marni Mullins would respond to this suggestion.

But Rory took it as confirmation of his agreement that Alex Mullins looked the most likely candidate for the attack.

He was probably right.

'Bring him in for questioning, and ask Tash Brady's parents what they know about the relationship.'

10

Sunday, 13 August 2017

Rory

Rory pulled open one of a pair of double fire doors and turned the corner into the trauma unit's main corridor. A red-faced nurse practically bowled him over.

'You can't come down here,' she said, without stopping. 'Please leave now.'

'Police,' said Rory.

She turned back to look at him. There were dark patches of sweat under both her armpits. 'I'm sorry, but that makes no difference.'

From further along the corridor, Rory could hear a woman crying hysterically. He wondered if it was Tash Brady's mother.

It was time to pull rank. He dug out his warrant card.

'I need to speak to the doctor in charge. Right now.'

The nurse sighed and gave him a malevolent look. 'This way.' She stalked down the corridor with short aggressive strides.

They passed the door to Tash's room and Rory slowed down to peer inside. He saw a woman bent over the bed, clinging to her daughter's body. A nurse was whispering something in her ear and another was silently gathering up the ephemera of a failed medical intervention.

'Come on,' snapped the nurse, making Rory feel like a rubbernecker.

He caught her eye. Neither of them wanted to be there.

A young woman in surgical scrubs came towards them. She looked half-dead with exhaustion, her feet practically dragging.

'Miss Parry,' said the nurse, 'this man's from the police.'

'Thank you, nurse.' Her tone was brusque and she looked Rory up and down, taking the measure of him. 'Tanika Parry.'

'I need to talk to the doctor in charge of Natasha Brady's treatment.'

'That was me.'

Rory quickly realised his blunder – people might talk about policemen looking younger, but for him it was medical staff.

'Right . . . sorry.' He glared at the nurse. She gave him a look like he'd pissed on her chips.

'How can I help you?' said Tanika Parry.

'Can you explain what happened to Natasha? Last update we had was that her wounds weren't life threatening.'

Parry gave him an intense stare. 'I can only release medical details to the next of kin.'

Rory felt a muscle in his jaw tighten. He took a breath to relax it. No point getting angry.

'Miss Parry, Tash Brady was brutally attacked. Now she's dead. If the cause of death had anything to do with that assault, we'll be looking at a murder charge.'

'Patient confidentiality rules actually extend beyond a person's death,' said Parry.

Bleeding jobsworth.

'Right, I'll ask you straight. Was Tash Brady murdered – because if she was, it makes it my business.'

Tanika Parry sighed. 'Come with me.' She motioned for him to follow her into a side room.

Once the door was closed behind them, she sank down heavily onto one of the plastic chairs and pulled her hair back from her face, redoing her ponytail.

'I don't know why Natasha died,' she said. She sounded upset. 'Her wounds were severe but not life threatening. The cut in her side nicked her liver, but we were able to stem the bleeding effectively. We gave her a strong dose of antibiotics to counter any infections that might have entered her bloodstream.'

'So why did she die?'

'Through the night she developed bradycardia.'

'Brady . . .?'

'Her heart rate slowed right down. It got worse this morning and then she suffered a massive heart attack. We did all we could, but we couldn't get her back.'

Rory waited a moment before going on. Tanika Parry got a tissue out of her pocket and wiped her nose.

'You have no idea why?'

Parry shook her head. 'She should have been showing signs of improvement by now – but we were seeing some odd things in her bloods. For one thing, her sodium levels were way too high.'

'Did something happen in the hospital?' Could Alex Mullins be responsible in some way?

She gave him a blank look. 'It's too soon to know what went wrong. You'll have to wait for the autopsy.'

'I need to have a word with Natasha's parents.'

Tanika Parry looked aghast. 'Their daughter died less than two hours ago.'

'And they're going to want me to do everything in my power to find whoever killed her.'

Ten minutes later Richard and Kath Brady were shown into the side room where Rory was waiting. The stroppy nurse from before gave him another filthy look as she made the introductions. Didn't she realise he was just doing his job, like she was doing hers? Or did she think he was just being unnecessarily nosy? She'd soon change her tune if someone murdered one of her family.

Rory watched Tash Brady's parents come in, then dither before deciding where to sit down. They looked around the room, not sure what they were doing there.

'Maybe we could get some tea, nurse?' said Rory.

She shot him a sour look and left the room.

There was no doubt in Rory's mind that Richard and Kath Brady were well off. Their clothes were undoubtedly expensive, even if they now looked the worse for wear. Watching a loved one die – it soon strips away your social pretensions.

Richard Brady helped his wife into a chair and then turned to Rory.

'Who are you?' His eyes were red-rimmed, but other than that his stiff carriage gave the impression of a man who kept his emotions on a tight leash.

'Detective Sergeant Rory Mackay.'

Kath Brady let out a cry, then clamped a hand over her mouth. Her shoulders shook convulsively.

'I'm sorry for your loss,' said Rory. It was something he had to say often in his job, but that didn't make confronting the bereaved with unpalatable truths any easier. 'I just have a few questions I need to ask you.'

'Is this really the time?' said Richard Brady. 'Perhaps you could send someone out to our home in a few days' time, when . . .' He glanced meaningfully down at his wife.

'I just want to check a couple of things while your memories are fresh,' said Rory, keeping his tone even. 'Let's sit down.'

He took a chair, and Richard Brady put a hand on his wife's forearm reassuringly.

'Please make this a quick as possible,' he said.

Rory took out his notebook.

'How old was your daughter, Mr Brady?'

'Tash was seventeen. But you should know, she's my wife's daughter, my stepdaughter.'

'How long had she been having a relationship with Alex Mullins?'

Kath Brady, momentarily in control, started to cry again loudly.

'I have no idea,' said Richard Brady. 'Until yesterday, we had no idea of his existence.'

Rory looked up from his notes. 'I was informed he was her boyfriend?' That's what the boss had said, anyway.

'Secret boyfriend, it turns out.'

'Why would that be?' said Rory, as if it wasn't already obvious to him. 'Why would she feel the need to keep that information from you and your wife?'

'Why do you bloody think?' snapped Richard Brady. 'Not quite . . .' He tailed off, suddenly cautious about what he'd intended to say.

But Rory understood him perfectly. The Mullins family were hardly in the same social bracket as the Bradys, and Alex Mullins – with his long dreadlocks and whiff of patchouli – would hardly be the sort of boyfriend they wanted for their princess.

'Do you have any idea at this point who might have attacked Natasha? Did she say anything in the last twenty-four hours that gave an indication of whether she knew the person?'

Richard Brady shook his head, but Kath Brady sniffed and stopped crying. She sat up straight and, wiping tears from her cheeks, she looked Rory directly in the eye.

'That boy. You need to be looking at that mixed-race kid.' She was referring to Alex Mullins – and it wasn't acceptable. Rory cleared his throat loudly to remind her who she was talking to. She ignored him and carried on. 'I caught him in her room, trying to attack her. He was fiddling with her heart monitor. I suspect he wanted to shut her up.'

'Shut her up?' prompted Rory.

'Before she could tell us what he was really like. What he'd done.'

'And what exactly had he done?'

'He was in the room when she died . . .' She tailed off, maybe not quite ready to make a direct accusation.

'Where is he now?'

'He ran off, didn't he? Disappeared in all the confusion . . .'

'Shhhh, darling,' said her husband. He looked at his wife, then at Rory, but Rory was hard pressed to tell whether he believed what his wife was suggesting or not.

II

Sunday, 13 August 2017

Alex

It was dark by the time Alex walked, with shoulders hunched and arms wrapped round his chest, up Selborne Place to the corner of Lorna Road. Despite the heat, he had his hood up and his dreads tucked down the back of his sweat top. His head ached from crying, but he needed to think. His mother's words echoed in his ears.

You need to get your story straight.

He crouched low and peered round the edge of the fence of the corner house. He would normally come into Lorna Road from the other end, from the town end, but he wasn't taking any chances. He didn't even really want to come here but he couldn't think of anywhere else to go. If he went home, he'd have to face his parents – Marni with her endless questions and his father contradicting her at every opportunity. He wasn't ready for that yet.

The street was quiet. Imposing Victorian terrace houses on the left, run-down and backing onto the railway track, and small, smug 1930s cottages on the right. The stubby streetlamps cast intermittent pools of orange light, but most of the road was in shadows. Most importantly, no sign of any police cars.

What the hell? Why was he acting like he was on the run?

He wasn't on the run. He just needed time to himself before

facing up to what had happened. Tash was dead. He shied away from the word, but it formed in his brain, kept forming in his brain, as it had done all afternoon. And the image of the doctors and nurses manhandling her in an effort to keep her alive. It was running on a loop – and he couldn't clear his mind to think of anything else. Like getting his story straight, whatever that meant.

He stood up and walked down the road, trying not to hurry, nonchalantly crossing it at an angle so he was walking on the railway side of the road. There was no one around. Lights were on in a few of the houses, the blue flicker of televisions. A peal of laughter from somewhere in a back garden, music from somewhere else, but no pedestrians and no cars driving up and down. A quiet Sunday evening.

He didn't need to check the house numbers as he walked and a few seconds later he slipped open a wrought-iron gate and walked up to the familiar front door. The black paint was chipped and peeling, and the doorbell didn't work.

He knocked and waited, pushing unwanted thoughts away without success, scrunching his eyes against the tears that threatened to start flowing again.

'Alex!'

Liv Templeton was his cousin. His mother's sister, Sarah, was her mother. He'd spent a lot of time at the Templetons' house as a child. Sometimes because his mother was working, but as often as not as a result of her chaotic lifestyle. It meant he and Liv were close. She'd been there for him through some of the roughest times.

She pulled him inside, and wrapped him in a tight embrace as soon as the door had closed behind him. She knew.

'It's true, isn't it?' she said, letting go of him and taking in his swollen eyes and heavy limbs. 'Tash's dead?'

'Who told you?' said Alex.

'Someone put it up on Facebook, bloody idiot. It got taken down pretty fast – I mean, how insensitive to her family – but then the news spread. Sally Ann told me.'

They went through to the living room. It was a typical student house, with sagging furniture, empty beer bottles on the hearth and a carpet that perpetually needed vacuuming.

Alex sank onto the sofa and put his head in his hands.

Liv dropped down to kneel in front of him. She put her hands on his forearms.

'What happened?'

'I don't know, I don't know.' His feelings were threatening to overwhelm him. It felt as if he wanted to be sick but it was nearly twenty-four hours since he'd eaten anything. His gut twisted and his hands were shaking.

'Sally Ann said you'd had a fight at the club.'

'It was nothing to do with that,' said Alex, sitting back abruptly so Liv's hands fell away from his arms.

She stared at him, wide-eyed.

He couldn't breathe. He bit on his bottom lip to try and regain control. Then he took a deep breath.

'I mean it was. But only 'cause it meant she stormed off on her own. I tried to go after her and I couldn't find her. Then she called in the morning. She was crying, saying she'd been attacked.'

'Oh my God . . .'

'If I'd found her, it wouldn't have happened. It's my fault.'

'It's not your fault, Alex. Don't say that.'

'It is.' He was crying again.

Liv got up and sat down on the sofa next to him, putting her arms round him. They sat like that until Alex wrestled back control. He sniffed loudly, and Liv stretched forward to get a box of tissues off the table.

'Your mum called,' she said.

69

Alex scowled.

'She's worried . . .' Liv faltered. 'She's desperate to know where you are. Can I call her and tell her you're here?'

'Wait a bit,' said Alex, wiping his nose with a tissue. 'I just need some time.'

'What was the fight about?' said Liv, after a few moments' silence.

'Nothing. It was stupid. She thought I was cracking on to this girl. But I wasn't. It was just the usual shit. I tried to tell Tash but she wouldn't listen.'

'Did you go after her?'

'I went outside and smoked a spliff. Then I was looking for her . . .' He fell silent.

'You smoke too much, Alex. It's poisonous shit.'

Alex glared at her.

'Then?'

'I don't know. I wandered about. I can't remember.'

'You didn't see her?'

Alex shrugged. He remembered smoking the joint. He remembered getting home later, trying to close the front door quietly so his mum wouldn't hear him. Then the phone woke him up and it was morning.

'I don't remember,' he said.

Other memories crowded in.

'Defib!'

The continuous, piercing tone of the monitor went on and on.

Tash was dead.

You need to get your story straight.

12

Marni

Hell! She was going to be late getting to the studio for her appointment. It didn't matter that most of her clients turned up late, Marni still felt that she should be there on time. If she kept them hanging around, chances were that she'd lose the business to someone else. There were enough tattoo parlours in Brighton, after all. It was a crowded market that had suffered after the Tattoo Thief case, and now at last it was getting back on its feet.

She gunned her ancient *deux chevaux* as the traffic started moving along Church Road, her thoughts going back to the events of the weekend. Why the hell would anyone want to attack Tash Brady in such a bizarre manner? She wondered if Alex was still at the hospital or whether he'd gone over to Liv's for the night – and made a mental note to give him another call as soon as she wasn't driving.

Something – somebody – caught her eye on the pavement.

Wait! What the fuck? Was that Thierry?

It was lunchtime on a Monday and she'd just seen Thierry standing on the pavement outside the Blind Busker. Who was he talking to? She glanced up to her rear-view mirror. Yes, that was definitely him – she knew the shape of the back of his head as well as she knew her own face. What was he doing there? She

71

thought he'd had an all-day appointment to finish off a back piece.

It didn't make sense. And who the hell was that girl he was with?

Parking the car behind the shop, she made her way round to the front with a definite feeling of unease creeping through her. It brought back all the feelings of mistrust in her husband she'd fought to banish over the previous few months.

Her client was waiting for her at the door and Marni silently thanked her stars that she'd finished off the final details of the design for her the previous evening. She quickly covered the massage bench with a fresh layer of cling film and prepared her tattoo machine with a polythene sleeve to protect it from blood spatter. Before starting to tattoo, she cleaned her client's skin with disinfectant and then applied a black stencil of the tattoo design they'd agreed on.

The girl, who'd come in for a wreath of peonies on her thigh, prattled endlessly about her mother, her boyfriend and her dog as Marni first outlined the flowers and then gradually started to build up the colour of the petals.

'Really?' said Marni, feigning interest in the chihuahua's health problems. She was finding it hard to keep her mind on the job. Instead, she was fighting with her imagination over the reasons why Thierry might have been talking to another woman on the other side of town when he was meant to be tattooing.

'Yeah, she's really suffering, poor little thing.'

Marni dipped the tip of her needle into the dark red ink and started shading another burst of writhing petals.

'I'm sure she'll be better soon,' said Marni, keeping her tone even.

'Yeah.'

What the hell had he been doing down there?

Even the buzzing of her tattoo iron failed to soothe her.

'Shit!' said Marni, pulling the tattoo machine back from her client's skin.

No tattoo artist is perfect. Every tattoo artist has made a mistake at one time or another. Marni Mullins was no exception. But a mistake while tattooing was permanent.

'What?' said the girl. 'What's wrong?'

'Nothing. Just . . .'

The girl craned her neck to see the part of her leg Marni was working on.

'What the fuck?' she squealed.

The mistake was obvious. A dark red line that overshot its limit onto the pale petal of a nearby flower.

'I'll sort it, don't worry,' said Marni, wondering exactly how she was going to fix it.

'Too bloody right you will. I'm not paying hundreds of pounds for a tattoo that's messed up.'

Marni disguised her mistake as a dark twig, then let the girl go with a hefty discount on the session. Her mind had been wandering and she should have stopped earlier. Where the hell was Alex? And why wasn't he answering his phone? And now it looked like Thierry was up to his old tricks. She'd had enough.

Coffee did nothing but jangle her nerves even further.

Who the hell would he have been talking to outside the Blind Busker? It wasn't one of his regular pubs. In fact, it was well off the beaten track for Thierry – and not even home territory for Charlie or Noa, the two other tattooists that worked with him at *Tatouage Gris*. But on the other hand, why was she even asking herself the question? How many times had he been unfaithful to her while they were married? Plenty that she knew of, probably a whole lot more she didn't.

Screw him!

Without thinking, she found herself heading towards Preston Street where Thierry had his studio. It only took her ten minutes to walk from her own place in Gardner Street, but by the time she'd reached the black-painted shopfront of *Tatouage Gris*, she was glistening with sweat and righteous indignation.

She slammed the door on her way in, making Charlie and Noa look up sharply from the drawings they were working on.

'Damn!' said Thierry.

He was tattooing a man's back.

I hope he's made a bloody mistake!

It was a thought she immediately regretted for the sake of his client – but that didn't mean she was going to let him off the hook.

She advanced towards him as he put down his tattoo iron.

'Let's take a break, Kenny,' he hissed to his bewildered customer.

'Thierry, a moment of your time,' said Marni through gritted teeth.

'Now? Look – I'm working.'

Kenny glanced from one to the other, then scurried for the door, pulling a packet of cigarettes from his pocket.

'And was that work this morning when I saw you chatting up a girl outside the Blind Busker?'

Thierry stood up, instantly removing her advantage of talking down to him, but the expression on his face was one of puzzlement rather than guilt. Had she got it wrong? No, it was definitely him that she'd seen.

'When exactly?'

'Just before midday.'

Thierry let out a grunt of contempt. 'Pah! I haven't been to the Blind Busker for months. What are you talking about?'

'I saw you there. With another woman.'

'It's bullshit, Marni. You saw someone else, who looks like me perhaps.' He glared at her. 'Go home. You're wasting my time.'

Marni felt certain he was lying. She'd seen what she'd seen.

And since getting back together with him, a part of her had been waiting for this to happen. It was practically inevitable with the man. She wanted to cry – with anger, with frustration, with the whole bloody gamut of feelings that he always managed to stir up in her.

'Why should I believe you?' she said. 'You've lied to me so many times before.'

Charlie and Noa pretended to carry on working. They weren't going to be drawn into a domestic.

'Outside,' he said, heading for the shop's front door. 'I'm not doing this in here.'

Once they were standing on the pavement, with his client Kenny eyeing them from across the road, he spoke again.

'Honestly, babe, I'm not lying. I haven't been near that shithole for months. You saw someone else.' He stood with hands on his hips, head tilted back so he was looking down at her.

'I know what you look like. You can't keep bullshitting me, Thierry. It can't work that way.'

Thierry shrugged. His dismissal infuriated Marni all the more.

'And you, Marni, you can't keep doing this.'

'What?'

He put both hands on her shoulders. 'You won't forgive me for the past and it's ruining our lives.'

'But you don't get it, do you? It's you that drags me back to the past.'

Thierry shook his head sadly. 'I don't know what to do about that. I can't erase what happened.'

Marni looked away from him, down the street in the opposite direction. She didn't want him to see that she was on the verge of tears. 'I know you can't.'

He tried to hug her but then she remembered the sight of him outside the Blind Busker.

'No, Thierry. We've got to find a better way. This is wearing me out. I want to trust you, but every time I'm nearly there, you go and do something to destroy my trust.'

'*Merde*! I told you – I wasn't there.'

He turned to go back into the shop.

'I don't know if I can go on like this,' she said, hating herself for saying it, even though it was true.

Their relationship always followed the same pattern. She would distance herself from him because she couldn't trust him. Which in turn would push him to find solace in other places.

'I need to get back to work,' said Thierry. He went back into the shop. 'We'll talk about it at home, okay?'

It wasn't okay, but she didn't know what to do.

Without another word, she turned and walked away down the pavement.

At this moment, she didn't believe she had a future with him – she needed to protect herself from any more pain.

'Marni!' It was Thierry, running up behind her. His voice sounded sharp and urgent.

'What now?'

'I just heard on the radio – Tash died yesterday afternoon.'

'What? How . . .?'

'The police are hunting for the man who attacked her.'

'Oh God, no.' Marni's legs felt weak. She put a hand out to steady herself on a shop window. 'No, that can't be right. She can't be dead.'

Thierry took her by the other arm.

'Come back to the shop and sit down.'

'Oh, no. No, Thierry.'

'What?'

'If Tash's dead, where the hell is Alex?'

13

Francis

By Monday afternoon, Tash Brady's dead naked body lay partially covered by a white rubber sheet, bathed in the harsh white light of the autopsy room. Forensic pathologist Rose Lewis was working on it as Francis and Rory came in. Francis drew a sharp breath and looked at Rory. His sergeant had a daughter of his own and an attack like this would be close to the bone.

'All right?' Francis said.

'I'll never get used to the smell in here.' Rory said, with an exaggerated grimace. He clearly didn't want to touch on how he was feeling about Tash Brady's death.

There was no music blasting out in the morgue this morning. It was as if Rose could sense the mood her colleagues would be in. She'd taken delivery of the body from the hospital over the weekend, and by the time Rory and Francis arrived she'd already made a start on the autopsy.

Their greetings were short and muted. Rose got straight down to business.

'The hospital sent me a copy of her notes with the body,' she said, 'so I've got a full record of her vital signs from when she was admitted up to the moment she died.'

Little over twenty-four hours, thought Francis. What had gone wrong? She should still be alive.

'Did you speak to the doctor who treated her, Tanika Parry?' said Francis.

'Briefly, this morning,' said Rose. 'She couldn't tell me very much. The symptoms Tash exhibited just before she died suggested some sort of toxic shock – but we'll need to wait for the blood and stomach content results to find out more. I've also sent samples of liver tissue for analysis – if there was something poisonous in her system, then it will show up there.'

'What can you say so far about the wounds and about that tattoo on her back?' said Rory.

'It's quite a piece of work,' said Rose. 'A full set of stigmata and a fresh tattoo. From the text across her shoulders – and its source – they're quite obviously linked, so it's probably fair to assume they were done by the same person.'

'You don't think she could have had the tattoo done at an earlier date?' said Francis.

Rose peeled back the rubber sheet and shook her head. The three of them studied the black scrawl across Tash's shoulders. The black letters were raised like welts and crusted with scabs and pus.

'Rory, get this photographed. If the attacker's sending a message, then we need to work out what it is.'

Rory grunted his affirmation.

'It might be nothing,' said Rose. 'Just an expression of his anger. I can't see any logic in any part of this attack. If he'd been trying to kill her, he could have been more efficient with the knife wound in her side.'

'So he wasn't trying to kill her? A warning perhaps?' said Rory.

'A seventeen-year-old girl? Is she really going to have the types of enemies that put out warnings like that?' said Rose.

'A message to her stepfather, maybe?' said Francis. 'Let's get the team digging into Richard Brady's business connections. He's an accountant, right?'

'That's right,' said Rory.

'On the straight and narrow?'

'We'll find out.'

'The tattoo's not healed and it's partially scabbed over,' said Rose. 'There's also evidence of an infection at the tattoo site. Possibly due to dirty equipment or exposure to dirt during the attack, or maybe an allergy to the ink he used. However, there's also a chance that it could be due to a hospital-borne infection.'

'A superbug?' said Rory.

'Possibly,' said Rose. 'Could be MRSA, but we'll have to wait for test results.'

'Tanika Parry mentioned some unexpected results in her bloodwork at the hospital,' said Francis. 'Would an infected wound account for those?'

Rose wrinkled her nose. 'Sounds odd – they would be alert to blood test results that suggested an infection.'

She walked across to the work bench at the side of the room.

'They were already treating her with antibiotics.' She rifled through a pile of hospital notes. 'But look here . . .' Francis went over to her. 'Her blood pressure kept falling for the duration of her time in hospital, and these figures indicate a severe acid-base imbalance, cardiac electrical instability and hepatic dysfunction.'

'Meaning?'

'Something out of the ordinary was happening inside her body. Possibly a toxic reaction – but, like I said, you're going to have to wait for test results for any more details.' Then she looked up at Francis. 'You might want your tattoo expert, Marni Mullins, to give you an opinion on this. She'll probably know a bit more about allergic reactions, and she might be able to tell us when the tattoo was likely to have been done.'

Rory coughed loudly, but Francis maintained his composure.

'Not sure she's the right person to help this time round. It's looking like her son might be involved.'

'You're kidding?' Rose's eyes widened.

'He was dating Tash Brady and we know they had a row just hours before she was attacked. What I need to know from you, as fast as possible, is this – did Tash Brady die directly as a result of the attack?'

Rose gave him a sharp look. 'It's too early to say what the cause of death was.'

Francis pursed his lips. 'I need to know whether I'm dealing with a murder case here, Rose.'

'You'll know as soon as I do.'

'Tell us about the wounds,' said Rory.

'The wound in her side measures four inches long, by about half an inch wide at its broadest point. It was made by a sharp blade, slightly serrated, and pierces her side to a depth of three and a half inches. Because of the angle of the thrust, the tip of the blade caught her liver.'

The wound in Tash's side gaped open where Rose had obviously cut the stitches during the autopsy. The skin on either side appeared waxy and blue, the cut flesh almost black.

'Was it life threatening?' said Rory.

'No, not once they'd staunched the bleeding. Untreated ... she could have bled out, though. The other four wounds were all very similar. They pass right through both hands and both feet, and all four are of an identical diameter. It's safe to say they were made with the same tool.'

'Tool?' said Francis. He studied the wound on the hand nearest to him. It was perfectly round and looked more like a bullet entry wound. Rose, who was wearing gloves, raised the hand and twisted it around so he could see the other side. Instead of a larger gunshot exit wound, there was a similarly round hole on Tash's palm.

'I can't tell you yet what the attacker used to make these. The flesh lining the passage through is chewed up. They're absolutely brutal.'

'And he did this while she was awake?' said Francis. 'That must have been agony. Any sign that he knocked her out or gagged her to stop her screaming?'

'She took a blow to the head at some point,' said Rose, 'but I can't tell how long she was out for.'

Rory looked like he was going to throw up and Francis could feel his own stomach churning.

'Jesus,' said Rory. 'Whoever did this is an animal.'

'And you really think it could be Alex Mullins?' said Rose. 'He's just a kid.'

'He's nineteen,' said Rory. 'He's got a background in tattooing and he's linked to the victim. We have him on CCTV following her when she left the club.'

'He was also in her hospital room when she died,' added Francis. 'He has to be our first port of call.'

He stared down at Tash's body until Rose covered it with the sheet. Then he snapped to attention.

'Rose, I need you to work as fast as you can on this to establish what exactly killed her. Rory, issue an arrest warrant for Alex Mullins. We need to talk to him right now.'

I4

Marni

Drawing was Marni's therapy. She could pour her angst onto the paper in dark, sweeping lines that would materialise into a spectacular tattoo. But when the lines didn't come and the pencil in her right hand faltered, she knew she was in deep trouble. Alex still hadn't come home – apparently, he was staying at Liv's. She desperately wanted to see him, to comfort him, but he wasn't even answering his phone. Things were no better with Thierry and the mood in the house was grim. Life seemed to be spiralling out of control and she needed to let her emotions out on the page.

Still unable to get hold of Alex, she took Pepper with her across to the studio. She felt calmer as soon as she let the door swing shut behind her, leaving the clamour of Gardner Street behind. Marching through to the back, she was itching to pick up a pencil.

But something was wrong.

She felt the draught of warm air on her face as soon as she opened the door that separated her workspace from the shop-front – the back door was open.

Pepper growled.

Hairs stood up on the back of her neck and she looked round frantically, but there was no one there. Everything seemed quiet.

She checked the door for signs of a break-in, but it was simply swinging open on its hinges, with no sign of damage. Had she left it unlocked? She thought back to the previous afternoon, when she'd left in a hurry to confront Thierry. She could remember locking up the front of the shop after the client left, coming through to the back and then leaving by the back door. Yes, she was almost certain she'd locked it.

What the hell?

It only took a moment to spot it. On the shelf where she kept her tattoo irons there were spaces. Two were missing. She went over to that corner of the studio and did a rough inventory of her equipment. A power unit was missing, and a set of cables. There seemed fewer bottles of ink on the shelf above.

'Bastard!' She slammed the door shut, but it didn't catch and bounced back open. Pepper moved forward to stand on the sill of the door, sniffing the air suspiciously. She called him away and closed it properly. She sighed. She must have left it open. Someone had come in and taken all they would need to start tattooing – but who would do such a thing?

She took her time to check the rest of the room, then went to her desk to jot down a list of what she thought had been taken. Was it worth the bother? There was no point calling the police – they wouldn't be remotely interested. And why claim on her insurance? No break-in meant negligence on her part. It would only mean an astronomical rise in premiums next time she came to renew. At least the burglar had simply come in, taken what they wanted and scarpered, rather than trashing the place.

She leaned back in her chair, staring into space. When was she going to get a break? She felt shaken, hating the idea that someone had been nosing around in her studio while she wasn't there. Some bloody kid who fancied tattooing his mates. That was all.

Any hope of concentrating was shot to pieces. She needed to

see Alex. She needed to know that he was okay.

Of course he wasn't okay.

Tash's death would have been a massive shock to him. He'd publicly argued with her just hours before she was attacked. And now he'd gone to ground. Was he hiding from her or from the police?

Her hands were shaking by the time she locked up the shop.

Liv Templeton, her niece and Alex's cousin, shared a house with three other students over in Hove. Marni drove there as fast as she could. When she banged her fist on the door, all she could hear was the sound of rock music coming from inside, certainly loud enough to drown out the sounds of her knocking. Marni bent down and peered through the letter box.

'Liv?' she yelled. 'Are you there?'

There was no response and the music carried on thumping through the wall.

'Liv? It's Marni.'

The door opened and Marni practically fell through it. Liv Templeton stood back as Marni straightened up. She was wearing a short bathrobe that showed off tanned legs that seemed to go on for ever. Her hair was a mess and there was sleep crusted in the corner of her eyes. Marni could smell weed.

'Aunt Marni?'

'Where's Alex? Is he here?'

Liv blinked. 'Alex?' she said, in some confusion.

Could she really have been asleep with this racket going on?

'Yes, I'm looking for Alex,' said Marni, trying not to lose her temper.

Liv answered through a yawn. 'He was here, but he's gone.'

'Was he okay when you saw him? When was it?'

Liv finally seemed to wake up properly.

'Oh God, he told me about Tash Brady,' she said. 'I can't believe she's really dead.'

'How is he?'

'He was talking about Tash, then he was talking about his father.'

'Thierry?'

'He said something like he didn't think Thierry was his real father. I don't know. He was stoned.'

Alarm bells went off in Marni's head. 'Tell me exactly what he said.'

'Something about a letter. That was all. I wasn't listening.'

What letter?

Liv rubbed her eyes. 'I need coffee. Do you want to come in?'

Marni shook her head. 'I need to find him, Liv.'

Liv Templeton shrugged and headed down the hall towards the kitchen.

'If you hear from him, call me, yeah?'

She pulled the front door shut behind her and hurried back to her car. Getting into the *deux chevaux* felt like climbing into a blast furnace. The steering wheel was practically too hot to touch and prickles of sweat broke out across Marni's top lip almost instantly.

All the way back to the house, her mind raced. What was the letter Liv had mentioned? Did this have something to do with Paul, Thierry's twin? Was this why Alex had seemed so distant towards her over the last few months? Thierry was the only one who could have told Alex anything about what had happened in France twenty years ago. But he wouldn't. Why would he?

It didn't make sense. She jammed her foot against the accelerator.

As she turned into Great College Street, she saw blue lights flashing halfway down the road. There was a police car parked outside her house. She pulled up behind it, fear making her cold as she fiddled with the door catch. A policewoman watched her from the pavement, but didn't step forward to help her open the door.

It was that bitch, Angie Burton.

Finally she got out of the car, drenched in sweat, hands shaking.

'What's going on here?' She made a move towards her front door, but Angie Burton blocked her path.

'Sorry, Mrs Mullins. I can't let you in quite yet. We're not finished.'

'Finished what?' said Marni.

Angie Burton pursed her lips and said nothing, so Marni simply pushed past her and went along the pavement to her house. The front door was open and as she came level with it, two figures emerged.

Francis Sullivan and Alex.

Alex was handcuffed.

Marni didn't stop to think for an instant. She blocked their way in just the same way Angie Burton had tried to block hers. But she wasn't going to let them get around her.

'What the hell, Frank? Let him go.'

'Marni.' Francis stopped in his tracks and put his left hand up to stop Alex.

'Why's he handcuffed? He hasn't done anything.'

'Sorry, Marni, but I need to take Alex in for questioning about Tash Brady's death.'

'Questioning? That looks like an arrest to me.'

'Mum,' said Alex. He sounded like a scared child and Marni felt like her heart was being ripped out.

'Alex, when did you come home? How did they know you were here?'

Alex shrugged, his face crumpling.

'We've been watching the house,' said Francis. 'We need to talk to Alex. He was with Tash Brady the night she was attacked and he was there when she died. He has to tell us exactly what happened.'

'But you're arresting him. Do you think he had something to do with it?'

'We intend to find out.' Francis's tone was grim.

Marni felt a sudden urge to slap him, but she knew it wouldn't help. She dug her hands into her jeans pockets to keep them under control.

'I'll come to the station with you,' she said.

Alex's eyes brightened for a second.

'I'm afraid not,' said Francis. 'Alex is over eighteen. He's an adult. Please, let us pass – the sooner we can get going, the sooner all this will be over.'

Never had a policeman's words rung more hollow in Marni's ears.

Defeated, Marni stepped to one side and then watched as Francis guided Alex into the squad car. He went around to the front passenger side and climbed in. Alex stared out of the car window at her, his brown eyes wide.

He needed a lawyer, quickly.

As the car drove off, Marni turned back to her front door. Angie Burton was once again blocking her path.

'You can't go inside yet, Mrs Mullins. We're still searching the property.' Beyond her, Marni could see movement behind her front windows.

'What exactly are you searching for?' said Marni.

'Tattooing equipment,' said Burton with bleak satisfaction. 'The attacker tattooed Tash Brady as part of the attack. We need to find the equipment he used.'

Marni staggered and would have collapsed if Angie Burton hadn't put a strong arm around her waist.

What if they found it in her house? In Alex's room?

15

Tuesday, 15 August 2017

Rory

Kath Brady sat opposite Rory in the interview room, legs crossed, top foot kicking at the air in a pointed, stiletto-heeled sandal. She looked strung out and, although her legs sported a healthy tan, her face was a couple of shades paler and her eyes red-rimmed.

'He did it and I want him brought in, Sergeant Mackay.'

This came at the end of a rant about Alex Mullins and his part in her daughter's death.

'With all due respect, Mrs Brady, DI Sullivan decides who gets brought in for questioning. However, rest assured, as soon as he turns up, we'll be talking to him.'

'I want him charged with murder, not just questioned. Whether or not he's the man that attacked her, it's plain to me he's responsible – he let her walk home on her own. He didn't protect her. And he was the one in her room, fiddling with her heart monitor right before she . . .' She couldn't finish the sentence, covering her mouth with her hand.

Rory listened with growing disbelief. They weren't even sure it was murder yet.

'Leave it to us, please, to do our job. It would probably be better if you went home, Mrs Brady.'

He stood up. Sure, he was sorry about what had happened to

the girl. But he'd had enough of humouring the woman while she told him how to do his job. She bristled at him, but followed him out into the reception area of the police station.

'Make sure you call me when you finally get around to charging him,' she said.

'Of course,' said Rory. *Not bloody likely.*

He put a firm hand on her back and started propelling her towards the double doors onto the street – which at that moment opened as someone came in. It was Francis Sullivan, with Alex Mullins by his side. The boy was handcuffed.

Oh, perfect fucking timing, boss.

'See, sergeant? Your inspector is a lot more on the ball than you are.' Kath Brady turned to Alex, who stood waiting as Francis went across to talk to the desk sergeant. 'I hope you rot in hell for what you did to my daughter.'

Alex scowled and looked pointedly at the floor.

Good for him, thought Rory, for not reacting. Not that it made the kid any less likely to have done it. Not with his family background.

The door swung open again and Marni Mullins burst into the station. She was panting, and sweat glistened on her brow and top lip.

Faced with a fresh audience, Kath Brady couldn't leave things alone. She jabbed a finger into Alex's chest. 'You killed my daughter, you bastard.' Her voice was harsh and shrill and the atmosphere in the reception area became electric.

Marni Mullins bridled with anger. 'What the fuck . . .?'

Alex Mullins stiffened and started working his mouth. Rory realised long before Kath Brady did what the boy was going to do. As Rory jostled Kath away towards the door, Alex spat with force. Instead of catching Kath right in the face, thanks to Rory's actions the glob of spittle landed on the shoulder of her linen jacket.

Kath Brady gasped, repulsed and shocked by the missile that had hit her.

Marni looked neither shocked, nor amused, by what her son had done.

'You'll charge him for that, sergeant?' Brady's voice was still shrill.

Rory had had enough. He bundled her towards the double doors that led out of the building.

'Wait.' Brady stopped level with Marni Mullins, eye to eye.

For fuck's sake!

In the confined space, the two women faced off. Kath Brady, the taller of the pair, looked haughtily down her nose at Marni. Marni practically snarled in return.

'Your son is going down for this,' hissed Brady, squeezing past her to the door.

Marni turned to follow her, fists clenched, mouth wide with surprise.

A well-dressed woman in a sleek grey business suit came in. She nodded at Marni as she assessed what was happening, then put a hand on Marni's forearm and held her back. 'Come on, Mrs Mullins. We came here for Alex.'

As Kath Brady left the building, the expression on her face turned to one of smug satisfaction.

Marni went to Alex and hugged him, while the smart woman addressed herself to Francis.

'Good afternoon, you're DI Sullivan?'

'I am,' said Francis.

'My name is Jayne Douglas. I'll be representing Alex Mullins.'

'Has he instructed you yet?'

'I've been retained by his mother.'

'Alex is an adult and will need to retain his own representation.'

The boss was good. Of course, he still had a lot to learn, but he showed flashes of potential.

'He will retain me.'

'Miss Douglas, please take a seat. I need to process him into the station. You can see him later if he decides to instruct you.'

Looking thoroughly pissed off at being dismissed in this way, Jayne Douglas turned to Marni. 'This is going to take some time, I think.' As Francis led Alex away through the doors on the other side of the reception area, she called after him. 'Don't think you can question my client without me being present.'

Francis stopped and turned back to her.

'Like I said, he's not your client yet. And he hasn't been charged. He's just helping with enquiries. If he co-operates with me, he'll be out much quicker.'

He pushed Alex through the door and banged it shut behind him. Rory pulled out his key card, reopened the door and followed him through.

Francis was waiting for him.

'Mackay, can you interview Alex Mullins?'

Rory was amazed. 'Why not you? He's our prime suspect.'

'It wouldn't be appropriate.'

'What? Because Marni Mullins helped out in a previous case? That's water under the bridge, boss.'

'Rory, I know the family.' His cheeks blazed bright red. 'Marni Mullins and I . . .'

Rory was about to say 'What?' but managed to bite his tongue – though not before his eyebrows had shot up. He took a deep breath and nodded. Had the boss just admitted to having some sort of affair with the Mullins woman? Seriously?

'Sure, I'll do the interview. No problem.'

Those two? He would never have put them together.

Rory and Angie sat on one side of the table. Alex sat on the other. The tiny interview room had no windows and with the door closed, the air seemed as thick as treacle. Rory stripped off his jacket and rolled up his sleeves – his armpits were already clammy and wet.

He dug into the breast pocket of his discarded jacket for his mobile and dialled the incident room.

'Kyle, see if you can track down a fan and bring it to interview room two, thanks.'

They'd offered to bring in the solicitor to sit through the interview, but Alex Mullins had declined. Not necessarily the wisest move, but Rory was good with it. At nineteen Alex was an adult and could make decisions for himself. And they'd made it clear to him, and the lawyer, that at this stage he was just being interviewed as a witness – even if it was obvious to everyone that he was currently their prime suspect.

'Hello, Alex,' said Rory. He was going to lead the questioning while Angie focused on the kid's body language and behaviour.

Alex looked up at him with a nod but hardly made eye contact.

Rory ran through the statement Alex had given at the hospital, in the first hours after Tash's abduction. Of course, there had been no mention of the fight they'd had, or the fact that Alex appeared to follow some time behind her after she left the club. But at that point Tash was still alive and no one had guessed it might become a murder investigation. Now, however, they needed the truth.

'Alex, can you tell me exactly what happened last Friday evening and in the early hours of Saturday morning?'

In short sentences, with frequent prompts, Alex told them about the early part of the evening when he'd been with Tash. They'd had a few drinks in the Mesmerist, where they met up with a group of friends, and had then walked around the corner to The Haunt.

'What time was this?' said Rory.

Alex shrugged. 'Eleven, half past eleven? I don't know.'

'What happened at The Haunt? Why did Tash leave the club without you?'

'She was tired. She'd been drinking on the beach all afternoon. I wasn't ready to go home at that point.'

'What time was that?'

Alex shook his head. 'No clue.'

'But you thought it was all right to let her walk home through Brighton on her own?'

'She'd done it before. It was her choice.'

Alex was sounding belligerent and he wasn't giving them any new information. Time to raise the stakes.

'Alex, we know from the CCTV footage in The Haunt that you and Tash had a fight.'

'So?'

'We know that you walked along the front a few minutes after she did.'

'I wasn't following her.'

'Really?'

Alex's eyes glazed over with exhaustion – shock and bereavement leaving their mark. Rory had seen it before, all too often.

'What time did you get home?'

The boy put his face in his hands, shaking his head. 'I don't know.'

He might be nineteen, but he was still just a kid. Rory felt uncomfortable watching his composure crumble, but it wasn't going to stop him. He was on Tash Brady's team now and he wanted to go in for the kill.

'Come on, Alex,' said Angie, firm but not harsh. 'You must have some idea. You need to try to help yourself here.'

'Alex, do you have any tattoos?' said Rory.

Alex rolled his head from one side of his shoulders to the other. It was clearly a question he'd faced often, given that both his parents were tattoo artists.

'No.'

'Have you ever worked in your parents' tattoo shops or given anyone a tattoo?'

Alex shook his head with a sigh. 'No.'

'Do you know how to use a tattoo gun?'

'Iron,' Alex corrected him. 'They're not guns.'

'Do you know how to use one?'

'Of course. I grew up in a tattoo studio, didn't I?'

'But you've never tattooed anybody?'

'It's not my scene. It's what my parents do.'

'You know your mother served time in prison some years ago, don't you?' Rory knew full well this was below the belt – and the way Alex's head snapped up told him that the kid hadn't known. 'She stabbed a man.'

Alex's eyes widened and his breathing became panicky.

'I don't believe you.'

'It's true, Alex. I wouldn't make up something like that. Is it something that runs in the family?'

Rory could feel Angie glaring at him, but he wasn't going to turn his head to make eye contact with her. It wasn't the strategy they'd agreed for the interview, but if he could wind Alex up enough, perhaps the kid would make the slip-up they needed him to make.

'Like mother, like son?'

With a yelp of rage, Alex stood up, knocking the chair over behind him. He leaned across the table and Rory thought for a second that he was reaching for his neck. He was wrong though.

Alex planted both hands flat on the table and snarled right in his face.

'I want my lawyer. Now.'

16

Francis

'I don't buy it.'

Francis nearly spat the words as he enumerated where Rory had gone wrong. Tempers were reaching breaking point in the tiny viewing space next to the interview room where Rory had just questioned Alex Mullins. Francis's superior, Detective Chief Inspector Bradshaw, was using more than his fair share of the oxygen and the air was rank with male sweat.

Rory blustered against Francis's every argument.

'You were supposed to be information gathering,' said Francis. 'Not setting him up to be a hostile witness.'

'Witness or suspect?' said Rory. 'That boy's looking good for charging to me.'

'Sure,' said Francis. 'We haven't even got the bloody cause of death pinned down yet.'

'Means. Motive. Opportunity,' said Rory. 'We know he would have access to tattooing equipment, and he's admitted knowing how to use it. Motive – he'd just had a very public bust-up with Tash and was probably feeling humiliated by that slap. Opportunity. Yes, he followed her home in the small hours of Saturday morning and he was in her hospital room when she died.'

'But that frames the attack on Tash Brady as a crime of passion, sergeant. Fine, if he'd run after her and knocked her down on the pavement. But this has all the hallmarks of premeditation.'

Francis had watched the interview through the one-way mirror between the two rooms, Bradshaw standing, sweating, by his side. He was incensed with the way Rory had casually wound Alex up and, now the boy had lawyered up, they had no hope of getting anything useful from him. But Rory and Bradshaw remained convinced of Alex's guilt.

'It's perfectly clear he did it,' said Bradshaw. 'Ockham's razor – heard of that, Sullivan? We go after the most likely suspect first and Mullins fits the bill.'

Francis pressed the heel of his hand against his forehead in frustration.

'Only he doesn't.'

'What is this? Your second or third murder case? Rory and I must have worked scores of cases between us. We know what we're talking about.'

Still they couldn't forgive him for being promoted young.

'With all due respect, sir,' said Francis through gritted teeth, 'we don't even know if this is a murder case. The PM results aren't in and Rose hasn't given us a cause of death yet.'

'So let's hear why you think it wasn't him,' said Rory. Francis didn't like the undercurrent of sarcasm in his voice.

'Tash slapped Alex in the club. You're suggesting he retaliated by attacking her, tattooing her with a Latin inscription and giving her stigmata?'

'Both his parents are tattoo artists,' said Bradshaw, letting a note of satisfaction creep into his voice.

'But Alex Mullins isn't. And what about the religious aspect to the attack? You didn't touch on that in the interview. Does he even believe in God?'

'Why are you so keen for it not to be Alex Mullins?' said Rory. 'Because you know the family? Is that it?'

Francis didn't care for the insinuation and headed for the

door. He wasn't going to expand on his relationship – or lack of it – with Marni in public. He needed some air.

'Marni Mullins is due to testify in Sam Kirby's trial next week. I don't want to do anything to derail it, and prematurely charging her son with murder would do just that.'

He pulled open the door, and took a deep breath of the comparatively fresher air in the corridor.

'Sullivan! Don't turn your back on me. Where are you going?'

Francis paused in the doorway. 'To release Alex Mullins.'

'It's my opinion that you should be charging him,' said Bradshaw.

'We need more evidence to do that, sir. I suggest waiting to see what Rose and the SOCOs come back with. Rory, I want the team looking at other possible suspects. What about Richard Brady – am I right in thinking he's her stepfather rather than her real father? What other significant men were there in her life?'

Rory stared at him, blank-faced. 'Richard Brady has an alibi – he was in London at the time of the attack.'

'Has that been confirmed by independent witnesses?'

'Hollins is on it.'

'Rory, we've got plenty of work to do. In the meantime, Mullins is free to go.'

'I think not,' said Bradshaw.

'Sir, I'm OIC on this case, so it's my decision whether to charge him or let him go.'

Bradshaw drew himself up to his full height. A drop of sweat flew off the end of his nose and landed on Francis's sleeve.

'You know, you're making enemies in all the wrong places, Sullivan.'

'Just as well I didn't take this job to make friends. Sir.'

Half an hour later, Alex Mullins left John Street station in the company of his mother and his lawyer. Francis watched them walking down towards Edwards Street from the window of the incident room on the third floor. He stayed where he was long after they'd rounded the corner and disappeared from view.

Why couldn't he get a handle on this case? The team were asking the wrong questions, looking at the wrong people. They weren't listening to him. Rory seemed certain it was Alex Mullins, while he didn't feel certain of anything at all.

He hoped to hell he hadn't just made a terrible mistake.

As he went back across the incident room to his office, his mobile signalled a text.

It was from Robin.

Come now.

17

Tuesday, 15 August 2017

Francis

He called Robin's number but there was no answer.

What'd happened?

He repeated the text message over and over in his mind as he hurried out to the car park. Did it mean his mother was dying? Would he get there in time? Shaking hands made him clumsy, and he dropped the keys as he tried to unlock his car. Grabbing for them, he grazed his knuckle on the tarmac, then crunched the seatbelt buckle in the door as he closed it.

'Damn!'

He made himself sit still, hands on the wheel, to take five deep breaths before turning the key in the ignition.

Did it mean his mother was dying?

When he arrived at the hospital, he ran up the stairs, too impatient to wait for the lift. The nurse at the nursing station came to meet him as he barrelled through the doors onto the ward.

'Lydia Sullivan? What's happened?'

'We think she might have developed pneumonia. She's running a high temperature.' The woman led him towards his mother's room.

'But she'll be okay?'

'It can be dangerous with her condition.'

The nurse was sugar-coating.

Francis stepped into his mother's room, muttering a prayer under his breath.

Please God, let it be a false alarm.

When did he last go to church?

Robin was sitting by their mother's bed, and she stood up when he came into the room.

'Fran,' she said simply, coming forward to embrace him.

He gave her a quick hug for form's sake, but he wanted to give his attention to his mother. A medic stood on the other side of the bed, listening to Lydia Sullivan's chest through his stethoscope. He looked grim-faced as he straightened up.

'Her respiratory rate is high, and I think she might have some fluid collecting in her lungs.' He gently placed an oxygen mask back over her face. 'I'll increase the dose of antibiotics.'

Francis could detect no note of optimism in the man's voice. He knew that with his mother's weakened chest muscles, pneumonia could take hold rapidly.

He turned around to look at Robin and for the first time noticed that Jered Stapleton, the verger at his local church, St Catherine's, was standing behind her chair. What was he doing here?

'Have you spoken to her today?' he said, addressing Robin.

'No. She's been asleep since I arrived.'

'It's better that way,' said Jered Stapleton. 'She needs all her strength for fighting the illness.' He was a tall man who stooped somewhat to hide it, and his hair was thinning on top.

Francis wondered when he'd become such an expert in geriatric care.

The medic finished writing up her chart and hooked it over the end of the bed.

'We're always on hand,' he said. 'Just press the bell if you need us.'

'Thank you,' said Francis.

He sat down by his mother's bed and took her hand. It was cold, already the hand of a dead woman.

You can't think like that.

He rubbed it gently to bring some warmth back. A feeble movement of her fingers made Francis look up at his mother's face. Her eyes fluttered open. She tried to speak.

Francis lifted the mask from her face and rested it on her chest.

'Maman.'

Lydia managed a weak smile when she saw it was him.

'Twice in one week,' she croaked. 'I really am dying after all.' Her breath wheezed as she struggled with the words.

No one laughed and Francis felt a lump forming in his throat. The exertion of speaking caused Lydia to start coughing.

'No more talking – you need to rest,' he said.

'I'll ... do that ... when ... I'm dead,' said Lydia, gasping for air between each chest-rattling cough.

'Don't talk like that,' said Francis.

He put the mask back over her face and her breathing eased a little.

'Don't tire her,' said Robin. She looked exhausted herself.

'How long have you been here?' said Francis.

'Most of the night,' said Robin.

'You should go home and get some rest. I'll stay with her.'

Robin's withering look spoke volumes. She wasn't going to leave her mother's side at this point. Francis wondered how long Jered Stapleton had been there, but he didn't ask.

'You could have called me earlier, you know,' he said.

Lydia closed her eyes and, in a moment, she was asleep.

They sat in silence. An hour passed. Jered Stapleton made himself useful, fetching coffee and a sandwich for Francis, when he admitted he hadn't eaten all day.

Robin felt her mother's forehead.

'She's not shaking off the infection,' said Robin. 'I'm worried.'

'But the antibiotics will kick in.'

'They should have done that by now.'

Francis didn't have to ask what this implied, and Robin's muted sniff showed that she was well aware how serious it was.

Lydia slept on, but Francis felt more and more aware of the labour each breath took. Despite the mask, he could hear the wheeze in her throat.

A nurse came in and checked her temperature and blood oxygen levels.

'Any improvement?' said Robin.

The nurse shook her head.

'Should we call Father William?' said Francis.

'If that's what she'd like, yes, I think it would be a good idea,' said Stapleton.

Robin got up and slipped out of the room, followed by the verger. Alone with his mother, Francis took both her hands in his and raised them up so he could kiss them. She barely stirred in her sleep as he placed them back on the sheet. As he stroked her hair, memories of his childhood crowded back, of being picked up from school by his mother in the smart little Volkswagen hatchback she had before she became too ill to drive, of the long days of summer spent down on Brighton seafront, him always begging for ice cream, her giving in to him with an indulgent smile, and of the darker times, after his father left. By then she was sick, and he could remember hearing her crying in her bedroom for what seemed like for ever.

His phone vibrated in his pocket. He ignored it.

It vibrated again. What could be so important?

To avoid disturbing his mother, he went out into the corridor, pulling his phone from his pocket. It was Rory.

'Is it important?'

'Where are you?'

'At the hospital, seeing my mother.'

'How is she?'

'Rory, what did you want?'

'It can wait. Are you coming back here?'

Francis hung up on him and hurried back into his mother's room.

He looked down at Lydia, sleeping. She wasn't wheezing now. Then it hit him. She wasn't breathing at all. And then Francis realised that his mother had died, simply slipped away on her own, with no one there to hold her hand. The room spun and for a moment he felt as if he couldn't breathe. He could hear his mother's voice calling his name but her lips weren't moving. He wasn't ready for this. He wanted to go back.

He should have had more time with her.

Robin and the verger returned.

'Oh, Fran,' Robin gasped, realising immediately what had happened.

Francis had lost all sense of time and place.

He was aware that Father William arrived, and Stapleton fussed around everyone with endless offers of cups of tea. Francis wished they'd all go away. The doctor who'd been in charge of his mother's care came and spoke to them about issuing the death certificate and what would happen next – Lydia's body would be collected and taken to the undertaker's, pending funeral arrangements. Francis took in only a fraction of what he said. It seemed like an efficient machine had been set in motion as their mother had drawn her last breath, and all he wanted to do was to stop time and scroll through his memories.

Father William prayed over the body, but Francis couldn't. The verger held Robin's hand and gave her his handkerchief. An unnatural quiet blanketed the room, as if his mother was simply asleep and everyone feared to wake her.

Finally, the priest and the verger took their leave, and brother and sister were left alone with her. Robin cried noisily. Francis chewed on his lower lip, unwilling to let the floodgates open, wondering what he could do for his sister.

'Shall I call Dad?' he said.

Robin snorted. 'Do you even have a number for him in Thailand?'

'Somewhere.'

'Well, don't expect him to come back for the funeral. He's moved on now, hasn't he? Living with someone new.'

'I thought they were married.'

'Living with? Married? What difference does it make? He's given up on us.'

Robin had always been far more bitter about their father's desertion.

'I'll call him,' said Francis. 'He has a right to know.'

'As you wish,' said Robin. Her nonchalant shrug turned into a racking sob.

Francis's phone buzzed insistently in his pocket again.

'Go on, answer it,' said Robin, a string of mucus trailing down her chin. 'Your work's more important than this.'

Francis put his hand into his pocket, but only to switch the phone off. Robin's comment hit him hard and the guilt about being out of the room when his mother died hit him like a tsunami. How could he tell her what had happened?

He couldn't tell anybody. Ever.

'Robin ...' He took a step towards her, open-armed for an embrace.

She came to him and cried on his shoulder.

'Sorry,' she said, sniffing, then gasping. 'It's just that I'm scared. It's been so hard with Mum ...' She sobbed again, clinging to him. He hugged her closer. 'Now that Mum's gone, Fran, I'm going to need you more than ever. I feel so alone ...'

'How can I help you?'

'By being more available. By being more present in my life.'

Francis knew his expression had betrayed his feelings when she backtracked immediately after saying it.

'No. Sorry. I don't want to take up too much of your time.'

She gathered together her coat and bag.

'Don't be silly, Robin. I don't want us to fall out at a time like this.'

She shrugged. 'You seem to be drifting further and further away.'

Francis felt his cheeks infuse with colour. 'I promise, Robin, I'll be here for you. Whenever you need me.'

But would he? His phone was burning a hole in his pocket and in the morgue was a dead girl who had just as much of a call on his time. His sergeant was railroading a suspect. His boss was driven by statistics. He still didn't know what had killed Tash Brady, let alone who.

He'd failed his mother and now he was making promises he couldn't keep. To Robin. And to Tash Brady.

Where could he turn for reassurance?

iii

19 July 1988

Aimée, sweet little Aimée, you're eleven years old today. You lie in your bed and think about what it will be like to be a grown woman. You're not sure you like the idea of it very much at all. The women you know – your mother, your aunt, your teachers – aren't joyous creatures. Where do they find their pleasures?

You get out of bed and go to the window. A gull whirls and screeches overhead but it's too early for people. You look through the trees to the end of the garden, trying to see the Maria *tied up at its mooring on the river. You imagine running away – taking a small bag of your favourite things, climbing into the motorboat and untying the rope that holds her. How far would you get? Along the coast to Brighton or Chichester? Or could its tiny motor chug you across the Channel to France?*

It's just a dream, isn't it? You're old enough to know now that little girls can't make their way in the world on their own. Not without bad things happening to them.

Because your mother is ill – she's been ill for soooo long – your father has prepared your birthday breakfast. There's a basket of croissants and pastries on the table, along with the expectation that you'll gorge yourself on them. Only you don't want to. The thought of the buttery, flaky patisserie makes you feel sick. You don't want breakfast at all.

Maybe just some coffee but your father has made you hot chocolate. He disapproves of children drinking coffee. He seems to forget that you won't be a child for very much longer.

Oh no, Aimée, you know that's not true, as much as you wish it were. That's not something he'll forget.

Jay grabs up two of the croissants and eats them greedily, crumbs flaking down his front and onto the floor. Your father looks over his newspaper disapprovingly but Jay doesn't care. He's perfectly happy to provoke. He takes a pain au raisin from the basket and starts unwinding the pastry directly into his mouth.

'Jay!' Your father's voice takes on a sharp tone that he never uses with you.

You use the distraction to give your pain au chocolat to your father's dog under the table. She wolfs it down as greedily as Jay.

Your father goes back to his paper.

He looks hurt when, a minute later, you leave the table, two thirds of a croissant left on your plate, the other third strategically crumbled into your napkin. You ignore his look of disappointment. You ignore the hunger pangs in your stomach. You don't eat any more, do you? It's your way of never growing up, never having to enter the adult world. If you do eat, you vomit it back up in secret.

But the problem with never growing up, Aimée, is that you'll stay daddy's little princess for ever. That might be even worse.

You wrap your arms around your ribs, practically cutting yourself on the sharp, protruding bones. You rub your forearms. They're covered in thick, downy hair that never used to be there. You're stiff and exhausted, bones aching as you climb the stairs.

You want to go to your mother's room, but she'll be asleep at this time. You never see her now in the mornings – she needs her rest is what your father says. She's always tired. Even her skin looks tired. She has no energy to mother you any more. Cancer does that to a person. It poisons them and takes away their spirit.

*

Your father's study has always fascinated you. The huge desk used to belong to his father, and his father's father. It has hidden drawers – Jay showed you once but you've never been able to work out the mechanism to open them yourself. What secrets do you think your father keeps in those drawers, Aimée? You know your father keeps secrets.

You're not supposed to go in there on your own. But you do. When he's at work and Mummy's resting and Jay's outside, sometimes you creep down the hallway and silently open the door. You've never been caught. You don't like to think what your father would say if he found you alone in his study. More disappointment. A punishment, perhaps. One of his secret punishments that you're not allowed to tell anyone else about.

Who the hell would you tell?

Once you tried to tell Jay. He wouldn't listen. He blocked his ears with his hands and said, 'Shut up!' over and over again. After that he avoided you and you heard him asking if he could go to your cousins' house. Then he was gone for almost a week. When he came back, you didn't dare say anything more about it. You couldn't bear for Jay to look at you that way he did before, with pity and with revulsion, all mixed together.

You can't turn to him for help.

Today your father calls for you after breakfast. He wants to give you a gift. Your heart thunders. In your father's world, gifts carry obligations. He'll want something in exchange. You try not to think about it as you pull down on the door handle.

'Happy Birthday, princess,' he says with a smile. He's sitting at his desk. On the blotter in front of him there's a small blue box tied with a white ribbon. You've seen boxes like that before. You know what's inside them.

You stand in the doorway.

'Come here,' he says. He pats his lap, for so long a favourite place of yours.

But now you understand. You don't want to sit on his lap.

Your reluctance causes him to tighten his jaw.

'Come here, Aimée.'

There's tension in his voice, so you go to him.

You climb onto his lap and he engulfs you in his arms. He smells your hair and exhales with satisfaction. His hands are warm, but you feel cold inside.

Whatever precious, precious gift is in the blue box, it can't be worth this.

18

Wednesday, 16 August 2017

Rory

If Rose Lewis summoned you to the mortuary, it meant she had news to impart. Rory thought she could just as well tell them things over the phone, but it was a power play – she liked to hold court. Frankly, Rory could do without it, but he didn't have any choice.

He parked his car next to hers, then looked round for Francis's wheels. The boss hadn't arrived, so Rory took advantage and lit up, wanting to put off the moment when he'd have to take a lungful of foul mortuary air. He leaned back against the bonnet of his car and though it wasn't yet eleven, he could feel the heat of the metal through his suit trousers.

It wasn't like the boss to be late for anything. Was his rather perfect facade beginning to slip?

He stubbed out his cigarette and went inside, peering through the glass windows in the doors to the morgue to see if Rose was at work on a body. Thankfully, she wasn't there, so he made his way up to her office on the floor above.

Rose was on the phone. She looked serious, but silently waved him inside when he stuck his head round the door.

Rory sat down in the chair opposite her desk, wondering how she kept it so neat with the number of cases she usually had going through.

'So sorry . . . Yes, I'll keep you posted, but take your time.' She listened for a few seconds. 'Bye.'

Instead of talking to him, she stared out of the window for a moment after dropping her phone onto her desk.

'Everything all right?' said Rory.

Rose looked round at him. 'You don't know?'

'Know what?'

'That was Francis. His mother died yesterday afternoon.'

Shit. That explained a lot. The missed calls. The fact that he wasn't here now.

'I told him he should take a few days off, but I doubt he will,' she continued.

'You're probably right.'

If only he would, then Rory could get this case wrapped up and Alex Mullins charged. It was bloody obvious the boy had done it, but the boss seemed to be lacking that gut instinct for the job.

'What have you got for us, Rose?'

She looked at him sharply, as if he hadn't expressed adequate sympathy.

'I'm worried about him, Rory. Bradshaw still riding him hard?'

Rory shrugged. 'He's still got a lot to learn – and the lad needs to grow a thicker skin.'

'He will. He's the brightest in the department. By a long chalk.'

She gave him a meaningful look that he didn't like – but he somehow managed to bite back the profanities that sprang to mind.

'You didn't ask me here to discuss the boss, did you?' If Francis was going to be absent for a day or two, he might as well try and take advantage of it. 'Got anything on the cause of death yet?'

Rose nodded and shuffled through a stack of papers on her desk. 'The ink used to tattoo her almost certainly caused her death.'

'An allergic reaction?'

'Not at all. The ink had been adulterated.'

'Deliberately? How can you be sure?'

'If it had shown an excess of one or other of the constituent ingredients of black tattoo ink, I would say it could be accidental. But not this. When we tested it, we found traces of a chemical called taxine in the tattooed flesh, in her blood and in her liver tissue.'

'Taxine?'

'It's found in the seeds of yew berries and also in the leaves. It's deadly.'

Rose let her words sink in.

'Deadly enough to have killed her?'

'Absolutely. It's been used as a poison since Roman times. Now it's harvested for anti-cancer drugs. It's not exactly something a tattoo artist would have in their studio.'

'So where would the attacker have got it from? If they used a particular drug, would you be able to identify it?'

'You can't get it in anything you can buy over the counter.'

'So they would need to have been prescribed the drug themselves, or have some sort of medical connection?' This could narrow the field.

Rose grimaced. 'I don't think it came from a drug,' she said. 'Otherwise I would have found additional ingredients. Looks more likely to have been processed directly from a yew tree.'

'How?'

'Probably by grinding the seeds or leaves of yew and then making a tincture to add to the ink.'

Rory digested the information.

'And you think that's what caused her heart to stop?'

'Yes. It's massively poisonous and the symptoms she experienced match up with those listed for oral poisoning with taxine – I've been through it with Tanika Parry on the phone this morning – dizziness, nausea, shortness of breath, tachycardia, respiratory arrest, cardiac arrest. We're in agreement that, given the presence of the poison in her body, taxine accounts for most of the symptoms the medical team observed.'

'And if there was taxine in the tattooing ink, someone added it on purpose? That means we're definitely looking at murder rather than manslaughter, doesn't it?' said Rory.

Rose looked at him over the rim of her glasses.

'Without a doubt.'

Rory took out his phone. 'Angie, I need you to go back to the Mullins's house. Check if there's a yew tree in the garden. Aye, that's all. Just a yew tree. I'll explain later.'

And when he next saw Francis – I told you so.

19

Angie

There was no yew tree in the Mullins's garden. Rory had made Angie double-check, unwilling to accept it when she told him over the phone. But walking to work this morning, she'd counted at least four in ten minutes – two in churchyards and two in gardens – so yew leaves and berries would hardly be difficult to come by. Still, that didn't build the case in the way the sarge wanted to build it, so he wasn't interested.

He was a bit too old-school for her liking, not that she'd ever admit it to any of the rest of the team. Not even to Tony, who'd worked with Rory for years. But with the boss away on compassionate leave, the sergeant was in command, steering things the way he wanted them to go.

Tony had been instructed to follow up on recent pharmacy robberies in the local area to see if any relevant drugs had been reported stolen. But Angie had another lead to be getting on with, one that had presented itself unexpectedly as she'd arrived at the station.

The girl sitting opposite her in the interview room was silent and unfocused. There were dark rings around her eyes and the rims were red, probably from crying. She picked at the frayed sleeve edge of her cardigan and even when Angie said hello to her, she didn't make eye contact.

Her name was Sarah Collins and she was Tash Brady's best friend. She'd come into the station with her mother because apparently she had something to disclose.

'Sarah, your mum told me you were worried about something,' Angie said. 'Something to do with Tash?'

Sarah didn't answer but gave her mother an appealing look.

Angie wondered if she'd be able to winkle anything of any use out of the girl.

'Come on, darling. Tell her what you told me,' said her mother. Angie wasn't wild about being referred to as 'her', but she kept a lid on her annoyance for the sake of getting the information. 'Tell her about Tash and Alex.'

Sarah sniffed. She looked close to tears, but then she had just lost her best friend.

'What about Tash and Alex?' said Angie, encouraging the girl to talk.

'It was nothing,' said Sarah, her voice a whisper, eyes downcast.

Angie started to wonder if she was wasting her time. She'd rather be back in the incident room, where at least they had a fan stirring the sluggish air.

Sarah's mother looked annoyed. 'It wasn't nothing, Sarah. It might be something important that the police should know about.'

Sarah continued staring at the tabletop, her face reddening.

'Why don't you want to tell me, Sarah?' said Angie.

Finally the girl looked up at her. 'I don't want to get anyone into trouble.'

'You mean Alex, don't you?'

She nodded, biting her bottom lip.

'I understand,' said Angie. 'But really, we need to know all the facts, so we can work out what happened to Tash. No one will be in trouble unless they've broken the law.'

Sarah sniffed and looked across at her mother. Then she started to talk.

'You know Alex was Tash's boyfriend, don't you?'

Angie nodded, not wanting to interrupt her before she'd even got going.

'They'd been together for about six months. Tash liked the fact that he was a bit of a bad boy, her 'bit of rough', she used to call him.'

'What was bad about him, Sarah?'

'Not so much,' said Sarah. Angie got the feeling she was backtracking slightly. 'He smoked a bit of weed, got it for other people.'

'You think he was dealing among his college friends?'

Sarah looked scared. 'Not really dealing, just getting small amounts of it, if people wanted it. Like doing them a favour.'

The fact that Alex was dealing came as no surprise to Angie. It seemed to run in the family – she knew that his father, Thierry, had a history of low-level drug convictions.

'Did Tash ever smoke weed with him?'

Sarah shook her head vehemently, a bit too quickly. 'No, not Tash. She wasn't into that.'

Angie didn't believe her, but decided to leave it. This couldn't be the reason why Sarah's mother had marched her into the police station – there must be something else, something more pertinent to Tash's death.

'Sarah, do you know if Alex was tattooing people at college?'

The girl's eyes widened. 'Tattooing people? No, I never heard that.'

There'd been enough beating around the bush.

'Sarah, do you think Alex was involved, in any way at all, in what happened to Tash?'

Sarah tugged harder at the sleeve of her cardigan and chewed on her bottom lip.

'No, of course I don't think that. But . . .'

'Yes?'

The girl took a deep breath. 'Tash told me that Alex had hit her.'

Pay dirt.

'When did she tell you this?'

'A couple of weeks back. About a week before she was attacked.'

'Did she tell you why?'

And when? Did it happen more than once? How often? How badly? Angie had so many questions but she needed to take it slowly – she didn't want her witness to take fright.

'It was after a party. Alex was drunk. Everyone was drunk – it was the end-of-year party, at the end of last term.'

'What happened?'

'There was this guy, he was interested in Tash. It was a boy from her tutorial group – he'd been messaging her and stuff. She'd said she wasn't interested, but at the party, he came on to her pretty heavily.'

'And?'

'She was drunk and she wanted to dance. Alex had gone outside with some of his mates for a smoke, so she danced with this guy instead. When Alex came in and saw her dancing with someone else, he went ballistic.'

'Did you see him hit her? Did he do it in front of everyone?'

Sarah shook her head. 'No, it didn't happen right then. It was afterwards, outside the house where the party was. He was still angry and when she said it was his fault for disappearing, he hit her. Not hard, not hard at all. But it shocked her. I think it made her start to think about breaking up with him.'

'But she didn't?'

'No . . . he was really sorry in the morning. He bought her flowers, promised he'd cut down on his drinking. They made up and everything was fine.'

'Did it happen again?'

'She never told me if it did. But I know they were arguing the night Tash was attacked.' She stopped and grimaced. 'I mean, I don't think Alex was the one that attacked her. But you need to know everything, right?'

'That's right,' said Angie. 'We know they argued that evening and Tash left the club. Were you there when that happened?'

'No, I just heard about it from a friend.'

'Okay. What you've told me has been really useful. Thank you for coming in, Sarah. If we need to talk to you again, we'll get in touch and if you think of anything else that might help us, I'm always here.'

She gave Sarah her card, which the girl passed straight to her mother.

'Thank you for bringing her in, Mrs Collins,' said Angie, standing up.

Sarah's mother got up and put out her hand.

'We just want to do all we can to help. It's awful what happened to Tash, and Kath's in absolute pieces about it.'

Angie wondered what the sarge would make of this. It would certainly add fuel to his fire.

20

Sally Ann

Sally Ann Granger was knackered. She hated her work – after-hours cleaning at the aquarium wasn't her idea of a dream job. Maybe it wouldn't be for long, once she got her YouTube channel sorted. The roar and vibration of the floor cleaner made her head ache, so she switched off, wiping sweat from her forehead with a clammy hand. Why did they have to keep it so damn hot in here?

And dark.

The lights in the fish tanks were lowered now the visitors had gone home. All she could see were shadowy outlines drifting back and forth, accompanied by the incessant bubbling that kept the tanks aerated. She leaned her arms and then her cheek on the cold glass of the nearest tank, jumping back when a piranha suddenly loomed up to her with its malevolent, sideways stare. Tiny, sharp teeth protruded from its open mouth and Sally Ann pulled away, feeling slightly sick.

She needed company. Maybe she could persuade Alex to come over. Of course, it was strictly against the rules, but so what? They had a laugh and it made the time pass quicker. And after what happened to Tash, he could probably do with that.

She sent a text, but he didn't reply. Disgruntled, she turned the floor cleaner on again and slowly made her way down the Victorian gothic arcade that formed the backbone of the building. On either side, the silent fish tanks reflected blue and green light onto the floor – and all that glass still to be polished. Halfway down, she needed to unplug the cleaner and move the cable to a different socket. She sighed as she battled to get the plug out of the wall.

A sharp, metallic click somewhere beyond the arcade made her turn. She took a deep breath. The place was full of odd mechanical noises – there were scores of pumps, generators and fans keeping the conditions in the tanks just right. She hated being alone in the building after hours. Of course, she wasn't alone. It was her and a thousand sea creatures. Not to mention the snakes. There was a giant anaconda . . . She shuddered. Her biggest fear was being alone here if it escaped. She'd read the information card about it squeezing donkeys to death. She glanced around nervously before continuing with her work.

At the end of the gallery, when she turned the polisher off, she heard another sound. An electric shriek, a high-pitched grinding. It made her jump. She thought she was here alone – she could have sworn she saw Roddy, the maintenance engineer, leaving before she started work. But maybe he'd come back to do something.

The electric whine started and stopped again.

She peered down the passage to the Seahorse Kingdom. She thought that was where the sound had come from.

'Roddy? Is that you?'

Nothing but the soft burbling of the tanks.

There was no one around the seahorse area, so she plugged the floor polisher into a new socket and carried on. She made her way up the long corridor towards the ocean pool, humming tunelessly under the roar of the cleaner. Reaching the steps at the end, she turned around and made her way back, still polishing, still humming.

A flicker of light around the corner caught her eye but she ignored it. The movement of the water in the tanks constantly caused the light to shimmer and flicker. She should be used to that. But she still felt a little jumpy as she coiled up the electric flex and pushed the polisher back in the direction of the tropical lagoon. This and the harbour section would complete the public areas, but then she still had to do the back area of the aquarium which was staff only. Her heart sank at the thought. She'd be here for at least another hour.

She heard a footfall on the tiled floor. Maybe Roddy was here after all.

'Roddy?'

There was no answer but she heard the footsteps again. They came from beyond the harbour area. She started cleaning the viewing platform around the tropical lagoon. Huge fish loomed up against the glass, adding to her sense of unease with their cold, dead stares as they slipped silently along the side of the tank.

With the sound of the polisher roaring in her ears, she didn't notice the man approaching her until he was nearly upon her. His reflection in the glass made her look round with a gasp. The shock of seeing someone looming out of the darkness made her stumble against the machine. She snapped it off. The man wasn't Roddy.

He was holding something in his hand. In the dim light, she could only see a silhouette. A gun?

'Hello? What . . .'

His other arm snaked out towards her and his fist slammed into her cheekbone. An explosion of pain in her head made her reel and she dropped to her knees, bones cracking against the tiled floor, her mouth flooding, sick with fear. She passed out.

*

It was pain that brought her back again. Pain in her head, dark, vast and throbbing. And pain in her left hand, sharp and burning. The rest of her body hardly registered – she seemed to be made up of just two pinpoints of intense agony.

Remember to breathe.

She gasped and, with the slight movement, the pain in her head splintered into shards. Her eyes were closed, and she was lying on her back somewhere. *What was happening?* It was difficult to think in the abstract when it was taking all her resources to draw a breath. She filtered information from the physical sensations. She was lying on a cold, hard floor, but she wasn't sure where. Still by the tropical lagoon or in the Victorian arcade? Virtually no light filtered through her eyelids. She listened for the gentle slapping and gurgling of the aquariums but her ears were ringing and she couldn't concentrate.

She was leaning to the right, with her right arm trapped underneath her body. She couldn't even feel her right hand. She tried to shift enough to free it and realised she was anchored by her left leg. Held in place, someone holding her down by the ankle, and beyond it, nothing but a fresh burning sensation. Pain seared through her foot, making her scream. She thrashed about, desperately trying to pull her leg away as the pain intensified.

She opened her eyes. They felt gritty and her vision was blurred. A dark shadow moved in the periphery of her view. Then a blinding light shone straight into her face. Terrified, she closed her eyes again, her cry of panic ringing in her ears.

The electrical screeching she'd heard earlier started up again, only this time it was right by her. It roared for a second or two, then stopped. Someone pulled her right arm free from under her and she rolled heavily on the hard surface.

Beyond the harsh glare of the light, she could hear someone

breathing heavily. She should try to get up, try to run away from him. What did he want with her?

The bright light blinded her again and fear gripped her. She couldn't move. She couldn't even find her voice to scream.

The light came closer.

Sally Ann gasped.

'No . . .' After a single word, her voice faltered, stifled in a constricted throat.

Abruptly she realised what the man had been holding. Her brain had matched the shape to the noise. Panic swept through her, loosening her bladder and stealing her breath. She felt she was going to suffocate, like she was fighting a weight of water crushing her chest.

Her right hand was held flat against the floor. The screeching sounded louder than ever. She screamed but it did nothing to blot out the sudden flare of pain in the palm of her hand or the feel of being spattered by her own blood like hot, stinking rain.

21

Friday, 18 August 2017

Francis

Francis lay with his eyes closed, elbows resting on the edges of the roll top bath, fingers steepled in front of him. The water had gone cold – goosebumps peppered his arms – but he was unable to move. A single tear rolled down his cheek and plopped onto his chest, merging into the larger body of water. He hated himself.

It was all fucked up.

A picture of his mother, dead in her hospital bed, floated behind his eyelids. He pushed it away brutally, trying to replace it with a living image.

She died on her own. You were supposed to be there with her.

He would never forgive himself for stepping out of the room to take that call.

Since when had work become so important? More important than his mother. His sister. In the moment of realisation that their mother had died, Robin had turned to Jered Stapleton for comfort. It should have been him. But that wasn't fair. She had a right to a social life, more than a social life even, if she wanted. His cock softly butted against his thigh in the chill water and he glanced down at it ruefully. What about his life beyond work? Nothing since that ill-judged ... thing, whatever it was, with Marni Mullins the previous year. But what did he have to offer somebody else?

His mobile vibrated on the stool next to the bath. He plunged his head under the water, willing it to go away, then emerged immediately amid a shower of droplets, determined not to miss a message from his sister.

It wasn't Robin. He saw it was from Rory and did his best to look away. But the word 'attack' sprang from the screen.

Francis grabbed a towel, thoughts of his sister forgotten.

'You shouldn't be here, boss,' said his deputy, as they met on the steps down to the aquarium entrance. 'I only texted to keep you in the loop – I wasn't expecting you to come in.'

The first responders had already taped off the aquarium fore-court with crime scene tape, and a gaggle of nosy tourists had gathered, craning their necks over the balustrade on Madeira Drive to see what was going on, disappointed that they weren't going to get the aquarium tour they'd booked.

'I can't sit around doing nothing, Rory,' said Francis. 'Just makes it worse.'

Rory looked as if he was about to say something further on the subject, so Francis ran down the steps and ducked under the tape. He didn't need to hear homilies from a man who made no bones about wanting his job.

Rory tossed a half-smoked cigarette into the gutter and fol-lowed him down.

'What d'you know about this?' said Francis, as Rory caught up.

'Young girl, a cleaner here, attacked while she was working last night,' said Rory, as they went through the doors. 'The manager found her when he opened up this morning. She's been taken to the County – they're about to operate.'

'Anyone talk to her yet?'

'Uh-uh.' Rory shook his head. 'The registrar called John Street as soon as she came in. It's an emergency situation – they won't hold off operating on her for us. She was stabbed in the gut, apparently. Lost a lot of blood. Might be touch and go.'

They showed their warrant cards to the manager of the centre. He was tall and blond, wearing shorts and a polo shirt with the aquarium logo. He sported a windsurfer's tan on his arms and legs, though his face looked ashen. He pointed them in the direction of the Victorian arcade, but obviously didn't have the stomach to go back in there himself.

The smell of blood and urine were by no means the worst thing about the crime scene, but when they invaded his nostrils, Francis momentarily winced. He could remember childhood visits to the aquarium, how much he'd loved it – the warm, soupy air that enveloped you as you went inside, the bright flashes of colour as tropical fish darted through twisted coral, and the vicarious thrill of looking a shark – albeit a small one – in the eye. Now, he knew he'd never want to visit an aquarium again.

The far end of the arcade was a study in blood spatter. Arcs of it swept across the flat surfaces of the glass, tiny globules clinging to their own reflections and larger drops that clumped into rivulets running to the floor. The stains looked darker on the sandstone pillars in the centre of the arcade – the droplets seemed to leach right into the porous stone. Near to the octagonal pool at the heart of the concourse was a slick of congealed blood, black and sticky, the edges smeared. The sharp, sweet smell of iron and plasma hung in the air. Not far away, a commercial floor polisher stood abandoned and speckled red. On one of the tanks a bloody handprint was being photographed by a SOCO in a white suit, bending awkwardly to get the best shot without treading in a smudge of blood on the floor near his feet.

'Jesus,' hissed Rory through clamped teeth. 'You say the victim of this is still alive?'

'Just.'

Francis wondered if the perp had left any footprints or finger marks or if they all belonged to the centre manager and the paramedics who'd treated the girl. As they weren't suited up, Rory and Francis couldn't venture further into the area to investigate. Rose Lewis came over to them.

'Find anything?' said Francis.

'Apart from haemoglobin?' She shook her head. 'No.'

'All this blood from the same woman, or could there have been another victim?'

'Looks likely to be from the one victim, given the spatter patterns and the progression across the floor – but we'll have to run DNA tests to find out for sure.'

'And no sign of a weapon?' said Rory.

'Nothing so far.'

They went back to talk to the manager. He filled them in on the girl's name, Sally Ann Granger, and told them she'd been working at the centre as a cleaner for the last three months.

'She's a nice girl,' he said, with a slight tremor in his voice. 'I can't think why anybody would want to do this to her.'

'Any idea how the attacker gained access to the building?' said Francis.

The manager shook his head. 'No signs of a break-in and because Sally Ann was in here cleaning, the alarm wasn't active.'

'Could she have let someone in?' said Rory.

The man shrugged. 'She could – but she wasn't meant to.'

There wasn't much more to be gained by hanging around at the scene, so they left it to the SOCOs and headed to the hospital. Tanika Parry hurried towards them as they came into the A&E reception area. Her hair was dishevelled and there was blood on her scrubs.

'You saw Sally Ann Granger?' said Francis.

She nodded. 'She's in theatre now.'

'How bad is it?' said Rory.

'Frankly, she was lucky she was found when she was,' she said.

'She was bleeding profusely from a stab wound in her side, and from wounds to her hands and feet.'

'The same as Tash Brady?' Francis felt the hairs on the back of his neck stand to attention.

'Exactly.'

'Shit!' said Rory. He looked accusingly at Francis.

Francis didn't have to ask what he was thinking. *You released Alex Mullins. Now this.*

'She was also tattooed,' said Tanika Parry, her face grim. 'We're testing her blood for taxine. If we find it at the same levels as Tash Brady exhibited, there's not much we can do.'

'Nothing?' said Rory. 'Even knowing what the poison is?'

'There's no antidote to taxine,' said Parry. 'A small dose might be survivable, but after a certain point . . .' She shrugged apologetically.

'We need to talk to her,' said Francis. 'When will she be out of theatre, and how long till . . .?'

'Till she dies? That depends on the dose. But it'll take a couple of hours for her to come out of the anaesthetic.'

'Can you do something to speed that up?'

'No.' Tanika Parry glared at them. 'My concern is for my patient and she's been severely traumatised. She might just have a few hours left to spend with her family.'

'And if we don't find out who did this, you might be seeing more girls with poisonous tattoos.' Francis tried to moderate the tone of his voice but failed.

Rory put up both hands to placate the medic but Francis was having none of it.

'One girl has been murdered. If Sally Ann Granger dies, that puts the body count at two. There's a killer out there that needs to be stopped. Don't obstruct us, Miss Parry – not unless you want to explain to more girls' parents why they need to say goodbye to their daughters.'

Tanika Parry took a step back from him, her face perfusing with blood.

'I'll see what I can do,' she said.

22

Friday, 18 August 2017

Angie

Tony Hitchins was supposedly at the gym. At least as far as his wife supposed.

Angie knew different. He was sprawled, naked, across her bed – and a fine sight it was. One she didn't get to see as often as she'd have liked.

'I swear I burn more calories when I come here than I do at the gym,' he said, grinning up at her.

'Just think how fit you'd be if you spent more time here,' said Angie.

Tony frowned, making Angie wish she hadn't said it. But did he think she was going to hang on like this for ever? It was time he made a decision. She turned away, heading for the bathroom.

'Ange?'

Her mobile sounded and, recognising the ringtone, she changed course and came back to the bed.

'That's Sullivan. I'd better take it.' She picked it up. 'Boss?'

'I need you to meet Tony down at the aquarium. Looks like Brady's attacker has struck again.' He briefed her on the details. 'I want you two to talk to the manager and check out yesterday's CCTV footage.'

'Sure. Have you spoken to Tony?' she said. She winked at him.

'He's not answering. I've sent him a text.'

Angie prodded Tony in the ribs with her bare foot. He grunted and she covered the microphone on her mobile.

"Kay, I'll let you know what we find.'

She disconnected and slid down the bed so she could reach Tony's mouth with her own. They kissed, but then she pushed him away.

'You'd better put your phone on. We've got to get over to the aquarium – there's been another attack, same as Tash Brady's.'

Tony groaned.

Ten minutes later, they drew up in separate cars outside the Brighton Aquarium. They parked and then greeted each other as if they were colleagues who hadn't just spent the better part of two hours in bed together.

'The manager of the centre's called Bill Faraday. He found the girl, Sally Ann Granger, when he opened up this morning.'

'Does she a have a link with the aquarium?' said Tony.

'She's the cleaner.'

A tall, blond man rushed over to them as soon as they went in through the double doors.

'You're the police?' he said. 'I'm Bill Faraday. I'm the manager here.'

Angie got out her warrant card. 'I'm DC Angie Burton and this is DC Tony Hitchins. We need to take a statement from you about finding Sally Ann Granger this morning.'

The man nodded.

'And we'll need to see whatever CCTV footage you have for yesterday, possibly the day before.'

'We can talk in my office,' he said.

They took a quick look at the attack site, but the crime scene crew had it cordoned off. Then they followed Bill Faraday into a small office situated behind the reception counter. There were only two chairs, so Tony stood.

'Sorry to make you go through this again,' said Angie, 'but we need all the details we can get.'

Faraday nodded. He pressed his hands palms down on the desk to stop them shaking.

'Is she going to be okay?' he said. He sniffed loudly, and Angie suspected he might be about to start crying.

'She's in good hands.' It was all the reassurance she could offer. She wasn't going to tell him that they suspected taxine poisoning. Or that if this was the case, she was probably going to die. There were moments when she hated her job.

'Just tell us what happened,' said Tony.

'I got here at half past seven,' he said.

'That's a bit early, isn't it?' Tony interrupted. 'What time does the aquarium open to the public?'

'Ten, but I wanted to get through some paperwork first so I'd be able to get away by lunchtime.'

'I'm afraid that's not going to happen, Mr Faraday,' said Angie. 'We're going to need you here until the SOCOs have finished with the site.'

Bill Faraday gave a resigned nod. He looked depressed, and no wonder. There was no chance the aquarium would be open today, and probably not tomorrow or for several days after that.

'Tell us about how you found her.'

'I came in, like I said, at half past seven – straight into the office. No one else was due in until half past eight to start preparing the day's feeds. I was working, maybe for about ten minutes, when I heard a noise.' He paused, remembering.

'What sort of noise?' prompted Angie.

Faraday drew a heavy breath. 'A squeak, sort of. It sounded like an animal, not human. I got up and went into the reception area to listen. We don't have any animals here that would make a noise like that.' He grimaced. 'I didn't hear anything more, so I came back to my desk. Then, after a while . . .'

'How long?'

'A few minutes – I heard it again. It sort of freaked me out a bit. I thought it might be a rat, come up from the sewers.'

'Has that happened before?' said Tony.

'Sometimes. I thought I'd better investigate properly and that's when I found Sally Ann.' He put his head in his hands. 'If only I'd gone to look the first time I heard the sound.'

'Where was she?'

'Down at the far end of the Victorian arcade. I didn't realise it was her at first – from this end, I could just see that there was someone lying on the floor, next to the rock pool.'

'What did you do?' said Tony.

'I went to her, of course,' said Faraday. 'As soon as I came close, I recognised it was Sally Ann.'

'Was she conscious?'

'Barely. I phoned nine nine nine straight away, then I fetched a towel to put under her head. I don't think she knew it was me.'

'She didn't speak?'

He shook his head. 'I don't think she could. But I told her not to. She was bleeding heavily from her side, and from her hands and feet. I spent the time waiting for the ambulance on the phone. They told me to get more towels, to try to stop the bleeding.'

Angie looked at him carefully. 'There doesn't seem to be any blood on your clothes.'

'I changed,' said the manager. 'This is a spare staff uniform. I gave the clothes I was wearing to one of your officers.'

'Can you tell us Sally Ann's routine? Is it usual for her to be working here so early in the morning?'

'She would have been cleaning last night,' said Faraday. 'She comes on at five and cleans till seven-thirty every day.'

'And she's here alone during that time?'

'Sometimes. But sometimes I'm here, or one of the other members of staff, working late.'

'What about last night?'

'I wasn't here. I'll have to check with the rest of my staff.' He looked suddenly horror-stricken. 'Jesus! You're not suggesting she was attacked by someone who works here?'

'No sign of a break-in anywhere?' said Tony.

'No, but . . .' Faraday's eyes widened at the implication. 'Look, I think she sometimes let friends come in here. In fact, I know she did. I once caught her drinking here with a couple of mates.'

'So it could have been someone she knew,' said Angie.

'We'll need to know who has access to the building,' said Tony. 'We need to know which doors were locked and which were open, and whether Sally Ann let anybody in while she was cleaning last night.'

'Do you have CCTV footage from inside the building?' said Angie.

'We've got three cameras. But we turn them off when the aquarium's closed. It's mainly to keep an eye on the shop and the till at reception.'

'Where's the other one?'

'Outside, trained on the front entrance, so the receptionists can see if there's a queue.'

It didn't sound like they were going to be of much help.

'Right – let's double check all the doors for any sign of forced entry,' said Tony.

They did, and found nothing. The main doors had been locked when Faraday had arrived at seven, and the two fire escapes were firmly shut.

Angie beckoned one of the SOCOs over to where they were standing, halfway down the arcade.

'Can you fingerprint all the door handles throughout the building?' she said.

'Of course,' said the man. 'But it's a public building – we'll probably get scores of prints with no way of identifying them.'

He was right. It would get them nowhere, but they had to do something.

She looked around, trying to imagine what it had been like for Sally Ann, here all alone and so viciously attacked.

'Where does that go?' she said, pointing to a solid-looking blue door on one side.

'That goes to the breeding and veterinary areas, and down to our reservoir.'

'Reservoir?' said Angie.

'We've got a tank of seawater in the basement that runs the whole length of the building.'

'But no way out down there?'

Faraday shook his head.

'Any access to or from the properties above you?' said Tony.

'Not at all.'

'What do you think?' said Tony, turning to Angie.

'I think she knew him. I think she knew whoever attacked her and let him into the aquarium, locking the doors behind them.'

'But then how did he get out?'

Bill Faraday looked from one to the other of them.

'The mortice lock on the front entrance wasn't locked when I arrived this morning, only the cylinder lock. So, the attacker could have opened it from the inside and simply pulled it shut behind him.'

'So if we take prints from that door, we might have our man,' said Angie.

'His and scores of others. Assuming he wasn't wearing gloves anyway.'

Angie shrugged. 'Look, either she let him in or he had his

own set of keys. I think she knew him. Come on, we need to take a close look at Sally Ann's circle – I have a feeling we'll find someone of interest.'

23

Rory

'Test results show positive for taxine.'

It wasn't what Rory wanted to hear.

Tanika Parry blinked at him, then rubbed her face with her hands, sighing.

'But you're treating her, right?'

'She's already showing symptoms – dizziness, shortness of breath, depressed heart rate.'

'But if you know what it is, surely you can do something?' said Angie. Her voice sounded a pitch higher than usual in the empty corridor.

'We're trying everything we can, but she's not responding to anything.'

'You can't just let her die,' said Rory.

Tanika Parry's face flushed and she tugged at the stethoscope hanging round her neck. 'I'm not letting her die. I'm doing all I can to prevent it.' She turned away from them. 'I need to get back to her.'

As she walked off, Rory called after her.

'We need to talk to her. Is that possible?'

Tanika Parry turned back to look at them. Scowling. 'I don't think so.'

Rory strode up to her, close, pushing his face into hers.

'He'll do it again. He'll attack someone else. It's my job to stop him. If I get five minutes with Sally Ann, she might just say something that'll make a difference, save another girl's life.' He always did his best to stay calm, no matter how angry the job made him. But right now he wanted to shake her.

Tanika Parry wiped a bead of his spittle off her face. She gave an imperceptible nod and walked away.

Rory and Angie followed her towards Sally Ann's room. At the door, she stopped them.

'She's awake, on and off, but I doubt you'll find her lucid. She's been through an enormous physical shock, piled on top of the mental shock of being assaulted. She's sedated right now and she probably won't remember anything of what happened.'

Inside the room, a single hospital bed was surrounded by a bank of monitors and equipment. Sally Ann Granger looked younger than eighteen years and only half alive to Rory's eyes. The blush of youth was missing – her face was wizened with pain, her skin almost grey, her eyes puffed up from crying. One side of her face was bruised purple and blue, and a ripe swelling bulged from her cheekbone like a plum. A middle-aged woman, sitting by the bed, looked almost as bad. Her mother, Rory guessed.

The woman stood up as Tanika Parry showed them in. She was small and timid, with untidy hair and faded clothes – and seemed unsteady on her feet. Tanika Parry introduced her as Danielle Ellis, then explained to her who Rory and Angie were.

'Officer, do you know who did it?' She sounded desperate.

'Not yet,' said Rory. *Alex Mullins? He'd been out of custody by the time Sally Ann was attacked.* 'This is DC Angie Burton, Danielle. She's going to ask Sally Ann what she remembers.'

Danielle sank back down into her chair with a look of resignation. She stroked Sally Ann's arm. 'Are you awake, love?'

A small sob escaped the girl's mouth but she didn't open her eyes.

'Sweetie? There's a policewoman here to talk to you 'bout what happened.'

Sally Ann closed her eyes tighter, crumpling her face. She tried to turn away from her mother.

Rory felt sick. The girl had been through hell but if Tanika Parry was right, she was dying. Right in front of their eyes. And instead of leaving her in peace, he and Angie had to prise what information they could out of her, no matter how it distressed her or her mother.

Angie moved closer to the head end of the bed.

'Sally Ann, can I ask you some questions?'

The girl opened her eyes and looked at Angie with a wounded expression that cut straight to Rory's heart. His own daughter, Vicky, was only a few years younger. What must Danielle Ellis be going through?

'Can you tell me what happened?' said Angie.

Sally Ann closed her eyes again and winced, as if every movement caused her pain. 'It's muddled,' she said, so quietly that Rory, leaning against the wall by the door, had to strain to hear her.

'Anything you can remember could help us find out who did this to you.'

'A man came in . . . while I was cleaning.' She started to cry.

'Where did you first see him?'

'I don't remember.'

'Did you know the man?'

Sally turned her head to the side, searching out her mother. Danielle gave her a reassuring nod.

'Can you remember anything about him?'

'It was dark. Then he had a gun . . .' Her eyes widened and her breath came in short, sharp gasps. 'But . . . it wasn't a gun.'

Did she mean the tattoo gun?

Rory glanced across at Danielle. She looked almost as

139

distressed as her daughter, but she had the presence of mind to take Sally Ann's bandaged hand.

'Shhhhhh, babes. He's all gone now.'

Angie seemed reluctant to press the girl further – and rightly so, thought Rory. She'd been through enough. This wasn't the way to spend her final hours, and it wasn't the final memory to leave her mother with.

But Danielle deserved to know the truth. If it was him, he'd want the chance to say goodbye to his child, however painful that might be.

But first there was one more question. He had to ask it.

Rory stepped forward. 'Sally Ann, do you know Alex Mullins?'

She looked confused for a moment, but then nodded. 'From college?'

Rory turned to Danielle. 'Was Sally Ann at Brighton Art College?'

'She was, for a couple of terms,' said Danielle. 'Then she dropped out.' She didn't elaborate, and Rory made a mental note to look into exactly what happened.

'Was she friends with Alex Mullins? Mixed-race boy with dreadlocks.'

Danielle looked blank. 'I don't know who her friends were.'

Sally Ann started to cry. Her mother leaned forward to give her a hug.

Watching them, Rory made a decision. He didn't want to, but he needed to tell Danielle Ellis what was happening to her daughter. To tell her Sally Ann was dying.

'That's enough for now,' he said.

Angie let out an audible sigh of relief. 'Thank you, Sally Ann. You've been really helpful.'

'Can we talk outside?' said Rory, turning his attention to Danielle.

She waited a few moments for Sally Ann to calm down and fall asleep again. 'Only for a minute,' she said. 'I wouldn't want her to wake on her own.'

In the corridor, Rory flagged down one of the nurses.

'Is there a family room we can use?'

'This way,' said the nurse.

'Will you watch Sally Ann and let us know if she wakes up, please?' said Rory.

The nurse nodded and showed them into an empty room.

More scared, even more desperate than before, Danielle looked from one to the other of them as they sat around a scarred coffee table.

'Danielle . . .' Rory started. 'When did you realise Sally Ann was missing?'

The woman looked broken. 'I didn't. I was working nights . . . sometimes we don't see each other for days.'

'Nights?'

'I work at a care home.'

Rory couldn't put it off any longer.

'Danielle, there's something you need to know.'

'Can I have a glass of water?' she asked.

Classic delaying tactic. She must have suspected she wasn't going to like what she was about to hear.

There was a water cooler in the corner of the room. Angie filled a plastic cup and brought it back for Danielle. She drank noisily from it, and Rory realised the poor woman had been here, and probably awake, all night. He wondered when she'd last eaten.

'Danielle, last week a girl was attacked in a very similar manner to Sally Ann.' He paused to let her digest the information.

'What happened?' she said.

'That girl was also tattooed, and she died. We have reason to believe the tattoo was made using poisoned ink.'

Danielle Ellis reeled with shock, her whole body slumping to one side.

'No? No ...' At first it was questioning. Then it became a drawn-out howl.

A nurse ran into the room.

'You need to come now,' she said sharply to Danielle.

The nurse took her arm and pulled her to her feet. Angie went to the other side of her and together they propelled Danielle Ellis back to her daughter's room.

It couldn't have been more different to when they'd left a few minutes before. The room was full of people and a male medic was leaning over Sally Ann, administering CPR. Danielle took a step into the room, then collapsed against the nurse who was guiding her.

Angie hovered on the threshold. Rory stepped away along the corridor and wiped the sweat from his brow with a shirtsleeve. He didn't need to watch Sally Ann Granger die.

iv

19 July 1990

Aimée, Aimée, Aimée! Today you became a teenager. How does that feel? Any different to when you were twelve? No, of course not.

Thank God.

This year you don't care that there's no party. Your friends gave up on you a long time ago, didn't they? No one comes to the house to see you. The only visitors are a stream of nurses and carers when your mother's home, then no one when she's in hospital. She's in hospital most of the time now, since she relapsed, so it's just you and Valentine alone in this huge house mostly. Jay spends as much time as he can anywhere but here – college, at friends' houses, just out.

Mummy was well for a while and everything seemed to go back to normal. On the surface, at least. She wasn't always in bed, and for a bit you all did things as a family. For a while you ate more. But it wasn't the same. She'd changed. You'd changed. And Valentine had stayed the same. He still followed you around the room with his eyes. You still never felt comfortable being on your own with him. He still tried to be alone with you as often as he could.

Then she got ill again. The cancer came back and poisoned her. It made Valentine sad and angry. For a while he left you alone. Did he think your mother's illness was his punishment for the way he behaved with you? It didn't last long. He can't keep away from your bedroom. And you have no one you can turn to for help. Not even your brother.

Jay is seventeen now. He thinks that makes him a grown-up, and though he's not mean to you in the way he used to be, he doesn't have much time for you. He has his own problems. When he's here there are fights with your father and doors being slammed. He's kind to you if ever he notices you. But really, you think he's forgotten you exist. And how your heart aches for that not to be true. How you wish he would act as your protector – if you could ever talk to him again about who you need to be protected from.

This year, instead of a party, your father takes you out to dinner. The restaurant is smart, the menu's in French. He asked you to wear something pretty but you read disappointment in his eyes when you came downstairs in your everyday clothes. Jeans and a sweatshirt large enough for you to hide your skeleton in. That's practically what you are now – you never eat. He doesn't start a row about it – just sighs, and leads you out to the car. Jay was supposed to be coming with you, but this afternoon they had another row. Maybe Valentine started it on purpose, just so he could have you to himself this evening.

You feel uncomfortable in the restaurant. The women at the other tables are different to you. Or more precisely, you're different from them. They have the shiny veneer of expensive grooming. You feel like a child, the only child in the room. Your father orders for you and, when the waiter's gone, he pours you a glass of wine.

'Thank you, Valentine.' You know he hates it when you call him Valentine.

You drink all the wine and ask for some more. You don't touch a morsel of the food that's put in front of you.

He gives you more wine and the rest of the evening becomes a blur. You knock over a glass, and stumble against another table on your way to the ladies. Your father laughs and gives you a silver bracelet in a blue box. Another piece of jewellery you'll never wear.

He takes you home.

You black out.

Things happen that you have no memory of.

But in the morning, there's blood on your sheets. When your father has left for work, you go into his bathroom and open his cabinet. You take a new razor blade out of the small paper package they come in. Sucking in breath, you drag the blade across the soft skin of your forearm. Not once, but three times.

The blood is bright red and so pretty as it drips onto the white china of the basin. Just like the blood on your white linen sheets. But to you, it's poison.

Is that what your father wanted, when he asked you to be pretty?

24

Sunday, 20 August 2017

Angie

Working on a Sunday was par for the course with a murder investigation ongoing. Angie didn't mind. Two girls were dead and she felt the team owed it to them, and to the killer's next intended victim, to solve the case. Bradshaw had called a team meeting for ten, so after picking up a decent coffee from the café over the road, she headed up to the incident room.

On the way up in the lift, she met Rory.

'Any word on the boss?' she asked.

'He came to the crime scene yesterday but he's not really up to it, so I told him to stay home till next week. A parent's death hits you harder than you think.'

'Tell me about it,' said Angie. She acted as Family Liaison Officer for the team, and had spent countless hours in the company of newly-bereaved parents, husbands, wives and children.

The lift came to a stop and the doors opened – but Rory didn't step out.

'Ange, can I have a moment?'

'Of course.' *What did he want?*

She stood and waited. Rory took a moment to find the words.

'You and Tony . . . that a thing?'

Oh, shit!

'I've seen the way he looks at you. I know his marriage is off the boil.'

She shook her head. 'It's nothing, Sarge. Honestly.'

She tried to act casual but he locked eyes with her. His expression was stern.

'Don't let it become anything. For your sake, Ange. I've seen it happen over and over in this station and others. Don't shit in your own nest – it always turns out bad. Worse for the woman than for the man.'

Inside, Angie bristled. Typical that the woman would bear the brunt of the blame.

'Like I said, it's nothing.'

Could he tell she was lying?

'Just be careful. If Sullivan gets a sniff of it, one of you will get transferred – and it won't be Tony.'

'Of course it bloody wouldn't.'

She wanted to close this conversation down, and more than anything she didn't want to cry in front of Rory. She was exhausted and it made her emotional. She took a sip of her coffee to put up a shield between them.

Rory stepped out of the lift. 'Come on, better not keep the chief waiting.'

Bradshaw was already holding court by the time Rory and Angie walked through the incident-room door. He looked pointedly at his watch as they made their way to join the group gathered round the whiteboard that ran the length of one wall.

'Get a move on, Mackay. You're the ranking officer in this team now that Sullivan's off. You should have been here before I was.'

Angie winced. Bradshaw's tone didn't contain an ounce of sympathy. There was a rustling of papers and general fidgeting – the rest of the team reacting to the chief's words. Much as she wanted to, she didn't dare catch Tony's eye in case Rory was watching. And anyway, Rory was right. They needed to be far more careful.

'Sorry, sir,' said Mackay. He turned his attention to the whiteboard. 'Two attacks so far, and both girls have died approximately twenty-four hours after being attacked. It's pretty safe to say that it's the same perp – both girls were given stigmata, both girls were tattooed using ink laced with taxine, a poison most easily available from yew trees.'

'What do these tattoos mean?' Bradshaw could always be relied upon to interrupt with an awkward question.

Rory studied the board. They now had an image of Sally Ann Granger's tattoo – one of the SOCOs had been given permission to photograph it in the hospital. Like the one on Tash Brady's back, it was gothic lettering. He assumed it was also in Latin.

> *Quid sum tibi responsurus,*
> *actu vilis corde durus?*

'The words tattooed on Tash Brady's back meant, "The nails in Your feet, the hard blows and so grievous marks I embrace with love",' he said, reading off the translation that was pinned up on the board. 'Kyle, have you got the translation of the other one, please?'

Kyle Hollins started searching through a fistful of documents. Bradshaw rolled his eyes.

'It's a line from the same piece by Buxtehude,' said a voice from the doorway. '"What answer shall I give You, Vile as I am in deed, hard in my heart?"'

It was DI Sullivan. Angie looked round at him as he came across the room to join Rory at the whiteboard. He looked as if he hadn't slept or eaten in days.

'Boss,' said Rory, 'you shouldn't be here. Not today.'

'I'm not going to sit at home and do nothing while the killer strikes again.' He sounded annoyed. Angie wasn't surprised – he wouldn't want to talk about his mother's death in front of the whole team.

Rory persisted. 'You should be with your sister.'

The sarge clearly didn't want to relinquish his moment in control.

'I'll be the judge of that,' said Francis, shutting the conversation down.

Bradshaw's condolences were conspicuous by their absence.

'Can we just get on?' he said.

Francis took control and Rory stepped back.

'As I was saying, they're verses from the same choral piece, but we can't say yet what their significance is. These are ritual killings with a religious element to them. The big question that needs answering is whether these particular girls are targeted for some reason or whether they're random victims, selected simply for being in the wrong place at the wrong time.'

'Weren't you looking at Brady's boyfriend?' said Bradshaw.

Of course, he'd want to tie things up as quickly as possible.

'We are,' said Rory.

'We'll need to reconsider in the light of this second attack,' said Francis. 'We've got no circumstantial evidence to tie him to the scene of either crime so far. And although we know he argued with Tash before she was attacked, what would be his motive for killing Sally Ann?'

'Just because we don't know what it is, doesn't mean he doesn't have one,' said Rory. 'She certainly knew Alex Mullins. She was at college with him and Tash Brady, before she dropped out.'

'Sir?' It was Kyle Hollins.

'What is it, Hollins?' said Francis.

'I've been checking Sally Ann's mobile phone record this morning. She texted Alex Mullins's number on Friday evening at twelve minutes past six. It was the last call she made.'

Bradshaw snorted indignantly. 'You need to be applying pressure to Alex Mullins. Get him back in here, and take apart his house for some kind of evidence – tattooing equipment, traces of the poison, weapons, whatever.'

'We'll talk to him again,' said Francis. 'But we still need some more convincing evidence. The Mullins house has already been searched. I think we need to keep an open mind and start looking further afield.'

Bradshaw scowled. 'You need to put all your efforts into finding the evidence on Mullins.'

Francis gave him an equally dark look but didn't respond. Angie knew they didn't have enough on Mullins yet and it seemed reasonable to open out the investigation – but if the boss defied Bradshaw yet again, they could all end up paying the price.

25

Francis

'I swear that the evidence that I shall give shall be the truth, the whole truth and nothing but the truth, so help me God.'

Francis swore the oath with one hand on the bible and his eyes on the jury.

So help me God. But God hadn't been there for him in recent days and weeks, and he wondered if he should have taken the affirmation instead.

It was the third day of the so-called Tattoo Thief trial, and Francis had been called to Court One at Lewes Crown Court, to give evidence against Sam Kirby, charged with three counts of murder and two counts of attempted murder. It had been Francis's first murder case in charge, and seeing her standing in the dock brought back memories. A wave of nausea flooded his mouth with saliva, as he relived the discovery of the abandoned farm where she was curing tattooed human skin into leather.

He stared across at her. Nudging six feet tall, Kirby's broad shoulders and sturdy legs lent her an air of strength. She wore a man's suit and tie, and her iron-grey hair was clipped even shorter than when Francis had last seen her. As she sat down, a smug expression settled on her face, and she looked around as if she were the star player on a stage and those assembled her adoring audience. George Elphick, her lawyer, grinned reassuringly at her, and she smiled back at him.

Elphick, a slime ball in a silk suit, was a clever man. He was orchestrating the defence case, priming his witnesses and conniving with his barrister to manipulate the jury to suit the needs of his client. Francis despised him – he'd been nothing but trouble through the arrest and interview process. Now he was trying to railroad the case with a verdict of diminished responsibility.

The lawyer twisted in his seat and gave Francis an ironic salute. Francis stared back at him, without returning the greeting. In this gladiatorial contest, he didn't want to let Elphick see any chink in his armour.

When he looked once more at Sam Kirby, her eyes were upon him. Francis saw a flash of hatred but then she smiled. A supercilious smile that reminded him of a snake. He looked away from her as the prosecution barrister stood up to question him. He wouldn't give her the satisfaction of looking at her again, if he could help it.

As the CPS-appointed barrister – a man called Don Martin – posed his first question, Francis felt his system flooding with adrenalin and his back prickled with sweat. What if it all went horribly wrong? What if Kirby walked free with a not guilty verdict? He needed a conviction against Kirby or his work as the Officer in Charge would be picked over, dissected and critiqued, not only by his superiors but also in the media. He wasn't sure he was ready for that.

'DI Sullivan, I'm going to run through with you the series of events that started with the discovery of a man's body in a dumpster in the Pavilion Gardens in May last year.'

Francis was prepared for this. Don Martin had schooled him with all the questions he intended to ask, as well as those they thought the defence barrister would ask when his turn came. He cleared his throat and the cross-examination began.

A couple of members of the jury had been doodling or looking at the ceiling, but they were all eyes forward as Sullivan started to speak. Slowly and clearly, prompted by Don Martin, he re-capped the harrowing events that had made up his investigation into the crimes.

'. . . the victim's skin had been flayed . . .'

'. . . a headless corpse under the pier . . .'

He faltered several times. The courtroom was as hot as a sauna and Francis desperately wanted to take off his jacket and loosen his tie. He had to get it right. Every last detail to make sure Kirby ended up in prison. Sweat beaded on his upper lip. She was watching him like a hawk with steely-eyed hatred.

'Tell us about Stone Acre Farm,' said Don Martin. 'What did you find there?'

Francis swallowed. His mouth was dry. 'We came across a locked barn. The appalling smell coming from the building suggested we should investigate further.'

'Did you get a warrant to open this barn?'

'We did.'

'What did you find inside?'

'What we saw inside the barn was horrifying – and will haunt me for the rest of my life.' Sam Kirby interrupted him with a bark of laughter. 'The place had been set up as a tannery, a small workshop for curing skins into leather. There were a number of plastic vats containing mixtures of chemicals and when we looked inside them, we saw pieces of tattooed human skin, which were in the process of being cured.'

Don Martin paused to let the full horror of the crimes sink in. The memories of Kirby's tanning studio made Francis's flesh crawl. Several members of the jury and a number of people watching in the public gallery looked repulsed. But Francis saw Tom Fitz, the crime reporter from the *Argus*, keying frantically on his mobile, filing his copy on what would be, without doubt, the year's most spectacular trial.

Sam Kirby grinned as a woman on the jury leaned forward, putting her head in her hands.

'Do you have images of what you found there?'

'Yes, we took lots of photos. You'll find a selection of them in the evidence file, for the jury to see.'

The clerk of the court took his cue and handed a package of photos to the jury foreman to pass around. Francis and Don Martin waited in silence, giving them a chance to look at the full horror of the Tattoo Thief's work. The people watching from the public gallery became restive. They wouldn't get to see the gruesome images and they speculated in low murmurs about what they might show.

The woman juror who'd looked distressed was handed the photos. She gave them only a cursory glance before passing them on to the man next to her. When they handed the sheaf of photos back to the clerk of the court, the judge cleared his throat.

'I'm sorry, members of the jury, that you had to look at those images, but it's important for your understanding of the crimes in question. However, I think now might be the right time to take a short break. We'll reconvene in fifteen minutes.'

Out in the corridor, Francis gulped down a bottle of water and checked his phone. Two messages from Rory, one from Rose – hopefully updates on the Sally Ann Granger case. He was about to listen to them when Don Martin appeared, his black gown flowing behind him as he strode purposefully towards Francis.

'Don,' said Francis, dropping his phone back into his pocket. 'Went okay, didn't it?'

'We've still got a problem,' said Martin. His expression was grim.

'Yes?'

'None of this mitigates the defence team's plan to argue diminished responsibility.'

'She's as sane as you or I,' said Francis.

'Not sure the jury will see it that way, not once Elphick has put his little spin on it. A young woman, betrayed and deserted by her family, ends up cutting tattoos off other people's backs. Not exactly a picture of rational behaviour. Easy to argue she's got a screw loose.'

Francis sighed.

A diminished responsibility verdict meant no conviction for Kirby – just an undetermined spell in the cushy surroundings of a high-security mental hospital, rather than a fixed tariff in prison. And no conviction would see his own career on the skids. A lot of people had felt he'd got his promotion to DI far too young, and if this case got ballsed up, they'd feel justified in that thought.

'How are you going to counter? What about the fact she killed them for money?'

Martin shrugged. 'Most people wouldn't do that for money . . .'

'Can I quote you on that?' said someone behind him.

Damn!

Recognising the voice, Francis whipped round to see that Tom Fitz had crept up on them. He was holding up his phone at arm's length, as he closed in.

'Are you recording?' snapped Martin. 'Switch it off now and piss off.'

Fitz scurried away. He knew what he'd been doing was uncountenanced, but as Francis was all too aware, he always worked close to the line. And crossed it more often than not.

Francis went back into the court, frowning as he thought about what the next morning's headline would be. At the same moment, Sam Kirby was being led back into the dock. When the policewoman at her side motioned for her to sit down, Kirby ignored it. She gripped the wooden rail across the front of the dock and Francis could quite clearly see the dripping, bleeding human hearts she had tattooed on the back of each hand. She was showing them off – for the jury's sake or for his? As if she felt his eyes upon her, she turned to face Francis and fixed him with a steely stare.

The muttering and general clamour in the courtroom prevented most people from hearing what she said. But Francis could lip read.

'Francis Sullivan.'

When she opened her mouth, he could see blood on her lips and teeth. He wanted to look away but he couldn't.

'You're on my list.'

Francis crossed the floor to stand directly in front of her, hands on his hips. Close up, he could see she was chewing at her bottom lip.

'What list would that be, Kirby?' He shouldn't be baiting her. He ought to know better.

She leered at him, blood running down her chin.

'You're in my sights. It's not over till it's over.'

It's not over till it's over.

Words he'd heard her say before, more than once.

'It's not over till it's over.' Her voice had risen to a shout.

Then she spat at him. A globule of bloody spittle landed right in his eye. And as he wiped it away, a flash of light made him blink, and he saw Tom Fitz holding up his phone again.

Now he had no doubt what tomorrow's headline would be.

26

Francis

When he got back from Lewes, Francis skulked into his office, leaving Rory to manage the team. The day in court had exhausted him, and perhaps Rory was right that he shouldn't be back at work yet. But staying home and giving in to his grief was out of the question. And he couldn't sit with Robin – watching her even more acute suffering was too painful.

Nor could he afford to let things drift. He would be giving more testimony tomorrow and, once he'd finished, Marni Mullins would be called. He needed to see her and go through the barrister's list of questions.

He was about to head off to Great College Street where she lived, when Rory came into his office. He dropped heavily into the chair opposite Francis's desk, uninvited. He didn't say anything for a minute, just looked around the scruffy office with pursed lips.

'What's on your mind, sergeant?'

'Just wondering. Bradshaw told you to pull Alex Mullins in for further questioning. But you haven't given the instruction.'

Francis nodded. He'd wondered how long it would be before someone – in fact, Rory – commented.

'Marni Mullins is due to give evidence in the Kirby case tomorrow. If we bring Alex in again, she'll go ballistic. I need her evidence in the bag before I can afford to let that happen.'

Rory pulled his vape out of his pocket and fidgeted with it nervously.

'It's not right, boss. If Mullins is involved in these attacks, we need him off the streets. I mean, what if Marni's evidence gets delayed?' This wasn't at all unusual with the slow pace of the criminal justice system. 'Just how long would you leave him out in the open? And what if there's another attack?'

'Put him under surveillance for the time being.'

'Have you okayed it with the chief?'

'No, of course I bloody haven't. He wants Mullins charged – but you know perfectly well we don't have enough evidence for that.'

'I suppose you know what you're doing.' Rory stood up to go.

'Yes, I do. I can't afford to have the Kirby case messed up by this one. As soon as Marni Mullins steps off the stand, I'll let you know and you can pick him up.'

'What if there's another attack? You're dealing with the trial, with your mother's funeral . . .'

Francis's head snapped up. Rory was angling to be put in charge and that was below the belt.

'Let me look after things for you, boss.'

'That won't be necessary, Rory.'

Francis still wasn't sure how much he could trust Rory when it came to Bradshaw. This would be a good test.

It was only a ten-minute walk to Great College Street, but Francis drove, not least so he could find five minutes of air-conditioned relief from the oppressive heat. He felt crumpled and sweaty after his day in court and couldn't face the hot pavements, jostling tourists and pub overspill the walk would entail. It also meant he could sit in his car and compose himself until he felt ready to face Marni.

She was expecting him. He'd messaged her earlier in the day to let her know he'd come round, and Don Martin had been updating her on the trial progress and when she was likely to be called. But that didn't mean she'd be pleased to see him.

She opened the door as soon as he rang the bell, then turned and led the way to the kitchen without saying a word. He understood. The police were hounding a member of her family, again. What did come as a surprise to him was to find Thierry Mullins, propping himself up against the kitchen counter, drinking a beer as if he belonged there.

Francis gave him a nod as he came in. 'Thierry.'

He and Thierry had together rescued Marni when Steve Harrington had tried to kidnap her after Sam Kirby's arrest. But they'd never been on easy terms, and Francis wondered what Thierry knew about him and Marni. He felt his face turn red as Thierry replied with a surly, 'Hello.'

'Beer?' said Marni.

'Sure.' It was hot and just the thought of holding a cold glass appealed.

Thierry finished his beer and thrust the bottle into a crate of empties by the back door. 'I'm going to the pub.'

Marni frowned. 'I won't wait up.'

The front door slammed as Thierry left and at least some of the tension drained from the air.

Francis took a sip of the beer Marni handed him. Did he dare? 'You and Thierry . . . are you?'

'Back together?' Marni glared at him. 'Not that it's any of your business, Frank, but, yes.' She didn't sound thrilled.

They sat out in the garden and when Pepper excitedly reacquainted himself with Francis, Marni's mood seemed to soften a bit.

'No, Pepper, you can't sit on Frank's lap.'

The dog barked and licked his hand. Francis ignored it.

'I've got a copy of your witness statement here – I thought you might want to refresh your memory before going on the stand tomorrow.' Francis drew a folded sheet of paper out of his back pocket and handed it to Marni. It covered how Marni had discovered the Tattoo Thief's first victim in a dumpster, to how she'd been instrumental in Sam Kirby's arrest, and what had happened after that when Steve Harrington had kidnapped her.

'How long do you think I'll be giving evidence for?' she asked, when she'd glanced through the statement.

'Most of the day, maybe even into Wednesday. You're our key witness and your testimony will be absolutely critical to getting Sam Kirby convicted.'

Marni drained her beer bottle. 'No pressure then. If I fuck up, Kirby goes free?'

'Not quite,' said Francis. 'She doesn't deny the killings – it's just a matter of whether she goes to prison or to a psychiatric hospital.'

'Does it matter?'

'Absolutely. I need to secure a prison sentence or Bradshaw will do his best to get me downgraded.'

'Really, Frank?' Marni got up to deposit her empty bottle just inside the door. 'This is just about your career then, is it?'

'Of course not.'

Her eyebrows shot up. 'And what about Tash's murder? How's your career faring there?'

Francis stood up. He'd wanted to avoid discussing the current case with Marni for obvious reasons.

'I'd better be going.'

'Are you still looking at Alex in relation to Tash and Sally Ann?' Her tone was downright hostile now.

She blocked the doorway back into the kitchen. Even when she was angry he found her attractive, but why had he ever thought they could have made a go of it?

'You don't have a single thing on him, do you?'

'Is he here?' said Francis.

She shook her head, but didn't move from her position in the doorway.

'You know he and Tash had a fight in The Haunt. Tash slapped him before she left.'

Marni's eyes widened for a split second. 'I knew that. It means nothing – they're teenagers.'

Francis wasn't at all convinced she had known.

'So I suppose you know that he hit her a couple of months ago, too?'

This time Marni couldn't hide her shock, and Francis regretted the words the moment they were out of his mouth.

What an idiot.

'I don't believe you.'

Francis shrugged. He felt terrible, but he couldn't discuss the case with her.

Marni stepped back so he could pass by her into the kitchen.

He turned to face her, looking down into her brown eyes. She avoided eye contact by turning her head to the side.

'My son had nothing to do with Tash's death,' she said, through teeth clamped tight.

'The investigation's far from over, Marni. Let's just get Kirby's case out of the way first.'

Back in his car, he wished Rory was there with him. Not because he wanted to confide in the sergeant or ask his opinion on what had just happened. Simply because he felt he could do with a cigarette. He might have, in a single sentence, destroyed all the good will he'd built to get Marni to testify willingly. And if Marni didn't give her evidence against Sam Kirby, he could probably assume his career was as good as finished.

Instead of turning out of Great College Street and heading

for home, he drove in the opposite direction to the Esso petrol station on Eastern Road, where he bought a packet of cigarettes and a lighter.

Damn!

27

Monday, 21 August 2017

Alex

Alex heard the front door slam and scooted across to the window on his desk chair to see who'd just left the house.

Francis Sullivan? What the fuck was he doing here?

He watched the policeman walk down the street and get into a dark blue Golf. He sat for a moment, then revved the engine aggressively and shot out of his parking space, practically clipping the rear of the car parked in front of him.

The bedroom door opened and his mother came in, without knocking first as she habitually did. He ripped his headphones off.

They both started speaking at once.

'What the hell was he doing here?'

'Alex, did you ever . . .'

'What? Did I ever what?'

Marni sank down on the side of his bed with a sigh. She looked around his room and he became conscious of how untidy it was – clothes all over the floor, wardrobe doors open, drawers open and overflowing. Bed unmade. Pretty much as usual. But she hadn't come in here to nag him.

'Mum?'

'The police are saying that you hit Tash.'

'No. No way. She slapped me, then she stormed off. Loads of people saw that.'

'Not at The Haunt. Some other time.'

Alex couldn't believe what he was hearing.

'I never hit Tash, ever. You can't believe that, Mum.'

'Of course I don't want to believe it. But why would the police be saying that?'

Alex spun on his chair, knuckles gripping the arms. His world was spinning out of control.

'Mum! You know they tell lies. They told me you'd stabbed someone. That you'd been to prison. That's bullshit, isn't it?'

'Jesus,' said his mother, shaking her head. She looked at him and her eyes were shiny. 'So you didn't hit her?'

'It's a lie. If someone told them that, they were lying.' Alex stopped his chair and leaned forward to rest his head on the desk, cradled in protective arms.

'Why was he here anyway?' he said, speaking into the crook of his elbow.

He heard the bedsprings creak, then felt one of Marni's arms snake around his shoulders. He raised his head and returned her embrace.

'I promise you, Mum, I didn't do anything to Tash.' She had to believe him.

'I know you didn't, bug.' She hadn't called him that in years.

Alex disengaged himself.

'Someone's been telling lies to the police,' he said. 'Someone they'll believe more than they'll believe me.'

'You don't know that.'

'You don't think Francis Sullivan made that up, just grabbed it out of thin air?'

She shook her head. 'No . . .'

'Right. Someone told them that.'

'Who would do something like that?'

'One of Tash's stuck-up friends.' He stood up. Anger rose like bile in his throat and he kicked a bag of books out of his way.

'Where are you going?'

'To find out who's shafting me.'

He grabbed his hoody and left Marni behind in his room.

'Wait!'

He was out of the front door in a minute and racing down the road in the direction of town. He pulled out his phone and tried calling Liv but she didn't answer. It was getting dark and he didn't see anybody as he trotted down College Street and Montague Place. Quiet residential roads on a Monday evening. There was more traffic as Bristol Road led him into St James's Street and there were groups of people drinking and smoking on the pavement outside the pubs. He slowed down to a walk and pulled off his hoody. He was hot now, and he knew that a black guy running in a hoody was never a good look in some people's eyes.

Goddammit.

He passed a newsagents with a sandwich board leaning up outside. Two murders, it screamed, city of terror.

Tash and Sally Ann. He couldn't believe they were both dead. Once again, the realisation caught him by surprise. For a moment he couldn't find a breath, the hard, heavy knowledge suffocating him. He stopped, one hand reaching out for the stability of a wall while he struggled to stay upright.

Deep, slow breaths. Stop the world from spinning.

He recovered, then looked around. St James's Street was still the same. No one took any notice of him. He felt invisible. And then he wondered. If the police thought he'd hit Tash, and if the police knew he knew Sally Ann – which wouldn't be hard to find out given she'd been at college with him and Tash, and had texted him that evening – then why hadn't they pulled him back in for more questioning? It didn't make sense.

He looked around again. Now a couple on the other side of the road were staring at him, so he started walking.

And when he saw a police car turning the corner into St James's Street, he instinctively ducked into an alleyway. He pressed himself against the wall, panting. Sweat soaked through his T-shirt, but he didn't dare move until long after the cops had driven safely by.

Was he a fugitive now, on the run? Did everyone think he'd done it? Even his mother?

Fuck you, Frank Sullivan.

He tried Liv's phone again, but still there was no answer.

28

Francis

Francis felt a wave of anxiety-induced nausea as he went down the stairs. He couldn't stand the thought of putting his mother away in a wooden box. The realisation that he wouldn't be able to see her again sliced through him anew every day when he woke up – but the idea that her funeral was supposed to give him some sort of closure on this absolutely terrified him.

He walked uncharacteristically slowly from John Street across to Saint Catherine's, smoking a cigarette as he walked. He was going there to meet Robin and Father William to discuss the arrangements. Heat oozed up from the paving stones – heavy clouds had blanketed Brighton all day, until even the sea breeze had seemed choked. As darkness fell it felt hotter than ever. The city was tired and fractious.

Francis looked at his watch as he walked up the brick path to the church. He was late, but at least he'd made it – he was determined to be as supportive to Robin as he could be. He heard the murmur of voices as he approached the vestry through the church, and he wished he could be anywhere other than this.

'Hello Fran,' said Robin, as he pushed open the door. 'I was worried you weren't going to show.'

He bent to kiss her on either cheek. He could have taken her remark as a dig, but he didn't want to bicker with her, today of all days.

'You smell of smoke,' she said, wrinkling her nose as he stepped back.

'Hello, Francis.' It was Jered Stapleton.

Francis was surprised to see him here. He'd been expecting to meet with Father William.

'Sorry I'm late.' He shrugged. Robin didn't need an explanation – she knew it would be work.

Francis pulled a wooden chair out from the opposite side of the table to where Robin and Jered Stapleton were sitting. He sat down.

'I've asked Jered to help us work out what we want,' said Robin. 'I talked it through with him yesterday . . .' There was an awkward pause, as if Robin was aware that she shouldn't have started planning without him.

Francis glanced from one to the other of them. They both looked sheepish.

'What have you come up with?' he said, keeping his tone even.

Robin pulled a notepad from her bag, on the first page of which Francis could see a long list.

'We were thinking of a wicker coffin,' said Robin.

We?

Jered Stapleton pushed an undertaker's brochure across the table towards him.

'Your sister likes this one,' he said, planting the end of a thick finger in the centre of an image of a coffin, effectively obscuring it from view.

Francis took the leaflet from under Jered's finger to take a look. He noticed the verger's nail had a rim of dark grime under it.

'It's nice,' he said, studying the picture of the wicker coffin, illustrated with an effusion of wild flowers trailing along the top and over the sides. It was pretty, but he wasn't sure it was what his mother would have chosen – Lydia would have been more the black coffin, white lilies type. He wasn't going to argue about it, though.

They went on to discuss the flowers, then the order of service. Throughout the meeting, it seemed to Francis that these weren't Robin's suggestions at all. The verger stepped in whenever he asked Robin a question and she seemed to defer to his opinion, particularly over the choice of hymns and music. It seemed out of character for Robin, making Francis wonder about the exact nature of their relationship. How long had they been this close? Watching someone wield influence over his sister in this way made him feel distinctly uneasy.

It took about an hour to run through everything.

'I can host the wake,' said Francis. 'It makes sense, being so close by.'

'But you can't cater for that number of people.'

'I'll use caterers.'

'I know a good catering company . . .' said Jered.

'It's fine. I'll sort it.' He hadn't meant to sound ungracious, but Robin gave him a look that told him that he had.

They wound up the meeting.

'Dinner?' said Francis to Robin as he helped her with her coat. 'I thought we might go to Polpo.'

Robin and Jered Stapleton exchanged glances.

'That would be lovely, Fran.' Robin turned to the verger. 'I'll see you tomorrow at choir practice, Jered.'

'Great,' said the verger. 'I want us to try out some new hymns.'

Once they were seated at the restaurant, Francis couldn't resist asking.

'Since when have you been a member of the choir? I haven't seen you singing at any services?'

'When were you last in church?' said Robin with a wry smile.

'Touché. I haven't been to the morning service for a few weeks.'

'Work?'

''Fraid so.' He studied the menu.

'Are you on that big case?'

Francis looked up. 'Which do you mean?'

'That was in the *Argus* this morning?' She leaned forward and lowered her voice, presumably so the young couple at the next table wouldn't hear her. 'The girls who were attacked and tattooed – at the bandstand and the aquarium.'

'What?' Francis exploded. 'Did you actually read those details in the *Argus*?' They hadn't issued any information to the press.

'Yes, look.' She pulled a folded copy of the *Argus* out of her bag. 'Full page, picture of the first girl who died, not so much about the other girl . . .'

Francis scanned the piece. Tom Fitz seemed to know altogether too much about both crimes. Where had he got the information?

He jabbed at his phone.

'Rory? Did you see today's *Argus*?'

The silence at the other end of the line told him that his sergeant had.

'Why the hell didn't you say anything to me? You didn't speak to Fitz about the case, did you?'

'Of course not.'

'So we've still got a leak in the department?'

'Maybe he got it from the families?' said Rory.

It seemed unlikely.

'Go through the article with a fine-tooth comb, then work out who could have known the facts that he covered. We need to close this down.'

'Right, boss.'

'I'll be with you in five.'

Robin's face fell and she bent over a corner of the menu in frustration.

'Seriously, Fran?'

He'd almost forgotten she was sitting there.

'Give me a moment, Rory.'

He dithered. His sister stared across the table reproachfully, not saying a word.

'Robin . . .'

She waited.

'Robin, I have to . . . I can't let this leaking go on indiscriminately.'

'What can you do, if you don't know who it is?'

'I need to find out, the sooner the better.'

Robin deflated visibly and Francis couldn't meet her eye.

'I could have been out with Jered this evening, but an offer from you is so rare.'

'So how long has this been going on?'

'What?' Robin's feigned innocence didn't fool him.

'This thing with Jered Stapleton?'

Robin frowned. 'It's not a thing. Jered's been helping me with . . . helping me come to terms with things. He's lost close family members, too.'

Francis pulled out his wallet. 'I'm sorry, Robin, but I've got to go,' he said. He put a couple of twenties on the table.

'Forget it,' said Robin. 'I don't need handouts.' She held out the money to him.

He didn't take it at first, just stood staring at it, his face suffusing with colour. Robin's arm showed a slight tremor, but she didn't withdraw it.

Aware that they were being watched by the other diners, he snatched it from her grasp and put it in his pocket. Then he left the restaurant without another word.

29

Tuesday, 22 August 2017

Marni

Marni was late for court, but she didn't give a damn. There were roadworks in two places, with temporary traffic lights and queues. The fact that she wouldn't have been on time even without the congestion was neither here nor there. They should be grateful she was turning up at all – it was going to cost her several days' work she could ill afford to lose. And at this point, she was more concerned with being available for Alex than she was over what became of Sam Kirby.

Truth be told, she was dreading the whole thing. Memories of another courtroom, in France, a long time ago, swirled into focus every time she thought about her summons to give evidence. She hesitated on the steps of the court building for a few moments before going in. She wanted to turn around and leave.

Damn. She couldn't let the past dictate her behaviour.

She made herself stand taller and, with a deep breath, stepped forward.

The foyer of the courthouse was busy with people coming and going in preparation for the day's business, but as soon as she'd passed through security, Francis Sullivan appeared at her side. Frowning.

'You're late.'

'At least I'm here.'

He winced.

Upstairs, he showed her into the witness room, where she would wait until she was called into court.

'It'll only be a couple of minutes,' he said. 'You should have been on the stand twenty minutes ago. I'll just go and let the clerk know you've arrived.'

She put a hand on his arm to stop him.

'Frank, I'm not sure I can do this.'

His eyebrows shot up.

'Marni, we need you,' he said. 'There's nothing to be afraid of. We've been over all the questions and you'll be standing at right angles to Sam Kirby, so you don't even need to look at her.'

Marni took her hand back and rubbed the scar that had distorted the tattoo on her left forearm. A gift from Sam Kirby.

'It's not her I'm worried about,' said Marni. 'It's being back in court. It brings back memories.'

Francis looked momentarily nonplussed.

'Marni, you'll be fine,' he said. 'You're our most important witness.'

Was there a note of desperation in his voice?

'But she's admitted killing them already . . .' She tailed off. She really didn't want to go in there. She knew how lawyers could twist your words, how they could trick you into saying things you didn't want to say.

Francis took hold of both her hands. It was the first physical contact she'd had with him since their short-lived affair had broken up. She took a step back and pulled her hands away.

'Marni, please do it. If not for me, then for her victims. She knew what she was doing and she deserves to go to prison.'

'People said that about me.'

'But that was different. You attacked Paul in self-defence.'

She shook her head. It hadn't been self-defence. It had been

173

several days after he'd raped her. She'd told Francis the whole story before.

She sighed. 'I'm here. I'll do it.'

'Thank you, Marni. I owe you a lot for this.'

'Then maybe you could lay off Alex.' The words came out of her mouth before her brain had engaged.

Francis's eyes widened for a split second.

'I tell the clerk you're here,' he said, disappearing from the room.

Walking into the courtroom and taking her place in the witness box brought back a flood of memories and a rush of anxiety. Despite the heat, Marni experienced a cold chill on her arms and a fluttering in her stomach. She could feel a hundred pairs of eyes upon her as she made the affirmation, looking down, only making eye contact with the clerk for the briefest moment.

Why had she agreed to do it? Her civic duty – and, yes, for the families of Sam Kirby's victims. Not for Frank Sullivan and his bloody career. She looked across the court to where he was sitting behind the defence barrister's table. He gave her an encouraging nod, then he looked to where Sam Kirby was sitting in the dock.

Marni's eyes followed his gaze. She'd avoided looking at Kirby so far, but as Don Martin shuffled through his papers in preparation to cross-examine her, her eyes came to rest on the killer.

Seeing Sam Kirby made her catch her breath. She had forgotten that the woman was so large – easily a foot taller than Marni and certainly far stronger. But that night in her tattoo studio, when Sam Kirby attacked her, suddenly seemed more recent than it was. She rubbed the scar on her arm where Kirby had slashed her with one of her specialist Japanese flaying blades. It was still painful when she applied pressure to it. Now she was glad she'd come, glad that she was going to play her part in putting the bitch where she belonged.

Don Martin stepped up to the witness box.

'Hello Mrs Mullins. I'm going to ask you a few questions about your involvement in this case. First off, can you tell the jury what you do for a living . . .'

Marni was on the stand for hours, labouring her way through how she'd first found the body in what became a spree of murders and attempted murders, then detailing Sam Kirby's attack on her in her studio, when her arm had been injured. She didn't enjoy it. She felt uncomfortable and put upon, as Martin fired question after question at her. The court was hot and airless – her mouth felt dry and her clothes stuck to the sweat on her body. There were moments, as she answered the questions about the Tattoo Thief's tanning workshop, when the room began to swim around her. She'd fainted that day when she saw her own picture pinned up as a potential target on Sam Kirby's wall, and now she felt the same thing was going to happen again.

'Some water, Mrs Mullins?' The clerk of the court was holding out a glass towards her.

'Thank you,' she said.

She took the cool glass and pressed it against her cheeks and forehead, before drinking from it.

'Can we continue?' said the prosecution barrister.

And so it went on, hour after hour. Every now and again, she would glance across at Francis. He was always watching her, always gave her a smile or a nod of encouragement. It helped.

When the defence barrister took over, Marni felt a change in the atmosphere of the courtroom. A sudden burgeoning of expectation – all the eyes in the public gallery were focused on her, ears straining to pick up every word.

Marni felt shaky, anticipation bound up with anxiety pulsing through her.

The questions started and the man wasn't pulling his punches.

'What were you doing in DI Sullivan's car when he went to investigate Stone Acre Farm?'

'Did you not attempt to strangle my client when she broke into your studio?'

'Would it not be the case that it would be you standing in the dock now rather than my client, if it hadn't been for the timely arrival of the police, who were able to drag you off her?'

'Is it true, Mrs Mullins, that you already have one conviction for attempted murder?'

'Objection, m'Lord.'

The prosecution barrister kept interrupting, and the jury would be told to ignore this question or that question. Marni felt hotter and hotter. How dare they bring up the case against Paul. That was ancient history, back when she'd lived in France when she was eighteen. How could it possibly have anything to do with Sam Kirby's case? And what was the point of the judge telling them to ignore it? Of course, it would be the first thing they'd remember when they got into the jury room to deliberate. It felt like she was on trial rather than Sam Kirby. She wished she hadn't agreed to do it.

And all the time, Marni was aware of Sam Kirby fidgeting in her seat, pulling faces and coughing loudly, so she was forced to repeat her answers. Although the judge threatened Kirby with contempt of court on a number of occasions, she kept finding new ways to needle Marni. Francis looked furious, sitting behind the prosecution table, glaring by turns at Kirby and the defence barrister. From time to time, Sam Kirby would stare straight back at Francis and give him a beaming grin.

Eventually, however, all the questions were spent. The prosecution barrister thanked her for her time and the judge told her she could stand down. Then, as she walked on shaky legs across the floor of the court towards the exit, Sam Kirby started to sing.

Frankie and Marni,
Sitting in a tree,
K-I-S-S-I-N-G.

The public gallery erupted with gasps and a few supressed laughs, while the jury did their best to look as if they hadn't noticed what was going on. Kirby sang it again, louder, if it could be called singing in her tuneless, rasping voice.

Marni swung round to face the woman in the dock. Sam Kirby's face was like a distorted mask with a joker grin – and Marni felt she'd never hated anyone more in her life. All the anxiety of her time on the stand was gone, replaced by cold, hard anger. Francis stood up to intervene, watching as Marni locked eyes with the killer.

'Frankie and Marni . . .'

'Order, order,' shouted the clerk of the court, but apart from Kirby the court was silent. All eyes were on the two women.

Finally, Marni wrestled her feelings under control and turned her back on Kirby.

As Marni left the court, Francis hurried out alongside her, texting as they walked back to the witness room to pick up her things.

It took Marni some time to calm down. She paced up and down in the small room, clenching and unclenching her fists at her side.

'What a bitch!' she said. 'So pathetic.'

'A clever bitch,' said Francis. 'The defence will now use her insinuation to attack our credibility still further. If the jury can be led to believe we had a relationship, all your evidence will probably be discounted in their eyes.'

'Oh, for fuck's sake – please don't tell me I endured all that for nothing. I need a cigarette.'

'Listen, it'll probably be fine. It's our best hope of having

Kirby convicted – and I can't tell you how grateful I am, Marni.'

Their eyes met. He still looked so young – and handsome. Sometimes she thought it was a pity that things hadn't worked out between them.

'Come on,' said Francis. 'I'll walk you to your car.'

Marni sighed, and rummaged through her bag to find her cigarettes.

As they came down the stairs from the witness room into the main foyer, Tom Fitz set foot on the bottom step.

'Inspector, I've been looking for you.'

'Don't harass my witness, Fitz,' said Francis. He sounded wary.

Marni was relieved that Francis was with her. She didn't want to have to answer the reporter's questions about the exact nature of their relationship. Her cheeks flushed – no doubt Tom Fitz would interpret that as something meaningful.

'If you need to talk about the case, maybe you could call me later, Tom,' said Francis. 'It's been a long day.' He paused and then added, 'And I need to talk to you. Who told you all that stuff you published yesterday?'

'Can't name my sources, Inspector. But maybe you'd like to comment on what I've just heard.'

'What might that be?' said Francis.

'Word is that you've just put out the call to bring Alex Mullins in for questioning.' Tom Fitz looked pointedly at Marni as he said it.

It took Marni about three seconds to work out what Francis had done – the text he'd been sending as they'd left the court.

'You fucking bastard, Frank Sullivan!'

30

Tuesday, 22 August 2017

Rory

Within fifteen minutes of Francis's text, Rory had the tactical firearms team ready for action outside the Mullins house on Great College Street. The boss had just been on the line again, asking if he had Mullins in custody yet – because if he didn't, his mother was likely to have warned him what was coming.

'I'll call you back, boss.'

Four armed officers surrounded the front door, while another two had gone around to the back of the house to intercept the boy if he made a run for it that way.

Rory gave the team leader the signal to start. The officer rang the doorbell. They waited fifteen seconds and then rang again.

'Open up, police.' The officer banged on the door.

The door remained firmly closed. One of the team stepped into position with a hand-held red battering ram – the Enforcer, as it was affectionately known. The team leader gave him a nod. He drew back the heavy metal tube and swung it with considerable force against the door. With a cracking sound, the door flew open and the team poured in.

Rory waited nervously, leaning against the side of his car, smoking. He wiped sweat from his brow with the palm of his hand, then wiped it on the seat of his trousers. Still anxious, he listened on his radio to the shouts and the banging of the internal doors being kicked open.

'Clear.'

'Clear.'

'Clear . . .'

'Got him, he's in his room.'

Thank God! Now he just needed to make sure Bradshaw knew it was him, rather than Sullivan, who'd brought the boy in.

There were sounds of a scuffle over the radio. Shouting and swearing.

Rory waited, confident that four armed men would be able to bring Alex Mullins out.

Finally, the armed officers emerged, leading Alex Mullins, handcuffed, into the street. One of them had a bloody nose.

Rory went over to them and looked the boy up and down.

'Did he do that?' he asked, gesturing to the man with the nosebleed.

The man nodded.

'Right, I'm arresting you for assaulting an officer.'

Alex sneered as Rory cautioned him.

'You got nothing on me,' he said. 'I was provoked.'

Rory turned to the team leader. 'Get him down to John Street now.'

He lit another cigarette and went back to his car. It was fine to feel a little smug – everything was going according to plan.

Alex Mullins didn't look as scared as he should have when Rory came into the interview room. In fact, the kid looked bored. Rory checked his watch. Now he had him under charge, they would have time to build some kind of case against him – then, if they managed that, they could hopefully get an extension to hold him longer. They would need it. Problem was, at the moment they didn't have anything linking him to either scene. They had to extract an admission from Mullins that would make a murder charge stick.

Rory sat down opposite him and rested his forearms on the Formica tabletop.

'I'm going to assume that your resisting arrest was an admission of guilt.'

Alex's eyebrows went up. So he had the same attitude problem as his mother.

'Then you'd be wrong,' said Mullins. He tilted his chair back, staring insolently across the table.

'In which case, why did you hit my officer?'

'Your lot broke into my house – you had no right to do that.'

'We had a warrant. You didn't answer the door.'

'A warrant for what?' Alex's look was a direct challenge. 'You think I killed my girlfriend?'

Rory studied the boy's sneering face for a moment. Was it the face of a double murderer? It could be. He'd encountered enough murderers in his time to know they looked just like anybody else.

'Did you know Sally Ann Granger?'

'I'm sure you know the answer to that already.'

'You were at college with her, weren't you?'

'You see, you knew.'

'Alex, you're in deep trouble. Now, drop the bloody attitude and answer the questions.'

'You don't have anything on me. You'll have to let me go.'

'Did you attack Sally Ann Granger last Thursday evening?'

'No.'

'You know she's dead, Alex?'

He nodded but didn't speak. Suddenly he was the frightened teenager he'd been the first time they'd questioned him, all bravado gone. He was only able to keep up the act for so long.

'I'd like to know exactly what you were doing last Thursday evening.'

'I want my lawyer.' Finally, he seemed to have realised the seriousness of his predicament.

'I'll ask someone to call her in a moment,' said Rory. 'But first, just tell me why you did it.'

Alex's head snapped up and his eyes met Rory's. He glared – the fear had been replaced with anger.

'You brought me in before because I was Tash's boyfriend. Don't you think you should be talking to Sally Ann's boyfriend this time?'

'She had a boyfriend, did she?'

'You didn't know?' The insolent look was back.

31

Francis

Francis was uneasy. Holding Alex Mullins for assaulting a police officer because they had nothing concrete to tie him to the murders was a typical Mackay manoeuvre – and not one he approved of. He'd been too heavy-handed. There was no reason to have smashed the Mullins's door down, but Alex Mullins had hit a police officer, so the arrest was completely justified. And if Alex Mullins had killed Tash Brady and Sally Ann Granger – about which Francis certainly had doubts – at least he wouldn't be able to attack someone else. But he'd be out soon enough if the team couldn't hold him for anything better than assault.

In the meantime, they needed to get back to investigating the case.

And he needed to get out of his bloody office. It was like a furnace and he couldn't think for lethargy.

'Rory?'

His sergeant appeared in his doorway in his shirtsleeves. There were dark patches under his arms and he leaned on the doorframe as if he was exhausted.

'Sally Ann Granger said she didn't know her killer, didn't she?'

'True,' said Rory. 'But it was dark in there when he attacked her.'

'But if our theory was that she let him in, that it was Alex, then she wouldn't have said she didn't know him, would she?'

Rory shrugged, not wanting to follow where Francis was leading.

Francis pushed his chair back and stood up.

'I'm going down to the aquarium for another look. Coming?'

Rory grunted, but went back to his desk to fetch his jacket.

As Francis went through the incident room, he stopped by Tony's desk.

'Any news on this supposed boyfriend yet?' he said. Tony had been given the task of going through Sally Ann's phone.

'Nothing in the call log,' he answered. 'I've just been in touch with the phone company to get details of deleted texts.'

'Keep at it,' said Francis. 'We really need a break in this case.'

Bill Faraday, the aquarium manager, was at lunch when they arrived. The sullen girl on the reception desk seemed unwilling to let them wait in his office, despite Francis showing his warrant card. But Francis didn't want to upset the staff.

'Fine,' he said. 'We'll take a walk around the aquarium. Ask him to come and find us when he gets in.'

For a moment, he thought she was going to ask them to buy tickets, but she just gave them a surly nod and went back to looking at her phone. After spending a few minutes examining the locking mechanism of the main doors, they headed back through the reception area towards the Victorian arcade.

'If Sally Ann let him in, he could have quite easily left through those doors and pulled them shut behind him,' said Rory.

'True . . .' said Francis, a note of hesitation in his voice. 'But that would be risky. Even in the small hours, there's some traffic on the roundabout out there. Remember, he would have been splattered with her blood from head to toe.'

'Perhaps he wore overalls,' said Rory. 'Or stripped off before attacking her.'

They came into the arcade. All the blood had been cleaned up. The aquarium had reopened and seemed busier than ever, as tourists milled around, wanting to see where it happened and looking for evidence of blood spatters that hadn't been properly cleaned away. Francis tried to picture how it had looked the morning Sally Ann had been found. Were there any indications in the blood traces that the attacker had gone somewhere to take off a bloodstained overall or wash himself before getting re-dressed? He'd need to confer with Rose and the SOCOs on this, and study the photos.

Francis prowled through the other areas of the aquarium, Rory tagging in his wake. If Sally Ann hadn't let the man in, then how the hell did he get in? Could he have come in earlier in the day and hidden somewhere till the centre had shut? It seemed unlikely and they'd gone over what CCTV footage there was and found nothing suspicious – no unaccompanied man with a heavy bag who didn't appear to exit. He inspected the fire escapes, but he knew they'd been carefully checked over by the scene-of-crime officers. They were of the push-bar kind that, once opened, wouldn't have closed behind him. Nonetheless, there were traces of fingerprint powder on the bars and the surfaces of the doors. The SOCOs had done an efficient job.

He went through a door marked 'Staff Only' and they found themselves in the backroom area of the aquarium. Water purifying and heating plant purred ceaselessly and the air was hot and humid. Rory mopped his brow with a handkerchief.

'I don't think the SOCOs found anything down here,' he said.

Francis looked around and went into the next room, wall to wall with glass tanks, most of which were empty. The whole building would have been thoroughly searched, so he didn't know what he was expecting to find.

They went down a narrow corridor. There was a door at the end. Francis tried it and found that it was locked.

Footsteps came up behind them.

'Detective Inspector?' It was the manager, Bill Faraday.

'What's in here?'

'That's the staircase down to our reservoir.'

'What happens down there?'

'We draw in seawater, use it to fill the tanks. And there's a drain that leads directly down into the sewers, for waste water run off.'

'Show me, would you?'

Bill Faraday's face took on a pained expression, but he got a set of keys out of his pocket.

'O-kay,' he said, drawing the word out. 'Follow me.'

They followed him down a short flight of stairs that led to an underground chamber. As he flicked on the light, Francis saw that they were standing on the edge of a vast tank of water.

'We bring fresh seawater in using a pump system via a pipe that goes out along the seabed some distance. We don't take water from right by the beach – too much litter and suntan lotion. This reservoir runs the whole length of the building.'

Francis was only listening with half an ear. He was looking around all the time for ways in which the killer could have got in if Sally Ann hadn't let him in. He saw something glinting along the crease where the wall joined the floor.

'Wait,' he said.

He bent to take a closer look. The corner was dark, what light there was blocked by his own shadow, but he could see a piece of metal. He pulled a latex glove from his pocket and put it on his right hand. Then he reached forward and picked the object up, turning round so he could hold it directly under the ceiling light.

'What have you got?' said Rory.

Francis stared at it. It was cylindrical, a bit smaller than a pencil. Congealed blood clung to the grooves that spiralled round it – and, horrified, sickened, Francis knew precisely what it was.

'It's a drill bit for an electric drill. I think we've just found out how he made the holes through Sally Ann's hands and feet.'

'Jesus,' said Rory.

Bill Faraday's mouth came open but he was stuck for words. For a moment it looked like he was going to vomit.

Francis found a plastic evidence bag in his jacket pocket and dropped the drill bit inside.

'He was down here,' said Francis. 'Is there a possible way in or out from here?'

Faraday snapped out his trance and shook his head. 'No.'

'What happens to the waste water?' said Rory.

'Here,' said Bill, indicating the far end of the tank. 'There's an overflow outlet there that connects to the sewage system.'

Francis headed towards where he was pointing.

'Is this locked?' said Francis, pointing at the grid over the main sluice outlet.

'Should be,' said Bill.

Francis bent down and grasped the steel ring that acted as a handle. He wrenched it up and the grid opened. With another tug, he was able to raise the grid up on its hinges to past the vertical point, where it rested.

Francis stared down the hole. Rory came to the other side of it and looked down. There was a metal stepladder attached to one side of the chute, leading down into the sewers. They could hear the sound of roaring water below.

'Jesus, of course,' said Francis. 'He used the sewers to gain access and to move around unseen.' He set a foot on the top rung of the ladder.

'You can't go down there,' said Bill.

Francis gave him a look. 'Just try and stop me, mate.'

Bill sighed. 'Then at least let me fetch you a torch and a helmet.'

'Okay,' said Francis, removing his foot from the ladder. 'Rory, get the SOCOs back to see if there's any sign that this could have been used by the killer as a way in or out. Let's get this drill bit up to Rose. I'd bet my life on it that it's Sally Ann's blood in those grooves.'

32

Wednesday, 23 August 2017

Angie

Angie didn't really enjoy her role as the team's family liaison officer. She found it stressful, having to be the main support for families who'd just lost a child, sibling or parent unexpectedly. It took a toll. But it was important – not only for the families she helped, but also for the investigations. Grieving relatives were often the best source of information on the deceased, and they needed to be handled with care. Angie spent time with the victim's close family and friends, gleaning what she could with a subtle approach.

Over a cup of instant coffee, sitting in a living room decorated with antimacassars and populated by a multitude of small animals made of coloured glass, Angie probed Danielle Ellis for information about her daughter. She asked about Sally Ann's job and how she spent her free time, and about why she'd dropped out of college, before finally getting around to the one thing she had come to ask.

'Did Sally Ann have a boyfriend?'

Danielle Ellis looked tired and wounded. Her drab clothes hung off her bony frame, suggesting recent weight loss, and the nail polish on her fingernails was badly chipped. As far as Angie had been able to ascertain, she didn't have anyone close to offer her support.

Danielle bit at a hangnail before answering.

'No, she wasn't with anyone. Not for the last few months.'

This didn't tally with what Alex Mullins had told them.

'Are you sure? Maybe she had recently started seeing someone?'

Danielle shook her head. Her hair fell into her eyes, and she hurriedly tucked it back behind her ears. 'She told me everything. We were like sisters. She hasn't been steady with anyone since she broke up with Alex Mullins, nearly a year ago.'

What the fuck? That was something the little prick had failed to mention when they interviewed him.

'She went out with Alex Mullins?' Angie had to be sure.

'He was a nice boy. I was sorry when they split.'

And now he was languishing in a cell in John Street suspected of murdering her.

Back at the station, Tony had received an email from Sally Ann's phone provider. It contained a list of all the texts she'd deleted during the past six months. There were no recent messages from Alex Mullins, but there were plenty from somebody else.

'Angie, come and take a look,' he said, almost immediately. 'She was definitely seeing someone, even if she hadn't told her mother about it.'

As they stared at the screen together, Angie surreptitiously breathed in her lover's scent as she bent over his desk.

'Look,' said Tony. 'Nearly all the texts she receives are from someone called Ben.'

He expanded a thread and they were confronted with a dick pic. Sally Ann's reply was a blushing, smiling emoji and another one blowing a kiss. Further up the thread, she'd sent him a selection of topless pictures. Looking at them made Angie feel a little prurient. This was a private message for the girl's lover. She would never have imagined them being blown up on a desktop screen in a police incident room.

'Right,' said Tony, closing the thread. 'I think we can safely assume these two were in some kind of relationship. Check his contact details on her phone and see if she's got an address for him. Otherwise, we'll work back from the mobile number he's using.'

Angie picked up Sally Ann's phone and clicked on the contacts icon. She scrolled through them, noticing Tash Brady's number among them, and Alex Mullins's. There was one Ben, no surname, but along with his number, there was a street address.

It took Angie and Tony just fifteen minutes to reach number seventy-six Hill Drive, in the Hove Park area of the city. Fifteen minutes of Tony telling her how unhappy he was with Barbara. She silently wondered why he stayed with her – and whether he'd ever leave her.

'Is she just as unhappy as you?'

Tony sighed. 'To be honest, I don't know. We don't talk about things like that any more.'

It sounded like her parents' marriage. People just growing bored and growing apart. Surely it would be better for them to go their separate ways and for Tony to find happiness elsewhere? Say with her, for example. They could make a fresh start somewhere else. In another city.

'Do you think you can get away for a bit this evening?' she said.

'I'll let you know.'

They pulled up outside a newly built, red-brick detached house with a sloping drive and a double garage to one side of it. The front garden was somewhat scruffy and overgrown, compared to the rest of the neighbourhood, and Angie couldn't guess when the windows had last been cleaned.

'Bit posh round here for someone going out with a college dropout, isn't it?' said Tony as they got out of the car.

Angie shrugged. 'The house doesn't look that posh though.

Might explain why Sally Ann hadn't told her mum about him. Maybe he's married.' It would explain why all the texts were deleted.

They went up to the house and rang the doorbell.

'Probably no one in at this time,' said Angie, but she was wrong.

A moment later the door opened and a middle-aged man stood blinking at them through round, horn-rimmed spectacles. He was wearing a polo shirt and longish khaki shorts, but in Angie's opinion they were still showing off too much of his gnarled and knobbly kneecaps.

'Good afternoon. I'm DC Burton and this is DC Hitchins. Would you mind telling us your name?'

The man paused, confusion written across his face. Angie raised her eyebrows.

'Benedict King.' he said. 'What . . . how can I help you?'

'Could we have a word inside?' said Tony.

It wasn't really a question and King stood back from the front door to let them enter.

'Is this your telephone number?' said Tony, reciting the number they'd taken from Sally Ann's phone.

'Yes. What exactly do you want?' he said, as he led them through to a large open-plan kitchen and living area. He dropped down onto a sofa but didn't invite them to sit. They both stayed standing. Angie looked around – the room was a mess, which came as no surprise after the state of the outside of the property. But what did come as a surprise was the artwork on the walls. There was a series of pictures, ink drawings of naked women, brought to life with flesh-toned colour washes, shaping the contours of their bodies with light and shade. She'd seen some of these before in a local gallery in the Lanes. They were good.

Tony led with the questions.

'Mr King, what do you do for a living?'

'I'm an artist.'

Artist. Art college. Could be the connection they were after.

'Do you have links to the Brighton School of Art?' she said.

'I'm a lecturer there.' He looked from one to the other of them. 'Why?'

'Do you know a girl called Sally Ann Granger?' said Tony.

Angie saw a shadow veil his eyes as he thought, or pretended to think, for a moment. 'Yes, I think I do. I think she might have been in my tutorial group for a while. She's dead, isn't she? I saw it in the *Argus*. What happened to her?'

'Are you married, Mr King?' said Angie.

The change of subject caught him by surprise and he tripped over his words.

'Yes. But what . . . why . . . my wife's not here. She's at work.'

Angie thought about the picture he'd sent to Sally Ann's phone. She'd heard all she needed to. Things were starting to fall into place.

Tony had obviously come to the same conclusion.

'Mr King, I wonder if you'd mind accompanying us to the police station to help with our enquiries.'

33

Francis

'Yes, bring him in for questioning,' said Francis.

He'd got back to the office from the aquarium at just after two to find that Angie and Tony had gone to question a man who'd been sending Sally Ann dick pics. It turned out that it was Benedict King, a local artist of some repute. Angie had called Francis from the car, while Tony waited inside with King.

'He was her tutor at the art college, while she was there. He's admitted knowing her, but we haven't pressed him further. He also knew Tash Brady, though he wasn't her tutor. We thought any further questioning should be down at the station.'

It was a no brainer. He knew both the girls. Now they needed to see if he had alibis for the critical time periods. Francis felt a frisson of excitement down the back of his neck as he disconnected from the call. Finally, a breakthrough – though that didn't mean he was letting Alex Mullins off the hook, especially since Angie had discovered that he'd dated Sally Ann before hooking up with Tash. They could still hold him for another seventy-two hours, and Francis knew better than to release a suspect prematurely.

While he waited for Angie and Tony to bring King in, he went out of his office into the incident room.

'Kyle, you've still got Tash Brady's phone, right?'

'Yes, boss.'

'Can you check if she had any contact with a man called Benedict King? Tony and Angie have got a number for him, if he doesn't come up by name.'

'Sure, I'll get onto it.'

Rory looked up from his computer screen.

'Who's that, then?'

'Tony and Angie are bringing in a man that Sally Ann was apparently seeing on the quiet.'

'Really?' Rory sounded unconvinced.

'We need to widen the search, Rory, given that there's nothing tying Mullins to the crimes.'

'Apart from the fact that he dated both the victims, has access to tattooing equipment, had a row with one of the victims . . .'

Francis ignored him and went back into his office to make a call.

'Rose, anything on that drill bit yet? Whose blood it was?'

It was nearly four o'clock by the time Tony and Angie walked Benedict King into the station. Apparently, he'd not been at all keen on accompanying them. They'd explained to him that they needed to ask him some questions and that he could either come voluntarily or they'd go back to the station and get a warrant.

Now he was sequestered in an interview room downstairs, while Tony and Angie filled Francis in on the details.

'When he asked about Sally Ann being dead, he looked genuinely sad,' said Angie. 'Not shocked, mind you – he'd seen it in the paper.'

'Not that hard to fake being sad, though,' said Tony.

Francis kept Benedict King waiting on purpose. His adrenalin levels would rise and fall, and his cortisol levels would rise – the longer he had to wait, the more stressed he'd become and the harder he'd find it to perform. That would make it easier for

Francis to judge whether he was lying or telling the truth.

Finally, at close to six o'clock, Francis and Rory went down to the interview room and introduced themselves.

The room smelled of his sweat.

'I've been kept sweltering in this airless little box for nearly two hours,' he blustered. 'Is that really the way you treat people who're helping you with your enquiries?'

'I apologise, Mr King. Things cropped up over the course of the afternoon that needed to be attended to. Policing doesn't always run to schedule.'

He sat down opposite Benedict King, and Rory took the chair next to him. Francis noticed that one of the artist's eyelids was twitching rapidly. The man was unnerved – and that would be to their advantage.

'Mr King, can you tell me, in what capacity did you know Sally Ann Granger?'

King moved restlessly in his chair, as if he was already fed up with being questioned.

'She was my student for a term . . . perhaps two, at the College of Art.'

'I understand you were her tutor, so you would have seen more of her than most of the other students. Is that right?'

'I usually have about eight students in my tutorial group – she was one of those. She would attend an hour's tutorial each week with the rest of the group.'

'Is that the only time you saw her?'

'To be honest, I don't remember seeing much of her then. She failed to attend several tutorials before she left the course.'

'Do you mind telling us why she left the course?' said Rory.

Benedict King gave him an incredulous look.

'I have no idea why she left the course. Personal reasons, I suppose. Her coursework was fine.'

'But you were her tutor. Didn't she discuss it with you?'

King shook his head.

Francis put his elbows on the table between them and leaned forward with his hands clasped.

'Isn't it true, Mr King, that you were actually having an affair with her?'

Anger flashed in Benedict King's eyes before he was able to bring himself under control.

'No, it isn't.'

'Did you send her photographs of your penis by mobile phone and receive in exchange photographs of her naked breasts?'

Benedict King was silent. It would be useless to deny what the police had seen on Sally Ann's phone.

'Mr King, please answer the question,' said Rory.

'That doesn't mean I had anything to do with her death.'

'Were you having a relationship with Sally Ann Granger?'

Benedict King's body language broadcast his reluctance to answer the question – he crossed his arms and his legs, pushing back into his chair. Francis stared at King's left forearm. It sported a scattering of tattoos – a bluebird, a heart with a dagger through it, stars, numbers, a key. American Old School style. They distracted him for a moment but then he carried on with the questions.

'Did your relationship with Sally Ann have anything to do with her leaving the course?'

The questions came thick and fast now – Francis wasn't waiting for King to answer. He knew they'd go over these questions again and again in the next few hours, but by showing King what he was up against, he could demoralise and scare him. Make him as vulnerable as possible before he had the sense to ask for a lawyer, which by law Francis didn't have to offer him as they were, at this point, only questioning him as a possible witness.

'Did you know Tash Brady?'

'No.'

'She was a student on the course you taught.'

'I don't know all the students by name.'

'Do you know Alex Mullins?'

'Have you ever tattooed anybody?'

'Do you own tattooing equipment?'

'Can you account for your whereabouts on Friday, eleventh of August, from ten p.m. until Saturday, twelfth of August, at eight a.m.?'

After this question, Francis let the silence stretch. Benedict King wouldn't or couldn't meet his gaze. Instead, the artist tugged at an imaginary thread on the stitching of his shorts pocket.

After more than a minute had passed, he said, 'Would you like me to repeat the question, Mr King?'

This time Benedict King raised his head and looked Francis straight in the eye.

'I'd like to call my lawyer.'

34

Thursday, 24 August 2017

Francis

Francis was staring at the details of the two murders on the whiteboard when Rory came into the incident room.

'I've secured another forty-eight hours on Mullins,' he said.

They'd already had him in the cells for almost forty-eight hours. Ninety-six was the maximum time they could hold him without charge – and at that point they'd have to decide whether to charge him with assault, with murder or simply let him go. This would mean a tough discussion the next day.

'He's asked for his lawyer to come in again.'

Francis shrugged. 'Fair enough. Get anything else from him?'

He returned his gaze to the images of the girls, their stigmata and the poisoned tattoos that had caused their deaths. There was a shot of Alex Mullins between them – the common link in both cases. Only now he added a picture of Benedict King in the same place. He knew both women and had been seeing one of them.

'Boss, does that mean you don't think Alex Mullins did it?' said Kyle Hollins.

'What do you think? I won't be sure he did it until he confesses or until we find something rock-solid that ties him to one of the scenes. But the fact that he tried to put some other man in the frame definitely confirms him as a person of interest. The long and short of it? We just don't know, so all other avenues of enquiry are still open.' He glared round at the team. 'So far we've got nowhere with this case. We need to go right back to basics again. Means. Motive. Opportunity. If we're going to prevent this happening to a third girl, we need to start answering questions. Who did both girls know in common and which of those have alibis? Why those particular locations? How does this killer choose his victims? Why the stigmata? Why the tattoos – what do they signify, if anything?'

'Aren't they just the means of administering the poison?' said Angie.

'Then why not simply do it with a syringe?' Francis countered. 'Both scripts are taken from a piece of choral music that references Christ's wounds on the cross – and the killer reproduced those wounds. That has to have some more meaning than just a simple signature. It seems unlikely to me that Alex Mullins would be using Latin references like that if these were simply killings caused by romance gone wrong.'

'What about Benedict King?' said Angie. 'He's an artist.'

'You need to look into his background. Is he, or has he ever been, religious? Does he have an interest in choral music? Has he studied Latin? If we can answer these questions, we'll find the killer.' He paused as they digested his words.

Rory answered his phone.

'Mullins's lawyer's here,' he said.

'I'll come down with you,' said Francis.

As Rory greeted Jayne Douglas, Alex's lawyer, in the reception area, Francis heard someone say his name.

'DI Sullivan?'

He turned around to find Tom Fitz bearing down on him. The last person he wanted to see. But he had a few things to say to the reporter. He hadn't had the chance to vent his spleen earlier, as he'd chased Marni out of the courthouse to try and explain. Only when he caught up with her, he had no explanation. What he'd done was vile and he couldn't blame her for being angry. While he stood in front of her, lost for words, she'd got into her car and driven off.

Now he felt a pressure in his chest – his anger returning.

'Fitz, how the hell did you know about the call out for Alex Mullins? Who told you?'

'Picked it up on the radio.' Fitz's mouth widened into a leering grin.

'Funny. But you know as well as I do police communications are encrypted these days.'

'I have to protect my sources.' Fitz raised his eyebrows and pursed his lips, making Francis feel the urge to punch the gurning idiot in the face.

'You're sailing close to the wind, Fitz. You know that.'

'Can you confirm that the two girls that died in the recent attacks had both been tattooed with poisoned ink? And also that they were both marked with stigmata?'

'No, I won't confirm those things. This information isn't for public consumption, Fitz, and if you print more critical details of the crimes, I'll charge you with putting a police operation in jeopardy.'

'So those things are true? I heard their toxicity tests came back showing massive amounts of poison in their systems.'

Where the hell was he getting his information?

This called for damage limitation.

'Tom, I'll talk to you off the record, if you can undertake to respect it.'

'Is there anything you can give me on the record?'

'You tell me what you've got and I'll see if I can confirm any of it.'

He couldn't afford to make an enemy of the press. And if he

knew what information Tom had, he might get a handle on where it was coming from.

Five minutes later, they were sitting upstairs in Francis's office, with the door firmly closed.

'I know that two girls have died after being attacked. Both had tattoos that were poisoned, both had injuries to their hands, feet and sides. One was found by the café under the bandstand, one was a cleaner at the Brighton Aquarium. Can you confirm any of that?'

'Off the record,' – he couldn't emphasise this enough – 'those facts are correct. I know news of the attacks and the deaths is public knowledge but I'm asking you not to publish any more details about the tattoos or the poison.'

'Why?'

'Come on, Tom, you know the drill. We hold stuff back to see if suspects know things they shouldn't.'

'But these are things the public have a right to know.'

'It's about timing. If you hold back on this stuff now, I'll give you first dibs when the time's right.'

'By which time every other journalist will have it too.'

'I don't want to cause a panic.'

'Panic sells papers.'

'Maybe at the expense of the next victim's life.'

'No way, Sullivan. If anyone can be blamed for the next one, it's you and your boys for not catching the killer.'

Francis pushed his chair back. He was getting nowhere.

'A few days, Tom. That's all I'm asking.'

He stood up and held out his hand for Tom to shake.

Tom Fitz gave him a begrudging nod and shook his hand.

'You scratch my back. I'll scratch yours.'

Francis let go of the reporter's hand abruptly.

'What's that supposed to mean?' said Francis.

Tom shook his head, grinning again.

'Nothing. Nothing at all.'

Francis stared at him.

'You know how the world works, Sullivan. Give me something good to print – it'll stop me printing other stuff.'

'What other stuff?'

Tom shrugged.

'That sounded like a threat, Fitz.'

'Take it how you like. Just make sure I get a good run at the story.'

He opened the door of Francis's office and left, leaving a sour taste in Francis's mouth and the conviction that Tom Fitz was a man he couldn't trust.

35

Thursday, 24 August 2017

Alex

It wasn't right. There were laws about how long you could lock someone in a police cell for – and after two days, Alex was sick and scared. Sick of the sight of four walls and a ceiling, all painted institutional grey, that seemed to be closing in on him, little by little. And scared that he was never going to get out. He'd shouted at the locked door and he'd thrown a cup of water at the PC who'd brought his breakfast to him. The cup had been made of paper and it had less than an inch of water in it, but it had made him feel better. For less than a minute.

He wanted clean clothes and he wanted a smoke. He wanted to see his mother and he wanted to talk to Liv. She was the only one who understood him. She believed him.

He lay on the hard, narrow bed, scrunching the threadbare blanket with his fists and staring at the pattern of peeling paint on the ceiling. The toilet bowl in the corner stank of sick – his own sick, from having released the contents of his stomach the previous day. Anxiety gnawed at his gut more fiercely than hunger and, since the water-throwing incident, they'd refused to bring him anything to drink.

He got up and banged on the door.

'Fucking bring me some water,' he shouted.

The heat was enough to do him in. His torso was wet with sweat and his mouth was dry.

'Water!'

Never had the grind of a key turning in a lock sounded so good.

But it wasn't a PC with a drink of water for him that came through the door. It was Jayne Douglas, the lawyer he'd seen when he'd originally been questioned. She walked into the cell and seemed immediately out of place, in her smart navy suit, high-heeled shoes, and carrying a soft leather briefcase. She smelled of something sharp and citrusy, but couldn't help wrinkling her nose at the rancid air that greeted her.

Alex stepped back from the door to give her some space.

'You're here to get me out – about bloody time.'

But the door clanged shut behind her and she gestured to Alex to sit down on the bed.

'Wait. What . . .?'

'They're not releasing you yet, Alex,' she said. 'They've had custody extended up to the full ninety-six hours. That means another day and a half. After that they'll have to charge you if they want to keep you.'

'No fucking way. There's nothing to charge me with.'

'Hitting a police officer?'

'They were all over me. I panicked.'

Her raised eyebrows told him that she'd heard it all before.

'They'll use what they can.'

'So if you can't get me out, what can you do?' Alex knew he sounded belligerent, and that she was on his side, but he'd had enough.

'Do you mind if I . . .' She pointed at the space next to him on the bed.

Alex gave a slight nod and she sat down.

'Listen, Alex, I can't get you out right now, but I can give you some advice.'

'What?' Did he want advice from Jayne Douglas? She had no idea what it was like to be in his situation. If she couldn't get him out she was just a waste of space.

'Alex, the police are building a case against you. They've got CCTV footage of you following Tash along the front before she was attacked, and they've found a witness who claims that you hit Tash on a previous occasion.'

'Who? Who said that? It's a bloody lie.'

'A girl called Sarah Collins. Do you know her?'

Alex nodded. 'That makes sense. She's a massive bitch.'

'But why would she come to the police with a lie like that?'

'I don't know. But it is a lie. I never hit Tash.'

Jayne Douglas's eyebrows went up a couple of millimetres. Didn't she believe him?

'Alex, the first and most important thing is for you to get your alibis straight. I've got the time frames of the two attacks here,' she said, opening the flap on her briefcase and pulling out a sheaf of papers. She flicked through them to find what she wanted. 'Right. Here's Sally Ann's. The hours in question are from five thirty last Thursday until approximately seven on Friday morning.'

'They asked me about that already.'

'What were you doing?'

Alex shrugged. 'I was at my cousin's house for some of the evening. Then I went home.'

'You'll need to be a little more precise with times than that.'

'I don't know the exact times.' He'd been over this so many times already, with the police and in his own mind. And each time it slammed it home to him that Tash and Sally Ann were both dead, and he started hurting all over again.

'Make an accurate estimate and then stick to it. And what

about witnesses? Is there anyone other than Liv and your parents who can vouch for you being in those places? After all, they're related to you.'

Alex sighed. 'No. It was just Liv and me at her house. And my parents were asleep when I got in, so they didn't even see me.'

Jayne Douglas glanced towards the cell door. 'Alex, we need to do better than this.'

'You mean lie. Or find someone else to lie on my behalf?'

She didn't answer him, but instead looked down at her piece of paper.

'What about the night Tash was attacked? I've got here that she left the club at just after one and was seen on CCTV cameras walking down the front. You were seen on the cameras following her, though several minutes later.'

'What?' This was news to Alex.

'You followed her.'

'I didn't.'

'Apparently you did.'

The ceiling and the walls rushed towards him and he couldn't breathe. He shook his head, desperate to speak but unable to form the words.

Jayne Douglas put a hand on his forearm.

'Take it slowly, Alex. Tell me what you told the police.'

'I told them what happened. I left The Haunt and had a spliff outside. Then I wandered around a bit and went home. That's it.'

'So how do you explain what's on the CCTV footage?'

Alex dropped his head into his hands. Had he walked along the front that night?

'I don't know,' he said. 'I can't remember where I went exactly.' He moved his arm to disengage Jayne Douglas's hand, then stood up and paced the short way to the opposite wall and back.

'I blacked out.'

The lawyer stared up at him, unblinking, for several long seconds.

'Never, never, never admit that to anyone else, Alex.' She stood up and put her hands on his shoulders. 'Not to the police, not to your mother, not to Liv. Never mention that fact to me again, either. Do you understand?'

Alex pulled away from her.

'Yes.'

Oh, yes, he understood all too clearly.

Like the police, Jayne Douglas thought he was guilty of the crime.

His own lawyer thought he was a murderer.

'Now get the hell out!'

The policeman who let Jayne Douglas out came back and handed him a cup of water. But Alex's hand was trembling too much to take it.

36

Marni

Marni knew about sleepless nights. She would count herself as an expert. She could chase sleep from one side of her bed to the other for hours on end. She knew about anxiety, gnawing at her belly, tightening her chest, making her feel cold, making her sweat. She greeted dawn like an old friend, with a dry mouth and a pounding head, more often than she would choose to. Pills were a temptation but she'd tried them before. Alcohol helped – occasionally, but not often. And it played havoc with her blood sugar levels.

The heatwave made things worse. Even a sheet was too much, and she lay awake, her body clammy with sweat that didn't cool her, thinking of Alex. She knew how he'd be feeling, how scared, how alone. Claustrophobia threatened to overwhelm her and she pushed the sheet to one side and sat up. How could she sleep? They had to release him soon or charge him – and what if they did that? She couldn't handle it.

Next to her, Thierry snored gently. He could always sleep. Drunk, high or sober, it made no difference. He was bored with her insomnia and there was no point both of them losing sleep.

She got out of bed and padded through the dark house. The upstairs windows were open, but there wasn't a breath of air. It didn't feel right. She could sense Alex's absence in the air, in the walls, floor and ceiling. Empty in the same way it was when she first kicked Thierry out as their marriage ran onto the rocks. There was a vacuum in the space Alex had taken up, an echo of his laughter just out of earshot.

Marni went into his room and seeing the outlines of familiar objects, but no Alex, broke her heart. Salty tears stung her eyes and her head ached, though not as much as her heart. She lay on his bed and buried her head in his pillow, taking a deep breath to get the smell of him, like she used to do when he was a baby.

Fuck Francis Sullivan. He had no grounds to hold her boy. He certainly had no grounds on which to charge him. Please God, let Alex be back in his own bed by this time tomorrow.

She slept.

In her dream, Alex was being taken away from her by armed police. They were in a courtroom and up in the public gallery, a row of girls with bleeding stigmata watched as Alex wrestled to break free. She had the dream over and over, but he never escaped.

When she woke, only fifteen minutes had passed. Insomnia rendered time elastic.

It was still dark outside. It would still be dark in Alex's cell. She tried to imagine herself being there with him, willing him to feel her presence and take comfort from it. Wide awake again, she slipped downstairs to the kitchen and drank vodka from the bottle, standing naked in front of the open fridge, welcoming the flood of cold air on her heated body.

Senses dulled by the alcohol, she went back up to Alex's room and climbed into his bed. This time she slipped under the covers, determined to sleep for longer than a quarter of an hour. She lay on her front and burrowed into the pillow. Searching for something cool to the touch, she slid her hand down between the mattress and the wall. It brought scant relief but as she was pulling it free, her fingers felt something. A piece of folded paper.

She pulled it out and dropped it to the floor by the side of the bed. She settled herself again.

Sleep didn't come, despite – or maybe because of – the heat of the vodka spreading through her body.

She turned on the light and picked up the piece of paper from the floor. An envelope. The stamp was French and it was addressed to Alex.

France?

The letter had already been opened and she pulled it out frantically, not caring that she ripped the envelope more in the process. Her hand shook as she unfolded it and then held it in the small pool of light created by the bedside lamp.

Mon cher Alexander,

You probably don't know who I am. Your mother and my brother will probably have never mentioned me during your childhood. No matter. I understand they must hide the truth from you.

Of what truth do I write?

Alexander, my name is Paul Mullins. I am your father. The man you know of as your father is my brother Thierry Mullins. He is not your father, he is your uncle. Your mother was with me, and we three are a family. I know this will come as a shock to you but, by God, I swear this is the truth.

Of course, you will want to meet me, just as I want to meet you. I will be coming to England soon. I will do all I can to come to Brighton. When I arrive, I'll write you again.

Mon cher fils, it's time that we got to know each other, do you agree?

Affectionately,

Ton père,

Paul Mullins

Marni gasped and dropped the letter. Paul was in prison in Marseilles. How could he have sent this? She studied the envelope. It had been posted in Aix-en-Provence, where Thierry and Paul's mother lived. That explained it and then she recognised that the writing on the outside of the envelope, different to that on the inside, was Paul's mother's. She would have happily smuggled it out of the jail for him. She'd do anything for her favourite son.

How long had Alex had this? She looked at the envelope but the postmark was obscured and she couldn't see the date. She thought about how secretive he'd become recently, how uncommunicative. Was this the reason why?

She looked around his room, trying to find answers in the abandoned trainers, kicked off into a corner, or in the jeans, discarded on the floor. Four brands of deodorant on the chest of drawers, his desk a muddle of books and drawings, pens and pencils. He'd tacked pictures to the wall – a sketch of Tash, photos of him and his friends at the beach.

No pictures from his childhood. No pictures of her, or of Thierry. She thought about the gulf that had opened between them. Was Paul the cause? Had he already sowed the seeds of doubt in Alex's mind about who he really was?

Paul was coming. Maybe he was already here.

Fear stole the oxygen from her lungs and made her hyperventilate.

37

Rory

Rory reached out to take the copy of the *Argus* that the boss was holding out to him. The paper trembled in Francis's hand and the colour had flooded back into his cheeks. He looked more alive than he had done for weeks.

'That bloody reporter. I shook hands with him on what was on and off the record and he's gone and printed the whole fucking lot.'

'You're kidding?'

Rory scanned the front-page article and sidebars about the deaths of Tash Brady and Sally Ann Granger, and he could see why the boss was enraged – Tom Fitz had included every damned detail. And furthermore, he'd added two plus two to make five, with a range of statements about the crime and the killer that were as much guesswork as anything else.

'There's worse. Page three.' Francis turned away from him.

When Rory opened the paper, he saw the true cause of Francis's anger. And his now very apparent embarrassment. As a sidebar to a separate article on Sam Kirby's trial, a series of grainy pictures with time stamps showed a man, unmistakeably Francis Sullivan, arriving at a small terraced house late at night, then leaving the following morning. Rory didn't need to read the caption identifying the property – it was Marni Mullins's house on Great College Street. Tom Fitz had linked Sam Kirby's taunts in the court to what he claimed was evidence of a relationship between Sullivan and Mullins. It ripped the prosecution's case to shreds.

'Jesus,' said Rory under his breath.

The boss crumpled like a football that had had the air kicked out of it. Hardly surprising, given the shitstorm looming on the horizon.

'Where the hell did he get those pictures?' said Francis.

Rory had seen them before. He knew exactly where they came from – on Bradshaw's instructions, he'd had Marni Mullins's house under surveillance for several weeks during the Tattoo Thief investigation. But the question was, who'd passed the images on to Tom Fitz?

'Come on, Rory,' said Francis through gritted teeth. 'We need to go and have word with the little shit.'

'Aren't you supposed to be in court?' It was the last day of Sam Kirby's trial.

'I've got time – I don't need to be there for the summing-up. It's just the verdict that counts.'

When Rory put on the blues and twos to cut through Brighton, Francis didn't complain about misusing them like he usually did – which in itself was a measure of just how shaken up he was. It was eight miles along the front to Lancing, where the *Argus* had its offices. The Friday morning school run was in full swing, and the not-yet-caffeinated mothers seemed oblivious to the flashing lights and siren. Rory swore softly under his breath as a gaggle of women with pushchairs dawdled on a pedestrian crossing, making him slam on the brakes.

'He made a veiled threat, but I thought he was bluffing,' said Francis. 'And the irony of it is, nothing happened between me and Marni Mullins that night.'

'The pictures tell a different story,' said Rory. *This was interesting.*

There was a moment's awkward silence, then the boss came clean.

'I got drunk, that was all.'

Rory bit down hard on his bottom lip. It would have been too cruel to laugh out loud, but he couldn't think of anything funnier than his super-square boss getting drunk with the tattoo artist.

'Listen, you can't trust the press as far as you can throw 'em,' said Rory. 'Why the hell did you tell him all that? Because of a threat he didn't put into words?'

Francis exhaled loudly in frustration. 'I was just confirming things he knew already. I thought if he knew what was true, he wouldn't publish a pack of lies. I asked him not to go public with certain aspects of the case. But he said he'd only wait so long. He wanted an exclusive and I had nothing to give him – so he's done this.'

'More to the point, who provided him with those images?'

'Who bloody took them, Rory? It's clear they're surveillance shots – from our department, at that.'

Time to change the subject, fast.

'We're going to have to start manipulating who knows what and then see what Fitz comes up with,' said Rory.

'That won't be easy. And we shouldn't have to waste time playing games like this.'

Rory indicated, turned off the main road and pulled up outside the building on the corner. A small newsagents and convenience store took up the ground floor. The offices of the *Argus* were located above, on the first floor. There was a door to the right of the shop and Francis was already banging on it with his fist by the time Rory had the car locked. The index finger of his other hand was pressing continuously on a buzzer. The intercom remained silent and no one came to the door.

Rory stepped back to the edge of the pavement and looked up at the first-floor windows. No signs of life.

'Damn!' said Francis, as he gave up hammering. 'Where does the bastard drink?'

Rory checked his watch. 'It's only eleven.'

'Yes, but Tom Fitz is an investigative journalist, Rory, and where does he do most of his investigating? In the pub.'

At that moment, the door of the newspaper office opened. Rory whipped round to see a woman standing in the doorway, a look of shock registering on her face as Francis barged forward and then pushed his foot into the narrowing gap of the rapidly closing door.

'Police. Open up.'

He pulled out his warrant card and thrust it under the woman's nose.

'I …' She didn't know what to say and resignedly stepped back to allow Francis to enter.

They took the stairs two at a time and burst into the newsroom. It was hardly a hive of activity – just two middle-aged men working on PCs, with the smell of burnt coffee hanging in the air. Neither of the men was Tom Fitz.

Francis strode around the office, looking at the empty desks as if he could somehow materialise the reporter into being at one of them.

'Police,' said Rory by way of explanation as the two men stopped work and gave them questioning glances. 'We're looking for Tom Fitz.'

The woman who'd opened the door had followed them up the stairs. 'He's not here,' she said.

'I can see that, love,' said Rory. 'Where is he?'

'I told him,' said one of the men.

'Told him what?' said Francis. 'Are either of you the editor?'

The other man, who was the older of the two, gave a cynical laugh. 'Us? You kidding?'

'Fitz?' said Rory, getting back to the point of their visit.

'Don't know,' said the second man and the other one shook his head.

'Are you expecting him?' Francis was getting more and more agitated.

'No.'

'But that's his jacket, isn't it?' said Rory, pointing to a garment hanging on the back of an empty chair.

Both men gave non-committal answers. Then Rory heard a footfall on the stairs. All eyes turned towards the door of the newsroom as Tom Fitz walked in with a McDonalds paper sack in one hand and a supersize coffee cup in the other.

As Rory watched, things seemed to go into slow motion. Tom Fitz's eyebrows shot up as he saw the two policemen, while Francis threw his now-very-crumpled copy of the *Argus* at the reporter's feet.

'You shit, you utter shit!' said Francis.

'Whoa,' said Fitz, raising his full hands in front of himself in an attempt to placate.

'You've probably blown both cases out of the water. How dare you print things you've been told off the record. I want a retraction in tomorrow's paper. All of that stuff that I told you.'

'No way,' said Tom Fitz. 'Not a chance. If I find something out independently of you telling me, then I get to print it, whether you say it's off the record or not.'

'I asked you not to print those things for the sake of the investigation.'

Tom Fitz shrugged and carefully placed his food on the nearest empty desk.

'Your career means more to you than us catching a killer?' Rory intervened.

'You've got two men in custody on this,' said Tom. 'Surely you believe you've got your killer?'

Francis's jaw tightened. 'And you've probably wrecked Kirby's trial.'

'You have. You were the one shagging your star witness.'

'Those pictures mean nothing.'

'I think most people who see them will think otherwise.'

'With your crude insinuations, they will.'

'You should have thought of that before you screwed Marni Mullins.'

Rory watched Francis snap. He lunged at the reporter, pulling his right arm back and clenching his fist. The punch, when it came, was almighty. Tom Fitz's jaw cracked as his head snapped back. He staggered and hit the corner of a desk with the back of his thigh, then, off balance, fell against the adjacent chair. It skidded out from underneath him and he sprawled ungraciously onto the floor with a loud 'Oomph!'

But Francis hadn't finished with him. After rubbing his bruised knuckles against his thigh, he bore down on Fitz and bent over him, grabbing a handful of his lapels on each side.

'I should fucking arrest you for obstruction.'

Fitz worked his jaw, already sporting a scarlet swelling that would no doubt develop into a spectacular bruise.

'No chance,' he said, his voice thickened and lisping. 'I'll lodge a formal complaint about this. I got witnesses.' Blood from a split lip dribbled down his chin.

Francis let go of one side of his jacket and balled a fist.

'I'll happily do it again, in case they didn't see it the first time.'

This was professional suicide.

'Come on, boss. Leave it now – you've made your point.'

'Shut it, Rory!'

Rory had to do something. He waded into the fray and pulled

Francis away by the arm. Francis glared at him and twisted out of his grasp.

'Boss?'

But Francis straightened up and brushed down his suit. Tom Fitz looked up, not bothering to get up and present himself as a target all over again.

Francis sneered down at him. 'That was your last chance for co-operation with us,' he said. 'I'll find your sources and I'll close them down. In future, you'll get nothing. No scoops, no priority information because you're the local man. Nothing. And if I was your editor, I'd seriously think about putting someone else on the crime desk. Because you're finished in this town.'

'You don't scare me, Sullivan,' said Fitz, still rubbing his jaw.

To Rory, it looked as if Francis was about to head in for a second go, so this time he got a firmer grasp on the boss's arm and propelled him down the stairs.

War had been declared in no uncertain terms.

38

Friday, 25 August 2017

Francis

Feeling more shaken by his encounter with Tom Fitz than he'd care to admit, Francis slunk into the back of the court just in time to hear the defence barrister summing up. As he sat and listened to the arguments concerning Sam Kirby's culpability, he rubbed his bloody knuckles. How could he have done something so stupid as punch Tom Fitz? And for all his and Rory's bravado, he was certain there would be consequences he didn't care to think about.

He tried to concentrate on what was going on around him in the court.

Certainly, the barrister argued, no one questioned that she was guilty of the murders of Giselle Connelly, Evan Armstrong and Gem Walsh, along with the attempted murders of Marni Mullins and Dan Carter. But an army of psychiatrists and mental health specialists had testified as to her state of mind when she committed the acts, all claiming mental illness.

As if the specialists could have any bloody idea of her state of mind, Francis thought, loosening his tie in a vain response to the stifling heat of the courtroom.

Francis could only see the back of the defence barrister from where he sat. The silk continued talking for about twenty minutes – too long – but finally he wound up and turned around to come back to his table. Then Francis saw it. The man, who'd been perfectly fine the day before, was now sporting a split lip. His mouth was swelling and bleeding, and the white jabot around his neck was spattered with blood. It must have happened just before he came into court and Francis could guess who was responsible. He looked at Kirby and noticed she was sucking the knuckles of her right hand. When she saw Francis looking at her, she dropped her hand to her lap and grinned at him. She was very pleased with herself.

What the hell had happened?

Francis's empty stomach curdled. Was the barrister's battered mouth the result of an altercation over strategy with his client, or was it a clever ploy, cynically administered to insinuate that his client was out of control? It made him even more nervous of the outcome. What if the jury made the wrong decision? How would that reflect on him? On his team? They had another killer on the loose and the last thing they needed was for this to undermine their authority. The town was twitchy, women were scared. All Francis could do was hope that Don Martin had made a better job of his statement than the defence barrister.

The judge began his final summation, addressing the jury about how they would need to reach a unanimous verdict. Some of them looked nervous, some bored. Probably most of them would be hugely relieved when the case was over and they could get back to their lives. They had no idea how much was riding on the decision they were about to take.

When the judge finished, the jury filed out of the courtroom to be sequestered in the jury room until they made their final decision.

The waiting began.

Francis couldn't second guess what the jury were thinking. There was a solid belief among his police colleagues that a speedy verdict meant a guilty verdict. And there was an equally solid belief that the longer the jury deliberated, the more likely the defendant was to be found guilty. Both seemed wishful thinking to Francis. No two cases were the same, and neither were any two juries.

Lunchtime came and went but Francis found himself unable to eat anything. A black coffee tasted bitter and the air in the courthouse was stale and warm. He longed to stretch his legs around the block but didn't dare in case the jury returned. He couldn't bear the thought of missing the verdict. He made do with smoking a cigarette out on the front steps. Then he tried answering emails, but his concentration constantly wandered back to the things he should have said on the stand but hadn't, the things he did say but shouldn't have, and the questions the prosecution should have asked him. Could it have made a difference? He was torturing himself but he didn't know how to stop.

Finally, when it was almost time for the judge to dismiss the jury to a hotel for the night, Francis caught sight of the clerk of the court in the corridor. He gave Francis a surreptitious nod, letting him know that the jury had finally reached their verdict. The buzz spread through the building and people hurried back into the courtroom and took their places. Tom Fitz was sitting, as always, at the front of the public gallery. Francis ignored him.

Don Martin came in and gave him a reassuring smile, while George Elphick looked pale and worried as he whispered to the defence barrister. Sam Kirby was led into the dock. She scowled as she looked around the room. Her moment at centre stage was coming to an end, and she had no control over what would happen next. From her perspective, neither option was particularly appealing – both involved a loss of freedom – but psychiatric hospital would be more comfortable, and she would no doubt relish the chance to parade her warped psyche in front of a rotation of doctors and psychiatrists.

The judge took his seat with a sombre expression and then spent some minutes consulting with the clerk of the court, a short man who had to stand on tiptoe for his hurried conversations at the bench. Finally, the judge nodded and the clerk scurried out through a door that Francis knew led to the jury room. A murmur of conversation started to build and the air became electric as every eye was focused on the door. Every eye apart from Sam Kirby's. She was, once more, staring right at Francis.

It's not over till it's over.

The phrase was easy for Francis to lip read as he'd heard her say it so many times before. But she was wrong. It was over – for her at any rate.

The judge frowned at the rising level of chatter in his court.

The door opened and there was a collective intake of breath as the jury came in. Francis looked at each one as they took their seats to see if any of them made eye contact with Sam Kirby. None of them did. *Thank God for that.*

'Will the foreman of the jury please rise?' said the clerk of the court.

An older man, wearing a tweed jacket and twill trousers, stood up.

'Have you reached a unanimous verdict on all charges?' said the clerk.

'We have,' said the foreman. He looked a little self-important, excited to be executing his civic duty.

'Please give me your verdicts,' said the clerk.

The foreman nodded and handed the clerk a folded slip of paper. The court was absolutely silent and the air in the room seemed to weigh heavily on Francis's shoulders like a warm blanket. The clerk walked across to the bench and handed the piece of paper up to the judge. He unfolded it and read what was written on it. Francis tried to read his expression but he couldn't

– the judge had been in the game long enough and knew better than to show anything on his face.

He folded the piece of paper again and turned to face the foreman.

With a nod from the judge, the clerk started to speak.

'Do you find Samantha Kirby guilty or not guilty of the murder of Giselle Connelly?'

'Not guilty.' The foreman said it a little too loudly and his words were greeted by a ripple of shock around the court.

'Do you find Samantha Kirby guilty or not guilty of the murder of Evan Armstrong?'

'Not guilty.' This time he needed to say it louder to be heard over the gasps and whispers in the public gallery.

'Do you find Samantha Kirby guilty or not guilty of the murder of Jem Walsh?' Even the clerk had raised his voice.

'Not guilty.'

Francis's world had started spinning at the first 'not guilty.' The other verdicts were a blur. He bit the inside of his cheek until he tasted blood, staring at the wooden rail in front him.

'Do you find Samantha Kirby guilty or not guilty of the manslaughter of Giselle Connelly?' This, as the judge had explained to the jury, was the diminished responsibility verdict.

'Guilty,' said the foreman.

The other two manslaughter charges also came in guilty, but none were salve to Francis's pain. The proceedings went into slow motion as he counted slowly to ten to anchor his mind.

One. Two. Three.

The public gallery couldn't contain its reactions. People gasped and one woman let out a shriek of unintended laughter.

Four. Five. Six. Seven.

Don Martin slammed his fist on the prosecution table. On the other side of the aisle, George Elphick had a grin as wide as a Cheshire cat.

Eight. Nine. Ten.

Tom Fitz was a blitz of fingers typing into his mobile phone.

Francis looked up at the judge. He could have been carved out of granite for all the emotion he showed.

Finally, he looked across the court at Sam Kirby.

Of course, she was looking straight at him. Her lips twisted into a sour smile. Then she started to move. With surprising speed and grace for a six-foot woman, she slipped to one side of the dock, cleverly dodging the slow reaction of the policewoman sitting behind her. She had the open floor of the courtroom to herself and she charged across it.

Francis realised her destination in an instant and stood up, ready to meet her head on. That was until he saw the look of murderous intent in her eye. He kicked his chair back and moved sideways into the aisle. Kirby adjusted her course. The dozy policewoman was finally running across the floor. The clerk and the judge were both shouting, ordering Kirby back to the dock. The public gallery gasped as one.

With a glint in her eye and baring her teeth, Sam Kirby launched herself at Francis. He turned his shoulder to her and moved to one side but she'd anticipated his feint. As her body crashed into his, she thrust an arm around his neck. Francis wrenched her arm off and pushed her back.

She glared at him, panting.

For three long seconds, nothing happened. No one moved. No one spoke.

Then, as the policewoman took hold of her, Sam Kirby hissed something that only Francis could hear.

'I will make it my life's work to find you and kill you.'

The words felt like soft bullets piercing his psyche. She spoke fast and before he could react or respond, she jerked her head back, then forward, smashing her forehead against his nose.

The policewoman yanked one of Kirby's arms behind her back

and snapped on a handcuff. Francis grabbed her other arm and held it until the second cuff was in place. Then he put a hand to his nose. It came away covered with blood.

'Just try it and you'll spend the rest of your life behind bars,' he hissed at her, now tasting blood as it ran into his mouth.

Sam Kirby's threat meant nothing to him – but the verdict could do real damage to his career and he'd been powerless to prevent it.

39

Friday, 25 August 2017

Marni

Marni could remember the days when Thierry's studio had been her favourite place in the world. When she fell in love with Thierry, she'd fallen in love with tattoos. One of those loves had stood the test of time better than the other. But now, as she looked round his current studio, she just felt confused. A few days ago, she'd felt sure she wanted finally to cut the ties that bound them together. He was unreliable. Unfaithful. Uncaring.

When she looked at him, too often she saw Paul – and that was something she was never going to get past.

But Alex was in trouble and her every instinct was to turn to her husband. If Alex was charged and had to stand trial, it wasn't something she could get through alone.

'Hey, Marni.' Noa's deep rumble brought her back to the surface. 'He's not here. He's gone to the cash and carry.'

He and Charlie were both working on clients and the sound of their tattoo machines soothed her.

'That's fine. Just came by to pick up some needles.'

She went over to Thierry's station and was overcome by a wave of nostalgia as she cast an eye over the rows of inks and neat lines of equipment. Always so much tidier in his workspace than in his personal life.

Wait a minute.

She went closer to the rack where he kept his tattoo machines – half a dozen or so, more than he needed – and there among them were two of hers. The two that had gone missing from her studio.

'Jesus Christ!'

'You okay?' said Charlie, looking up from the girl's leg he was tattooing.

Marni picked up the two irons and looked around for the rest of the kit that had gone missing. It was there – the charger and the cable, the foot pedal. She shoved the whole lot into her bag and then grabbed the box of blister-packed tattoo needles she'd come for.

'No. Yes. I'm fine, Charlie. Just . . . fuck Thierry.'

'I'd rather leave that to you, babe.'

But Marni was already out of the door.

She set off up Preston Street in the direction of her own studio at a brisk march, but she only lasted twenty metres before she had to stop. She bent forward, resting her hands on her knees, hyperventilating. Because it was only with the wave of relief she felt at seeing her equipment that she realised the full extent to which she'd doubted her son. She'd actually believed that Alex had taken the tattoo equipment from her studio, burying the thought deep within her psyche so she didn't have to confront it.

Only now she did. She'd doubted her son.

The pavement was crowded. Tourists and shoppers pushed past her, no one stopping to see if she was okay. She leaned back against a wall and fought to get her breathing under control.

If she'd believed Alex had taken the equipment, did it mean she'd believed he was capable of murder? She couldn't imagine a worse betrayal of the person she loved most in the world. But now she was one hundred per cent certain of his innocence. One hundred per cent.

She started to run along the pavement, weaving through the

people, buffeted by the sheer swell of them heading down towards the front. All oblivious of the mission Marni had set for herself.

She would prove her son was innocent if it killed her.

Ten minutes later, she was sitting in her studio with her head in her hands. She'd cancelled the appointment she'd had for midday, all thought of work abandoned. The police, as usual, were failing to do their job and her son's freedom was on the line. It was time to step in and if Frank Sullivan didn't like it, he could go to hell.

She scanned the *Argus*'s website for information on the case. Where should she start? Someone had tattooed these girls with poison ink. Why? There were no pictures of the tattoos in the paper. She needed to see them, and she knew exactly where to go.

When Rose Lewis came back from running lunchtime errands, Marni was waiting in the mortuary car park for her. She'd met Rose when she'd helped Francis on the Tattoo Thief case. That time, the police had asked her to look at the tattoos on the victims' dead bodies and she hadn't been keen. This time, she would be asking Rose if she could look at them, and she had a feeling that Rose wouldn't be so keen to show her.

'Hello, Marni,' said Rose, when Marni fell into step with her as she walked across the baking tarmac. 'What are you doing here?'

Marni took a deep breath. 'It might sound like a strange request, Rose, but I was wondering if I could see the tattoos on Tash Brady and Sally Ann Granger's backs?'

Rose took a moment to unlock the door to the mortuary before answering.

'Why?'

'I'm sure you know Alex is being questioned about the deaths.'

Marni struggled to stop her voice from cracking. 'He didn't do it, Rose. I know that. I want to see those tattoos because they might give me a clue as to who did do them. I need to get Alex off the hook.' She restrained herself from sharing her views on the crap job the police were doing.

Rose tilted her head to one side. 'Okay, I understand, Marni, but it's totally against regulations. I'm sorry, I couldn't really show them to you without Francis's say so. Does he know you're here?'

'Please. Those tattoos must have a meaning and that meaning might just lead us to the real killer.'

'Us?'

'Don't you want to find out who did this?'

'Of course I do. But Francis and his team are on the case.' She paused, looking sheepish. 'I'm sorry that he's arrested your son, but he wouldn't have done that if he didn't have a good reason to.'

'You've got a son, Rose, haven't you?' She left the implication of the words hanging in the air between them, but she held Rose's eyes with her own.

Rose dropped her gaze, then capitulated. 'Okay, let's take a look at them,' she said. 'I can spare ten minutes for this, then I've got to get started on a PM scheduled for this afternoon.'

She led Marni into the mortuary and told her to wait in the vestibule while she took her bag upstairs to the office. Marni's heart was pounding. The tattoos had to tell her something.

'Right, come on then,' said Rose, appearing at the bottom of the stairs in a white lab coat. She unlocked the inner door to the morgue and ushered Marni inside. The smell of chemicals and death made Marni wince. It reminded her of Sam Kirby's barn, though it wasn't nearly as powerful as the stench of Kirby's skin-tanning operation.

'Here,' said Rose, handing Marni a pot of Vapor Rub and a white coat.

Marni knew the drill and rubbed the oily ointment along her top lip, while Rose pulled open a couple of the stainless-steel drawers in which the bodies were stored.

'This is Tash Brady.'

Rose pulled on latex gloves, then gently turned the body so Marni would be able to see the tattoo on Tash's back. Marni stood away while she did it – she didn't think she could bear to see Tash's face. She hadn't known her very well, but she'd liked her, and Alex had been happy while he was with her.

'Come and look,' said Rose.

Marni stepped forward and stared down into the metal drawer. Tash's skin looked grey and waxy but there were also mottled patches of purple-reddish skin on her back and buttocks.

'What are those?' said Marni, pointing to one.

'Lividity,' said Rose. 'Where the blood pooled after she died. It's normal – she was lying on her back and that's where her blood settled. If you can't see the tattoo properly, I've also got photos of it that the police took when she was still alive.'

'Thanks,' said Marni, turning her attention back to Tash's back.

'It's Latin, right?' said Marni, as she read the ornate script that stretched across the shoulder blades.

Rose nodded.

Alex had never learned Latin at school.

Marni studied the work. 'The handwriting's good enough – quite even in terms of the size and shape of the letters – but the tattoo isn't well executed. It's not professional work.'

Rose raised her eyebrows and Marni explained. 'Look, at these points the needle was pressed in too hard and the tattoo's gone too deep.' She indicated some areas that were crusted with scabs. 'She would have bled quite freely when it was done. But for these letters the touch was too light, not taking the ink deep enough into the dermis for a permanent fix.' She pointed with her finger to a different part of the tattoo.

Marni scanned the rest of Tash's back.

'Has Frank's team found out anything about the UV tattoos?' she asked.

Rose's head snapped up. 'The what?'

Marni pointed to some faint scratches lower down Tash's back. 'These bits. She's been tattooed with ultraviolet ink.'

Rose studied the area. 'They just look like scratches. What makes you think they're tattoos?'

'Have you got a magnifying glass?'

Rose fetched one.

Marni peered through it at the marks on Tash's back, then held it out to Rose. 'Look closely, just there. You can see needle marks.'

Rosie studied the skin, then nodded. 'I see them.'

'And if we shine a UV lamp on them, you'll see tattoos.'

Rose's eyes widened and she took a deep breath. 'Oh God,' she said. 'We missed that. Shit.'

'UV lamp?' said Marni.

'Hold on.' Rose stripped off her gloves and left the room.

Marni continued to study the marks on Tash's back while she waited. Rose was back in less than a minute, with a small, hand-held UV lamp. She plugged it in at one of the side benches and unfurled its cable. It was just long enough to reach to the steel drawer containing Tash Brady's body.

Marni found herself holding her breath as Rose switched off the room's main lights, then switched on the UV lamp.

Luminous white lines, circles and dashes sprang to life across Tash's back. It wasn't writing.

'What the hell is it?' said Rose.

Marni shook her head, studying the marks from a variety of angles.

'What about Sally Ann?' she said.

Rose handed her the lamp and pulled open another drawer.

She quickly put on gloves so she could turn Sally Ann's body over. Marni shone the lamp on her to discover that she too had been tattooed with UV ink. The glowing markings on her back were similar but not identical to Tash's.

'What do they mean?' said Marni. 'A message?'

Rose nodded. 'He's telling us something but I'm damned if I know what.'

40

Friday, 25 August 2017

Francis

Francis left the court without speaking to anyone. Of course, he should have thanked Don Martin for prosecuting the case, but he couldn't trust himself not to speak his mind. That they'd screwed up. He sat in his car in the car park and rested his forehead against the steering wheel. Then he lit a cigarette.

Damn!

If they couldn't manage to put away a serial killer who'd admitted her crimes, what hope in hell did they have with the current case, where so far there wasn't a scrap of evidence tying anyone to the scene?

His phone buzzed with messages and missed calls but for once he ignored it. He didn't want to hear Rory moaning or some other member of the team asking a question that they already knew the answer to. A reminder chimed – he was supposed to be meeting Robin at their solicitor's office for the reading of his mother's will. Grief washed through him all over again. How could she be dead?

He threw the car into gear and backed out of his space. He was going to be late.

He was only ten minutes late, but earned himself a disapproving look from his sister as he was shown into the wood-panelled office of James Baines – who was both their solicitor and a cousin on their father's side. Robin was drumming her fingers against the side of her chair and he thought she looked pale and so much older than when he'd seen her last. She'd been dreading their mother's death for a long time and, as inevitable as it was, she was taking it badly.

He apologised to James, who he hadn't seen for more than a year, despite the fact that they lived less than five miles from each other. James Baines was his senior by ten years, the cousin he'd looked up to as an older brother in their childhood. But they'd seen less of each other as Francis had reached adulthood and though James worked as a solicitor in Brighton, their paths hadn't crossed professionally. He'd put on weight, Francis noticed as they briefly shook hands. Then he sat down, avoiding Robin's stony look.

Once his PA had sorted coffees, James Baines got down to business.

'I've got your mother's will here, and she named me as executor some years ago, when she made this will. I have no reason to believe that she's made any other subsequent will.' He looked at them questioningly, in case they knew otherwise.

Francis shook his head.

'No,' said Robin. 'She told me she'd lodged her will with you, so go ahead.'

'Do you already know the provisions?'

Both siblings shook their heads, and James unfurled a folded document that had been lying in front of him on his desk. He scanned the contents, as if checking all was as he expected it to be.

'This will is dated the seventeenth of April 2014. The first paragraph states that it revokes all previous wills. The second paragraph appoints me as executor. Right, here are the provisions.' He started to read aloud from the document. '"I hereby bequeath to my son Francis Frederick Sullivan a gift of my grandfather's pocket watch.'" James paused in the reading. 'I have the watch here,' he said, opening a drawer in his desk.

He pulled out a leather presentation case and handed it to Francis. Francis knew the watch well – it had lived in his mother's bureau throughout his childhood, but he still opened the box to look at it. The eighteenth-century gold pocket watch had an ornate gold case and an engraved mother-of-pearl face. It had been passed down the male line of his mother's family since it had been first purchased by a distant cousin in the early 1700s. It had been well cared for and still worked, as far as Francis could remember. He felt the heft of it in his hand like a direct link to his antecedents.

'It's beautiful,' said Robin, smiling at him for the first time in weeks.

He passed it across the table for her to look at. Then he looked over at James. It seemed an odd thing to start with – just a small detail really.

James cleared his throat and picked up the will again.

'Moving on to the fourth paragraph,' he said. '"Subject to the payment of my funeral and testamentary expenses, I give all my residuary estate to my daughter, Robin Alice Sullivan, if she is still living at the time of my death."'

'What?' Had he heard that right?

Robin gasped and dropped the pocket watch onto her lap. It slid off and hit the wooden floor with a clatter. She put a hand up to her mouth.

'Oh my God!' Her words were muffled by her fingers, her face suddenly drained of colour.

She bent forward to pick up the watch, but Francis beat her to it. He pretended to examine it for damage, looking down intently so he didn't have to look either James or Robin in the eye. There was a slight dent in the case, where the metal was worn thin. He slipped it into his jacket pocket without showing Robin.

'It's fine,' he said, settling back into his chair. His heart was pounding. This was not what he'd expected.

'It's not fine,' said Robin. 'It's not fine at all. I had no idea Mum was going to do this, Fran. Really I didn't.' Her voice quavered. 'Of course, I'll give you half, that goes without saying.'

'No, you won't,' said Francis. 'You'll have far more need of the money than I will and she obviously wanted to make sure that you'll always be provided for.'

In fact, Robin would now be a wealthy woman – Lydia had inherited a considerable sum from her own parents and had invested well.

The tears that had been hovering on Robin's lower lids over-flowed onto her cheeks.

'Fran,' she said. The word was fraught with both gratitude and remonstrance.

'Don't say anything,' said Francis, a little too curtly. He didn't want James to think he cared about the money – because he didn't. It was something else . . . The feeling he'd always had, and tried to suppress, that Robin had been Lydia's favourite child.

The solicitor put down the will and pulled a folded hand-kerchief out of a pocket. He pushed it across the table towards Robin, who took it gratefully.

'That's it, really,' he said. 'She's left some instructions for her funeral, which aren't binding, and that's all.'

'Of course, we'll honour them,' said Robin, still sniffing.

Francis wondered how his mother's stipulations would fit with Robin and Jered's plans for the service, and whether they really would be honoured. Of course they would. Robin wouldn't go against her own mother's wishes, despite her new-found attachment to Jered Stapleton.

And it was right that the whole inheritance should go to

her. Robin had always hated pity and had never wanted to be seen as a charity case. But as she was getting older, she seemed to understand that her illness meant she sometimes needed to swallow her pride and let people help her. Lydia had made the right decision – it would give Robin the independence she craved and would mean a more equitable relationship between the siblings, as Francis would be spared the burden of supporting her financially. Just as well, considering his stellar career was no longer quite so shiny.

She hadn't done it to hurt him.

They chatted for a few more minutes about the funeral arrangements and then Francis helped Robin out to her car. She thanked him and remonstrated with him again as she got into the specially adapted Mini she drove.

'She shouldn't have done that, Fran.'

He shook his head. 'I don't need the money. I earn quite enough and I'm living rent-free in Dad's house. Talking of which, we need to get in touch with him.'

Robin bristled at the mention of their father.

'I don't want him at the funeral.'

'Come on, Robin – they were married for nearly twenty years.'

'And then he deserted her. And us.'

'He has a right to be there, if he wants to come.'

'No.' She glared up at him through the open car window. 'If he comes, I won't.'

'For God's sake! You're being overdramatic.'

'Don't do it, Fran. Please.'

She wound up the car window, cutting off what he was going to say. He doubted their father would come all the way from Thailand, but he still had a right to know that his ex-wife had died.

As Robin drove away, he went back up to James's office to collect the watch case.

'Thank you, James,' said Francis.

'I'm not sure that was entirely fair,' said James. 'It's more money than Robin needs and by rights some of it should have come to you.' Then seeing Francis's look of discomfort at the suggestion, he quickly changed the subject. 'Have you heard from your father? Will he come to the funeral?'

'I've got a number for him in Thailand, but I haven't been able to reach him.'

James's eyes widened in surprise. 'But he's over here at the moment. Haven't you seen him?'

'He's here?'

'Yes, he's over with his wife for a few weeks.'

His new wife. His other wife.

'Have you seen him?' said Francis, desperately hoping his voice wouldn't convey the surprise he felt.

Why hadn't he been in touch?

James shook his head. 'No, but I spoke to him on the phone.'

'Have you got a number for him?' It practically killed Francis to have to ask this, but thankfully James restrained from commenting on how strange it was that he should have to furnish Francis with his own father's mobile number.

'Thanks,' said Francis. 'You didn't mention this to Robin, did you?'

'No. We talked about your mother while we were waiting for you.'

Francis went home and sat at his kitchen table, staring at the new number in his contacts list. But he didn't dial it. He felt overwhelmed. His mother was dead. His father had a new wife. Two women had been murdered. A serial killer might escape justice because of some misjudged behaviour on his part. And if Tom Fitz lodged a complaint . . . Things that had seemed certain no longer were. He had too many balls in the air at once. And now, as they were all tumbling down around him, he realised with a jolt that the only person he wanted to talk to wasn't talking to him because she believed he was about to charge her son with murder.

41

Marni

'Whore!'

'It was before we were back together. You were with that slut with the mermaid tattoo.'

Thierry's double standards never ceased to amaze Marni. She was expected to remain chaste, despite the fact they were divorced? While it was okay for him to shag anything with a pulse?

'But you slept with a *flic*.'

'Nothing happened – that whole thing in the paper is bullshit.'

She went out into the garden and lit a cigarette to get away from him. The lawn was brown, bone dry, and despite her occasional attempts at watering, the flowerbeds were parched and cracked. She squinted into the sun as she exhaled a plume of acrid smoke. What she'd really taken exception to in Tom Fitz's piece was the fact that he'd named Alex as a 'person of interest' in the current case.

But that hadn't bothered Thierry as much as the insinuation that she'd taken Francis Sullivan to her bed. She wasn't lying when she'd said nothing had happened, but he was never going to believe her.

'*Putain*,' said Thierry, standing in the doorway.

'Remind me, would you, why I thought it was a good idea to

get back together with you?' she said.

'You know we're good together,' said Thierry.

'This is good?'

Marni ground out her cigarette angrily and left the butt lying on the patio. She shoved past him into the kitchen.

'We're a family,' he said, following her in.

'For sure,' she said. 'You stand by and leave it all to me. And now your bastard brother's trying to claim him.'

'*Merde*, forget Paul. He's nothing. You're living in the past.'

Marni bit down hard on her bottom lip. How had it come to this? Alex was in custody. Paul was threatening to come to Brighton. And Thierry was kicking off over a non-event that had happened more than a year ago.

'I want you to leave.' It came out of her mouth with no thought at all, but she knew straight away she was making the right decision. She needed all her energy for her son – Thierry was just a distraction, and not in a good way. 'It's over, Thierry.'

'Come on?'

'I need space. I need to help Alex. And I don't need any more of your shit.'

Thierry scowled at her, but half an hour later he came down the stairs with a bulging grip bag.

'I'll be at Noa's, when you change your mind.'

The front door slammed behind him and Marni gave a sigh of relief that instantly turned to tears. Damn the man.

She made coffee to clear her head and tried to work out what she should do next. Francis Sullivan had never shown up at the morgue the previous evening, so she still had no idea what the UV tattoos on Tash and Sally Ann's backs signified. Rose said she'd let her know as soon as she found out, but she'd believe that when it happened. There was no reason for the pathologist to keep her in the loop and, with Alex in custody, there was every reason not to.

She drained her coffee and picked up her phone.

'Liv, do you know Sarah Collins?'

Liv sniffed at the other end of the line. Marni's call had obviously woken her. 'I do.'

'Can you fix up to meet her for coffee? I need to talk to her.'

'What . . . why?'

'I think she lied to the police about Alex. I want to know why.'

'No way, Marni. This doesn't sound like a good idea . . .'

'Liv?' She paused, listening to the static on the connection. 'Liv, I'm scared they're going to charge him with murder.'

'They can't do that.'

'They can.'

'Okay.' She sounded resigned. 'I'll fix up for you to talk with Sarah.'

'Today, yeah?'

Liv was as good as her word, and at three o'clock Marni arrived, as arranged, at Pret on East Street. The coffee shop was heaving – Saturday afternoon on a bank holiday weekend and the whole town was at bursting point. Marni joined the queue behind two girls in full mod regalia and scanned the ground floor for her niece. A hand waved at her through the throng of bodies – Liv was sitting at a corner table and opposite her sat a girl who must have been Sarah Collins.

Marni looked at her with interest, though she could only see her from the side. Glossy black hair swept back from an immaculately made-up face, tight jeans and a skinny lycra top showed a strip of taut, brown flesh between them. She picked at the edge of a plastic cup on the table in front of her – some kind of green juice – and then twisted a strand of her dark hair round her finger. She was nervous, making Marni wonder what Liv had said to her.

So she should be nervous, the little cow.

Marni got to the front of the queue and asked for a black coffee, though a hot drink was the last thing she needed. Then she went over to the girls' table.

Deep breaths. Stay calm. Don't make any accusations.

Liv stood up as she arrived and moved to the next seat so Marni could sit opposite Sarah.

'Sarah, this is my aunt, Marni Mullins.'

On hearing the name Mullins, Sarah Collins flinched in her seat. Her hand shot back to the plastic cup and snapped the rim of the lid.

'Hi Sarah,' said Marni. She couldn't quite smile at the girl – she wasn't here to be friendly – but she sat down and made a conscious effort not to sound as aggressive as she was feeling. 'You probably know what I want to talk to you about, don't you?'

Sarah Collins stared at her cup and didn't speak. Liv raised her own cup to her lips. Her cheeks were flushed and she looked almost as uncomfortable as her friend.

Marni was walking on a knife-edge. She wanted to shove Sarah Collins against a wall and ask her why she'd lied to the police about her son. But if she did anything that showed her true feelings, the girl could just get up and walk.

'Sarah,' she said gently. 'You spoke to the police about Alex, didn't you?'

Finally the girl made eye contact with her and nodded. Marni could read fear in her eyes. Why was she afraid?

'You told them Alex had hit Tash, didn't you?'

She nodded again, working her mouth nervously as if she wanted to say something but couldn't.

Marni waited.

Liv put down her cup.

'Why did you say that, Sarah?' Liv burst out. 'You know Alex well enough to know that he'd never do that. Now the police are trying to blame him for Tash's death.'

Marni stayed quiet. Sarah might respond better to Liv than to her.

Sarah started to cry and Liv grabbed hold of one of her hands.

'I didn't want to say that,' said Sarah, gulping down air as she sobbed. 'I knew it was wrong.'

'Then why did you do it?' said Liv.

Sarah sniffed and dabbed her nose with a paper serviette that was lying on the table. She pressed her index finger under each eye to stem the flow of tears and mascara.

'Kath came to our house . . .'

'Kath Brady?' said Marni.

Sarah nodded. 'She came to see Mum a few days after Tash died. Mum called me down to talk to her. Kath said Tash had told her that Alex had hit her once.' Sarah paused and blotted her eyes again. 'But she said if she told that to the police, they wouldn't believe her because she'd already said stuff to them about Alex.'

'Stuff?' prompted Marni.

'That she thought Alex had done it, that he'd attacked her.'

Marni cursed silently, digging her nails into her palms underneath the table.

'She said that if I told the police about Alex hitting Tash, they would believe me.'

'But you would be lying, Sarah.'

'My mum said I should do it.' She started to cry more loudly, without reservation.

The couple at the next table stared across at Marni with accusing looks. Marni fished a clean tissue out of her bag and passed it across to Sarah.

'It's okay, Sarah,' said Liv. 'It was right of you to tell us.'

Sarah snorted loudly and tried to gain control of herself.

Now Marni had what she wanted from the encounter, but she had one last question.

'Sarah, would you come with us to John Street and tell DI Sullivan what you've just told us?'

Sarah shook her head violently. 'They'll lock me up, won't they?'

'Of course not. They'll be the first to tell you you've done the right thing.' Marni didn't know or care if Sarah would be charged with perverting the course of justice. All she cared about was Alex.

'Please, Sarah. Alex could go to prison for years. And meanwhile, the real killer's still out there somewhere, getting ready to attack another girl.'

Sarah's wide, dark eyes flared even wider, then she nodded.

'Okay, I'll come with you.'

42

Saturday, 26 August 2017

Rory

Rory stared at the clock on the incident-room wall and decided the hands hadn't moved since he'd last looked up at it. Still four fifteen. Bloody thing must need a new battery again. He checked the time on his phone. The clock was right and it felt like the afternoon had ground to a halt. He should have been in his back garden with a beer, not stuck in the office reviewing crime-scene data.

The investigation had pretty much ground to a halt. The SOCOs had been down into the sewers and come back empty-handed. Rose had nothing for them from the crime scenes, apart from a partial footprint in blood from the aquarium. Size ten, generic lugged sole. It could have come from the shoes of a thousand men. In other words, it wasn't a lead. And now there were these weird UV tattoos apparently that no one understood.

There was a single link between the two girls and the two suspects. The School of Art. Angie, Kyle and Tony were scheduled to go there first thing Tuesday morning, after the bank holiday, to get a list of Tash and Sally Ann's classmates and teachers. But why had the killer targeted those two girls, out of hundreds? They had missed something, somewhere. A critical fact, a small piece of the jigsaw . . . and until they found it, they weren't going to make any progress.

The clacking of Kyle's keyboard was setting his teeth on edge and the clattering of the fan only served as a reminder of how useless it was. It just shunted the hot air around with no cooling effect at all.

'Can't you give it a rest, Kyle?'

'What, sarge?'

'Nothing,' he muttered. 'Make us a coffee, would you?'

Kyle nodded and scraped his chair back on the floor.

Blessed silence for two minutes. Then his phone rang. It was the boss. Wasn't he in his office?

'Yeah? Where are you?'

'Can you process Mullins for release, Rory?'

What the fuck?

'But . . .'

'No. Just do it.' Francis cut the connection.

It took Rory a couple of calls to track him down, but according to the desk sergeant the DI was in one of the interview rooms with Marni Mullins and two young women.

Rory rapped on the door with his knuckles and went in without waiting to be invited.

Francis glared at him. 'Yes?'

On the other side of the table from the boss sat two girls. He didn't recognise either of them, but Marni bloody Mullins was standing behind them, leaning against the wall. She had Sullivan wrapped around her little finger and Rory could smell trouble.

'A word?' he said, nodding his head towards the door.

Francis stood up.

'Can you just wait here until we've got a statement for you to sign,' he said to one of the two girls.

She nodded. There were black smudges of mascara down her cheeks and her eyes were bloodshot.

Francis followed Rory out of the room.

'What's happening?' said Rory.

'That's Sarah Collins,' said Francis. The name rang a bell – the girl Angie had interviewed, who'd said Alex Mullins had hit Tash Brady. 'She's just retracted her previous statement.'

'Because Marni Mullins got to her?'

'Because Kath Brady asked her to lie.'

'You believe that?'

'Yes, as a matter of fact I do.'

'And now you want to let Mullins go?'

'We don't have much choice, Rory. We didn't have much on him to start with and now we've got even less.'

Rory shook his head. This was wrong. They were going to be releasing a killer out onto the streets.

Francis looked at his watch. 'Process him out. King, too. Put eyes on both of them.'

'Both of them? That'll need overtime. You gonna square it with the chief?'

'Enough, Rory.' He took a step forward and for a second Rory thought he was going to lose it like he had in Fitz's office. 'This is my bloody investigation and I know exactly what I'm doing. Now get out of my sight.'

Rory went back to his desk. The boss was cracking up over this case. But if that was the way he wanted to play it, more fool him. It wouldn't be his problem when Bradshaw blew a gasket.

Rory fingered his mobile, opening the list of contacts at 'B'. But he didn't dial.

Instead, he got on with the paperwork to release Mullins and King from custody.

He organised a surveillance roster.

He wondered what Sullivan was up to. Was he playing the most dangerous game of all? Was he going to try and catch the killer in the act?

*

249

At five to five, Rory led Alex Mullins from the custody suite to the reception area of John Street Police Station, where Marni Mullins was waiting impatiently for his release.

Alex stood sullen and silent as Rory took his handcuffs off. Behind him, the heavy security door that separated the reception area from the rest of the station opened.

'Mackay, what are you doing?' It was Bradshaw.

'Releasing this man,' said Mackay.

'Couldn't you get an extension?' said Bradshaw, ignoring Marni who was now stepping forward in protest.

'Sir, we've been holding him for ninety-six hours.'

'Can't you charge him?'

'No grounds. DI Sullivan instructed his release.'

'Where is Sullivan?'

'In his office, I believe.'

Without another word, Bradshaw stormed back the way he'd come. Rory pulled out his phone to text a warning to the boss, then thought better of it.

He got the cuffs off Mullins and handed him the paperwork.

'Released under investigation,' said Rory. 'You're to stay in Brighton and remain available to us if we need to talk to you again.'

Mullins nodded.

'Come on,' said Marni, stepping towards Alex to give him a hug. 'Let's get home.'

For the first time since coming out of the custody suite, Alex Mullins looked up at his mother. His expression was cold and hard.

'Get lost,' he said. 'I'm not going home.'

43

Lou

Lou Riley huddled in the doorway of the empty shop, shivering as she lit her last cigarette. She was coming down hard and fast, and she had no more caps to take and nowhere to go. There was no way she was going back to her mum's, not with Derek in the house. Last time she'd snuck in after a night on X, he'd been getting up for his early shift – and while her mum lay snoring upstairs, he'd pinned her up against the kitchen wall and put his hand down her knickers.

She gagged at the memory of his stinking breath.

St James's Street was quiet. It was gone three, so nobody was around. But she was out on the street alone. She didn't want to think about the stories going round, of a maniac grabbing women off the street. Girls from college, though she didn't know them. Mostly people were staying in. Scared. Fear, seeping through the town like poison. Stupid really. If she tucked up small in the corner of this doorway, she could hunker down until it was light. No one would see her. Then, when it was past the time that Derek went on shift, she could go home. What did her mum see in him?

She took a last drag of her cigarette. She'd smoked it right down to the nub, and the smoke burned the back of her throat, setting off a coughing fit. She tossed the filter across the pavement to the gutter, then checked her pockets for her fag packet.

No, that had been the last one.

Was she going to go home? She wanted her bed desperately, wanted to be warm and asleep. Cramp clenched her lower bowels and she pushed herself further into the corner of the doorway, wrapping her arms around her knees. No one could see her here. The stone step was cold to sit on, and it crept slowly through her, but she was too lethargic now to move.

The headlights of a passing car woke her with a jolt. Every bone in her body ached. She hunted for a cigarette and then remembered.

Fuck!

'Hey, you okay?'

Her eyes snapped open and she pulled her cardigan defensively against her body. There was a man looming in the doorway above her. He blocked the light from the streetlamps so she couldn't see his face. But he seemed to know her.

'It's fine, don't be frightened.'

She struggled to her feet. It only made her feel marginally less vulnerable.

'Have you got a cigarette?' she said. 'Got any E?'

He moved back and the light caught the side of his face. No, he wouldn't have any E. She knew him – she'd seen him round college.

'You don't want E, not now. What are you doing out here? Can I take you home?'

'I can't go home.'

He didn't ask why. Maybe it was obvious. Maybe he could see how worthless she was.

'What time is it?' she said.

'Do you want to stay somewhere dry?' he said.

Lou stiffened and shook her head.

'Don't get the wrong idea,' he said quickly. 'Nothing like that, believe me.'

'Where?' she said. Could she trust him? His voice had a friendly quality. Reassuring, not threatening. She virtually knew him.

'Just a few minutes' walk from here,' he said. 'There's a cricket pitch round the corner, with a pavilion. I've got a key for it, and I could let you in. You could stay there for a couple of hours till it gets light.'

She thought about it for less than a minute. Anything had to be better than being out here in the cold.

'Thanks,' she said awkwardly. She wasn't used to people being nice to her.

'This way.'

They walked east along St James's Street, away from the city centre. The man was carrying a heavy black bag. Neither of them said anything for a while, but she felt warmer just walking by his side. Then Lou said, 'What's your name?'

'What's yours?'

'Lou,' she answered. 'D'you live around here?'

'Not far,' he replied.

His monosyllabic answers discouraged further conversation and they continued in silence. After a few minutes, they turned left up Montague Place and then right along Eastern Road. Lou wondered how much further it was. Her whole body ached and her mouth felt dry. Comedown hell.

'Just another couple of minutes,' he said.

They passed the posh boys' school and turned left. Fifty yards up the road, an open gate led onto a sports field. It stretched away into inky darkness, but the streetlights along the right-hand side illuminated a small building set halfway down the side of the pitch.

'That's it,' said the man. 'You'll be out of the wind in there.'

She followed him towards the pavilion and waited as he unlocked the door. He led her inside without turning on a light. They wouldn't want to attract attention from the houses across the road.

'You can even grab a shower, if you like,' he said, 'though I don't know if the water will be hot.'

The thought of a warm shower was like a balm.

'Thanks.'

Lou was still smiling as the first blow came out of nowhere. A smash with his fist to the side of her head, and she dropped to the floor. Pain cut through her like a knife. And hindsight. She should have known better. He'd taken her for the fool she was and now . . . oh, shit! What was he going to do to her now?

She wasn't the girl that people were kind to, that people took pity on. She was the girl they hurt. Because she was stupid.

Blinking back tears of pain and anger, she tried to get away. But he bent over her and slammed his fist into the same side of her head again. Her skull smacked back onto the wooden floor and consciousness spun away.

She woke up in agony, and she didn't know where she was. She wasn't in her own bed. She wasn't in a bed at all. Pain bit deep into her side, as if her guts were on fire. She could smell blood. She could taste it, too. She must have bitten her tongue. She panicked and screamed, opening her eyes, but it was too dark to make out where she was.

Someone moved in the shadows.

'Who's there?'

Memory flooded back. Crouching in a shop doorway. A man looming above her. Then what?

A bright white light blinded her and she put a hand across her eyes.

'What're you doing?' she said.

Something was terribly wrong. Her body shook and her mouth went dry. The light moved. It was coming at her. Her bowels turned to water and she started to retch. She had to get away but she was paralysed.

'Relax. It won't hurt much.'

A hand grabbed her shoulder and rolled her over onto her front. She felt him pulling at her cardigan and her top to expose her back. She tried to crawl away but he hit her again. Her head spun and she lay, panting, still. Somewhere behind her, a sharp metallic buzz started in the darkness. She'd heard that sound before. She remembered it, thought of the little image of a strawberry on her ankle.

It was daylight outside when Lou opened her eyes, but the small room she was in remained gloomy. She tried to sit up but felt a stab of pain when she pushed up on her right hand. She looked down and, in the half-light, she saw that it was covered with blood. Both hands. A burning sensation on her left side made her gasp and, as her eyes got used to the light, she saw more blood. Everywhere. Her head spun and for a moment she couldn't draw breath.

Then she screamed for help, terrified and confused. What had happened to her? What was this place? She felt dizzy and sick. She called for help again.

The door swung open. Three little boys in cricket whites jostled for position at the threshold. Then, taking in what he was seeing, the first boy, probably no more than twelve years old, let out a scream as long and as loud as any that Lou had managed. Memories jostled for space in her addled brain. The man. The dark pavilion. Blows to her head. The electric whine in the shadows.

The familiar burning pain of a fresh tattoo on her back.

She'd heard the stories. She'd read about what had happened

to Tash Brady and Sally Ann Granger. About the man taking girls. Tattooing them with poison. She knew what it meant.

Now it had happened to her. She knew she was going to die.

44

Rory

The head of the sports department at Brighton College was scowling and it was easy to see why. His pristine cricket pitch was being chewed up by a fleet of emergency vehicles. An ambulance, three police cars – and now the forensics team were spilling out of a van, as Rose parked carelessly across one of the creases. Rory had parked his own car on the street for an easier getaway, and he and Angie had walked in past a gaggle of boys being escorted off the pitch. They were overexcited by the sudden police presence, craning their necks to see what was going on and showing off in loud voices. All of them, apart from one boy, walking by the teacher's side, who looked like he'd been crying.

Rory flashed his warrant card at the master.

'I'm DS Rory Mackay and this is Detective Burton. Are you the person who called this in?'

'I am,' said the man. 'I'm Dale Gillingham, Head of Sports.' He didn't sound local to Rory. Sounded like he'd spent his whole life in the bastions of the public school system, never having to step outside into the real world. Well, this would be a rude awakening then.

'Could you tell us what happened?'

'Of course, though one of your PCs has already taken it down.'

Rory tilted his head. 'We'd prefer to hear it for ourselves, if that's okay.' He wasn't really giving the man any choice.

'Right, sure. Three of my boys heard a woman's voice, screaming, coming from the pavilion. The door was open and they looked in.' He shook his head. 'I wish to God they hadn't. They called me over and I went in. There was a woman in there, covered in blood. Horrifying injuries.' For a moment, it seemed like Dale Gillingham was going to vomit. He battled for control, then carried on. 'God knows what she was doing in there, or what happened. Blood everywhere.'

'Was she still conscious when you went in?'

He nodded. 'She wouldn't stop screaming, "I'm going to die. I'm going to die." I dialled nine nine nine straight away but she wouldn't calm down. I asked her what her name was but she never told me.'

'What did you do to help her?' said Angie.

'What could I do? I'm not a doctor.' There was no blood on Gillingham's clothing – evidently his had been a hands-off approach. 'I rang the office and asked them to send the school nurse out with some towels.'

'That's all?' said Angie.

Gillingham gave her a sharp look. 'My responsibility is to the boys in my care, not to some random woman who got herself into a fight. She looked like a druggy. The boys who found her were shocked and upset. They were my priority.'

Rory could sense Angie's fury at the man's attitude, but he wasn't surprised by it. His type were incredibly tribal when it came to looking after their own.

'Any idea how she got in there? I take it you normally keep the place locked?'

'No idea,' he said. 'The door must have been left open. It only had a single Yale lock – there's nothing of any real value kept in there.'

'Thank you,' said Rory. 'We might need to talk again, and DC Burton will need to interview the boys who found her.'

'Will that really be necessary? It'll only upset them more, and they won't be able to tell you anything useful.'

'Yes, it'll be necessary. And in the meantime, if you remember anything else that could be relevant, please call me.' He handed Gillingham a card.

They walked over to the pavilion and watched as the stretcher team loaded a woman into the back of the ambulance. Rory caught one of the paramedics by the arm.

'Is she lucid? Did she tell you anything?'

The woman mopped her brow with a forearm. Her green uniform was stained with blood – patches on her knees where she must have knelt in it, and other smudges on her front and arms.

'She's in shock. She was hysterical when we arrived, so we immediately gave her a sedative. I didn't catch anything coherent from her.'

'What about a name? Any ID?'

'Nothing on her. From what she was wearing, it looks like she was out partying last night.'

'How bad are the injuries?' said Angie.

'She's got a knife wound on the left side of her torso, and injuries to her hands and feet . . .'

'Shit!' Rory interrupted her. 'That's not a random attack – that's the guy. What about tattoos?'

The paramedic gave him a puzzled look but then realisation dawned across her features.

'You mean like those girls in the paper?'

'We need to check if she's got a tattoo,' said Rory.

The woman started to shake her head.

'Yes,' said Rory. 'Right now. This could be the work of a serial killer.'

The paramedic's eyes widened, but she climbed up into the back of the ambulance. Rory stood in the doorway, craning his neck to see inside. She spoke hurriedly to her colleague. Having been sedated, the woman – or as Rory could now see, the girl – was barely conscious. Gently, the two medics turned her onto her side and pulled up her top.

Rory heard a sharp intake of breath.

'Yes, she's got a tattoo,' said the paramedic they'd been talking to.

'Oh God!' Angie clapped a hand over her mouth. 'She knew. That's why she was screaming that she was going to die.'

Rory thrust his phone at the paramedic. 'Take a picture.'

It only took a couple of seconds. Then the paramedic climbed out of the back of the ambulance and went towards the driver's door. 'I've got to go. We need to get her to theatre.'

Rory and Angie watched as the ambulance chewed up more of the pitch making a three-point turn, and drove off, blue lights flashing. Then Rory checked the picture the paramedic had taken.

Even though it was smeared with blood, there was no mistaking what they were looking at. Three lines of ornate script. Latin verse, just like the others.

'Fuck!' said Rory, letting out the frustration he'd held under check in the presence of the medics. 'Same MO. She'll be dead within twenty-four hours.'

'Maybe they'll be able to save her,' said Angie.

'Wishful bloody thinking. Let's hope Rose can get something from the scene this time – this bloke's too clever by half.'

The SOCOs had already cordoned off the pavilion with crime-scene tape, beyond which they were busy taking photos and sweeping the ground for clues. Rose emerged from the open door and came over to them.

'Treat it as a murder scene,' said Rory, his expression grim. 'She's got one of those Latin tattoos.'

'I guessed that was the case,' said Rose. 'I saw her hands and feet when they were loading her onto the stretcher. The wounds looked very similar to Tash's and Sally Ann's.'

'Did you get any pictures of her or the wounds?'

'No. They needed to stem the bleeding quickly and I didn't want to get in their way. We'll get them later. I'll send one of the boys down to the hospital to photograph her.'

'Find anything of interest in there?' said Rory.

'Blood,' she said. 'Everywhere, and I'm pretty certain it's all the victim's blood.'

'Any sign of weapons? Finger marks?'

'Nothing so far,' said Rose, 'but the boys'll go over it with a fine-tooth comb. If there's anything there, we'll find it.'

'Thanks,' said Angie. She sounded subdued.

Rose turned to go back in, but paused.

'There was one thing,' she added, with a wry smile. 'A team photo featuring Francis Sullivan – believe it or not, he was captain of the first eleven here in 2004.'

'Nob,' muttered Rory, under his breath.

Rose disappeared into the pavilion.

'Right, let's go and talk to the kids who found her,' said Rory.

They set off across the now less-than-pristine pitch towards the school buildings.

'If it's the same as the other tattoos, it proves one thing,' said Angie.

'What's that?'

'That neither Alex Mullins or Ben King are the killer. We'll have to let them go.'

Rory stopped in his tracks, scowling. Angie had been off the previous day. She didn't know what Sullivan had done.

261

'No,' he said. 'The boss released them both yesterday afternoon. It could actually be either of them.'

And if this latest victim did die, Rory would have no scruples about laying the blame squarely at Francis Sullivan's feet.

45

Monday, 28 August 2017

Francis

'We need a word.' Rory rose from his chair to intercept Francis as he walked into the incident room late on Monday morning. It might have been a bank holiday Monday, but the whole team were in and at their desks – and Bradshaw had called for a briefing at midday.

'Now?' Francis had wanted some time to put his thoughts in order before discussing a new course of action with the team. Rather, he desperately needed to come up with some new course of action.

He'd spent all of the previous night and half the morning waiting outside Lou Riley's hospital room for the chance to speak to her, if only for a couple of minutes. He hadn't got that chance. Her condition was deteriorating fast and the registrar in charge of her case, Tanika Perry, had decided it was in her best interests not to be forced to relive her ordeal under police questioning.

'Don't you get it? Some small detail could save another girl's life.'

'I get it, but the chances of you getting anything useful are so remote . . .'

'I'll be the judge of how useful anything might be.'

'She's in shock, she's dying. Now, I need to get back to my patient.'

Parry was adamant, and Francis had finally given up and returned to John Street.

'Yes, now,' said Rory, following him uninvited into the tiny office off the incident room.

'Give me a moment. I need to change my shirt.'

In the small room, Francis was acutely aware of the smell of his own body odour and how long it had been since he'd last showered. He should have gone home, but even the thought of it had seemed wrong given that Lou Riley's life was ebbing away in front of their very eyes.

Rory leaned on the doorframe, hands deep in his pockets, as Francis untucked and unbuttoned his sweat-soaked shirt. He went to the filing cabinet and took a fresh one out of the bottom drawer. He gazed at Rory as he unfolded and unbuttoned it, trying to assess his deputy's mood. The look he got in return was hostile to say the least.

He turned his back on the sergeant and peeled off his dirty shirt. The smell of his sweat became more immediate.

'Jesus, that explains everything.' Rory's voice was tight with supressed anger.

Francis dropped the dirty shirt on the floor and whirled round. 'What?'

Rory was pointing, shaking his forefinger in the direction of Francis's shoulder, his cheeks flushed red.

'That. On your back.'

Shit! He meant the tattoo.

Why had he ever let Marni persuade him to let her do it? She'd spent several hours working on the black outline of a sinewy, twisting, suckered beast – a writhing octopus, anatomically correct and infinitely detailed down to the last sucker and siphon. Rendered side on, it had one dark eye that seemed to

264

stare out malevolently, and one of its tentacles stretched over the top of his shoulder to touch his clavicle at the front. But the way things had worked out, he'd never gone back for the colour.

Naturally, it wasn't something he'd shared with the rest of his team.

'You and Marni Mullins. There was something going on, wasn't there? No wonder you released Alex Mullins without pressing charges.'

Francis pulled on the fresh shirt. He was kicking himself for letting this happen – and he wasn't going to engage with Rory's insinuations.

'It's got nothing to do with it.'

'Sure thing. You let Alex Mullins go.' His eyes narrowed. 'And now it all makes perfect sense.'

Francis did up his shirt buttons slowly. It looked bad. And now Rory had seen the tattoo, he could deny a relationship with Marni till he was blue in the face, but Rory would never believe him.

'If that girl dies, it will be your fault.'

'Jesus, sarge!' Angie Burton was standing in the doorway.

'Leave it, Angie,' said Francis quickly.

'No,' she said, shaking her head. 'No way. He shouldn't have said that.' His unlikely defender.

'What?' said Tony, appearing over his shoulder.

'It's nothing,' said Francis.

'It's not bloody nothing,' said Rory, 'and you know it.'

Francis didn't answer.

Rory took his silence as arrogance and exploded. 'We had two bloody suspects in custody. You released them and within hours there was another attack. We're supposed to protect the population of Brighton, not unleash killers on them. We're not doing our job.'

'It's true,' said Tony, pushing past Angie into the office.

The tiny space seemed crowded. Francis felt at a disadvantage, so he stood up.

'Sure, you're right – we're not doing our job. But it has nothing to do with that bloody tattoo on my shoulder. You want to know what the problem is?'

Rory glared at him. 'Go on then,' he challenged.

'It's you, Rory. You're the problem. From the very outset, you decided Alex Mullins was guilty and you've gone out of your way to try and put him in the frame. We don't have anything on him. We ran out of time.'

'We could have charged Mullins with assault.'

'Barely.'

But what if they had? If he'd still been in custody, and Lou Riley had been attacked, it would have cleared him.

'Come on, boss. We've ballsed this one up, haven't we?' Tony could be relied on to echo any sentiment of Rory's.

'By which you mean, I've ballsed it up, I suppose?'

Tony shrugged.

Behind him, Francis saw Bradshaw looming in the doorway.

'Get out here now,' he said with a scowl.

The team shuffled out for the meeting, but Bradshaw stayed in the doorway.

'Lost control of your team, Sullivan? I'd never let my men talk to me like that.'

I bet you wouldn't, thought Francis to himself as the chief turned his back. But the sharp truth in Bradshaw's words cut like a knife. He'd certainly lost control of the case – and he didn't know how he was going to convince Bradshaw otherwise.

In fact, he'd just handed the chief the perfect opportunity to indulge in his favourite pastime – undermining him in front of his own team. Bradshaw positioned himself near the back of the room. Just another team member. Simply checking in to keep abreast of what was happening in his own department. *Was he fuck!*

Francis stood next to Rory and looked around at the assembled group. He cleared his throat.

'Right, let's run through where everyone is on current cases.'

So far, so good. Bradshaw was nodding approvingly.

'Last week, I was over in Lewes for the Kirby trial. That's now ended with a verdict of manslaughter due to diminished responsibility. As you know, that wasn't the verdict we were hoping for.'

'I heard she was running her trial like a three-ring circus,' said Bradshaw. All heads turned towards him. 'According to the *Argus* – which is not where I should be getting my information on things like this – Kirby managed to discredit the evidence of the main prosecution witness. Can you explain, DI Sullivan?'

The bastard!

Francis's cheeks flamed and he stumbled over a couple of words before speaking.

'It was nothing, and the jury was told to ignore it.'

'What exactly?' said Bradshaw.

'Sir, with all due respect, I'd like to move the meeting forward so the team can get on. Sam Kirby's behaviour in court had no effect on the trial outcome.'

'Not what the *Argus* implied.' Bradshaw was like a dog with a bone.

Kyle Hollins supressed a snigger, badly. It was clear that the whole team knew what Bradshaw was referring to.

Francis breathed in deeply and took control.

'More importantly, I'll be meeting with the CPS to discuss whether it's worth appealing the verdict – and whether an appeal could be used to keep her in the prison system rather than releasing her to a secure hospital.'

'Either way, you didn't get the verdict we needed. I'm severely disappointed in that result, Sullivan.'

Would Bradshaw never not be disappointed in his performance?

The team were getting restive – people were fidgeting and surreptitiously checking their phones. He needed to move things on.

'What's next?' said Bradshaw.

'Brady/Granger. As you know, sir, the killer struck again in the small hours of yesterday. A girl called Lou Riley. She's in the County, under sedation.'

'Got any useful information out of her?'

'Not yet, sir. She realised she'd been tattooed and, because of the leaks to Tom Fitz, she knew that the tattoo was poisoned and that she was likely to die. She was hysterical when the paramedics arrived. She's been sedated ever since.'

'What leak? What are you talking about?'

'We've reason to believe someone who has access to the case information has been passing on details to Tom Fitz of the *Argus*. I don't know who it is yet, but I intend to find out.'

Francis scanned the room. Rory followed his gaze. Kyle Hollins was staring out of the window.

'You've got enough to make the assumption it's an attack by the same individual?'

'Yes, sir,' said Francis. 'The tattoo is definitely by the same hand. There's some Latin verse, tattooed in conventional black ink, and we think there's also some UV tattooing underneath it.'

'You think?' said Bradshaw.

'We don't have access to Lou Riley to make sure. We can't tell until we get a better image of her back. She's also got identical wounds on her hands and feet, made by a drill using the same size of drill bit as the one we found in the aquarium.'

'What about that one? Get anything useful off it?'

'It had traces of Sally Ann's blood on it. That was all.'

'No finger marks?'

'No, sir. The drill bit looked brand new, according to Rose Lewis. No marks from previous use, no finger marks, nothing apart from Sally Ann's dried blood.'

'And what about the verse on Riley's back?'

'The verse comes from the same Buxtehude cantata.'

He pointed at the whiteboard, where Rory had carefully transcribed the new verse from the photo on his mobile.

Grates ago plagis tantis,
clavis duris guttis sanctis
dans lacrymas cum osculis.

'What does it mean?' said Bradshaw. He looked uncomfortable, as he always did when he needed to defer to a member of his team.

'"I give thanks for the terrible wounds, the hard nails, the holy drops, shedding tears with kisses." It's from the third movement,' said Francis.

'How many movements are there, sir?' asked Angie.

Francis thought for a moment. 'Seven in total.'

'So we can expect four more attacks?' she said.

Bradshaw was evidently feeling left out of the conversation. 'Not if you get those bloody suspects back in custody. If you hadn't released them both, this third attack wouldn't have happened.'

'Actually, sir,' said Rory, 'Ben King has an alibi for Saturday night through to Sunday morning. We had him under surveillance and he didn't leave his house.'

He hadn't mentioned that when he was busy throwing out blame for the attack.

'What about Mullins? Were you watching him?'

There was an awkward silence for a few seconds.

Bradshaw's face darkened. 'Good God, don't tell me he gave you the slip? He's just a kid. You're bloody useless, the lot of you.'

Another thing Rory had failed to mention. Francis gritted his teeth while Bradshaw wound things up, willing himself not to speak out of turn.

As the team dispersed back to their desks, Bradshaw came up to where Francis and Rory were standing.

'A word in my office,' he said. It wasn't a request.

They followed him up the stairs. Francis hung back a bit and Rory turned to look at him.

Francis spoke in a low voice so the chief wouldn't hear. 'For fuck's sake, Rory. If your team had kept Mullins in sight, we might know now whether he was the killer.'

'You were the one that put him out on the streets again – the buck stops with you.'

Francis carried on up the stairs, staring straight ahead. He was too angry even to glance in Rory's direction, and they reached the chief's office without exchanging another word. Bradshaw looked from one to the other of them as they stood stiffly in front of his desk.

'I've had a complaint about you and your team, Sullivan. And after what I've just seen downstairs, it frankly comes as no surprise.'

'Really?' said Francis. He was unable to retain the veneer of good manners any longer, while inside he was seething.

'Yes, really,' said Bradshaw. 'Tom Fitz, of the *Argus*, is accusing you of assault and threatening behaviour.'

'That's bullshit,' said Rory. 'I was there – there was no assault.'

'That bruise on your knuckle, Sullivan?' said Bradshaw, ignoring Rory's intercession.

'I punched a wall,' said Francis. He felt like doing just that, right now. 'And as for threatening behaviour, yes, I threatened him – with prosecution if he continued to obstruct my operation.'

Bradshaw bristled with anger. 'You're a fool to have made an enemy of the press, Sullivan. Tom Fitz has always been a good friend to this department. I've worked closely with him for years.'

Not that many years, presumably, because Fitz was considerably younger than Bradshaw. But had they been close? Is that where Fitz was getting his information? Perhaps it was time to manage their updates to the chief a little more strategically.

'Now he's planning to write a piece on how the police are incapable of doing what they're paid for.'

'He's making our job tougher, sir, by printing off-the-record information,' said Francis. 'He's put the killer's MO in the public domain – can you imagine what Lou Riley's going through because of that?'

But Bradshaw was bored. He rarely showed any empathy for the victims of the crimes his team was investigating.

'I expected better of you, Sullivan. And of you, Mackay. You were bickering like bloody kids in front of your team. I need you two working together to pull this case back from the brink. If you think it's likely that the killer's planning four more attacks, it's your job to stop it. Now get out and do something before he strikes again.'

As much as Francis hated him, Bradshaw was right. The personal enmity between him and Rory was poisoning the case when they desperately needed to work together. They had to prevent another death – or another four – and on his own Francis had no idea how he could achieve that.

As they went down the stairs, Francis's mobile rang.

'Hello?'

He stopped in his tracks.

'Shit. Shit, shit, shit.'

He shoved the phone back in his pocket.

'Lou Riley is dead.'

And it's all my fault.

V

19 July 1993

Sweet sixteen. My dear, sweet Aimée. Every girl's dream is your nightmare, isn't it? The worst birthday ever and, by God, you've had some poisonous birthdays before this one.

Things have been getting worse for a while, haven't they? Your mother is dying, for real this time. There have been remissions in the past but now her doctors have run out of options. She's at home, but you don't see her. She won't have you in the room. You've barely seen her at all over the past year. Valentine tells you how she's feeling, and how she's thinking of you. But you know full well when Valentine is lying. He tells so many lies. It's a little harder to know when he's telling the truth. That doesn't happen very often.

Your sixteenth birthday is the day your mother chooses to die. The cancer has finally run its venomous course.

How does that make you feel?

How does that make Valentine feel? This question is easier to answer. He comes to you in the middle of the morning, his eyes red-rimmed, and tells you she's been dead an hour. He says she died peacefully and the doctor is coming. You think it's a bit late for that. It's not pleasant to see your father cry. And worse when they're crocodile tears.

You feel hollowed out.

From a distant room, you hear Jay's roar of anguish. Doors slam. You hear his feet running across the gravel. When you look out of the window, you see him, standing on top of the flint-stone wall at the end of the drive, his arms outstretched. It looks as if he's howling into the wind, though you can't hear him. He drops out of sight on the other side of the wall.

You feel that you've already spent your grief for your mother. You grieved so long ago when she didn't read to you. You grieved when she went into hospital the first time. When she wasn't at your school play. When she stopped smiling. When she became a stranger. There's very little left, and that grief you keep for yourself. It's behind the wall you've been building to protect yourself.

Sixteen today, in a silent house.

The doctor comes and goes. You don't see him. But later you watch from an upstairs window as your mother's body is carried out. Valentine asked if you wanted to see her before she left. Why? To steal another small piece of the memories you have of when she was really your mother? He didn't ask you if you wanted to see her while she was still alive. Now she's a cadaver and you feel numb.

No birthday party this year. But you haven't had one for years. No dinner with Valentine in a swanky restaurant. That wouldn't be appropriate on the day his wife and your mother died. In the dining room, he's set a place for you in your mother's seat, opposite him at the far end of the long table. A setting too grand for the cauliflower cheese he's dug out of the freezer. He pours you a glass of wine. Jay won't come out of his room.

'Why aren't you drinking your wine, Aimée?'

He tries to top up your glass.

Your mother's death has precipitated a hard, sharp pain in your side which you counter with hard, sharp cuts to your forearm using your father's razor blade. You are determined not to succumb to his will.

'You look so like her when she was sixteen,' he says.

You don't eat but he doesn't even notice any more.

He gives you your mother's ring.

Valentine has been drinking. He wears it lightly, but you know. It makes him a little more talkative. A little more demanding. Things happen when he's drunk, things you don't like.

Later, your father comes to your room and rapes you. Then he lies in your bed, crying for his dead wife.

Poor, sweet Aimée. Where is Jay when you need him most? Did he hear the muffled shriek of pain when Valentine forced himself on you? Silenced by your father's hand over your mouth.

You cry for yourself and make plans.

This wasn't the first time Valentine has raped you. But it will be the last.

46

Tuesday, 29 August 2017

Francis

Francis was late to his own mother's funeral. Stinking hot and unable to sleep through the night, on this morning of all mornings he overslept. He slapped off the alarm, tired and angry, for an extra ten minutes. Ten minutes became half an hour, until he was finally roused by the dull ache in his knuckles from punching Tom Fitz.

Remembering what day it was, he cursed and rolled out of bed. His black suit hung in the wardrobe, back from the cleaners, but a white shirt needed ironing. Glancing out of his bedroom window, he could see people arriving at St Catherine's for the service. He recognised some of them, but he didn't have time to stop and stare. He was supposed to be there, greeting them at the door. At least he didn't have far to go. He knotted his tie as he ran down the stairs, making it to the church with just a minute to spare.

Father William caught his arm in the porch.

'Francis, slow down and take a moment with me.'

Francis looked at his watch.

'Your mother won't mind waiting.'

The vicar was right. But Robin would.

'How have you been, Francis? I've not seen much of you in church.'

'Sorry, Father William. Work has me by the . . .' His usual excuse, but now wasn't the time to tell Father William that he'd lost his way and felt abandoned.

'You look like you've been burning the candle at both ends. You need to take some time for yourself. Come and talk to me soon, Francis. You're looking troubled.'

Francis gave the older man a quick embrace. 'I need to go to Robin.'

'Do that,' said Father William. 'I'll give you a few minutes before I start the service. And I'll see you after.'

Francis hurried up the aisle to the front row, where seats had been reserved for the family. His was between Robin and James Baines, but Jered Stapleton currently occupied it. Robin looked up from their conversation to glare at Francis as he arrived.

'I thought you were going to miss it,' she hissed. 'And you have the shortest distance to come.'

As he bent to kiss her cheek, Stapleton stood up to vacate his place on the pew.

'It will be a beautiful service,' said the verger.

'Thank you,' said Robin.

Francis couldn't help but notice their hands brushing as Stapleton moved away. They seemed close, something Francis should have been happy about. Robin needed some stability in her life – and much as he wanted to, he couldn't be there for her all the time.

He leaned forward and bowed his head in prayer. It was easier today than it had been recently, but he knew what he was praying for. His mother lay in front of them in a simple wicker coffin, crowned by a profusion of white hydrangeas, her favourite flower. Robin had organised everything because, although he'd promised to help, he'd missed countless calls and most of the meetings about the arrangements. Looking back down, he prayed for his mother, then for his sister. He left it at that. What

277

prayer could he say for himself? The problems he faced were his to solve, not God's.

When the time came, Francis rose and went to the lectern to deliver his mother's eulogy. He took a sheaf of notes out of his breast pocket, but he didn't need to refer to them. He could speak about his mother from his heart – the lessons she'd instilled in him and Robin, the jokes she told them and, for him, the best feeling in the world, the moments when he knew he'd made her proud.

'She was, overall, a remarkable woman who shaped not only mine and Robin's lives, but the lives of all who were close to her. Her humour and grace carried her through a long and difficult illness, and we'll both miss her more than words can say.'

He looked at Robin. Her eyes were shining bright with tears, but she smiled at him and he smiled back. Then he looked up at the rest of the congregation as he folded his unused notes.

His heart stopped in his chest.

A man was standing at the back of the crowded church.

A man he hadn't seen for at least six years.

His father.

Robin immediately whipped her head round to see what had caused such a change in his countenance. Francis heard her gasp as she recognised him.

Francis stared. His father didn't look a day older. In fact, he looked slimmer and fitter, with a healthy tan. Standing next to him was an Asian woman, considerably younger than him. In her arms was a child. A boy who looked to be about four years old. He had black hair like his mother, but his face had been unmistakeably inherited from his father. From their father.

The rest of the service rushed by in a blur. Next to him, Robin sat stiffly, her knuckles white as she gripped the edge of the pew. He sang the hymns on autopilot and if anyone had asked him afterwards, he wouldn't have remembered a single word of Father William's blessing. He didn't dare turn around to look in case he wouldn't be able to face the front again. As they filed out behind the coffin, as he supported Robin down the aisle, he looked for Adrian Sullivan. Their father was nowhere to be seen.

Francis stood impatiently at the side of the grave as the coffin was interred, scared that his one living parent had left while he attended to the needs of his dead parent. Robin sensed his distraction and tightened her grip on his jacket sleeve, as if to stop him running off.

'. . . we therefore commit her body to the ground. Earth to earth, ashes to ashes, dust to dust, in sure and certain hope of the Resurrection to eternal life, through our Lord Jesus Christ.'

Francis bent and picked up a dry clump of earth from the neat pile by the side of the grave. It clattered as he threw it down onto his mother's coffin. 'Amen.' As he did it, the images of Tash Brady, Sally Ann Granger and Lou Riley came to the forefront of his mind. Soon to be buried by their families. Who would be next?

Robin followed suit, then James Baines and the rest of his family. In the distance, dark clouds massed on the horizon, making Francis wish the rain would come. It was muggy and there wasn't a breath of wind. The graveyard was silent apart from the sounds of dirt hitting wicker, and the soft murmurs of the mourners as they turned and made their way back to the path. His mind wandered to the case.

Robin started sobbing and Francis took her hand, waiting alone at their mother's graveside until she could get her tears under control.

'I won't speak to him,' she said with a sniff, as they walked round the corner of the church.

'Come on,' said Francis. 'He's made the effort to be here.'

'And brought his other woman.'

'His wife,' said Francis.

'And what about that child? Whose is it?' Robin's tone was accusatory.

It was quite clear to Francis whose child it was, so he said nothing.

Finally, he saw his father standing by the gate. Robin let go of his hand as he changed direction to go over to him. Instead, she turned to say something to James Baines's wife, Amanda.

Greeting his father felt awkward. Francis didn't quite know how to address him as they shook hands. It didn't seem like he was 'Dad' any more, but it would be equally strange to call him by his first name. They both let it pass as Adrian introduced the woman by his side.

'This is Nita, my wife,' he said.

The woman was older than he'd thought from a distance, and she had an engaging smile.

'Hello, Francis,' she said. 'Adrian's told me a lot about you.' Her English was good. 'I understand you're a policeman?'

'That's right. Do you work, Nita?'

'I'm a doctor,' she said, 'but only part-time since Kip came along.' She smiled at the small boy who was currently hugging her leg, overwhelmed by the strangeness of everything around him.

Francis squatted down.

'Hello, Kip,' he said.

The boy hid his face in his mother's skirt.

'Don't mind him,' said Adrian. 'You used to be just as shy.'

Francis stood up again.

'Are you over here long?' he said.

'We fly back tomorrow. Nita has been speaking at a medical conference.' Adrian Sullivan looked at his wife with pride. 'Keynote speaker, in fact.'

That look told Francis everything.

This was his family now, and he was proud of them and delighted with himself. What was he even doing here? Paying his respects to a dead wife, whom he'd deserted? Showing off his replacement kid? Certainly not here to see a sick daughter and a son who'd inherited none of his brilliance. A son who'd tried to forge his own path and was failing. He didn't have a clue what to do next to solve this case.

His father didn't come to the wake and, when the mourners had left, Francis looked for the answers at the bottom of a whisky bottle.

47

Marni

Marni had given up trying to sleep. Thierry had gone. Alex had taken refuge at Liv's and wouldn't come home. She'd cancelled her appointments for the rest of the week. She withdrew to her bedroom, seeing and speaking to no one, and even Pepper couldn't pull her out of her dark mood.

She gathered up all Thierry's belongings and crammed them into bags for him to collect. This time, the split was for good. She had no room in her life for him, and she would never be free of the shadow of Paul if she continued to live with his twin. But a small voice at the back of her mind contradicted her. She'd never managed to turn her back on Thierry in the past. They were locked in an endless cycle of coming together and falling apart.

She wanted an end to it.

Maybe she and Alex should leave Brighton, if she could persuade him to come with her. But he was shaken to the core – accused of murder, interrogated by the police, receiving a letter that told him his father wasn't actually his father. No wonder he'd escaped to Liv's. He needed time to straighten his head out, but in the meantime, she needed to deal with the threat from Paul.

She struggled off her bed and threw open the window. It was nearly dark outside, the air hot and heavy. She could taste rain but the ground was still dry and the leaves on the tree by her window rattled ominously in a breath of wind. A storm was coming and she was scared of what it would bring.

In the early evening, thunder rolled in the distance as she walked the length of St James's Street and across Old Steine. The town was busy – there were still plenty of tourists staying on after the bank holiday, and the restaurants and pubs hummed with the sound of voices. As she strode up North Street, she rehearsed what she was going to say. She didn't feel bad about the thought of lying. She'd do far worse if she needed to, to protect her family.

Marni had been to Francis Sullivan's house once before. It belonged to his father, in fact – and he had seemed like a teenager playing house while his parents were away. He'd cooked her dinner, not long after the Sam Kirby case had drawn to a close. The evening hadn't gone particularly well, as they both realised the differences between them carried more weight than the things they had in common. It had more or less spelled out the end of their burgeoning relationship.

Just as well, Marni thought to herself as she walked up to the row of grey Georgian terraced houses. He was a policeman and he came from a totally different background to her. They would never be able to make it work.

She knocked on his door and tugged the bell pull, noticing there were lights on inside. She wondered about having a quick cigarette while she waited, but thought better of it. He didn't appear, so she took a few steps back and craned her neck to look at the upstairs windows. His bedroom was lit up, the curtains open. She couldn't hear anything from inside, so she knocked and rang again. Perhaps he'd gone out and left the lights on, though that didn't seem very much like the Francis Sullivan she knew. She waited another couple of minutes, looking round at the other houses along the terrace and up towards St Catherine's churchyard. A fresh grave was almost obscured by bunches of wilting flowers.

Finally, after a third attempt, she heard the sound of footsteps on the flagstones of the hall. She peered through the frosted glass panels of the front door and saw a blurred figure approaching.

'Who's there?' It was Francis but his voice sounded slurred.

'Frank, it's me.'

'Who?'

'Marni.'

The door opened. Francis Sullivan leaned against the edge of it unsteadily and looked her up and down. His hair was a mess. He was in a black suit and a white shirt, top button undone. He held a lit cigarette in one hand and there was a white smudge of cigarette ash on his trouser leg. A plain black tie hung undone around his neck and she made the connection. The new grave. He'd just buried his mother.

'What do you want?' It was hardly friendly.

'I need to talk to you.'

'It's not a good time.'

He started to push the door shut, but Marni stuck the toe of her Doc Marten in the way.

'Please, Frank. I need your help.'

'If it's police business, go to the station.'

'You know I can't.'

Francis sighed. 'Come in, then.'

She followed him down the hall and into his large kitchen. The Aga made it even hotter inside than it was outside, and Francis pulled off his jacket and tossed it over the back of a chair. A near-empty bottle of whisky stood on the kitchen table, a cut glass tumbler next to it. Empty.

'Francis, I'm so sorry about your mother.'

He stared at her with red-rimmed eyes, but said nothing. It was none of her business.

'Drink?'

She nodded and he opened a cupboard to get a second glass. He split the remains of the bottle between them, then sat down and motioned for her to do the same. He pushed the fresh glass towards her, and gulped down the contents of his in one go.

'What can I do for you, Marni Mullins?'

'It's Paul.'

'Your brother-in-law?' Francis got up and rather unsteadily walked across the kitchen to a tall larder cupboard.

Marni nodded. 'He's out of prison. He's here in Brighton.' She stated it as a fact.

'The guy you stabbed?'

'Yes. I saw him talking to a woman outside the Blind Busker.'

Francis emerged from behind the cupboard door with a fresh bottle. 'This is of interest to me?'

'I'm scared. He told Thierry once that he wanted revenge for what I did to him.' It was a lie, but Marni was a good liar. And in his current state, Francis wasn't going to see through it. 'I think he's here to come after me.' It made more sense than saying he wanted to steal her son away.

'So you want our protection this time?' Francis was referring to the fact that when Sam Kirby had been coming after her, she'd fought against having a police protection detail.

'I want you to find him.'

'I can't arrest him on the basis of hearsay.'

'But you could warn him off. I'm worried he'll go after Alex to get to me.'

Francis took a mouthful of whisky. 'Good luck to him with that.'

'What the hell do you mean?'

'Maybe if you'd tell me where Alex was, I could protect him.'

'I don't know where he is.' She wasn't going to tell Frank Sullivan where Alex was in a million years. The bastard would only go and arrest him again. 'Some tattooing equipment was taken from my studio. I think Paul took it. You could arrest him for that.' One lie, or half a dozen. What was the difference?

'You reported it when it happened?'

Marni shook her head.

'For God's sake, Marni. Sure, if there were prints at the scene, we could arrest him. But if you don't tell us about a crime . . . You know another girl has died? Tattooed with poison ink.'

'What?'

'She was called Lou Riley. She was also at the art college. I need to find Alex . . .'

'So you can try and pin a third murder on him. You're a bastard, Frank Sullivan.'

'I don't want to "pin" murders on anyone, Marni. I just want to get to the truth.' Francis covered his face with both hands.

Marni couldn't feel any sympathy for him.

'If you'd stop trying to implicate my son and go after the real killer, things might be better for everyone.'

Francis slammed his fist down on the table. 'What the hell do you think I'm doing? Listen, Marni, I'd be delighted if I could rule Alex out, believe me. But so far he can't explain his whereabouts when any of those girls went missing.'

'So that's how you'll get your killer? By ruling everyone else out, one by one? How long will that take you?'

A silence stretched between them and Marni reached for her drink. The whisky was good quality, slipping smoothly down her throat without the customary burn.

'I'm sorry.'

'Sorry for what? For victimising my kid?'

'For everything. I fucked up, Marni.'

He took his hands from his face and looked at her squarely, making her remember how much she liked his blue eyes. Even bloodshot as they were at the moment. She put down her glass.

'What? What did you fuck up?'

'Us.'

Now?

'No way, Frank. We're not doing this. Nothing happened. Nothing can happen.'

He looked like he was going to be sick and she took pity on him.

'You need coffee, don't you?'

'Would be good.'

Neither of them spoke while Marni set his espresso machine to work. She remembered where the coffee was, and the mugs, and left Francis to his own thoughts while she worked.

'How was the funeral?' she said, setting a cup of black coffee in front of him.

When he looked up, she saw his boyish, vulnerable side. The part he worked so hard to keep hidden.

'My father was there.'

'I thought . . . he was dead. You never talk about him.'

Francis took a sip of the coffee. 'He left my mother, about ten years ago. I hadn't seen him for six years and I had no idea he would be there.'

'Was it good to see him?'

Marni brought a mug over to the table for herself and sat down again.

'He had his new wife with him.'

'At your mother's funeral. Oh God, I'm sorry, Francis.'

Francis shook his head. 'And his new son . . .' His voice faltered and he gulped in air as if he was about to sob.

Marni waited for him to go on as he fought to control his emotions.

'Kip. He's four years old. I have a brother. He's four years old and my father didn't even tell me about him.'

'Jesus, your father sounds like a piece of work.'

'I don't know why he came.'

'Are you going to see him again?'

Francis shrugged. 'They fly back to Bangkok tomorrow.'

Now Marni understood why Francis was upset and why he was drunk. They sat in silence for a few minutes, Francis slowly sipping his coffee.

'Sorry, Frank. I shouldn't have come here, should I?'

'It's okay,' he said, staring into his cup.

Marni finished her coffee.

'I should go.'

Francis put a hand out, placing it over one of hers on the table. 'Maybe you could stay.' His eyes pleaded with her.

Marni pulled her hand away and stood up.

'I don't think so, Frank.'

His face crumpled but all Marni felt was a hot flash of anger.

'You need to sort yourself out. You need to sort this case out. My son didn't kill Tash. And he didn't kill Sally Ann or this other girl. I think you know that – so now it's up to you to bloody find out who did.'

She went towards the kitchen door, but then turned back.

'Drinking is a grown-ups' game, Frank. You're not ready for it, so get your head out of that bottle.'

She slammed the front door as she left. The last thing she needed in her life was another man who wanted mothering.

48

Francis

Why whisky? Why in the name of God had he thought that was a good idea? Now his head was pounding and his vision didn't seem quite right.

After a shower that was as long and as cold as he could bear it, and a coffee that was as hot and as strong as he could make it, Francis began to believe he might be human again. He threw the half-smoked packet of cigarettes in the bin, took two ibuprofens and climbed into his car, not caring that his blood alcohol would still be over the limit. He knew exactly how long it would take to clear his bloodstream. But at least Marni's visit had stopped him from finishing off the second bottle.

He pushed the thought of her from his mind as he parked outside the morgue. No good would come of thinking about Marni Mullins.

'God, you look like death warmed up,' Rose said, as she unlocked the front door.

'You're the expert,' said Francis. He wanted to throw up, so he gritted his teeth and followed her inside.

'You want to know about Lou Riley's autopsy?' Rose had performed the PM the previous day while Francis had been at the funeral.

'Yes. But first I want images of the UV tattoos from all three girls. They've got to be the key.'

Rose led the way to her office.

'We've examined them closely, Francis. There's nothing – just a series of random jabs and scratches. There's something very aggressive about them.'

'Did those tattoos also contain taxine or was it just the black ones?'

'Just the black ones,' said Rose, dropping down into her black leather desk chair.

Francis was too fidgety to sit. He went to the window and came back again without looking out.

'Right, so the UV tattoos weren't a vehicle for the poisoning. That means they had some other purpose.'

Rose produced photos of the three tattoos, taken with a UV light shone on them to make them visible. Francis snatched up the images and studied each one in turn.

'Tracing paper.'

'What?'

'Now, Rose. Come on – another woman's life could depend upon this.'

Rose's eyebrows shot up, but she spun her chair and opened a small wooden stationery cupboard behind her desk. 'I think I've got some.'

Francis paced to the window again, this time looking out over the graveyard that lay beyond the back of the building the morgue was housed in.

'Here.' Rose held out a few sheets and finally Francis sat down.

'Pencil?'

She handed one to him.

Over the next five minutes, Francis sat in silence as he traced the smattering of curved and straight lines that made up Tash

Brady's UV tattoo, along with a couple of larger shaded areas. When he'd finished, he held up the tracing paper, first one way and then rotating it through ninety degrees.

'See anything in it?' said Rose.

Francis shook his head. 'I don't expect to at this point.'

He took the image of Sally Ann's UV tattoo and studied it. Then he handed it to Rose. 'Can you make a copy of this to the exact same scale as Tash's? And Lou's as well, please.'

Each tattoo had been photographed with a ruler along one side to give the measurements of the area pictured. Rose went out of her office to use the photocopier in the hallway and returned a couple of minutes later. Francis took the two new copies and quickly traced them both on to separate pieces of tracing paper.

'Now we'll see,' he said, switching on the lightbox that sat on one end of Rose's desk.

He put the tracing of Tash Brady's tattoo down first, then layered the other two tracings on top of it. Rose leaned over from her side of the desk and they both considered the composite picture the three images created.

It looked like nothing more than a series of random lines, curves and circles.

'Damn!' said Francis.

He lifted the top two tracings and then turned them this way and that to see if he could make anything in the images line up and make sense.

'Wait,' said Rose.

Francis paused.

'Look, put this one here,' she said, taking the tracing of Lou's tattoo from his hand, 'and this one like this . . .'

They both gazed down at the light box. Francis could make out some order in the combined image now. He moved Lou's tattoo slightly and as if by magic, some of the lines joined and some circles were almost completed.

'Oh my God,' said Rose. 'You've done it.'

'But what is it?' The realisation hit him before he'd even finished speaking. 'It's a map, isn't it? Do you see that?'

'Yes.' Rose was nodding her head. 'It's definitely a map.'

'It looks like a map of a river or waterway somewhere. But where the hell is it meant to be? And what's the meaning of it? Why would the attacker be drawing a map on his victims?'

'There are still gaps in it, so it's going to be hard to work out where it is.'

'Still gaps – that means he's planning to attack again.' Francis stared down at the broken image. 'As many times as it takes to complete this map.'

He looked up and Rose's eyes met his.

'We can't let that happen,' he said. 'We've got to work out where it is now – and use it to identify the killer.'

'How's the map going to do that?'

Francis's frustration bubbled up into anger and he stood up abruptly.

'I've got no bloody idea.' His head was throbbing and Rose's small office seemed suddenly airless. 'I need a minute,' he said.

Rose looked at him but didn't speak.

Francis went to the men's toilet at the rear of the building. He splashed cold water onto his face and had a long drink from the tap, uncaring of how much he spilled down his front.

No more whisky. Never again.

When he got back to Rose's office, she was still studying the tracings.

'Look at this, Francis,' she said, pointing with her finger to one corner of the joint image. 'It looks like a small bird or something.'

Francis looked. She was right. There was a shape in the top corner, not complete, but what there was of it suggested the silhouette of a small, dark crow, wings folded, with one leg raised out in front as if it were striding along.

'I know that bird,' said Francis. 'I've seen it somewhere.'

If only he didn't have this ruddy headache.

He racked his brains. Where had he seen that crow before?

Rose switched off the lightbox. It was making the small room hot. She pushed her hair back from her brow and watched Francis, waiting.

'Where, where, where?'

'Take it back to the office and get Kyle to do an image search for you,' said Rose.

'We don't have the whole image.' He turned his back on her and concentrated.

A small black crow.

He could see it in his mind's eye, painted on stone.

It was in a church somewhere. A church that stood by water.

He looked at the partial map.

'It's Bosham,' he said. 'The crow – it's on a plaque commemorating King Cnut's daughter, who drowned there. This is a map of Bosham Water.'

Rose snapped the light box back on and they looked again.

'You're right.'

She quickly found the spot on Google Maps and they compared the images.

'Look,' said Francis. 'There, in the water along Itchenor Reach.' He pointed at a dark mark on the composite of the tracings. 'What's that?'

'There's nothing on the Google map that corresponds,' said Rose. 'It looks like it could be part of an X. Do you think he's showing us something?'

Francis picked up his jacket from the back of the chair where he'd carelessly thrown it.

'Come on, let's go. I think this killer's starting to give up his secrets.'

The fog was finally lifting.

49

Rory

Not all the mud fringing the estuary was dry and cracked. Rory Mackay's foot suddenly sank beneath him, and he almost overbalanced. He felt moisture seeping into his shoe and soaking through his sock. He looked down with disdain – grey, stinking mud up to his ankle.

'Fuck's sake,' he breathed, flexing his foot to release his trapped shoe with a loud squelch. It was his own fault – the SOCOs had laid some planks across the mud for walking on but he'd tried to cut a corner.

Rose Lewis waved at him from where she was crouching at the water's edge fifty yards or so further up the half-dried river course. Francis was with her, bending to look at something she was uncovering.

'Sergeant,' she called, 'over here.'

Rory was sweating inside his scene-of-crime suit. This wasn't his idea of fun, and it was probably a wild goose chase, but the boss had demanded his presence. Thought it was a big break. Time would tell. Apparently, X really did mark the spot and they'd quickly come across what looked like a bone emerging from the mud of the dried riverbed.

Rory had driven just under forty miles along the coast from Brighton to get to Chichester Harbour, though it still fell within their jurisdiction. It was the combined estuary of a number of small rivers that joined the sea at West Wittering, but in the prolonged drought, several of them had run dry. Now there was more mud than water and the rivers were sharing their secrets.

'What is it?' said Rory, as he got closer to Rose. 'Just a dead dog, I assume?' He was yet to be convinced that the tangle of UV scrawls across three girls' backs had really been pointing to this precise location.

Rose shook her head. 'No, we've got what looks like a full set of human bones here.'

'Brought to the surface as the river dried?'

'Correct.' She was carefully cleaning the mud away from a dome-shaped fragment – which even Rory's untrained eye could see was part of a human skull. She had a camera hanging round her neck, and she stopped frequently to take photographs.

'So they've probably been in there for decades?' said Rory hopefully. If they could go straight to a history museum rather than crossing his desk, he'd be more than happy.

Francis shrugged. 'Too early to say.' His SOCO suit was heavily splattered with mud, but the cadaver-like pallor of the past few days had gone. He straightened up and pulled a folded photocopy out from within his white suit.

'Look.' He held it out to Rory. 'We've now got a link to Bosham Church, and the map led us here.' He pointed to a dark spot on the map and Rory could see that it approximated to where they were now standing. 'These bones are going to lead us to the killer.' There was new determination in his voice. Something had changed.

Rose carried on with her work in silence, finally lifting the muddy piece and placing it gently into a large plastic box. She scribbled something on the box's label and handed it to one of the SOCOs loitering nearby. Rose was stuck into the painstaking task of carefully extricating each individual bone from the mud so it could be taken back to the forensics lab for analysis. The human body had two hundred and six bones in total, and all Rory could think was, *rather her than me.*

'First assessment, Rose?' said Rory, handing the map back to Francis. 'The bones telling you anything yet?'

Rose stood up and flexed her back. Despite having a plank to kneel on, her white suit was besmirched with river mud, and she swatted at a couple of flies that buzzed round her head. Her red hair was damp with sweat, tendrils sticking to the nape of her neck and her forehead.

'Definitely human, can't tell you the sex yet,' she said, unscrewing the cap from a small bottle of water that one of the SOCOs handed her. She took a long draught. 'Too early to determine age, apart from saying that it's not a teenager, and nor is it a very elderly person.'

'Cause of death?' Rory asked tentatively.

'You're kidding?' The look Rose gave him told him he shouldn't have bothered asking.

Without warning, Francis plunged through the mud towards the river bank. Rory and Rose watched him, puzzled.

'Get the hell away and stop taking pictures,' shouted Francis.

Rory looked to the bank in the direction the boss was running.

Tom Fitz was standing between two trees, his camera raised in front of his face.

Rory looked round and spotted a uniformed PC. 'Go and escort that man far enough away that he can't take any more pictures.'

'Yes, sir.'

Fitz was already backing away, but not before he'd taken a number of candid shots of Francis struggling through the mud.

The reporter held up a hand. 'I'm going, I'm going. But just one question. How did the girls' tattoos lead you to these bones?'

What the hell?

The boss's reaction reflected Rory's own disbelief – he clambered up the bank and gave chase, his face darkening with the exertion. Tom Fitz turned and ran through the trees, pursued by Francis and the uniformed PC. Francis's fists were clenched and Rory knew exactly what would happen if he caught up with Fitz.

Ten minutes later, he rejoined them at the excavation site. He was red-faced and dripping with sweat, but he didn't look like he'd been in a fight.

'He got away,' he said, panting heavily. 'But how the hell did he know we were here?'

Neither Rose nor Rory answered him, but Francis was looking at Rory.

'Mackay, who did you talk to after I called you here?'

Rory wasn't sure he wanted to answer, but he did.

One word.

'Bradshaw.'

50

Thursday, 31 August 2017

Alex

Nothing seemed right. Nights spent on different sofas, waiting for the crash of the door being broken down. Days spent in a twilight existence of rooms with drawn curtains. His mother kept texting and texting, even his father had left a voicemail. Another girl was dead. Supposedly someone who'd been at college with him, but he didn't remember her.

And now this. A text message from his father's brother, suggesting they meet.

He wasn't even sure he wanted to meet this Paul. His uncle. Or maybe his father. Was this really the way to go about things? He wished he could ask his actual father, Thierry, about it, but he didn't dare.

Liv said to give the guy a chance.

Alex didn't know the Hove pub scene as well as he knew the bars in Brighton, and he'd never been to the Blind Busker before. He walked over from Liv's flat, hyper-aware of people and traffic on the streets, constantly looking out for a police car coming around the next corner. For most of the way he'd had a creeping feeling that someone was following him, although whenever he looked around, there was no one there. Why had he even come here? He stepped into the pub with some trepidation. How were you supposed to feel when you were going to meet the man who claimed to be your father for the first time?

The interior of the pub was dark – and seemed even darker after the piercing sunlight outside. The walls were mainly painted black, as was the bar and the ceiling, and the space was lit by a series of large chandeliers that had been set at the low end of the dimmer switch. Alex blinked and looked around. He didn't see anyone who could be his father's brother. The whole thing was doing his head in – his uncle claiming to be his father and suggesting that the man he believed to be his father was actually his uncle.

He went up to the bar.

'Peroni, please,' he said to the barman.

'ID?'

Alex dug his student card out of his pocket with a sigh. He knew he looked older than his nineteen years, but it would be a while before he looked over twenty-five.

'You're Alex,' said a voice in his ear. A French accent.

He turned to see the man that had come up behind him. It was like looking at his father, but not. If anything, perhaps it was looking at his father a few years into the future. Age hadn't been so kind to Paul Mullins – his face was more hollowed out than his brother's, his eyes more lined. Thierry's hair was showing a sprinkling of salt and pepper, but this was more pronounced in Paul's shorter hair.

'You're Paul?'

'I'm your father.'

The man's statement made Alex instantly uncomfortable.

Paul must have guessed this, as he turned his attention to the barman, ordering a Peroni for himself. He thrust a hand into the pocket of his jeans and pulled out an assortment of coins. Then he looked at Alex apologetically.

'*Pardon*, it's all Euros.'

Alex paid for the beers with shaking hands.

Could this man really be his father?

Paul picked up his bottle of Peroni and led the way to a small corner table towards the back of the bar. He started talking before Alex had even had a chance to sit down.

'What your mother and my brother have done is wrong. You're my son. Thierry took your mother and he took you. I want you both back.'

Alex stared at the label on his beer bottle. He could see his father in the way Paul moved and hear him in the sound of his voice – though Paul's French accent was much more pronounced. It distracted him from what Paul was saying.

'I'm sorry. Confronting this untruth, this lie, it must be very hard for you. You are shocked by what I say?'

Alex nodded. 'How can you be sure you're my father?' The familial resemblance he shared with Thierry had always been clear visible evidence that Thierry was his father. But when he looked at Paul, the resemblance could just as easily be to him, as the brothers were identical twins.

'I know because of the dates. I'm not an idiot. I know when you were born and when I was with your mother. We were together at the time you were conceived.'

What if he was telling the truth? Alex's world rocked on its axis. The foundation on which he'd built his life was slipping away like sand through his fingers.

'Why would my mother lie to me about something so important?'

Both beers stood untouched on the table.

'To you? To everyone. She lied to everyone about the father of her child, because she wanted it to be Thierry. She made to change history.'

'But even if that's true, you can't expect to turn back the clock,' blurted Alex.

At last Paul picked up his beer and took a long drink from it.

He put it down and wiped his mouth with the back of his hand.

'We could have a fresh start, Alex. You and me. Come back to France with me.'

Alex didn't know what to say. He'd only known of Paul's existence for a short while, yet here was this stranger, a weirdly familiar stranger, suggesting that he leave his mother and move to France. He grabbed for his beer and knocked the bottle over. The pale liquid ran like piss down his leg. Paul laughed and held out his own bottle for Alex to take.

Alex didn't like the way he laughed, but he took the beer and downed what was left of it.

'You need some time to think,' said Paul. 'You need to ask your mother why she lied to you. And why my brother claimed you as his own, when you're not his child. But don't wait too long, Alex. I can't stay here for ever.'

'I don't know,' said Alex. 'I'm at college here.' It sounded like a feeble excuse. And maybe it would be a good time for a spell out of the country.

'Pah! We have schools in France. Better schools. You must come to Marseille with me. I'll show you where I grew up. You're half French – it's as much your country as this one is.'

Paul's face had lit up when he mentioned Marseille. Alex had always begged Thierry to take him there, but for reasons best known to his parents, they'd always refused to go back to France. Was Paul the reason?

'But my mother . . .'

'She could come too. Pah, I know she won't.' Paul's eye's narrowed. It was an expression Alex had never seen on his father's face. 'Come on, Alex, you're a grown man. Don't be tied to her at your age.'

Suddenly Alex was swept by a feeling of revulsion for the man. Something wasn't right about the way he was going about this. Something wasn't right about him as a person. Alex studied the small black cross tattooed between Paul's left thumb and fore-finger. His nails were grimy, his clothes unkempt and unwashed.

'I've got to go,' said Alex, standing up abruptly.

Anger flashed in Paul's eyes. '*Merde!*'

'I don't know you.'

'You were stolen from me. Believe me, Alex, you're mine. That's a truth you'll never escape from.'

His words echoed in Alex's ears as he walked away, and all the way back to Liv's flat.

51

Friday, 1 September 2017

Francis

September. Autumn couldn't come soon enough. Though the days were already getting shorter, the heatwave seemed to have intensified. Eight in the morning and Francis had needed the air conditioning on in his car. He parked in the morgue's small car park, next to Rose's dusty four-by-four. An unexpected blast of heat enveloped him as he opened the car door and he was sweating by the time he reached the entrance.

He went into the lobby. Deliciously cool – it almost made up for the smell. Almost, he thought, as he opened the double doors to go through to where he could see Rose already at work. The camouflage effect of wearing a white lab coat against the white tiled walls and floor made her flame-red hair stand out all the more, and her long ponytail bobbed slightly in time with the music blasting from her wall-mounted speakers.

She looked up and saw Francis approaching, so she reached for the control to turn the volume down.

'Jefferson Airplane,' said Francis by way of greeting. 'Bit before your time?'

She ignored the comment and pulled a white rubber sheet over the cadaver she was working on.

'Here,' she said, leading him across to one of the other mortuary tables.

She pulled back the covering sheet to reveal a collection of stained and broken bones, arranged in the approximate layout of a skeleton.

'The skeleton from Itchenor?' said Francis.

Itchenor Reach was the particular stretch of Bosham Water where the bones had been found.

Rose nodded.

Francis studied the bones. There were a few missing.

'Tell me what you know so far,' he said. *It had to lead to something.*

'He's been on the riverbed for maybe a decade or two, though I'll probably be able to narrow it down a bit further when the test results come back. No sign of clothing or ID in the mud around him – just a few fibres clinging to the bones here and there.'

'They're probably not going to help us, are they?' said Francis.

Rose shook her head.

'Cause of death?'

'Blunt trauma to the skull,' said Rose. She pointed and Francis could see a gaping hole in the cranium. Fragments of bone lay alongside it – the caved-in portion that would have fallen away as the soft tissues rotted.

'Murder?'

'Could have been accidental.' Rose sounded tentative at best.

'How?'

'If he was sailing on his own . . . maybe something hit him on the head, knocked him overboard.'

'A falling branch?' Francis shook his head. 'Then his boat would have been found and the river searched for his body.'

'I agree,' she said. 'Murder looks more likely – someone coshed him, then threw his body into the river.'

'Was he weighted down?'

Rose gave him the look that she generally reserved for pointless questions. 'If there were rocks in his pockets, there's no way of telling now.'

'And no sign of a weapon?'

'Nothing obvious.'

'Any indication of what the killer used?'

Rose picked up a fragment of the skull and turned it one way, then the other, in the bright light.

'It could have been done with any number of things and the forensic evidence, in terms of blood and hair, would be long gone.'

Francis looked down at the bones.

'This is getting us nowhere.'

'Don't be impatient,' said Rose.

'Of course I'm impatient. I don't want to watch another girl die.'

'I've only just started. I should get some information from his dental records. Both jaws were intact, so I've been able to send x-rays and images to the forensic odontologist. If he's ever been reported missing, they'll be able to get a match without too much difficulty.'

'What about his age?' Francis was rocking backwards and forwards on the balls of his feet. He wanted so much more than he was getting, but there was no point in taking out his frustration on Rose.

'Looking at the bones and teeth, he was a fully adult male, over thirty years old, but not showing signs of bone loss, so not elderly. Assessing the level of fusion of the intact sutures of the skull, I'd say we're looking at someone maybe in their forties.'

A man in his forties who went missing ten or twenty years ago. Probably murdered. No ID, no idea where to start looking.

'Lean on the odontologist, would you, Rose? Hard. Until we get an ID, we can't even begin to trace the threads back to our current investigation. I need to know who he is right now if I'm going to prevent another killing.'

52

Friday, 1 September 2017

Rory

Rory just wanted it to end. The heat. This case. The office politics. It all made getting out of bed in the mornings that much harder. He wasn't often late but, of course, the one morning he was, Francis was already in, looking freshly scrubbed in a pristine shirt, syphoning black coffee from a large takeaway cup. Rory watched him add some information to the whiteboard under the heading 'Itchenor bones', then quickly assign a string of tasks to the members of the team who were already in.

'The clock's ticking,' he said, addressing the room and, it seemed to Rory, him in particular. 'It's the Speed Trials tomorrow – the town'll be crowded, and it'll be our attacker's perfect opportunity to strike again. Let's stop him before he gets the chance.'

The boss's change of demeanour was reflected in the incident room, where activity suddenly seemed to ramp up a gear. Now, rather than a graveyard, it was a hive, with the team following up on every scrap of evidence offered by the Itchenor bones, by Lou Riley's scene of attack, and by the increasing level of detail they were digging up on the three dead girls. Even Rory found himself ploughing into the case files with a renewed sense of urgency.

Francis crooked a finger at Rory, beckoning him into the small corner office.

'Any sign of Alex Mullins yet?'

There had been an APW – all ports warning – on Mullins since the attack on Lou Riley, and finding him was a priority Rory had set the uniform branch.

'No, but the woodentops couldn't find . . .'

Francis cut through his comment. 'Keep 'em on it, though I'm not convinced he's our man.'

That Francis had thought this had been obvious for some time, but it was the first time he'd had the balls to say it out loud.

'That leaves us with no one.'

'Then we've got to work harder and pull all the stops out.' Francis looked at him and sighed. 'We've got to work together as a team, Rory. I don't know what I did to get on the wrong side of you along the way, but believe me we're not enemies – and we can only succeed jointly.'

That came out of nowhere and Rory wasn't quite sure how to respond. He cleared his throat.

'I'm right though, aren't I?' said Francis.

Rory nodded. He'd had to admit to himself that he'd been impressed with the way Francis had deciphered the UV tattoos to discover the map and then the skeleton. At last things seemed to be stirring in the case.

'But there's still a hell of a long way to go.'

Francis tilted his head in agreement. 'When's the appointment with that art-college woman?'

'Faye Roderick? In ten minutes.'

'Good.'

Faye Roderick was the principal at the Brighton College of Art. As well as getting a list of all the girls who attended the college, Francis wanted to see if she could suggest any link between the three dead girls apart from the fact that they all knew Alex Mullins and Ben King.

While Francis checked his email, Rory went back out to the incident room.

'Angie?'

'Yes?'

'Tracked down Lou Riley's parents yet?'

'I've got an address for them. Tony and I are going to go and see them in a minute.'

Tony and Angie – still glued together at the hip. That was another problem brewing, but now wasn't the time.

'Dig around a bit and find out who she was dating, and if she ever had anything going with Alex Mullins or Ben King.'

'Sure.'

'We need to go, boss,' said Rory, sticking his head back into Francis's office.

The art college was on Grand Parade, just around the corner from the station, so they walked. Having just put his jacket on, Rory peeled it off again almost as soon as they were outside. The heat was smothering. What had he been thinking?

Ten minutes later, they were ushered into a bright, cluttered office on the ground floor of the modern School of Arts building. Faye Roderick stood up to shake hands with them as they introduced themselves, then invited them to sit down opposite her desk. She was a tall woman with spiralling blonde hair and a narrow face – and she was dressed in a sharply tailored skirt and a sleeveless silk blouse. The jacket to match the skirt was draped over the back of her chair. To Rory, she looked more like a bank manager than custodian of the next generation of artists.

'I'm glad to see you,' she said, as she sat down. 'This has all come as a terrible shock to us and to the students. Do you have any idea why our girls are being targeted?'

'It's why we wanted to talk to you,' said Francis. 'There have been three victims so far, all present or past students here.'

'Three?' Faye Roderick straightened in her chair.

'I'm afraid so,' said Rory. 'A girl called Lou Riley was assaulted in the small hours of Saturday morning.'

The principal covered her mouth with a hand. 'Oh my God, no. I read in the paper she'd been attacked. I had no idea she'd died.'

'I'm sorry,' said Francis. 'Was she a current student?'

Faye Roderick shook her head, pursing her lips as she fought to get her emotions under control. 'She was excluded at the end of last term. She had some problems.'

'What was the nature of the problems?'

Roderick became instantly more businesslike. 'I'm not really at liberty to discuss that with you.'

'She's been murdered. We're investigating it. So unless you want to see more of your students ending up in the morgue, I suggest you get over your scruples, Miss Roderick.' Rory wasn't going to mince his words with a jobsworth.

Faye Roderick drew in a deep breath through her nose. It expressed her displeasure more than words could have. 'I seem to remember she had some attendance problems.'

It didn't sound like enough of a reason to chuck someone out. He felt she was holding back on something – and the look on Francis's face suggested that he felt the same.

'Go on.'

Roderick shrugged. 'That's it. We expect our students to put in a regular appearance. If they don't . . .' She trailed off.

Francis leaned forward, crowding her desk. 'Of the women who've been murdered so far – Lou, Tash Brady and Sally Ann Granger – can you think of anything they had in common that might explain why they came to the killer's attention?'

'Of course not,' she replied immediately. 'I know very little of my students' personal lives.'

'Two of these girls were no longer attending college,' said Francis. 'They had some sort of problem. Would you say Tash Brady had similar problems?'

'Nothing I've heard about. You might want to talk to her tutor about that.'

'I think we already have,' said Rory. 'Ben King was her tutor. Was he also Lou Riley's tutor?'

'I think so,' said Roderick, after a moment's thought. 'I can check. But you can't possibly think Ben had anything to do with these crimes.' It wasn't a question.

'He has an alibi for the time when Lou Riley was attacked,' said Francis. 'And we're fairly certain all three girls were attacked by the same man. Do you know if Lou Riley ever dated or went out with Alex Mullins?'

'No idea, I'm afraid.'

'Okay, thank you. We'll send a policewoman here to interview her friends, and the rest of your female students. If we can discover the link between the victims, we can hopefully prevent further attacks. In the meantime, Miss Roderick, could you ask all your female students to take care not to go out on their own?'

'Of course – we've already advised that, but I'll make sure we give them the message again.'

'That was a waste of time,' said Rory, as they walked back to John Street.

'Maybe Angie can get some more out of the students themselves. There has to be a link between the three girls, other than the fact that they all knew Alex Mullins and Ben King. Those connections probably cover nearly all the girls at the college – so why these three in particular?'

'And who next?'

A blast of music from Francis's phone put paid to further speculation. He took the call, then ended it abruptly.

'Got your car here, Rory? Rose has something for us.'

'And God forbid she should simply tell us over the phone.'

*

Rose was fidgeting in her office when they arrived, and from the shine of her eyes, she had something significant to tell them.

'Valentine Montgomery,' she said, before they'd even had a chance to sit down.

'Who's he?' said Rory.

'Sounds like a fifties film star,' said Francis.

'The man in Itchenor Reach,' said Rose. 'Got a dental match through.'

Rory let out a low whistle. 'Fast work.'

'Are you going to enlighten us?' said Francis.

'He went missing in July 1995. Presumed suicide, so the case was dropped pretty sharply. But as we now know, it wasn't suicide.'

'Why did they think it was?' said Rory.

Rose shrugged. 'That's all I've got for you. Here's the file – not much in it. Just his personal details. Reported missing by his business partner when he failed to show up for work for a week.'

Francis took it from her.

'I'll put Kyle onto it,' he said. 'I hope the trail hasn't gone cold.'

vi

19 July 1994

Poor Aimée. A year has passed since your mother's death and now every birthday has been spoiled. You're diminished, a vanishing girl who nobody sees. You don't go to school any more. You hide in your room. You want to disappear. Cease to exist. Poor, poor child.

Valentine tries to make you happy. He buys you presents – clothing and jewellery you refuse to wear. He suggests holidays and trips that you refuse to go on. There are arguments and recriminations. It almost seems as if your mother's death was in some way your fault – at least in his mind. Sometimes he's sad, sometimes he's angry. Both are your fault. When he's angry he hurts you. When he's sad, he lays his head on your breast and cries. It sickens you. His mucus and saliva on your clothes. On your skin.

But he goes away a lot, too. Business trips to God knows where – you don't care. You only wish he'd stay away longer and not come back, panting and hungry to be in your room at night.

You hate him.

But you hate yourself more. Poor Aimée.

Jay doesn't come home often any more – he's at art college now and spends as much time there as possible. You can't blame him for that. He hasn't become the son Valentine wanted him to be. Just like you haven't become the daughter he longs for. But with you, Valentine is

313

still trying. With Jay, he's given up. They argue whenever Jay's home. Valentine caught Jay drinking his whisky and laid into him. Jay came home with a tattoo and Valentine hit him. As much as you want to see your brother, you can't stand the fighting. You retreat to your room until the house is silent once more.

You miss Jay desperately when he's away. He misses you. You talk on the phone. You implore him to come home. Once you visited him and for three whole, blissful days you became a girl without a care in the world.

Jay knows what your father does to you. You told him again, more than once. He says he doesn't believe you, but that's just because he doesn't want to believe you. You've asked him for help. He's thinking about what to do, how to get you away. But it's hard. You'll need a place to live and Jay is still studying. He can't afford to support you.

You've begged him for help.

He feels sorry for you and says he'll help as soon as he can. But he's not the one Valentine comes to in the night. He's not the one so tired and damaged and hurt.

That's you. And you can't go on for much longer. You cut your arms and the pain soothes you. You wonder if you'd have the nerve to make a deeper cut.

Why won't Jay help you?

You start to hate him too.

Your birthday's in the summer and this year, at last, Jay has come home for it. Maybe this will be a better birthday. While Valentine is at work, he asks you what you want to do. You ask him to take you out on the river, in the Maria, *the little motorboat moored at the end of the garden.*

'Let's have a picnic,' you say.

'Let's run away,' you say.

It's the brightest of summer days, but you still feel the cold. You're always cold because you're so thin. There's a breeze out on the estuary and you pull your fleece around you. Jay tells you about a job he wants to apply for when he finishes his studies. It would mean moving to London. You're only half listening. You trail your hand in the cold water, staring into its glassy depth. There's another world under the surface.

Jay starts to show off, driving the boat in circles, faster and faster. You shriek with delight. It's like being on the waltzers at the fair, back when you were six or seven, before it all began. You want to go there again, and then you think of a way in which you can . . .

'Aimée!'

Jay's panicked voice is silenced as the cold water closes over your head. The propeller blades churn the water and bubbles rush past your ears. You twist and turn in the current and quickly become confused as to which way is up, or where the surface lies in relation to you. But you don't care. You're not looking for the surface.

The water's so cold it hurts.

The first blade hits your ankle with a crack, and a plume of red colours the water. Then your other knee. Pain flares, then fear. As the propeller slices across your left arm and into your ribs, you gasp, sucking in water. You choke. Your eyes search for the surface.

It's too late, Aimée. Too late even to take comfort that you'll never see Valentine again.

You've gone.

53

Friday, 1 September 2017

Francis

'You owe me one, Sullivan.'

'Sorry, sir?' Francis was advancing into Bradshaw's office to update him on the progress of last twenty-four hours.

'I've just had Tom Fitz on the phone . . .'

I bet you have.

'. . . and I've persuaded him not to press charges against you.'

'How did you manage that, sir?' Francis fought but failed to keep the sarcasm out of his voice.

A sour frown swept across Bradshaw's face. 'I told him it would be his word against yours and Mackay's, and that the jury would naturally believe two police officers.'

Francis gave a scant nod at this and Bradshaw's frown became darker.

'Oh, holier than thou, are you now? You put me in this bloody situation – punching a reporter in the face. Bringing the force into disrepute . . .'

Blah, blah, blah . . . Francis had heard this lecture several times since the incident with Fitz. But what was interesting to him was that Bradshaw seemed to be sanctioning him and Rory to lie about it. It made him wonder if there was something more to the deal. What information might he have given to Fitz to make the charges go away? He was certain it had been Bradshaw that had told Fitz they were digging up bones at Itchenor Reach. What the hell did the reporter have on him?

'You're lucky I'm not instigating disciplinary action against you, Sullivan.'

'Sorry, sir. It won't happen again.'

Bradshaw gave him the side-eye. He clearly didn't believe a word.

'Right, update me. There better have been some bloody progress. How close to an arrest are you?'

Francis took his time in answering. He was calculating what he would tell the chief. Not the precise facts, certainly. Nothing yet about the discovery of the identity of the Itchenor bones. Now was the time to plant a false fact and then wait to see if it appeared in the *Argus*.

'Come on then – I haven't got all day.'

'Right. Sorry, sir.' Francis crossed his legs. 'Lewis has been examining the bones we uncovered at Itchenor Reach. So far it appears to be a middle-aged man who suffered a blunt trauma injury to the skull. We're waiting for dental matching on any missing persons in the right time frame.'

'Listen, Sullivan, it's the Speed Trials tomorrow. Chasing a cold case isn't going to lead us to the killer overnight. You need to find out why he targeted those girls – they're what'll lead us to the bastard.'

'We're working on that too,' said Francis, struggling to stay patient. 'Brighton Art College has confirmed that Riley was a student there and that she was excluded a few months back for non-attendance. I've got Burton and Hitchins investigating the girls' social lives to see if there's anything else that links them, that might explain why these girls were chosen in particular.'

'Hmm ...' Bradshaw nodded his head. 'You're too bloody slow, Sullivan.'

Francis didn't rise to the bait. It was a fair comment, but up to now they'd assumed that Alex Mullins was the link between the girls. He possibly still was.

'I'll let you know what they come up with.'

'Do. We need to get this killer into custody before he tries again.'

Francis couldn't get out of Bradshaw's office fast enough. Keeping things from his superior made him feel uneasy. He hadn't envisioned a career in skulduggery on joining the police, and having to take such measures didn't sit well with him. Hitting a reporter didn't sit easily with him either.

'Rory, in my office,' he said, as he passed through the incident room.

Behind his closed door, he told his sergeant what Bradshaw had said.

'Don't mention this to the rest of the team.'

'Of course not.'

'You and I need to do some digging. Somewhere in Bradshaw's past, Tom Fitz has protected him.'

'Or has some information on him that Bradshaw would rather didn't go public.'

'Take a sniff around his early cases, would you? Find out when Fitz got the crime beat and check out anything from there onwards.'

'On it, boss.'

Someone knocked on the door.

'Come in.'

It was Angie, and Francis could tell from the way she carried herself that she had news to impart.

'What is it, Angie?'

'Two things.' She was practically out of breath. 'First, I've just been talking to the welfare officer at the art college. It seems like the three girls were all having counselling at some point, which suggests that they were all troubled in some way.'

'No surprise there,' said Rory. 'Sally Ann had dropped out because of her affair with Ben King, and Lou Riley had been excluded – and according to Rose, had traces of drugs in her system.'

'But what about Tash?' said Francis. 'Was she in some sort of trouble, apart from having a stormy relationship with Mullins? Angie, talk to her friends again – see if there might be something else. Drugs or some other issue, maybe?'

'Go and talk to the counsellors as well,' said Rory.

'They probably won't tell us details of the girls' problems,' said Angie.

'Then get them in here and I'll sort them out,' said Francis. 'Three girls are dead and we have reason to believe the killer will strike again. Make this your top priority.'

'Absolutely, boss.'

'And you had something else?'

'This,' said Angie. She'd been clutching a fold of papers since coming in. Now she unfurled them on Francis's desk. Francis pulled them across to read them.

The first sheet was a photocopy of an old newspaper article. The date was in July 1995. It was short and to the point.

A local businessman has been reported missing by his business partner after not returning from a business trip abroad. Valentine Montgomery failed to show up for work last week after a scheduled trip to France, according to his partner Eric Davis. When he couldn't get Montgomery on the phone, he contacted his clients in France who said Montgomery had never arrived. Police are checking flight records to see if Montgomery actually left the country. Montgomery lived alone after losing his wife to cancer and his daughter to suicide in recent years. He has one son, Jay Montgomery, studying in America, who has been informed of his father's disappearance.

'Interesting.' Francis passed the photocopy to Rory, and read the second sheet, another copy of a newspaper article. It was from 2002, and the piece was even shorter.

Chichester businessman Valentine Montgomery, who went missing more than seven years ago, has finally been declared dead. It has long been presumed that Montgomery committed suicide following the deaths of his wife and daughter in 1993 and 1994. Montgomery's surviving son was unavailable for comment.

He showed it to Rory.

'Well done, Angie. We'll need to talk to the business partner and the son – see if you can track them down. Someone killed Montgomery and our killer led us there. We need to work out why – and we're running out of time.'

54

Marni

Marni heard the key turning in the lock, then the front door opened.

Please be Alex, not Thierry, she thought as she ran from the kitchen to the hall.

'Mum? Are you home?'

'Alex?'

She swept him into her arms, but he pulled back from her. There was a hardening to his face and a sharp look in his eyes she'd never seen before.

'Alex, what is it?'

'Why did you choose Thierry over Paul?'

Marni couldn't believe what she was hearing. She shook her head. 'Oh, no. No, no, no.' Her whole body heaved with a great sigh. 'You've seen him, haven't you?'

'Didn't you think I had a right to know who my father is?'

'Jesus!' Marni slapped a hand against the hall wall in frustration. 'It's not that simple, Alex.'

'No? He says you were with him when I was conceived.'

Marni turned and went back to the kitchen. She didn't want Alex to think that Paul was his father. She didn't want to discuss with him the fact that she had sex with both brothers within the time frame in which he'd been conceived. She didn't want to have to tell him that Paul had raped her. And she didn't want to tell him that there was no way of knowing which brother was his father, because they were identical twins with identical DNA.

It was a conversation she wasn't ready for. It was a conversation she'd never be ready for.

Alex followed her into the kitchen, his eyes demanding an answer.

'Where's Paul staying?' she said. 'I need to talk to him.'

Marni stood on the step of the hostel smoking a cigarette as if she belonged there. It was her second cigarette in ten minutes, but she'd smoke as many as it took until someone came out. She'd almost finished it when the door opened from the inside and two men emerged. Perfect. She dropped the butt and caught the door as they let it swing shut behind them.

'Ta,' she said, as she pushed inside.

They ignored her and walked away. People came and went in a matter of days at these sorts of hostels. No one kept track. No one cared.

Once inside, with the door shut behind her, Marni looked around. She was in the narrow hall of a run-down Victorian terraced house. A cork board hung on the wall with scruffy notices pinned to it – no smoking in the rooms, a cleaning roster for the kitchen, a clutch of other instructions that were no doubt routinely ignored. The hall, and the staircase leading up from it, were dark. All the interior doors were shut, and the ones she could see had plastic numbers tacked up on them. Every room rented out – no communal space apart from the kitchen and bathrooms. The air smelled of damp and cheap cooking fat.

This looked like the sort of place Paul would stay. He'd be short of cash. And it was the sort of place where nobody asked questions.

The kitchen, as Marni expected, was on the ground floor at

the back. It was empty. Marni looked around. A stack of dishes, thick with congealed grease, stood by a sink half full of dirty water. A stained and crumpled tea towel lay on the table. Dirty mugs. A plate with a toast crust left on it. In the corner, the bin was overflowing. Whoever's turn it was to empty it hadn't read the roster.

Marni went back to the hall, her boots squeaking on the grimy linoleum. She stopped outside the first door she came to and listened. There was no sound coming from inside. She tried the handle. The door was locked. She moved on to the second door. This would have been the house's front room in better days. This time when she listened she could hear a baby crying – the soft mewling of a newborn, rather than an all-out howl. A moment later, a woman's sing-song voice comforted the child in a language Marni didn't understand.

She went up the stairs, feeling for the handle of the knife in her pocket to keep the dark flutterings of foreboding at bay. Somewhere from higher up in the house she could hear the blaring of a radio, but on the first floor all seemed quiet. There were four doors, all numbered, and she tried them in turn. The first two were locked, suggesting that their residents were out – maybe working, maybe sitting on a park bench somewhere drinking.

The third room seemed quiet, but when she pushed down the door handle, the door opened. She squinted through the crack.

The room was large, with a bay window looking out over the street. Marni could only see a narrow strip – and didn't dare open the door further – but what she could see triggered a surge of adrenalin to cascade through her body.

Fight or flight? She'd come here to fight.

A scruffy armchair, with pilled red upholstery and worn arm-rests, faced the window. A man was sitting in it and, though

323

Marni could only see a quarter or so of his profile from behind, she knew immediately who it was. The shape of his head was as familiar to her as the shape of Thierry's.

Paul Mullins was wearing an expensive-looking pair of headphones – *stolen?* – and as Marni slipped silently into the room, she could hear the tinny beat of heavy rock music leaking out of them. She closed the door softly behind her. No need for witnesses to see what was about to happen. As she drew the knife from her pocket and stared down at the blade, an uncanny sense of déjà vu threatened to overwhelm her. How many more times would she have to confront this man to protect her family?

'Paul.'

She spoke loudly enough for him to hear her over the music he was listening to.

He jolted out of his chair, ripping the headphones off and dropping them to the floor. As soon as he realised it was her, his expression changed from one of shock to a dark scowl. Every single muscle in Marni's body clenched tight. She squared her feet on the floor, sinking her weight as low as possible. Her right hand tightened its grip on the knife as she held it protectively in front of her.

'*Pute!*' Paul took a step forward, using the advantage of his height to menace her.

Marni stood her ground.

'Stay away from my son, Paul.'

'Your son? You mean our son.'

'He's not.'

'You can't know that.'

'If you go anywhere near him again, I'll use this on you.' She brandished the knife.

'You don't scare me, Marni. I survived your last sorry attempt. This time it will go worse for you.'

'And you think you can win Alex over by hurting me?'

'You've done the damage yourself already. Alex has agreed to come back to France with me.'

'You're lying.'

Paul shrugged, then laughed. '*Ne soyez pas trop sûr.*'

Don't be too sure.

'Oh, I'm sure, Paul. If he'd agreed to leave with you, you wouldn't still be here.'

She'd caught him out and Paul lunged forward, thrashing an arm sideways to knock her knife arm out of his path. Marni danced back as he came at her.

'Don't be an idiot. You know I'll use this.'

'Fuck you!' he said.

Marni had the upper hand. She held the knife out in front of her, remembering the feeling of power it had given her once before. She took a couple of deep breaths to steady herself, all the while never letting her gaze stray from Paul's face.

He was also breathing heavily, now standing in a half-crouch, watching her, watching the knife. She couldn't read fear in his eyes, but he must also be remembering what had happened. She wondered if he still carried the scar of what she'd done to him. It had been a deep cut into his abdomen. It must have left its mark on him.

Damn it! Don't get distracted.

They circled slowly, each waiting for the other to make a move. Marni's hand was shaking and she felt light-headed. Her blood sugar was low. She couldn't project the outcome of this little dance in her mind – but she needed to. If she couldn't control her breathing, if she started to hyperventilate . . .

No.

She centred herself, counting slow breaths as she watched Paul watching her. They moved round another quarter-turn of the circle.

Too late she realised the position she'd put herself in. Paul was between her and the door. She would have to go through him to get out. He was taller. He was stronger. Even though she had the knife she knew her odds weren't good.

She should never have come here.

'I'll kill you, Paul, to get out of this room.'

'It doesn't have to be this way, Marni,' he said.

'It does,' she said, fear making her voice tremble.

'Say you and Alex will come away with me.'

'You'd know it was a lie.'

Paul's features darkened and Marni saw his left eyelid start to twitch. She'd seen this happen before and fear cloaked her with its cold breath.

She passed the knife to her left hand so she could flex the fingers of her right hand. It might have been Paul's chance but he seemed wrapped up in his own thoughts. She didn't want to wonder what they were. With the knife back in her right hand, she felt safer. She reached into her pocket and pulled out her phone.

'I take it you're calling Alex,' he said. 'Tell him to come here or . . .'

Marni didn't answer. Without looking down, she pressed the sequence of keys she knew best, dialling the number of the one man she knew would come to her aid.

55

Saturday, 2 September 2017

Liv

Liv had gone to the annual Brighton Speed Trials for as long as she could remember. Fast cars and bikes racing for a straight, hair-raising quarter-mile stretch down the front. Coke when she was a kid, beer now, sunshine, the roar of engines and the stink of petrol. Hot guys revving their hot rods and leather-clad bikers giving her the eye. What wasn't to like about that?

She'd spent the day cruising Madeira Drive with a couple of girlfriends, feeling like they were on the set of *Grease* and wishing the summer would go on for ever. But the sky was a hot and heavy blanket. Sweat stuck her T-shirt to her back, and the incessant droning of engines was precipitating a dull ache behind her eyes.

When Alex called at just gone five, upset and angry, she wasn't sorry to leave. She made her way home to drop off some stuff, then headed out to meet him at the Hope and Ruin.

She was in a hurry. Alex had sounded distraught on the phone. This guy turning up, claiming to be his father, was really messing with his head – the idea that he'd never know who his real father was was cutting him up.

As she crossed Clifton Place, her phone buzzed in her bag. She pulled it out and checked the screen. It was Alex again. Impatient.

'Be with you in five, okay? I've just reached Clifton Terrace and I'm cutting through the memorial garden.'

He was still sounding fucked up, and she quickened her step as she went through the small wrought-iron gate into the gardens. The air was clammy and she felt sweat running down between her breasts, even though she was only wearing a light vest. Her jeans clung to her legs uncomfortably. In the distance, thunder rumbled and the sky seemed to swell with the promise of rain.

Then, halfway across the empty memorial garden, it finally happened. A large, warm raindrop landed on her arm. A second later another slapped her on the opposite shoulder. She looked at the ground. Dark circles appeared on the path around her, then as if finally given permission, the clouds let loose the weight of water that had been building for days. Within seconds, the dusty tarmac became black and shiny, and water ran from Liv's hair down her forehead and dripped from the end of her nose. Walking as fast as she could, she followed the sweeping path down to the lower level of the garden. It would take her past the creepy Victorian sepulchres – she and Alex had played ghosts here when they were kids – but it would bring her out opposite Church Street, from which it was just a five-minute walk to the pub.

If only she'd thought to bring an umbrella.

A man walking towards her was closing his. That seemed weird, as the rain was getting heavier still, bouncing up from the path now to splash her legs. She veered to the left of him as they came nearly level – he would walk straight into her if she didn't get out of the way. Bloody men, always assuming they had the right of way. She scowled at him, taking in his dark raincoat and an old-fashioned trilby-style hat. He probably worked for one of the firms of accountants . . .

The blow came from nowhere and she staggered sideways with the impact, grunting with pain.

What the fuck?

Before she'd got her balance back, an arm snaked around her neck. Out of the corner of her eye, she saw the closed umbrella, with which he'd hit her, rolling to one side on the wet grass.

She tried to scream but the man tightened his arm about her throat, and only a guttural moan escaped her. She attempted to break free but he was taller and stronger than her. He dragged her along the path. As she kicked her feet, trying to gain purchase, a terrifying thought sprang into her mind. Could this be the guy, the Poison Ink killer? The police thought it was Alex, which was bollocks. It was someone else. This man?

They were at the end of the row of Victorian sepulchres now, where they abutted the garden's high brick wall. Between the last tomb and the wall, there was a narrow doorway with a battered steel door – she'd always wondered where it led. Now, she heard the click of it being opened and a rush of cold, rancid air washed over her. He was pulling her inside and down some steps. The door clanged shut behind them, plunging them into total darkness, but he still seemed to know where he was going.

She turned her head to the side and the pressure on her vocal cords eased.

'Who are you?' Stinking air choked her lungs, making her want to vomit.

The man didn't answer.

The steps had given way to a flat surface beneath their feet, but it still sloped downwards. The air became more fetid still – and the stench told her where they were. He was taking her down into the sewers. Cold sweat erupted from every pore with the realisation. There would be no one down here to help her. No one would hear her screams. Her only chance would be what she could do by herself. She had to get away from him.

When he stopped without warning, Liv almost fell. She gripped his arm to steady herself and then wondered why she'd done that. If she fell, he would fall, and that might be her chance to escape. But as if he guessed what she was thinking, he hit her again, this time with his fist. Sparks cascaded past her eyes and for a moment she thought she was going to be sick. She struggled for breath as the world spun around her.

He pulled her further down into the darkness.

'Someone's ... waiting ... for me,' she said. Speaking was a struggle.

'Death's waiting for you.' It was only a whisper but the words seemed to echo in the dark.

With a snap, the beam of light from a small torch lit up the sewer. They were in an oval-shaped channel constructed of red bricks. To one side of them, a torrent of raw sewage rushed by – brown water churning with faecal matter and disintegrating paper. The sight of it made Liv want to throw up even more. Ahead, the way divided, two forks stretching away further than the feeble beam of light could reach. Still disorientated by the struggle, Liv had no sense of direction and no idea where either of the tunnels might lead. The man seemed to be weighing up which one to take, so she used the time to regain her strength. Then they were off again, the torchlight bobbing ahead of them and the man grunting in her ear with the exertion of pulling her along. She fought every step of the way, finally allowing herself to become a dead weight against the arm that supported her, making it even more difficult for him to move.

'You little bitch,' he hissed.

It lit a touch paper inside her. She wasn't going to let this man snuff out her life in a stinking sewer, damn it! She raised both arms to grab the arm that was around her neck. Using all her strength, she was able to pull it away enough to tuck her chin in behind it. This meant she could bite it, which she did, as hard as possible, for as long as she could. The man yelped with pain and loosened his grip. Liv broke away, turning to run back the way they'd come, skidding over the slippery floor as she felt her way along the wall in the darkness. The bricks were slimy under her fingers, but she had no choice other than to touch them.

Behind her, his torch beam swept in an arc as he searched for her. His footsteps crunched on the uneven stone surface, coming at her from behind.

Could she outrun him? She had no choice.

She could hear him panting behind her, getting closer.

The torch went out. She stumbled on, blind to where she was going.

She heard his intake of breath as his steps sped up. Then nothing.

A split second later he crashed into her, throwing his arms around her knees, rugby-tackling her to the floor. She landed with a thud that winded her and her head smacked against the wet stone.

When she came round, she was lying on her back. She blinked and opened her eyes. The light from a dozen candles illuminated a barrel-vaulted stone ceiling. The air she breathed in was cold and damp, though not so rancid. She could see a dark silhouette in the candlelight. The man was bent over a stone bench, doing something. It wasn't a bench – it was a tomb. She was also lying on a similar tomb. It was a crypt. They were in a crypt somewhere.

She felt cold stone underneath her shoulder blades. Where was her vest? Her bra was also missing. She felt for her jeans with one hand . . . at least they were still on.

A soft electrical buzzing cut through the silence and the man turned towards her.

Please, God, no . . .

She started to sob.

In the dim and flickering light, she could see that he was smiling.

And she knew she'd have one chance – only one chance – to lash out and get away.

56

Saturday, 2 September 2017

Alex

It was barely six o'clock but the Hope and Ruin was heaving with people who'd been watching the Speed Trials all day. Most of them were already half drunk and the noise levels made conversation impossible unless you were prepared to yell. Alex had secured a corner table with two stools, but as time passed and he reached the end of his beer, he was having a hard time defending the empty seat.

Where the hell was Liv?

He tried her phone again for the seventh or eighth time and, again, she didn't answer. He'd sent three texts, which had also been ignored. Twenty minutes had passed since she'd spoken to him from Clifton Terrace – she should have been here long ago.

The weather had broken. People were coming in with hair plastered to their heads and their clothing soaked through. Virtually no one had had the foresight to go out with a coat or an umbrella. People had forgotten such things existed. Was the rain affecting the mobile network? That didn't make sense – and if it was just an issue with her phone, Liv would have arrived by now.

Alex finished his pint and wondered what to do. He really needed to talk things through with her. Should he leave the pub and go and search for her? He stood up and a pair of sodden biker girls swooped on his table with high-pitched thanks. Maybe Liv was sheltering somewhere rather than walking the rest of the way in the rain? Hardly likely. She wasn't a little princess who'd balk at getting her hair wet. He went outside and stood under the overhang of the porch, trying her phone once more. Nothing. Now he was starting to get worried. What could have happened to her?

He bent his head against the rain and started running, only looking up occasionally to scan the faces of figures hurrying in the other direction. People were sheltering in doorways all the way along Queens Road, but when he turned into Church Street the pavements were deserted. He ran on, blinking water out of his eyes, splashing through puddles that hadn't been there an hour ago. He traced the route Liv would have come from the memorial garden, then crossed Clifton Terrace into Victoria Road. There was no sign of her.

It wasn't cold, but Alex shivered. His wet shirt was sticking to his body and his shoes were starting to let water in.

He stopped under a bus shelter to check his phone again.

Ten minutes later he was knocking on the front door of Liv's flat. Could she have gone back home for some reason? Frustration and fear churned in his gut.

What the fuck was she playing at?

Suze, one of Liv's flatmates, opened the door, wide-eyed with surprise at Alex's appearance.

'I thought she'd gone to meet you for a drink?'

'She never showed up.'

Sarah shrugged. 'D'you want to come in and get dry?'

Alex shook his head. 'I'll try her mum's. Tell her to call me, yeah, if she comes back?'

He ran on. Liv's mum only lived around the corner but it seemed like miles. The rain didn't let up – a constant deluge, weeks' worth of water being dumped on the city in minutes.

Running was hard in wet jeans and his feet squelched in his water-logged trainers.

Sarah Templeton had just got in from work when he arrived.

'Is Liv here?'

She went to the bottom of the stairs and yelled up. 'Liv? You there?'

No answer.

'I don't think so, love. What's the matter?'

'She was supposed to meet me at the Hope and Ruin.'

'You know Liv,' said her mother. 'Running late.'

'But she called to say she was on her way.'

'Then she's probably there now. You'd better get back or you'll completely miss each other.' She gave a girlish laugh at the thought, not the slightest bit worried about her daughter's whereabouts.

Maybe she was right. Maybe he was overreacting. But why wasn't she answering her phone? Something didn't feel right to him. He didn't want to scare Sarah Templeton, but he had to tell her.

'I think something's happened, Sarah. If she was running late, she would have called me. I'll go back and look again, but in the meantime, can you call the police? You know, with what's been happening . . .'

Sarah Templeton's smile disappeared in an instant.

'Go,' she said. 'Go now. I'll get onto the police.'

Short of breath, Alex started walking back towards the centre of town. Then a thought struck him. He stopped at Liv's flat again and banged on the door.

Suze let him in.

'Is Liv's laptop here?'

"Spect so. Try her room.'

Suze followed him through to the back bedroom. Liv's laptop was sitting open on the desk.

'Why d'you want it?' she said.

'Just need to try something.'

He sat down in front of the computer and booted it up. He knew Liv's password as he'd borrowed it once or twice when he'd stayed over. The screen lit up and he scrolled through her apps.

'Find My Phone,' he said, clicking on a round green logo.

He typed in Liv's password again and waited.

A compass spun on the screen.

Locating phone . . .

'Come on.'

The screen filled with a map. In the centre of it was a small circle with a picture of a phone at the centre.

Liv's iPhone.

Alex studied the map for a second. Liv's phone was in the memorial garden apparently – at the south-eastern corner, just near the old sepulchres.

So why hadn't Liv been there too when he'd just run through?

57

Francis

'You were counselling all three of these girls?'

'Yes, I'm afraid I was.' She expelled a long sigh. 'I wish I could have helped them more.'

Damn! This was a link they should have discovered a week or two ago.

He'd been treading water.

The woman looked beyond retirement age, making Francis wonder how well she could have understood the concerns of today's teenagers – but Marcia Cornwallis was the contact the art college had given him and she'd very generously agreed to see him late on this Saturday afternoon. Her hollow chest was draped in a fuchsia twinset, though she wore it with large plastic beads rather than the regulation pearls. When she'd come to the door to let him in, she'd been leaning heavily on a stick and her breathing was short from the exertion of walking down the hall. Even if she was the connection between the girls, she certainly wasn't the attacker. Was he speeding down a dead end, while the killer had more work to do?

'Can you tell me a little about their problems?' he said.

She frowned at him.

'I'm not being prurient – if we know what issues they were dealing with, it might give us a lead to the killer.'

'Oh, I see,' she said, but still she pursed her lips in disapproval. 'Tash Brady was having some problems at home. With her stepfather.'

Francis thought about Richard Brady. He'd come across as overbearing.

'And the other two?'

Marcia Cornwallis narrowed her eyes. 'Lou Riley – the same, only her problems were with the man her mother moved in with. He was making her life a misery.'

'Abusing her?'

'Physically? She never admitted that to me, but I had my suspicions. Sally Ann was different. She lived alone with her mother.'

'But she was having an affair with her tutor?'

'Yes, there was an older man involved.'

Ben King. Who had a firm alibi for the attack on Lou Riley. He was getting nowhere.

Francis stood up to leave.

'Just one other thing, Miss Cornwallis . . .'

'Yes?'

'Did you discuss these cases with anyone else or did anyone else have access to your files on the girls?'

'Of course I never discussed my clients with other people.' Marcia Cornwallis's eyes flashed. 'Only my supervis . . .'

Francis's phone trilled in his pocket. Rory's ringtone.

'Excuse me,' he said, raising the phone to his ear.

'Boss?'

'Not a good time, Rory. I'll call you back.'

'No, boss. A girl called Liv Templeton, Alex Mullins's cousin, has gone missing. Her mother just called it in. We've triangulated her phone. It's stationary, just at an entrance to the sewer system.'

Francis didn't need any more to know what was happening.

338

His gut coiled painfully as his pulse suddenly quickened. They were going to be too late.

'Where?'

'There's a door into the system in the memorial gardens opposite Saint Catherine's. You nearby?'

'A minute away. I'll meet you there.' He terminated the call. 'Sorry, Miss Cornwallis. I've got to go.'

He rushed out of the room and down the hall, Marcia Cornwallis following slowly with her stick. When he reached the door, he turned back to her.

'Just one last question. Are you seeing a girl called Liv Templeton?'

'I can't discuss existing patients with you.'

'Tell me. She's been abducted, damn it – I need to know.'

Marcia Cornwallis stopped in the doorway between her living room and her hall. She leaned forward with both hands gripping the top of her stick. She looked hard at him, eyes wide, face impassive.

'Yes, I've been seeing Liv Templeton.'

58

Saturday, 2 September 2017

Thierry

Thierry ran through the rain like he'd never run before. He had known in an instant. This had his brother written all over it. Marni had been scared and there wasn't much, apart from Paul, that scared her. Paul had promised he'd stay away from Marni. But when had his brother ever kept a promise?

Merde!

He banged on the door of the hostel but when no one came he took a step back, followed by a good, hard kick to the latch. The door flew open, slamming against the hall wall and rebounding. He ran up the stairs two at a time, calling Marni's name.

He got no response so he tried each door he came to. The first was locked. So was the second. Behind the third door he heard a scrabbling for the lock, so he kicked this one too. It held fast, but not quite – someone was pushing from the other side.

'Paul?' It had to be.

'Thierry?'

Marni's voice. Thank God.

Without warning, the person on the other side stepped away. The door flew open and Thierry fell into the room, sprawling and skidding in a pool of blood. Whose blood? He looked up quickly, glancing around the chaotic room.

An overturned chair.

An unmade bed, bloody bed linen.

By the time Thierry looked up, Paul was standing by the window. There was a knife in his hand. He had a cut lip, and there was blood trickling down his chin – but not enough to account for the blood on the floor and bed.

'Marni?'

A moan from the corner of the room made him look in the direction of the bed. Thierry scrabbled to his feet and went towards the noise, never taking his eyes off his brother.

'Leave her and listen to me,' said Paul, his voice harsh and guttural.

'Marni, are you okay?'

Paul took a step forward, the knife stretched out in front of him.

Thierry stopped in his tracks.

'Thierry?' Marni didn't sound right.

He stepped sideways and looked over the end of the bed. His wife was curled in a ball in the corner, pressed back against the wall as if she was trying to put as much distance between herself and Paul as she could. A blood-soaked sheet was bundled in her lap, but Thierry had to look back to his brother before he could work out the source of the blood.

Paul held out a phone to Thierry in a bloody hand. It was Marni's phone.

'Call Alex.'

'No,' said Thierry.

Paul's scowl became uglier.

'Call my son.'

'He's not your son,' said Thierry. He turned his head. 'Marni, what did he do to you?'

Marni pushed herself up slowly until she was standing, her back still jammed into the corner.

'My hand,' she said, still clutching the balled-up bloody sheet.

Thierry could see from the way she held it that it was her right hand bound up inside the fabric.

'*Merde*, Paul. *Qu'est-ce qui ne va pas?*' What's wrong with you.

'Your wife is a bitch.'

'Thierry, he wants me and Alex to go with him to France.'

'*S'ils ne viennent pas, je les tue et je me tue.*'

Thierry hoped desperately that Marni's French wasn't as good as it used to be – but her gasp told him otherwise.

'If you believe Alex is your son, you wouldn't kill him,' said Thierry.

'What good is a son that I don't have?'

Paul stepped forward with the knife. The room was practically dark now, but there was enough light still from outside for Thierry to see the glint of the blade.

'You first,' said Paul. He took another step towards Thierry. 'Then her. After that, I think it will be easy to persuade Alex to come with me to France.'

'*Tu es fou.* If you do this, you'll spend the rest of your life in prison. Think of our mother.'

Thierry couldn't move any further back – his calves were already pressed up against the side of the bed. He took a step sideways and Paul lunged at him. As the blade came at him, Thierry dropped backwards onto the bed and rolled. Paul dived at him, landing across his body. Thierry continued the roll, grabbing Paul's shoulder and hip to throw him off.

He heard Marni screaming.

Metal flashed close to his face. Searing pain ripped across his chin. He grabbed for Paul's wrist and slammed it against the wall. Paul let go of the knife with a roar of pain, slumping on top of Thierry once more. Thierry brought his knee up sharply, hoping to catch his brother in the groin. It worked and as Paul gasped and struggled to breathe, Thierry was able to roll out from under him. He immediately felt down the side of the mattress and retrieved the knife.

Marni ran and picked up her phone from the floor.

'I'll call the police,' she said.

'Wait,' said Thierry. He could feel blood running down his chin and dripping onto his T-shirt.

'What?'

'He's my brother.'

'He just tried to kill you.' She started dialling.

'I said wait.' Without a second's thought, Thierry pointed the knife blade towards her.

Marni froze.

'Jesus, Thierry.'

He ignored her and looked at Paul, who was cowering at the far end of the bed, his hands cupping his groin.

Thierry dug a hand into his jeans pocket and Paul immediately tensed. Slowly, Thierry pulled his hand out and held it up to show his car keys.

'Take these and go,' he said. 'Head north, or go south and get on a ferry to Spain. You can have my passport.'

'What the hell?' said Marni. 'You're helping him now?'

'Shut up and stay out of it,' said Thierry. 'This is between me and Paul.'

Paul watched them both with wary eyes.

'I came here for one thing. Alex has to come with me,' he said.

Thierry shook his head. 'Uh-uh. He won't.'

Paul leaned across and grabbed Thierry's car keys from his hand. Then he stood up and stared at Marni. Thierry thrust a hand into his other pocket and pulled out a handful of crumpled notes and change.

'Take this.' He pushed the money into Paul's other hand. 'Now go.'

Paul thrust the keys and money into his own pocket.

343

'I'll come back for you all,' he said. He looked at Thierry. '*Je ne vous laisserai pas vous en sortir. Vous avez pris ce qui était à moi.*'

'Get out!' said Thierry.

'Fuck you, Thierry,' said Marni, as Paul's footsteps receded down the stairs. She looked as if she was close to tears but there was a steely edge to her voice. 'You're letting the bastard go? He's threatened to kill me and to kill Alex if we don't go with him. I think you'd better go too. I never want to see either of you again.'

As she spoke, the sheet fell from her right hand and Thierry saw what Paul had done. A deep cut between her thumb and forefinger looked black with congealing blood. It was her tattooing hand.

Marni looked down at it and fainted.

59

Alex

Alex ran from Liv's flat back to the memorial garden. This was where Liv's phone had showed up on the Find My Phone app, so this was where Liv should be. Under cover of the rain clouds, dusk had fallen rapidly and it was dark by the time he got there. The garden was deserted. He walked up and down the paths, calling her name. Where the hell was she?

After a complete circuit of the small graveyard, he headed back towards the gate he'd come in by. He must have missed her. He kicked an abandoned umbrella that lay on the path. Maybe she'd been sheltering somewhere round here, and now she'd be waiting grumpily for him at the pub. He tried her phone. No answer. Though he was completely alone in the garden, somewhere nearby he heard a phone ringing.

It was the same ringtone as Liv's.

'Fuck.'

The ringing stopped so he redialled, running through sheets of rain towards where he thought the sound had come from. As his call connected, he could hear it again. At that point, he felt certain it was Liv's phone. The sound was coming from the end of the row of ancient tombs. He veered off the path and across the wet grass, the ground squelching under his feet.

'Liv?'

Then he saw it. Liv's phone was lying on a threadbare strip of gravel that led to a small metal door at the end of the row of tombs. The glass was cracked, something which he was sure wasn't the case when he'd stayed at her flat the night before. He picked it up, but the mobile couldn't tell him anything about where she might be.

'Liv? Where are you?' His voice was getting hoarse from shouting her name so often.

In desperation, he tried the metal door. It came open with a creak of protest and he peered into the dark beyond. The cold air that caressed his face smelled rotten. He could see nothing, so he got out his own phone and switched on the torch app. A brickwork path sloped away into the darkness beyond the feeble beam of his small light. Rainwater had run in under the door and the first few feet of the path were wet. But beyond that, it was dry. Alex peered further and walked inside a few steps, holding his torch out in front of him. The smell made him want to retch but he wasn't going to let that deter him if Liv was down here.

On the dry stones of the path there were footprints. Two sets of them, one large, firm and steady. The other set smaller and scuffed, not moving in a single forward direction, but instead looking as if the smaller person was almost dancing round the larger one.

Or being pulled along against their will.

He bent down and looked more closely at the smaller prints, trying to see something in the marks that might suggest what type of shoe the person was wearing. In one clear print, he saw the logo of a little-known sports brand. But he knew it. He'd seen it on the sole of Liv's shoes only the day before.

'Liv . . .' It came out as a whisper this time.

He had no time to lose, so he set off at a run, holding his phone out in front of him for light. If Liv had been dragged in here straight after he'd called her from the pub, whoever had taken her had one hell of a start on him. But he should be able to catch them up, as it looked like they'd been struggling.

Jesus. What if Liv had been grabbed by the Poison Ink killer?

He ran faster, using his phone torch to see where the footprints led, but then the tunnel bottomed out in a large puddle that stretched ahead into the darkness. The air down here was foul and Alex realised he'd come down into the old Victorian sewer system that cleared the city's waste. The water he was running through looked inky black in the half-light, and he tried not to think about what it might contain. The tunnel he was following opened out into a much larger tunnel and he found himself on a walkway along the side of one of the main sewage channels. The smell was overpowering and, as he looked around, he had no way of knowing which way Liv had been taken by her abductor.

He didn't dare call out her name – he didn't want to alert the attacker to his presence. But maybe if he did call for her, she could call back, if she was in earshot. Then he'd be able to find her. He stopped to catch his breath.

Was that a flicker of light off to his right? He shone his torch in the direction from which it had come, but he couldn't see anything moving. Then, realising his error, he switched his light off and was plunged into absolute darkness. There was no light in that direction or any other, but he figured that if he had seen a light down there, that was the way to go.

He set off again at a gentle jog. The walkway along the side of the larger channel was wet underfoot, but he wasn't actually running through water like he had been before. However, the roaring torrent of sewage was wider and faster here – probably strong enough to sweep a man away. Then he saw it again – the edge of a flicker of light where the tunnel went round a corner. He ran faster, feeling sure that he had nearly caught up with them. He hoped he'd be in time, that the bastard hadn't hurt her yet.

'Liv!' he shouted, without thinking that he would be giving himself away.

'Stop! Who's there?'

'Who's that?' he called, but he knew the voice from somewhere.

He rounded the corner. A light flashed on in front him, aiming straight at him and blinding him with its glare.

'Alex Mullins,' said a voice he knew all too well. It was DI Sullivan.

Fuck!

What were the police doing down here?

'I had a feeling it was you we'd come across,' said another voice from somewhere in the darkness.

Alex turned away from the glare and started to run, but a man stepped out from the shadows ahead of him.

Rory Mackay.

He was trapped.

Mackay was holding a baton, ready to strike.

'No,' cried Alex. 'You've got it wrong. Someone's taken my cousin Liv – I'm trying to find her . . .'

He heard a loud crack, and the tunnel seemed to spin around him as pain radiated through his skull. Then the world went black.

60

Angie

The man from Southern Water whom Angie had called on to let them into the sewer system hadn't been overjoyed at the prospect of a load of policemen descending into the tunnels.

'Not in this rain,' he said grumpily. 'I really wouldn't recommend it. If it carries on like this, we'll probably see a flood surge and I can't guarantee you'll be safe down there.'

Drowning in sewage wasn't exactly Angie's idea of fun either, especially as it meant working late on an evening that she and Tony had managed to secure for themselves. But it looked like another girl had been abducted, and she would be damned if she didn't do all that she could to find her.

She printed out a schematic of the sewers, and she and Tony left John Street in the direction of the front. She'd agreed with Rory on the phone that they'd head into the sewers from the entrance under the pier. This was where the sewer tours started from and the man from Southern Water had agreed to meet them there to unlock the door.

The rain hadn't let up and by the time they got there, they were both soaked to the skin.

'Fucking great,' said Tony, blowing a drop of rainwater from the end of his nose. 'The timing of this couldn't have been worse.' His wife had gone to see her mother, making it easy for him

349

to have an evening with Angie without needing to make up a complex excuse.

Angie sighed, shaking her wet hair and raking through it with her fingers. This had the potential to stretch long into the night. There were thirty miles of sewers under the city, so a thorough manhunt would take hours. Using dogs had been mooted, but they didn't have a guide scent for the killer, and the sewers were so overflowing with different smells that the handlers thought the dogs would simply be overwhelmed.

'So it's down to us stupid mutts,' Tony had murmured when he'd heard.

Mr Grumpy was waiting for them by a black metal door just on the left-hand side of the walls under the pier. They showed their warrant cards and he opened the door for them.

'How long will you be?' he said.

'There's a girl missing. We'll be searching until we know she's safe,' said Tony.

Angie shrugged. 'Two or three hours, maybe. You going to wait here to let us out?'

The man looked horrified by the suggestion. 'I'll leave the door unlocked. Just make sure you pull it shut after you come out, so it's not obvious.'

'No way. We're looking for a potential murderer down here – do you understand?' Tony's tone was gruff. 'You leave the door unlocked and you're giving him an escape route. We need you to wait here until we return.'

'But what if we leave by a different exit?' said Angie, ever pragmatic.

Tony shrugged. 'Then we'll call.'

Mr Grumpy scowled. Angie sympathised but it couldn't be helped.

He opened up and showed them inside, issuing them with hard hats and strict warnings about what to do if they heard an alarm going off. 'Depending on where you are,' he said, 'if the high-water alarm goes off, you'll have just minutes to clear the main sewer tunnels.'

They set off down the passage, Tony leading the way with the torch they'd brought from the station.

'God, it stinks down here,' he said.

Angie couldn't answer him. She was retching. She switched to mouth breathing but it hardly helped. The brickwork floor was wet and slimy and even the walls and the top of the tunnel seemed to be dripping.

Tony marched on relentlessly, setting a pace Angie found it hard to keep up with.

'Sooner we're out of here, sooner we can get to doing something a whole lot more pleasurable,' he said, waiting for her to catch up.

He shone the torch ahead.

'Look, the tunnel splits here. What does the map show?'

Angie got the printout out of her pocket. 'Where are we supposed to be headed?'

'Rory said to cover the southern part of the system. He and the boss are searching these tunnels to the north.'

Tony switched off the torch, plunging them into darkness. 'Come here,' he said.

He embraced her and for a moment they clung together, Tony stroking her wet hair.

'I'm sorry about this evening,' he said. 'I was really looking forward to it.'

'Mmm … me too. Maybe we'll still salvage some time later on. Come on, let's get going.'

When they broke apart, Angie couldn't remember which direction they'd come from and which way they were meant to be going. Tony switched the torch back on and they consulted the map. She couldn't work out which junction they were at.

'Did you bring a torch?' he said.

'I've got my phone,' said Angie. 'I can use the torch app.'

'Okay, let's each go fifty metres up one of the tunnels. If we're here' – he pointed at the map – 'one of us should hit a dead end. Then we'll know to follow the other tunnel.'

'I'll take the left one,' said Angie, fishing her phone out of her jacket pocket. 'You're right, let's get it over with as quickly as possible.'

'Okay, see you in moment,' said Angie, as she headed off up her chosen tunnel.

She didn't think they had their location right. The tunnel she was in twisted sharply away to the left. That wasn't what it showed on the map. And as she went further into it, the gradient tilted steeply upwards. The sewage in the bottom of the channel here had less space so it ran faster. She wondered where she was in relation to the surface. When she hit fifty or so metres, Angie continued a little further, just to see around the next corner. Nothing if not thorough, she thought to herself. She shone the small beam of light in front of her, alternating between checking where she was putting her feet and trying to see further into the darkness ahead.

Another thirty metres on and the light showed, if not exactly a dead end, the end of the walkway. The sewage channel continued, but a rusted grating stretched across its path, so Angie couldn't have gone further even if she'd wanted to. Which she didn't, as it would have meant wading in the sewage. She needed to head back anyway. If Tony had stuck to fifty metres, he'd be waiting for her already.

As she retraced her footsteps, she realised that the light from her torch was weakening. She walked faster. She wanted to get back to Tony, who had the proper torch, before hers ran out.

Nearly there.

'Tony?' she called. 'Find anything?' Her voice echoed in the brick vault.

He didn't respond.

Just as she came to the junction, her torch gave out. She was plunged into darkness, and despite looking round in all directions, there didn't seem to be a glimmer from Tony's torch.

'Tony? My torch is out of juice. Can you turn yours on so I can see where you are?'

Still no answer.

'Tony, this isn't funny. Turn on the torch.'

In the distance, along the other tunnel, she heard something splash into the water. She put a hand out until she felt the wet brick wall and began gingerly to feel her way in that direction.

'Come on, Tony.'

What the hell was he playing at? It wasn't the time or the place for messing around.

She started to feel nervous. Could something have happened to him? If his torch had run out too, surely he'd give her a shout to let her know where he was. The wall she was skirting along started to curve. She carried on following it round, feeling sure she was nearly fifty metres into the tunnel.

When her foot struck something, she very nearly tripped over. She stopped in her tracks and felt what she'd come across with the tip of her toe. It wasn't solid – it gave a bit. It lay right across the path. And with creeping dread she knew what it was.

She dropped to her knees.

'Tony?'

She put out her hands and felt clothing, an arm. She ran her palm up his sleeve, across his shoulder to his neck. When she felt for his pulse, her hand encountered wet, sticky, warm blood. Her fingers felt the edge of a gaping wound and she snatched her hand back.

'Tony!' she shrieked. She tried to shake him. 'Tony, wake up.'

She knew he wasn't asleep. She knew she was wasting her time. 'I'll go for help.'

Tony didn't answer. He was dead.

61

Francis

They found Liv Templeton's phone in the back pocket of Alex Mullins's jeans.

In Rory's eyes, there was now no question of his guilt, but Francis wasn't so sure.

'He told her mother she was missing, right?' said Francis, trying to work out exactly what might have happened. For Marni's sake, he desperately didn't want to reach the same conclusion as Rory.

'That's what Sarah Templeton told me,' said Rory.

'So, if he was holding her captive somewhere and was about to tattoo her and drill holes in her, why would he go to her mother?'

It didn't make sense.

Alex was slumped on the brickwork floor between them, groaning but conscious.

'Right, we going to arrest him now?' said Rory, as it became clear the boy was lucid.

'Let's see what he's got to say about Liv's disappearance.'

'He did it, obviously. We've caught our main suspect in a place we already thought the murderer was using, when another girl with a link to him has gone missing. What more d'you want? I can't believe there's some other villain lurking down here.'

'Fuck's sake,' Alex grunted from the floor.

Francis squatted down. 'Okay, Alex, tell us what happened.'

355

Alex pulled himself up into a sitting position. His clothes were soiled with filthy water, and so was one side of his dreadlocks.

'I was meeting Liv for a drink, but she never showed up. I went looking for her. I checked her flat and her mum's house and she wasn't there.'

'So how do you come to have her phone in your pocket.'

'I traced it using Find My Phone on her laptop. It showed up as being in the memorial garden. I think she's been taken by whoever took Tash and Sally Ann.' He was talking so fast the words were almost garbled.

'You expect us to believe that?' said Rory

A distant scream stopped Francis from making any response.

'Liv!' said Alex, scrambling to his feet.

'Come on,' said Francis.

The three of them set off at a run in the direction of the scream. The beams from their torches bobbed up and down across the greasy walls and black water. Francis took the lead. Alex was slightly unsteady on his feet after Rory's punch, so Rory grabbed him by one arm to keep him upright.

'Liv?' shouted Francis. 'Are you there?'

They splashed through the mucky water, their footfalls making it hard to hear anything else. Francis strained his eyes and ears, desperately trying to catch a flicker of light or a sound in the darkness ahead.

'Liv?'

'Boss?' The voice that echoed out of the tunnel ahead wasn't Liv Templeton's.

'Angie? Where are you? Put on your torch.' She'd sounded distressed. 'Are you okay?'

'Boss . . .' She sounded like she was crying now. 'Tony's dead.'

'What the fuck?' said Rory behind him.

Finally, round the sweeping curve of the wall, Francis's torch beam picked up a kneeling figure silhouetted against algae-covered bricks. He ran faster towards her.

'Jesus, Angie, what happened?'

In the light, he could see her properly now. She was covered in blood. Next to her lay a body. He moved his torch to see who it was. Tony Hitchins was lying in a puddle. His head was at an angle and his throat had been slashed. The water underneath him had turned a brackish red.

Angie was crying insistently now and couldn't even talk. Francis pulled her into his arms.

'We're here, Angie. We're here. You're safe.'

'Who did it?' said Rory.

'I don't know,' said Angie between gasps. 'I was in the other tunnel.'

'We need to find Liv,' said Alex.

Francis helped Angie to her feet.

'Rory, is your radio working?'

Rory unclipped his radio from the harness he was wearing under his jacket and tried it.

'No, boss. No signal down here.'

'Right. Rory, you head out and get help fast. Call an ambulance for Tony and get this tunnel network flooded with uniform branch. See if you can get some armed officers down here.'

'Got it,' said Rory.

'Take Alex with you and get someone to take a statement from him.'

'Right.'

'Then go, go now! Angie, can you stay here with Tony until Rory comes back?'

Angie nodded and sniffed loudly. Rory started heading down the tunnel towards the exit by the pier, one arm holding Alex roughly by the elbow.

'What are you going to do?' said Angie.

'I'm going to find Liv Templeton.' He embraced Angie again,

and whispered in her ear. 'I know about you and Tony, Angie. I'm so, so sorry. I won't rest till I get the cunt.'

'Thank you,' said Angie, struggling to get the words out.

'They won't be long,' he said, hoping that would be the case.

It seemed immediately obvious to head up the tunnel in the direction Tony had been going when he met whoever had killed him. Francis was in no doubt that the person who'd slashed Tony's throat was the Poison Ink killer. He was sure it wasn't Alex Mullins, though for protocol's sake they needed to keep hold of him until they could properly exonerate him.

He shone the torch beam to show the way ahead, as other questions churned through his brain. If the killer wasn't Alex, who was he? What had they missed? There had to have been a clue to his identity somewhere. Was he even still down here or had he scarpered after running into Tony? And what the hell had become of Liv Templeton? For the first time in weeks, Francis felt able to send up a heartfelt prayer.

Please God, don't let the killer have tattooed her yet.

He ran on, following a system of always taking the left branch when the tunnels forked. He hit dead ends and retraced his steps, returning to the last junction to take the right-hand option instead. Every tunnel looked identical to every other one. The constant rush of the sewage, now bloated with gallons of rain, made it hard to think. He saw no glimmers of light, apart from his own torch. He switched it off at regular intervals to see if he could see signs of any other lights. The only sound he heard was that of his own feet running on brickwork and splashing through the stinking puddles. But gradually he realised that the sound of his footfall was being completely drowned out by the growing roar – the rain that was falling so heavily across the city was running down the drains into the sewers, swelling the volume exponentially.

He stopped for a moment, out of breath. The tunnel he was

in was narrow, and the slightly raised edge he was running along was close to the level of the rushing water. He wondered if it was still raining outside and how the system coped with such a prolonged downpour.

'Liv? Can you hear me?'

The only answer was the splosh of sewage slapping against the bricks.

He carried on, wondering if Rory had managed to get a search party into the system. He was determined to find whoever had been down here and taken one of his men. And if the killer escaped them today, he would hunt him down relentlessly until justice was served.

'Liv?' he shouted. 'Are you here?'

He wondered how many entrances and exits the system had. He would need each one cordoned off until they were absolutely sure there was no one still down here.

A noise up ahead in the tunnel startled him. A stone sliding against another stone. It might be nothing or it might be everything. He turned off his torch and tried to listen but the din of the water was too loud. He turned the light back on and kept going. He felt sure he could sense something ahead – the hairs on the back of his neck were rising.

He carried on running in the direction of the sound.

He very nearly missed it, but above his head he caught a brief flicker of light – then it was gone. He stopped in his tracks and shone his torch upwards. There was an iron ladder bolted to the wall a couple of feet back. He craned his neck to see where it led. A circular opening cut through the roof of the tunnel, a way out. Shoving his torch into his jacket pocket, he grabbed the bottom of the ladder and started climbing up the narrow chute.

He could see no light above him and he was ascending in total darkness. The rungs were slimy and hard to grasp. The whole structure seemed shaky and he wasn't convinced it would stay on the wall. He climbed as quickly as he dared and as quietly as he could, all the time listening for sounds above as the roar of the water diminished below him. But he couldn't hear anything.

After about fifteen feet, the chute widened and he stopped to get out his torch. A couple of feet above him, there was a metal hatch. Gripping his torch between his teeth, he stretched a hand up to push against the rusty opening. It gave way, opening a crack, through which he could see flickering light. The hatch was heavy, but by bracing his back against the wall of the chute and his feet on the ladder, he gained enough purchase to be able to push it up.

The hatch opened, grinding on rusty hinges. Then, before he could stop it, it carried on back to fall with a clang onto a stone floor.

Damn!

He'd given himself away. If there was anyone up here, they knew he was coming. He stepped up another rung and put his head through the opening. Then he got one arm up onto the edge so he was able to shine the torch round the space he found himself in.

The white beam of light played off stone walls and across the sides of sarcophagi.

Francis knew this place.

He was in the crypt of St Catherine's.

Footsteps sounded on stone beyond a doorway at the far end of the brick-vaulted space. Francis pushed himself up from the chute and onto the stone floor. He looked around. A black sports bag had been left in one corner, gaping open, and a cordless drill was lying on the floor next to it. Further along the same wall, on a low stone tomb, a tattooing iron and battery pack, a small glass bottle, bits and pieces . . .

He swung the torch beam to the other side of the crypt, and his breath caught in his throat.

Lying bound and facedown on a larger tomb was a young woman. At first, in the flickering light, Francis thought she was wearing jeans and a white top, but as he went towards her, he realised she was naked from the waist up. Her hair covered her face in dripping skeins and she was shivering violently.

'Are you Liv Templeton?'

62

Saturday, 2 September 2017

Alex

Alex was furious. Beyond furious. They hadn't gone more than a hundred yards down the tunnel when Rory turned back.

'Where we going?'

Rory hadn't answered him. Instead, when they reached Angie, Rory unclipped his cuffs from his belt. Then he looked around until he found what he was looking for. A few yards up the tunnel there were the iron fittings for an old ladder. There were only the bottom three rungs – the rest was long gone.

'Alex, come here.'

'What the hell?' said Alex.

Rory had held the cuffs out. 'Sorry, mate,' he said. 'But until things are totally clear . . .' He gestured towards the metal frame-work on the wall.

'No way, man,' said Alex. 'I haven't done anything. I need to find Liv.'

'I'm not giving you a choice,' said Rory. 'I don't want to leave Angie down here on her own. Let me cuff you voluntarily. If you don't, I'll charge you with resisting arrest.'

'Fuck you,' said Alex, but he'd grudgingly held up one wrist.

Now he wished he hadn't complied so easily. He employed his full body weight to yank at the metal fixing he was handcuffed to but succeeded in doing nothing but grind the rusty metal against his wrist. He roared with pain and anger.

'I didn't do it. You need to let me go.'

His scream echoed through the sewer, incoherent above the noise of the torrent less than three feet from where he was standing. Mackay was long since out of earshot and the policewoman seemed oblivious to his presence as she bent over her dead colleague. He tried again to wrench himself free, then kicked the brickwork of the tunnel in frustration.

'Fuck!'

Liv was somewhere down here and at the moment he could do nothing to help her. He didn't trust the police to put her interests first. The man had killed an officer and Alex knew what that meant. They would be out to get him. They'd probably send armed police in after him and Liv would be caught in the shootout.

'You!' he shouted at the woman, desperate to make himself heard. 'Hey!'

She didn't even look up. In the faint light of the torch that lay beside her on the ground, Alex could see that her shoulders were shaking. She was crying. He felt bad about that, but it wasn't going to help Liv.

There was a slight lull in the noise of the water and he tried again.

'Hey, officer!'

This time she heard him. She wiped her nose with the back of her hand, then used her other hand to smudge the tears from her cheeks. She stood up ponderously, like a woman sleep walking. Alex watched her, willing her to come to him, to do the right thing. The noise level had risen again and when Alex looked down, he realised that the course of filthy water was creeping closer to where he was standing.

The woman stood still, staring at him.

Alex took a deep breath of the fetid air and pointed at the

water. 'You need to let me go. The level's rising. I think we should get out of here.'

She didn't answer him but looked down at the body of her colleague. Raw sewage was lapping along the length of one of his legs. Finally she reacted. But instead of coming to release Alex from the cuffs, she turned back to the dead policeman. She went to his head and inserted her hands under his shoulders. She tried to drag him clear of the encroaching water, but the floor was slippery and she couldn't gain enough purchase. She skidded, a foot flew from under her and she sat down heavily, with one leg extending into the stinking channel.

'Take these cuffs off me and I'll help you,' said Alex.

She didn't hear him, but struggled to her feet and made another attempt to move the body. This time she was marginally more successful, shifting her colleague almost a foot back from the edge of the flow. Then she stopped, overcome with emotion as she contemplated his dead form. Alex could tell she was crying again.

'Please,' he shouted. 'We need to get out of here.' He drummed his frustration on the wall with a fist. *Liv needed him*. He'd failed Tash – and now he was about to have another death on his hands. The fight drained from his body and he leaned against the brickwork, trying to keep his weight from tugging against his wrist. The smell was getting to him – he wanted to throw up. The water was rising faster now. He slid his feet back against the wall to avoid letting his trainers flood, but there was little more he could do if the volume of sewage continued to expand.

In the distance, a sudden loud roar finally made the policewoman look his way. The noise was rushing towards them.

'Undo me,' shouted Alex. 'There's a surge coming.'

She picked up the torch and came over. He recognised her from when he'd been in custody.

'You're Angie, aren't you?'

She nodded. 'You've got to help me, Alex,' she said. She put the torch on a ledge halfway up the sewer wall and rummaged in her pocket.

'We need to get out now, or we could drown.' It wasn't the death he'd envisaged for himself.

'We're not leaving Tony.'

'Tony?'

She looked over at the body.

Jesus.

Alex bit his tongue. There was no point arguing with her until she'd released him, but there was no way he was risking his life over a dead copper. The sewage level had risen rapidly and was now lapping at his ankles. He could feel the strength of the current already tugging him downstream. Once freed, there would be nothing to hold onto and they'd have to battle their way upstream to the nearest escape ladder.

Angie grabbed hold of him as she fought the onslaught. She still hadn't found the keys, but she looked across to where Tony had been. His body was gone and she let out a cry of anguish.

Pulling her hand out of her pocket, she lunged forward and grabbed at something in the black water. With a shriek of exertion, she pulled on it. She had the body by the foot and then, with superhuman effort, she dragged him back towards where Alex was still cuffed to the wall. She was soaked, head to toe, in sewage, and Alex could see her retching as she struggled with her colleague's body.

'Let me free and I'll help you,' he shouted.

'I can't let go of him,' she said.

'Pull him here and put him behind my legs,' said Alex. 'I'll keep him steady while you undo me.'

The water was halfway up his calves and the force was growing stronger. Angie was nearing exhaustion point and he was still trapped.

'I don't know,' she said.

Did she really still think he was the killer?

More likely the woman was in shock and it was making her indecisive.

'If you leave me here, I'll drown.' Alex could feel the sewage level creeping up his legs. He was starting to panic. He shut his eyes and counted to ten, willing Angie to do the right thing in the meantime.

When he opened them again, she was pulling the body towards him. In the strong current of shit, piss and rainwater, she was making slow headway but, inch by inch, they were getting closer. Alex's heart was in his mouth as he watched her battle with the flood – would she get to him before it became too much for her and knocked her off her feet? If that happened, he might as well give up hope.

Seconds turned to minutes as she moved one way and was then tugged back just as far or further the other way.

'You're going to have to let him go,' said Alex, but she couldn't hear him.

Finally, she was close enough and reached out to grab one of Alex's legs. He braced it against the tunnel wall as she pulled Tony's body closer. Once he was able to, he hooked his other leg over Tony's torso and pressed the body back hard against the wall.

'Now undo these bloody cuffs so we can get out of here.'

Angie looked up at him blankly.

'The keys . . .'

'In your pocket,' said Alex.

Something inside her snapped awake.

'Of course,' she said. She put a hand in her pocket and drew it out again. Alex saw a glint of metal in her fingers and breathed a sigh of relief.

But he breathed it too soon. A sudden surge took the water

level above his waist. A heavy torrent of filth hit Angie in the small of her back. The breath was expelled from her lungs with a loud 'Oomph!' and she catapulted forward. Alex saw the hand-cuff keys fly from her hand, into the mire. She disappeared under the surface, arms flailing, then bobbed up again.

Alex stuck out one of his legs as far as he could, desperately hoping she'd be able to reach for it. As he did so, the strong rush of filthy water snatched his other leg from under him, where he was pressing Tony against the wall. The body was swept away, crashing into Angie as she reached for Alex's foot. He was left hanging by his wrist from the ironwork on the wall. Alone. And the sewage level was rising faster than ever.

63

Saturday, 2 September 2017

Francis

Francis untied Liv and gave her his jacket to put on. It was soaked with sewage but at least it would cover her and give her some warmth. The girl was in shock, and even when Francis had explained who he was, she continued to shake with fear.

'You're safe now, Liv.'

She nodded but her eyes were blank.

There was no question that he could leave her here on her own while he chased down her abductor, so he helped her to her feet and guided her towards the doorway at the far end of the crypt.

'No,' she said, stopping abruptly.

'What is it?'

'That's where he went – when he heard you coming.'

'He won't be there now, Liv. That leads up into the church, and he's sure to be trying to put as much distance as he can between us.'

Reluctantly and still shivering, she let him lead her up the steep stone steps that emerged against the south wall of the vestry. The church was dark and silent, so Francis switched on the lights in the small, cluttered room. It seemed mundane and homely, a world away from the events of the last hour.

But things were far from over.

He turned to Liv. She was clutching his jacket tightly across her chest and seemed to be waking from the stupor of shock.

'Are you hurt?'

'I'm okay, I think. He hit me a couple of times.' Francis could see the beginnings of a bruise forming at her hairline on the left side of her forehead.

'He didn't tattoo you?'

She shook her head. 'He was going to, but he heard you coming.'

The girl's back had looked untouched when Francis had found her. She'd had a lucky escape.

Over the next five minutes he got busy on the phone, arranging for an ambulance and for a female police officer to come and take Liv's statement. He instructed the duty sergeant at John Street to call Liv's mother. He spoke to Rory briefly – the sergeant had organised all the available uniformed officers to search the sewers.

'But, boss, there's a problem. Southern Water have advised me to get everyone out – the sewage levels have been swollen by the rainwater. They're dangerously high and a lot of the tunnels will become impassable. I've put out the order to evacuate.'

'Quite right. What about Angie?'

'I've sent a team in for her.'

'And Tony?'

There was a long pause. 'They'll bring the body out too.'

'Shit.' Angie and Tony. He should never have sent them down there. 'Get everyone out of there now.'

'What else?'

'Did you leave Mullins at the station?'

'No, I left him with Angie, so she wouldn't be alone.'

'What?' Francis bit back an expletive. 'I told you to take him in. D'you think he stayed with her? He's desperate to find Liv.'

'I cuffed him to the wall.'

369

This time Francis couldn't restrain himself. 'Jesus Christ, Rory. The water's rising fast. If the rescue team doesn't get there in time . . .'

There was silence at the other end of the line.

'Fuck!'

'Sorry, boss.'

'We don't have time now. We'll talk about it later. The killer escaped through St Catherine's, so organise a city-wide search. I'll try and get a description of the man from Liv.'

He couldn't afford to stay here and wait for the ambulance. He needed to be coordinating the search.

'Liv, I've got to go back to the police station. I'm going to call the verger here to come and sit with you until the ambulance or your mother arrives. Is that okay?'

She nodded. She'd been crying while he'd been on the phone. She needed warm clothing, a hot drink and a familiar face. The shock and cold were taking their toll.

Jered Stapleton was happy to oblige when Francis called him and took only a couple of minutes to get to the church from where he lived nearby. Francis shook his hand and thanked him for coming.

'I've got another officer on the way here, but in the meantime, would you be able to sit with her?'

'Of course,' said Jered.

He cleared a pile of vestments off a small armchair and motioned to Liv to sit down.

'I should have a cardigan around here somewhere,' he said, rifling through the discarded pile of garments.

Francis hurried down the front path of St Catherine's. In the round arc of the streetlights ahead, he saw the rain still billowing in slanted sheets. His shirt was soaked through in minutes – but he rejected the thought of running into his house to grab dry clothes. His phone told him he'd missed a call from Rose

Lewis while he'd been talking to Jered Stapleton – it would just have to wait. A killer was roaming free somewhere on Brighton's streets and Francis had to find him. But at least Liv Templeton was safe.

64

Saturday, 2 September 2017

Alex

When the sewage level reached halfway up his chest, Alex started to panic. He had exhausted himself trying to rip the rusty ladder away from the wall, and his cuffed wrist was a bloody mess. Now the current was so strong that he had to cling on to the top rung with both arms. The filthy brown water sloshed against him, splashing his face and making him feel sick, and his whole body felt slapped as solid particles of muck pelted against him and wedges of soggy paper wrapped round his legs.

This wasn't how he wanted to die.

He blinked. The splashes of water stung his eyes and his throat burned from constantly retching.

He thought about Liv and felt a fresh surge of agony. Had Francis Sullivan managed to save her? Or had they all been carried away by the tide of waste water?

But the person he thought about most while clinging to the side of the sewer in the pitch black was his mother. He had distanced himself from her, horrified by the thought that for the last nineteen years she hadn't even known who the father of her child was. It wasn't that he believed what Paul had told him and it wasn't that he didn't want to believe that Thierry was his father. He just didn't know what to think.

But what the hell did it matter whether his genes had come

from Paul or Thierry? Their genes were the same. He would have been the same person no matter which one of them fathered him. But they weren't the same people. Thierry had been a good father to him in a way that he doubted Paul would have been. Paul had raped his mother, and he was the result of that rape.

And now he was going to die down here, without getting the chance to say sorry to her, or to tell her that he loved her, that she was the most important person in his life.

Despair flooded him and he wondered if it wouldn't be easier just to submerge himself in the torrent and embrace what was coming.

The thought made him retch again and he clung onto the rusty ironwork a little bit tighter. If the rain stopped, the water levels would recede. It could still happen, so he wasn't going to surrender just yet.

He wondered how long he had left. Every second would be precious to him. A few fleeting minutes to remember all the good things that he could. Only he couldn't think of anything good. Even his memories of Tash were overlaid by the image of her in the hospital, as the medics fought desperately to save her. He'd soon be dead like her. His teeth were chattering and he had to keep spitting out the foul-tasting water splashing into his mouth.

'Help . . . Help me!'

He'd shouted over and over again, but it was a waste of energy. There was no one down here to hear him and the roar of the sewage would drown out his shouts even if there was.

He was going to die.

He was going to die alone and covered in shit.

He closed his eyes and did something he hadn't done since he was a kid. He prayed, urgently and fervently. If there was a god, now was the time he needed to do his stuff.

And miraculously, his prayers were answered. A flicker of light in the distance told him there was someone else down here.

'Help. Help me . . .'

He didn't even care if it was the killer. He just wanted to see another person.

The light became brighter. It was coming closer.

'Help . . .'

'Alex Mullins, is that you?' called a voice.

'Yes! I'm here.' He yanked at the metal ladder, desperate to get free, desperate to go towards the source of the voice.

Finally, he could make out what looked like a small rubber dinghy heading towards him on the current. There were two men in it, both using paddles to steer the craft as best they could. When they came close enough, one of them picked up a rope from the bottom of the boat.

'We've got one chance, Alex. You need to catch this and hold onto it or we'll go straight past you.'

He threw the rope, shining his torch so Alex could see it. It had a knot at the end of it and Alex stretched out an arm to grab it.

'I can't hold it.'

It was slipping from his grasp. The dinghy was level with him, rushing past him. He snatched his arm back to his chest so his shackled hand could grab the rope as well. His bloody wrist had to take his full weight and the pull of the boat and men. For a few seconds, he thought his wrist would snap, but then one of the men was able to reach for the bottom of the ladder.

'We're here, Alex,' he said. 'We're going to get you out.'

It was the best thing anyone had ever said to him.

65

Saturday, 2 September 2017

Francis

'Talk to me, Rose.'

Francis was pounding down North Street, outstripping the torrent of rainwater that rushed down the gutter like a small, fast river. His white shirt was plastered, transparent, against his chest and his trousers clung to his legs like wet towels. He could hear the scream of sirens and blue lights flashed in almost every direction. The city centre was being flooded by police manpower. If only they knew who they were looking for.

'Finally!' said Rose Lewis at the other end of the line. 'Right, you need to hear this. I've done some digging on Valentine Montgomery since the dental match came in.'

'Be quick.' His voice jarred as his feet thudded on the pavement.

'He was a successful businessman, electronic components, import/export, and he lived in a pile just on the edge of Bosham Hoe.'

'So the bones were found pretty much in his back garden?' Francis spoke breathlessly, not slowing down.

'Absolutely. He went missing in 1995 . . .'

'We know this.'

'What you don't know is that the year before, his seventeen-year-old daughter Aimée died on the same stretch of water.

375

There's some confusion over what exactly happened. Montgomery's son was driving the boat – she went overboard and got chewed up by the propellers.'

'Jesus.'

'At the time, the son, who was then twenty-one, claimed that she'd thrown herself out of the boat and into its path. He could do nothing to prevent it – but he's the only witness to what happened.'

'Implying?'

'Could have been an accident due to bad driving, for which he didn't want to take the blame. But the girl was known to have mental health issues. She was anorexic and had a record of self-harming. Also, Montgomery's wife died exactly one year to the day before his daughter.'

'Cause?'

'Cancer. The date, which was also Aimée's birthday, gives credence to the suicide claim.'

Francis had reached the bottom of North Street and was waiting to cross Old Steine as a fleet of police cars sped by.

'But this doesn't get us anywhere with Montgomery's murder – or how it's linked to the Poison Ink killer.' Francis was impatient for facts he could work with.

'It might,' said Rose. 'Listen, when the police investigated his disappearance, they found nothing of interest in his business dealings, or those of his partners. But his family had imploded. I think you need to talk to his son at any rate.'

'Okay. I'll get the team onto that next week. Thanks, Rose.' He was about to disconnect.

'Wait.'

'What?'

'I've done some digging on the son.'

'Slow week, was it?' Francis hurried across Old Steine as a gap in the traffic presented itself.

'The reason your team couldn't find him was because he changed his name – not surprising, given his possible part in his sister's death – but I found one thing that could help. 'Jay' wasn't his given name. It was just a nickname, the letter 'J' in fact. His actual first name was Jered . . .'

Francis stopped in his tracks in the middle of the road.

'. . . Stapleton. It's Jered Stapleton.' The realisation hit him with the shock of an ice bath. The Latin. The Buxtehude. The religious symbolism.

'What the? How did you . . .'

Francis cut Rose off and shoved the phone back into his pocket. He turned 180 degrees in the middle of the road and started running. A police car blared its horn at him and he turned again, digging out his warrant card. He ran up to the passenger door.

'Get out now,' he screamed at the WPC sitting in the passenger seat.

'What?'

'Now!' He climbed into the car as the woman was still pulling her second foot out of the door. 'Drive up to St Catherine's. Put your siren on and your foot down.'

There was a sharp ringing in Francis's ears and for a moment he couldn't breathe. He clamped his teeth down on his lower lip and tried to calm himself but it proved impossible.

'Faster!'

'Yes, sir.'

The PC driving the car gripped the wheel tighter as he took a sharp corner. Francis was flung against the passenger door – he hadn't even had time to get his seatbelt on. But he didn't care. They had to get there in time. They had to get there before Jered Stapleton could start tattooing Liv.

The car screeched to a halt by the entrance to Wykham Terrace. Francis leapt out.

'Come on,' he shouted to the PC. 'And call back up, now.'

'What . . .?'

'The Poison Ink killer. He's in the church.'

Francis ran up the brick path past the top end of the terrace of houses, and through the gate into the churchyard. His chest burned but he ran faster. The PC trailed behind him, talking on the radio as he ran. Francis lunged at the double doors to push them open and crashed into them. They were locked.

'Damn, damn, damn!'

He turned around and looked at the PC coming up behind him. He was a big bloke, well over six foot and built to match.

'It's locked,' he said.

His meaning was clear to the PC, who quickly re-hooked his radio to his belt. He looked closely at the double doors.

'The left one?' he said.

'I think so,' said Francis, looking at the arrangement of the lock and door handles.

The copper took a step back, then launched a ferocious kick at the left-hand of the two doors. His momentum burst the lock and carried him forward into the church. Francis followed him in.

The place was in complete darkness.

'Liv? Stapleton?'

Francis felt his way along by putting a hand out to find the back of the nearest pew. He moved as fast as he dared through the silent space, turning to go up the nave when he reached the end of the pew. The PC blundered behind him, swearing as he bumped into the font.

'What's your name?'

'Gavin. Gavin Albright.'

'Get the lights, Gavin,' said Francis. 'The switches are by the doors in the north transept. Directly opposite.'

'Yes, sir.'

Francis carried on towards the vestry, straining his ears for any sounds that Stapleton and Liv were still in the building.

He heard nothing.

The lights came on and he was able to move more quickly. As he expected, the door to the vestry had been locked from the inside, but it only took another quick kick from his companion to break through.

'This way,' he said, running to the steep staircase that led down to the crypt.

From somewhere below, he could hear the whining buzz of a tattoo machine.

Please God, no!

At the bottom of the stairs, he went around a corner. There was light here, bright and white, but flickering with movement. As he entered the part of the crypt, he saw why. A tall man – Jered Stapleton – was bent over the largest of the stone sarcophagi, where Liv Templeton was lying, once more bound and stripped naked to the waist. The figure turned in his direction and the glare of a head torch shone directly into his eyes.

'Stapleton, stop now!'

Jered Stapleton turned back to Liv and gouged the tattoo machine across her shoulder blades. Liv screamed and thrashed against her bindings.

Francis had no choice. He threw himself at Jered Stapleton with all the force he could muster. Stapleton swore loudly and tried to sidestep the onslaught, but Francis caught his left shoulder, causing the taller man to stagger. He dropped the tattoo iron, which clattered away over the slab-stone floor, and the two men followed it down with a crash. Francis was underneath, his arms pinned to his sides by the weight of Stapleton's body.

He moved his legs and found the side of the stone sarcophagus Liv was lying on. Pushing off from it with his feet, he was able to squirm out from under the verger just in time to see Stapleton's hand reaching for the tattoo machine. Without a foot on the pedal, the machine had stopped whining, but it didn't stop Stapleton from jabbing it in the direction of Francis's eye. Francis whipped his head to one side and felt the needles rip across the skin of his cheekbone.

As Stapleton raised his arm to try again, Gavin Albright loomed towards them out of the dark and grabbed the verger's wrist. Yanking his arm back hard, the policeman dragged the verger away.

Francis struggled to his feet and put a hand up to his cheek. He felt warm blood course through his fingers.

Albright had Stapleton face down on the floor.

'Cuffs, sir. On my belt,' he said.

Francis unhooked a pair of handcuffs from the policeman's belt and attached them to first one, then the other, of Stapleton's wrists. Outside, a wail of sirens heralded the arrival of the ambulance and the police backup team.

'Jered Stapleton, I'm arresting you on suspicion of the murders of Tash Brady, Sally Ann Granger, Lou Riley and Tony Hitchins, and for the attempted murder of Liv Templeton. You do not have to say anything, but it may harm your defence if you do not mention when questioned something which you later rely on in court. Anything you do say may be given in evidence.'

He hoped to God that the last charge remained attempted murder and didn't become an actual murder charge. But he was by no means certain that it would.

66

Sunday, 3 September 2017

Rory

Jered Stapleton filled the tiny interview room with his presence. From his fingers, stained black with tattoo ink, drumming on the Formica tabletop, to the stench rising up from his sewage-soaked shoes.

Rory stared at him from the door, gripping the doorframe as he struggled to get his temper under control.

'Murdering bastard,' he muttered under his breath.

Tony Hitchins was dead. Angie Burton was still missing. The boss, and Liv Templeton, had been rushed straight to hospital, along with the tattooing equipment and ink bottle that Stapleton had been using. Tanika Parry was doing what she could, but if either of them died . . .

'I heard that,' said Stapleton.

'Good,' said Rory, as Kyle Hollins followed him into the room. The tape recorder wasn't switched on yet, so Rory didn't have to mind what he said.

The two policemen sat down, both of them instinctively moving their chairs back from the table to be further from the rancid stink of sewage. Rory explained what would happen and Kyle snapped on the recording device.

'It's two a.m. on Sunday the third of September, 2017. In the room: DS Rory Mackay and DC Kyle Hollins to interview a suspect in an attack on Liv Templeton. Please state your name for the record.'

'Jered Montgomery Stapleton.'

So he was going to co-operate?

'You have been arrested on suspicion of four murders and two attempted murders. You can request to have a lawyer present.'

'I don't need a lawyer. God will be the only judge of my actions.'

'I think you'll find there'll be plenty of people judging you for your actions down here on earth, Mr Stapleton. But if you don't want a lawyer that's up to you.'

There was a sharp rap, and the door opened.

'Rory?'

Rory's head snapped around. It couldn't be.

'Boss?' He got up and slipped out into the corridor to find Francis Sullivan standing outside. 'What the hell? You should be at the hospital.'

Sullivan had a bandage taped to his cheek where Stapleton had gouged him with the tattoo iron. His complexion was grey, but at least he'd changed out of the drenched and filthy clothes he'd been wearing when Rory had last seen him.

'No, I shouldn't. I need to see this through.' His voice betrayed his absolute exhaustion. 'There's nothing they can do for me. It's just a waiting game.'

'Nothing they can do? What about a blood transfusion?' Rory couldn't believe what he was hearing.

Francis shrugged. 'Parry didn't think that would make a difference. The dose is much smaller than the ones that killed the girls. I discharged myself.'

Rory shook his head. 'You shouldn't be here.'

'I feel okay. Not great, but well enough to interview Stapleton. If my condition deteriorates, you'll have to take over.'

They went back into the room and dismissed Kyle.

Rory turned the tape back on. Stapleton stared at them both

from beneath heavy lids. Something had changed – it was as if he didn't recognise them. As if he was drugged.

'I want to talk to you about the murders of Natasha Brady, Sally Ann Granger and Lou Riley,' said Francis. 'Do you know the women I'm talking about?'

Stapleton took a deep breath and sat up, ramrod straight, on the chair.

'I killed them. I saved them.'

A shiver of excitement ran down the back of Rory's neck. A confession. He glanced across at Francis. Nothing betrayed how that statement must have made him feel. His hands were steady, one rolling a pencil between finger and thumb, the other flat on the table in front of him. The eye contact between him and Stapleton was like an electric charge in the air between them.

'Saved them from what?' Sullivan's voice was calm, even conversational.

'*Vulnerasti cor meum, soror mea.*'

'"You have wounded my heart, my sister." It's from the Buxtehude, isn't it?' said Francis.

Stapleton nodded.

'You killed your sister, Aimée, as well?'

Stapleton was aghast. 'No. Never that.' His face crumpled. 'I failed my sister. I could have saved her but I didn't act. I was indecisive and she couldn't wait any longer.'

A tear rolled down his cheek and he brushed it away impatiently.

'What could you have saved her from?' said Rory.

'Our father.'

For a second he thought Stapleton was starting to pray, but then he realised.

'What was he doing to her?'

'He defiled her.' Stapleton's voice rose and took on a tone of bitterness. 'I heard them. I heard what he did to her. But I closed

383

my ears to it. I didn't know what to do when she asked for help. Not helping her while she was still alive is something I've regretted every single day since her death. I only realised what I had to do after she had died.'

'You killed your father?' said Francis.

'It was easy.'

They waited for a few seconds, but Stapleton leaned back in his chair, closing his eyes.

Rory couldn't make sense of it.

'You know your father's bones were recently discovered?' said Francis.

'I know. I saw them. He rose from the waters to remind me of what I needed to do.'

'And that was?'

Stapleton looked at them both as if they were idiots. 'To save the girls, of course. To make up for failing Aimée. That was my mission.'

'And you saved them by killing them?' Rory's eyebrows were in danger of colliding with his hairline.

'How did you know which girls needed saving?' said Francis.

A look of sly cunning passed over Stapleton's face. His eyes narrowed.

'They were troubled girls. They were prey. I saved them from the beasts that were killing them slowly. The fathers and protectors who were anything but.'

'They all went to the same college. They were all seeing the same counsellor. Do you know Marcia Cornwallis, Jered?'

'I do. I'm her supervisor. You know every counsellor has to be supervised, don't you?' His supercilious smile made Rory's skin crawl. 'Marcia told me all about the girls she was helping. We discussed their problems and worked out how she could best help them. Of course, I didn't tell her I had a better way of helping them.' Stapleton leaned forward to put his elbows on the

384

table, interweaving his hands as if to pray. 'By saving them, I've been atoning for my own sin. Soon, I think, my sister will be able to forgive me for what I did.'

'Where did you learn to tattoo?' interrupted Francis.

'A long time ago I went to art college. I did a project on tattooing. It's a skill you never forget, like riding a bicycle.'

'And the stigmata. Why?'

'Like Christ, and like my sister, these girls had suffered . . .'

Rory had heard enough cod-religious babble.

'Your sister's dead, and now three other girls have also died. Not to mention one of our officers. You can't claim you were helping him, can you?'

'God rest his soul.'

Rory's fist slammed down on the table. 'You pious bastard. You'll pay for this. You'll spend the rest of your life in prison.'

Francis flicked off the recorder.

'And were you intending to save my sister too?'

What was the boss talking about?

Stapleton shook his head. 'Your sister is pure. She doesn't need saving.'

'She needs saving from you.' There was venom in Francis's voice. Rory glanced at him and saw he was swaying slightly on his chair. He shouldn't be here.

'I think we need a break.'

Francis led the way out of the room, Rory following close behind.

Stapleton shouted in their wake.

'I saw blood in the sink when my sister sliced her own flesh. I heard her screaming the night my mother died. I did nothing. I deserve to be punished . . .'

67

Francis

Francis's vision blurred and he was acutely aware of every heartbeat in his chest. Each breath he took felt laboured. He leaned on the wall of the corridor outside the interview room and bent forward with his hands on his knees.

'Boss, you all right?'

He licked his top lip. It tasted of salt, and sweat dripped off the end of his nose.

'Just give me a minute, Rory.'

It took a supreme effort but he straightened up.

'You don't look well.'

Bradshaw appeared from the next-door room, where he'd been watching the interview through the two-way mirror.

'He's making a full confession. Now isn't the time to bloody stop.' He looked Francis up and down. 'What's wrong with you.'

'Nothing, sir. We'll get back in there.'

Rory looked as if he was about to say something, so Francis glared at him. Bradshaw couldn't be trusted with any sensitive information and he wondered how he could continue the interview without the chief listening in.

'Rory,' said Bradshaw, 'find out what's going on with the search for Burton.'

Rory nodded and drifted further down the corridor, pulling out his mobile.

Francis took deep breaths. The walls and the ceiling were closing in and there was a pulse throbbing in the corner of his eye.

A uniformed sergeant came up to Bradshaw and spoke a few hurried words. The chief followed him, leaving Francis on his own. His mouth was dry. His heart was pounding like a slow drumbeat. He needed to sit down, so he staggered back into the interview room, grabbing for the nearest chair.

Jered Stapleton opened his eyes.

'Oh, Francis, you don't look good.' He leaned forward over the desk and put a hand out to feel Francis's forehead. 'Oh dear, oh dear. Methinks I'll soon be helping your sister arrange another funeral.'

'Stay away from her.'

Francis felt like he was drowning.

'I'm sure she'll visit me in prison. That's what good Christian girls do, isn't it?'

Francis grabbed the edge of the table and heaved himself up. He took a swing at Stapleton, but he missed the verger's face by miles. He slumped forward. Somewhere far away, he heard a man laughing.

'I hear the voice of my vengeful sister. She whispers in my ear at night. She tells me to take a life to save a life. I was too late to save her, but I took my father's life anyway. She comes back to me in the dead of night and talks to me. A thousand times I've told her to leave me alone, but she only stops her clamour when I save a girl for her. She's talking to me now, Francis Sullivan.'

Francis slid down onto the chair, but he couldn't hold himself steady and he carried on sliding down to the floor. Black mist was creeping in at the periphery of his vision. Far above him a face loomed, then receded.

'She's telling me to kill again . . .' His voice changed, taking on a sickening tone as if he was speaking to a child. 'Is that right, Aimée? Is that what you want me to do? You know I'd do anything for you, my darling.'

Francis concentrated on breathing. The floor was cold under his cheek, but then the world turned upside down and his face was pressing upwards against the floor, which was now above him.

'Oh, Aimée, you're right. I shall.'

Francis struggled to turn his head. Stapleton seemed to be stripping off his shirt.

What?

He heard him walk across the room. He shut the door firmly.

Francis twisted, suddenly suspicious of the verger's intentions. Stapleton was twisting and knotting his shirt.

'No!'

'Goodbye, Francis.'

He closed his eyes. Someone kicked over a chair. Someone banged on a door. A man grunted. A moment's silence. Then people were shouting.

Rory was somewhere above him.

'Boss, boss!'

Francis opened his eyes. He could see the floor, back in its rightful position. He could see one of Rory's shoes.

It moved back.

'Get a medic!'

Francis sank back into darkness, the drum beating more slowly in his chest.

'He's dead. No pulse.'

That wasn't right. He couldn't be dead. He was thinking and he was breathing. He opened his eyes.

'I'm not dead. Rory? I'm here . . .'

'Boss, stay where you are.'

Francis struggled up into a sitting position. Beyond the table leg, a figure lay slumped on the floor. What was going on? He pulled himself up using one of the chairs and then leaned on the table, looking down at the prone figure.

It was Jered Stapleton.

His shirt was knotted around his neck.

'Short-drop hanging,' said Rory. 'From the back of the chair.'

'Couldn't he still be alive?' How long had he been out for?

'No pulse,' said Rory. 'Even if he was he'd have probably sustained brain damage.'

Francis stared at the verger's back, blinked, then stared again. It wasn't the huge tattoo that had caught his attention – though it was indeed worthy of it. A black and grey back piece depicting Christ on the cross, surrounded by a phalanx of angels and weeping women, stretched from the top of his shoulders to disappear into the top of his trousers. But what stood out more were the scars that criss-crossed and obscured the finer details of the picture.

'What the hell are those?' said Rory, looking at them too.

'Self-flagellation scars,' said Francis. 'Looks like Jered Stapleton had been punishing himself for years.'

'Jesus Christ.'

The door opened and a medic burst into the room. He rushed over to Stapleton's body and squatted down.

'You're too late, mate,' said Rory.

'I hope not,' said another voice from the door.

Tanika Parry strode into the room and took Francis by the arm.

'You foolish, foolish man,' she said. 'We need to get you right back to the hospital to start treatment now. What were you thinking, discharging yourself like that?'

Francis tried to recall what he'd been thinking but he couldn't.

In fact, he couldn't make sense of anything. He just needed to lie down.

His legs gave way under him, only this time, Rory and Tanika Parry were there to ease him down to the floor.

68

Francis

They should have discharged him two days ago. He was fine. He felt absolutely better and now he was bored. Francis couldn't stay in bed and he couldn't concentrate on any of the pile of rubbishy thrillers Rory had brought in for him to read. Robin had had the sense to bring him in a copy of *A Ship of the Line*, his favourite of the Hornblower series, but he knew it too well to try to read it while his mind was wandering. Instead, he got out of bed and paced the room and then the corridor beyond, itching to get back to work and go through the fallout of what had happened.

Of course, Rory had been in every afternoon to discuss things with him, but it wasn't quite the same as being in control. His sergeant always timed his visits for when he knew the tea trolley would be coming around, and he always made sure to turn up with a packet of Hobnobs.

'How's Angie?' said Francis, watching with undisguised disapproval as Rory dunked a biscuit in his tea.

Angie had been flushed down the main sewage channel and into one of the vast overflow tanks that the council had built underneath the beach. She'd been pulled out half drowned and rushed straight to hospital.

'She's getting better, gradually. They pumped her stomach and put her on maximum doses of antibiotics. Apparently, she'll need check-ups for parasitic infections for months to come.'

Francis nodded. He'd been given antibiotics as well, having got thoroughly soaked in filthy water while he'd chased through the sewers.

'But it's not the physical effects she's going to have trouble getting over,' continued Rory. 'She's blaming herself for Tony's death.'

'That was hardly her fault – I'm more to blame for that than she is.'

'I'd pretty much lay blame with Stapleton,' said Rory. 'You took the best decisions you could to save Liv's life. Which you achieved.'

Thankfully, Liv had also survived Jered Stapleton's attack.

Tanika Parry had explained. 'Taxine poisoning is dose related,' she said. 'Both you and Liv were lucky enough that he didn't have the chance to give you a full tattoo. The amount of taxine in that scratch on your cheek was enough to make you pretty ill, but you weren't going to die from it.'

Francis had studied the wound on his cheek in the mirror. The gouge was healing but the scar would be black. He now had two tattoos, but this one he would have lasered off. Until then, he'd have to get used to having a black streak down his left cheek. The shape of it reminded him of the little marching bird in Bosham Church.

'Rory?' he said.

'Yes, boss.'

'Bradshaw.' The more Francis had thought about it, the more he'd become convinced that Bradshaw was the source of the leak to Tom Fitz.

Rory let out a low whistle. 'Impossible problem,' he said.

He was probably right. 'We'll see.'

Rory cocked an eyebrow but didn't say anything. They ate Hobnobs in silence.

'There was one thing he said though . . .' said Rory.

'What?'

'We need to pull together as a team, instead of competing against one another.'

There were so many ways Francis could have responded to this, but instead he just nodded. His sergeant was reaching out with an olive branch, so he wasn't going to kill the moment.

Someone knocked on the door.

'Come in.'

'I'll be going,' said Rory. 'See you back at the office.'

The door to Francis's room opened and Robin came in. Rory left.

'Brought you grapes,' she said.

'I hate grapes,' said Francis. 'You know that.'

'Fine.' She dropped the brown paper bag she was carrying into the bin.

'Sorry. That was rude of me.'

'It's reassuring. Means you're on the mend.'

She sat down on the chair Rory had just vacated.

'How are you?' she said.

He shook his head. 'No. How are you? I'm so sorry, Robin. I realise you were growing fond of Jered. If I'd had any idea . . .' It was the thing that made him most angry about Jered Stapleton, the fact that he'd toyed with Robin's affections while all the time he was on a killing spree.

Robin was still looking pale and washed out, as she had done since their mother's death, but there was a determined jut to her chin.

'No one knew. He seemed completely normal on the surface, didn't he?'

'They always do. "Such a nice boy." It gets said about virtually every serial killer.'

'I'll get over him. It wasn't like it was a "proper" relationship.'

She made quote marks with her fingers in the air. 'We'd only been out a couple of times.'

But he hated the thought of Robin being so alone. So lonely.

'You know that idea you once had, about moving into Dad's house with me?'

Robin shook her head.

'No, Fran. That was just a stupid thought I had when I was feeling vulnerable. I wouldn't want to cramp your style.'

Francis laughed. 'What style? With who?'

'When do you go back to work?'

'I'm being discharged this afternoon. The doctor's suggested I should take the rest of the week off, but there's a lot to do at work.'

'Which Rory couldn't possibly manage on his own?'

Francis shrugged. 'I'm fine.'

'Good. But you work too hard, all the time. Just take a short break, recharge.'

'It's lovely that you care.' Then, putting the sarcasm aside, he said, 'Let's do something at the weekend, right? Go for a drive, a pub lunch?'

Robin smiled.

Before leaving the hospital a couple of hours later, Francis went down to the ward where Angie was slowly recovering from her ordeal. She was sitting up in bed, staring unseeing at the television screen on the wall opposite. The sound was muted and it was a football match, a sport that Francis knew she took no interest in. On one side of her forehead there was a livid graze, and one of her arms was in a sling. The other arm, bruised and scratched, lay limp across the bed covers.

Francis knew she'd taken quite a beating as she was swept through the system to the overflow tank. She'd also swallowed a dangerous amount of raw sewage and, though they'd pumped her stomach, she'd been desperately ill for several days because of it.

'Hi Angie,' he said, moving in front of the screen to catch her attention without shocking her.

'Boss.' She struggled to push herself further up on the mound of pillows behind her.

Francis didn't offer to help her. He knew that would embarrass her even more, so he waited until she'd settled herself and then sat down on the chair by her bed.

'How are you doing?'

Angie's eyes brimmed with tears. Francis knew what the problem was but couldn't think of any words of comfort. He picked up the box of tissues on the night stand and held it out to her. Angie took one and blew her nose.

'Thanks, boss,' she said. 'I'm getting better slowly. Afraid this,' – she lifted her plastered arm a few inches from the bed – 'is going to keep me off for a while.'

'No problem,' said Francis. 'Take as long as you need.'

'When's Tony's funeral?' she said.

'Friday week. You'll be well enough to come, won't you?'

She shook her head, the tears threatening again. 'I don't think I should . . . In fact, I can't. I wouldn't be able to face Barbara.'

'I understand. I'll tell the team you're still too ill.'

'Thanks,' she said, and blew her nose again. Then she looked up at him. 'How are you doing?'

'I'm okay. Going home, thank God.'

'Are you sleeping all right?'

'Not great.' It was true. Francis had suffered broken nights ever since it had happened. He was plagued with the vision of Jered Stapleton's back, criss-crossed with the scars of a broken mind.

'Me neither,' said Angie. 'If I do sleep, I have nightmares about being chased and about drowning in sewage. And when

I'm awake I relive every moment I spent with Tony down there, and how I lost his body.'

'It'll take time,' said Francis. 'But I'll give you as long as you need. I'll be here for you, Angie, every step of the way.'

'And the worst thing,' she continued, 'I know I'm clean now – I must have had a hundred showers – but I just can't get that stench out of my nostrils.'

Francis knew exactly what she meant.

69

Francis

Twenty-four hours back in the real world, and Francis was already getting used to people staring at his face. The black mark on his cheek wasn't huge, but against his pale complexion, it stood out – and now that it had scabbed over it looked more like an ugly cancer than a tattoo.

When he'd appeared in the incident room that morning, for the first time since Jered Stapleton's attack, half the team didn't know which way to look, while the other half simply stared at him unabashedly. No one asked him about what had happened – there were just a few quiet 'good mornings'. Rory had filled them in on the events down in the sewer and the mood was subdued. Tony was dead and Angie would be off for the foreseeable future. The killer had short-changed them by taking his own life so, though the case was over, there was nothing to feel celebratory about.

A morning in that dour atmosphere was enough for Francis. After making inroads on the mountain of paperwork the case had generated, he left at lunchtime for an equally sombre destination – Tash Brady's funeral. Rose had released her body and finally her family were going to be able to pay their last respects. The funeral was being held at St Peter's on York Place. St Catherine's was nearer to where Tash had lived, but the family had chosen not to have it there for obvious reasons.

Francis walked up to the church from John Street, marvelling at how fresh and cool it had become ever since the storm. The rain had lasted for a couple of days and now, in the sunshine, Brighton looked freshly washed, a layer of dust swept from the streets and pavements and down the drains. And without the oppressive blanket of heat, everything felt lighter.

The mourners were still congregating outside the church when Francis arrived. He hung back, on the other side of the road, and watched them filing inside – Kath and Richard Brady in elegant black clothes that did nothing to hide their despair. A lot of people he didn't recognise. Faye Roderick and Marcia Cornwallis, from the art college, flanked by a number of what looked like colleagues. And Tash's friends, some more, some less appropriately dressed.

He scanned the faces. There was no sign of Alex Mullins. But then Kath Brady had more or less accused him of murdering her daughter, so he would hardly feel welcome here. It was a shame. The Bradys owed Alex an apology. The world owed Alex an apology.

Once the last mourner had disappeared inside, Francis went across to the church and slipped in at the back. At the top of the aisle, Tash's white coffin was already in situ, covered by a profusion of flowers, and with at least half a dozen wreaths lined up on the steps in front of it. Tash had been a popular girl. Francis knelt and sent up a prayer for her, for her family and for all the people who had been affected by Jered Stapleton's actions – not least his sister. When he opened his eyes, he noticed the back of Tom Fitz's head a couple of rows in front of him. It gave him a sour taste in his mouth.

The organist stopped playing the funeral dirge they'd walked in to. There was a second of silence, then 'Lord of the Dance' thundered out and gave life to the huge portrait photo of Tash at the front of the church. The congregation stood and started to sing.

As he filed out at the end of the service, Francis saw Marni standing outside in the small parking area at the front of the church. She must have come in the back after the service had begun. He looked round for Alex – he wanted to talk to the boy if he could.

'Hello Marni,' he said. He noticed that her right hand was heavily bandaged.

She nodded at him and there was an awkward moment when he didn't know whether to embrace her or not. She stepped forward and did the job for him.

'That doesn't mean I've forgiven you,' she said.

For arresting her son? Or for the car crash he'd made of their relationship? Both?

'Isn't Alex here?'

She nodded in the direction of a group of Tash's friends. Francis looked but couldn't see the boy. And then he realised – Alex Mullins had cut off his dreadlocks. His black hair was cropped close to his skull, and in a dark jacket and black jeans, he looked like a completely different person.

'Do you think he'll talk to me?'

Marni shrugged. 'Don't ask me. He's his own man.'

Alex saw them talking and came across to where they were standing. But there was no friendly greeting. Instead he focused on his mother.

'Come on, let's go,' he said, taking her arm. 'We won't be welcome at the wake.'

'Alex?' said Francis.

Alex looked at him properly for the first time, making eye contact with a fierce gaze.

'Alex, I wanted to say sorry for what happened in the sewer.

You should never have been cuffed down there.'

'No, he shouldn't,' said Marni, but Alex shot her a sideways glance to shut her up.

'I wasn't the bad guy,' said Alex. 'We were on the same team.'

'I know,' said Francis. 'I'm sorry.'

Liv Templeton beckoned to Alex and he turned away.

Francis looked back at Marni.

'He looks good with his haircut.'

Marni laughed. 'You would say that, Frank. But after the sewer, his dreads stank. We couldn't get them properly clean.'

'Will he grow them back?'

'Probably not – but who knows?' She peered up at his cheek, then ran a finger lightly over the black mark. 'Are you okay?'

'Getting there,' he said. 'What happened to your hand?'

Marni's expression clouded. 'I had an encounter with my brother-in-law and a knife.'

'Paul was here?'

'I told you he was coming.'

'Will you report this? Then we can try and bring him in.'

'He's long gone.'

'Will it affect your work?'

Marni glanced down at her bandaged hand with a rueful shrug. 'It's too early to say. I just have to let it heal.'

Their conversation ran out of steam and they took leave of each other with a couple of nods.

Francis walked back to John Street. He felt exhausted. It would be a while before he was totally well again and he was supposed to be taking things easy. He thought about the events of the previous couple of weeks. They'd messed up. Maybe, if they'd worked faster, Lou Riley wouldn't have had to die. Maybe Tony Hitchins would still be alive. Maybe Angie would still be happy.

But he'd saved Liv's life.

They'd taken a killer off the streets.

And wasn't that, after all, why he'd become a police officer?

Then he wished he'd asked Marni out for a drink while he'd been talking to her, and wondered how she'd answer. He pulled his phone out his pocket and dialled her number.

Acknowledgements

It's no secret among writers that the second book can be 'the difficult one'! After the excitement of seeing one's debut published, one comes back down to earth with a bump – there's a blank sheet of paper waiting to be turned into a novel, and this time it comes with a deadline and a weight of expectations. Thankfully, throughout the writing experience, I'm lucky enough to have had a great many people cheering me on, willing me forward and helping me out in all sorts of practical ways.

First and foremost among these is my brilliant agent, Jenny Brown of Jenny Brown Associates, a dispenser of reassurance, excellent advice, coffee and stronger drinks. Likewise, thanks are due to my two amazing editors at Trapeze – Sam Eades who shepherded me through the early writing stages and, when Sam went on maternity leave, Phoebe Morgan, who stepped in to pick up the baton and keep things on track. Much gratitude also to the rest of the Trapeze/Orion team, which includes, but is not limited to, Jennifer Kerslake, Laura Gerrard, Kim Bishop, Alex Layt, Jessica Tackie, Paul Stark, Jessica Purdue, Hannah Stokes, Richard King and Krystyna Kujawinska. And huge thanks to long-time and rediscovered friend Candida Gubbins for her brilliant reading on my audio books.

Her Last Breath went through several incarnations as I wrestled with a badly behaved plot – and I had a huge amount of help from my 'super-editor' Karen Ball, of Speckled Pen. Sometimes, as a writer, you can't see the wood for the trees and Karen is an expert at unpicking plot threads and straightening out tangles!

Once again, there was invaluable input from my expert witnesses – Doctor Jo Harris, Dean of Medical School, University of Buckingham, who showed immense patience with me over all things medical, and Superintendent (Retired) David Hammond of Staffordshire Police, who set me straight on my police procedure.

As always, a huge number of other writers, friends and family have given their time and support to my writing endeavours – probably far too many people to mention here. But notable among them are my brother Nick Higgins, who read almost as many versions of this book as I wrote, my fellow writers Jane Anderson, Vanessa Roberts, Jane Bradley and Gill Fyffe, my head cheerleader and unofficial PR Katie Wood, my hugely supportive friends Sarah Simpson and Caroline Wilkinson, and the members of my longstanding book group (of which I'm now an absentee member!) – Diana Barham, Amanda Hyde, Jo Harris and Sue Collier. Sue, finally after seventeen years, I think I've got your name right this time!

And, of course, love and thanks to Mark, Rupert and Tim for always being there for me.

I know as I write this, I will have missed someone critical off the list – so forgive me if it's you!